a CHANGED life

MARY A. WASOWSKI

Copyright ©2013-2017 by Mary Wasowski
Cover Design by Okay Creations
Editing by Joe Marron
Formatting by JT Formatting

First Edition: August 2013
Second Edition: September 2017
Library of Congress Cataloging-in-Publication Data

Wasowski, Mary
A Changed Life/Mary Wasowski – 1st ed
ISBN-13: 978-0989623803

1.   A Changed Life—Fiction. 2.   Fiction—Romance
3.   Fiction—Contemporary Romance

This book is dedicated in loving memory to my big sister, Jeanie.
You are always in my heart. I love and miss you every day.

Prologue

I was greeted with soft kisses to my face and the smell of the ocean coming from Simon's skin. My gorgeous husband had been night surfing again, as I sat up waiting for him to return.

"Come to bed. It's late. You have your big meeting in the morning, and you'll want to bring your A-game to the table," he said to me.

"Simon, I don't know if I could do this. It sounds like an amazing opportunity, but when I wrote *A Changed Life*, that story was meant just for me, and for us. It's our life—one I am not sure I will ever be able to share with anyone but us and the people that were involved. Speaking engagements are a lot different than publishing your story in black and white. Any anonymity I have would be no more once my book hit the bookstores. Also, members of our family don't exactly lead a quiet life."

I watched my husband let out a sigh of relief. Was he worried that I wanted to publish my story and tell the world what I went through after being attacked? Simon would never hold me back from anything I wanted to do, but that didn't mean he didn't want to protect me either. He would move heaven and earth to ever allow anyone to hurt me again.

"I love you, Simon, and the look on your face just told me that I had my answer. I will not be publishing *my* story. It's *ours*. Besides, I wouldn't be the only one that this book would affect. There's Uncle Jack to think about and my parents. Too much heartache to relive and our life is about living in the now and moving forward to becoming a family."

"Oh, baby, we already are. I promise you we will be parents someday, and our children are going to be so loved because you are going to be an amazing mother. You do so much good for all the women you help through the C.A.L.I. Center, and a book or no book, that's not going to change. Now, come to bed. I want to love on you until you fall asleep and dream of good things. No more sadness, okay?"

"Okay, but what about this?" I pointed to the nearly four-hundred-page manuscript that was penned by me and was now bound in a thick leather binder.

"It belongs to you, Nicolette. I can't tell you what to do with it."

"Thank you, Simon. I guess after hearing the new revelations in my case, it brought it all back. All that bad for me to relive again."

He picked me up from off the couch and placed me down onto his lap, wrapping his arms around my body.

"Listen to me baby, please. I know you like no one else, and I know when you are at your lowest and most vulnerable point. It's easy to remember just the bad parts of your story, but you know that's not all true. We had the good too, right? We found each other and fell in love. You're here with me, and I am never letting you go. Remember, you were the missing piece to my puzzle, and now we are complete. You read that book of yours as much as you need to, and when you are ready to put it away, I will still be here loving you…forever. You are my life, Nicolette, and I have never been the same since the day I found you sitting on that beach. You changed my life on that day. I fell in love."

"God, how did I get so lucky to have found you? I love you so much, Simon."

"I know you do. Let's. Go. To. Bed." He smiled and kissed me beautifully on my lips.

"Okay, I'll join you in a few minutes."

"I'll be waiting." He kissed me again and began stripping down out of his board shorts, giving me quite the view.

God! I loved my sexy husband. As I began to shut the lights off, I glanced down at my open book and couldn't help getting lost once again.

It was New Year's Eve. I made my way through the crowded bar, needing a quiet moment to myself. I discreetly made my exit down to Uncle Jack's private office. I should be happy, right? But I'm far from being happy. I had never been so sad in all my life, knowing this would be the last holiday in Chicago with all my family under one roof. My parents would tell me that I was worrying too much over our upcoming move, but I was seventeen years old and felt as if my life was completely being replaced with someone else's. I had no choice but to go with it.

My cell phone buzzed in my pocket, and I ignored the call. It was my mom looking for me. Talk about worry, they literally had me on GPS and one very tight leash. I just needed some air and a few minutes to think.

I had ten minutes of solitude, and then Uncle Jack knocked on his own door before entering. He just smiled and opened his arms for me to walk into. He knew this was what I needed.

"There's my Nickel. Come here, sweet girl."

I hugged him hard and didn't want to let go of the one person who never let me down.

"That didn't take long. I knew eventually someone would find me," I said as Uncle Jack continued to hug me in his strong embrace.

"I had to beat them off with a bat from charging in here to get you. I told your parents to give you a few minutes, and then I promised to bring you back to the party. Besides, I have to make my big announcement on stage, and you know I need my number one girl to cheer me on."

"Aunt Sara is your number one, but thank you for saying that."

"You both are. I love you so much. Dry those tears, and let's go ring in the New Year together, like we have done your entire life."

"That's just it, Uncle Jack. It all changes after tonight. I will never have another moment like this again, not with you and Aunt Sara," I said as I began to cry uncontrollably and separated myself from his hold. I knew I was being melodramatic, but I had finally reached my breaking point.

"Now you listen to me, Nicolette, and believe me when I tell you that this is not our last holiday together. I know you feel as if no one is listening to what you want and you are being forced to just go with it, but maybe some good will come from it. A new beginning. I bet you will meet someone, and they will probably fall in love with you at first glance. I don't want to have to come out there and crush some skulls."

How did he do it? He always knew what to say to make me feel better. For the first time all evening, I finally smiled, and he was right: I found some good.

"Thank you, Uncle Jack. I love you too."

"You ready to go back upstairs? It's about that time."

"Lead the way."

Uncle Jack took my hand and escorted me through his crowded bar to the VIP section that was reserved for our private party. I didn't miss the relieved look from my father as he watched his brother give me one more hug and kiss and then made his way up to the *stage. Aunt Sara was laughing with my mother and toasting with champagne after Uncle Jack stepped up to the microphone.*

"Thank you all for coming out tonight to not only ring in the New Year in the best bar in Chicago but to support one of our own. You know her from her times of entertaining you right here on this very stage when we hosted our Open Mic Nights. Who would have thought that singing a few songs on the piano would lead to our shining star, Zoe Madsen, signing with Sony Music? It's all thanks to my beautiful sister-in-law, Christina Vanelle, and my kid brother, Mason Vanelle of Vanelle Records. Zoe was the very first artist to sign and record under their label, and now all their hard work has paid off as we celebrate not only Zoe's success and wonderful future, but my family's as well."

My mom and Aunt Sara were crying and hugging one another as applause rang out. This was a huge moment for them, and I quietly sat back trying to fight back my own tears while my heart was silently breaking.

"Now with Zoe's help and yours too, let's ring in 2008 with the loudest countdown Chicago has ever heard."

I watched my family celebrate with love and affection for one another. Zoe led off the count as Uncle Jack now stood with Aunt Sara, and my father was spinning my mom in a dance around the room. They looked so happy. Five, four, three, two, one... Happy New Year!

Zoe began singing her number one hit, "Be Yourself," as the crowd listened to the beautiful melody co-written by my parents. My parents and their label had taken her as far as they could, and now she was on her way to New York City to record her first mainstream album with Sony Music. I was so happy for my family and for Zoe, but as I watched their dreams come true, I knew my life was going to change too.

My parents had been offered a chance of a lifetime: to write songs and the score for an upcoming Paramount Pictures movie. I didn't want to go. I didn't understand why they couldn't just go to California and write the songs while I remained in Chicago with Uncle Jack and Aunt Sara. It sounded simple in my head but not in reality. After my parents sold their label along with Zoe's contract and music to Sony, they decided to make a change and move us to California permanently. I wanted to stay in Chicago, but my reasons fell on deaf ears, and I had no choice but to follow and support their dreams, forgetting what I wanted.

Five months later, I watched the rest of my belongings get loaded into the back of the moving van. As the van drove off, my eyes focused on the "Sold" sign on my front lawn. This was really happening. I was leaving and had to say goodbye to not only Chicago but to Uncle Jack.

After tearfully hugging Aunt Sara, I walked with Uncle Jack to have a few minutes with just him.

"You'll visit me, right?" I asked as I wiped away more falling tears.

"Of course, we will, you never have to worry about not seeing us. We will always be with you. We love you, Nicolette. We have loved and protected you since the day you were born. Moving to California will not change that."

I hugged him back and prayed he was right.

"Nicolette, come, we need to leave for the airport," said my father, whom I tried to ignore until he called out for me again, and I knew my time with stalling the inevitable was over.

As my father made his way over to us, I tried one last time. "Please, Uncle Jack, make them listen to you. Convince them that my place is here with you and Aunt Sara. I don't want to leave you."

I cried, again and again, breaking my Uncle Jack's heart. With a strong resolve, he calmed me down and wiped away my tears, holding me in place so I could look at him.

"You will always have a home here, and I am not going anywhere. If you should ever need me, I am a phone call and a flight

away. Now, your parents are waiting. Please promise me that you will try to find the good and to not give them such a hard time. We will talk tonight, I promise."

"Okay, I will try for you, Uncle Jack. I love you so much."

My father reached for my hand and began walking me to the car. I pulled away and ran back to my uncle to hug him one more time, further angering my father.

"Nicolette, get in the car," my father loudly ordered.

I entered the car and stared out the window to witness my uncle hug my mother and shake my father's hand. Uncle Jack pulled my father close to him, and it appeared like he whispered something into his ear. I watched my father nod and turn away from his brother, not looking all that happy with whatever was just said. Once my father was seated beside my mother, the door closed and my heart sunk.

"It's going to be alright, Nicolette. You'll see, in time."

I half smiled and said nothing more. Uncle Jack waved to our departing car. I watched him until his image faded away. My parents began a conversation between them as their excitement for our new life was about to begin. I remained quiet and already missed what was my old life.

Bye, Chicago...

PART ONE

My story begins...

One

Nicolette

The sun shimmered through my room early one Saturday morning. I was now living in a modest Beverly Hills home, so removed from my old life back in Chicago. The sun was so bright, I was kicking myself that I had forgotten to close the room-darkening drapes the night before.

I hit the snooze button again as I heard my mom call from outside my room. To stop her from barging in, I called out that I was awake and would be down in a few minutes. I certainly wasn't up for another argument with her over attending this party today. It had been lonely since I arrived in California. I remained close to home and hadn't really met anyone new, not that I cared to either. Yeah, I was being stubborn and not giving our new life a chance, but since my parents didn't really care how I felt about the move, then why should I plaster a smile on my face to appease them? I played the role of the sullen teenager quite well.

When I finally made my way downstairs to the smell of coffee and delicious banana muffins, I took in my parents, who were already seated at the table and going over the paper and the entertainment news.

"Good morning, daddy," I said as I wrapped my arms around his neck.

My father put his paper down and smiled back at me.

"Good morning, princess. Did you sleep well?" he asked.

"I slept fine," I lied, but played it off well to make him happy. My fake façade didn't go over well with my mother, who greeted me with a disapproving glare.

"Did you forget what today is?" she asked.

Rolling my eyes, something neither of them appreciated, I responded, "How could I forget? You've been reminding me daily for over two weeks."

"Don't be snarky today, Nicolette. You know how important today is for us and the good impression we need to make."

"Oh, yes! A party with the plastics of Beverly Hills. You know, mother, I've heard that if they smile too hard, their faces crack."

I couldn't help myself, that was a good one. Of course, it angered my mother and received disapproving looks from my father from across the table.

"That will be enough from you. We have been invited to Clayton St. Clair's home for his annual Fourth of July party. We will be surrounded by musicians, movie producers, studio heads…you name it, and they will be there. This is so exciting and an amazing way for your father and me to network."

"Why do I have to go? I'm seventeen, and my days are supposed to be spent working on my tan and lounging by the pool, not rubbing elbows with a room full of snobs." Well, that earned another annoyed glare from my mother. I was on a roll. "It's my summer vacation. Why am I even here in sunny California when I should be back home in Chicago with Uncle Jack and Aunt Sara?" I said, not regretting my snarky tone one bit.

"Mason," she enunciated very slowly, "she's your daughter. Please talk to her."

It's funny how I was always my father's daughter when my mother and I reached a standoff in our many arguments. My poor dad, always the mediator between us. At least now I could enjoy my coffee and breakfast in peace.

"We need to talk, Nicolette," my father said as he reached for my hand. He was trying, and I wasn't. "Sweetheart, we have had this discussion over and over again. Don't you think we have exhausted it by now?"

"No, I don't. Daddy, if you would have allowed me to live in Chicago with Uncle Jack, everything would've been okay. Did you ever consider how this change would affect my life by moving out here? Being removed from my school, my friends, and our family?"

"There you go again, exaggerating your point. We did not kidnap and bring you against your will. Before we made this decision, we did discuss it as a family. You just didn't want to bend on anything we suggested. And now, here we are once again arguing over it. It's done, Nicolette. You need to accept that we live here now and going back to Chicago is just not going to happen."

"So, that's it? Is your word bond? After all the valid reasons, I gave to you and mom, you still made the decision for me. Don't you know how much I wanted to finish out my senior year with my friends? You don't get it, do you? You ruined everything for me."

His face had fallen to a sadder one.

"Do you honestly see it that way? Because we never knew moving out here would make you this unhappy. Please, baby, can't you try?"

"I will be eighteen in a few months, and then you will not be able to stop me from going back home. I can move in with Uncle Jack and Aunt Sara. They said I would always have a home with them, and it's more than I have here with you." I raised my voice higher, and I knew I pushed my father too far.

He slammed his hand down on the table and looked at me with a disappointed and angry look as he said, "You know, I really thought I heard it all until right here and now. You listen to me, Nicolette, because I will not repeat myself again. This attitude and whining end right now. Uncle Jack is not your father, I am. I make decisions for you. You are my daughter; do you hear me? Your place is with us, not across the country with your uncle. We do not work as a family if we are apart."

"But, daddy…"

"No! End of discussion. Finish your breakfast, and do as you are told. Your mother was right about today. It's important that we make an appearance at this party, and young lady, you will behave as one and be on your best behavior. Do you understand me?" he said with his curt tone not changing.

"Yes, daddy," I responded.

He got up from the table and left me on my own. Shit! I knew I had hurt his feelings just now by constantly bringing up his brother, but I loved and missed him so much. Uncle Jack was my godfather and the best uncle a girl could ever have. He and my Aunt Sara owned The Neighborhood Bar and Grille, kind of my second home. She was the head chef, and her Rooftop Burger Buster was phenomenal. You certainly couldn't get gourmet burgers out here like the ones my aunt made.

My coffee turned cold, and I lost my appetite. I walked outside and sat by the pool. It was quiet out here, and after my argument with my father, I needed a few minutes to myself.

As songwriters and then finding success with their independent label so much happened for my parents. I mean, I always knew they were talented, but after the song that my mom wrote for Zoe went gold, it was a non-stop whirlwind after that. One open mic event changed all their lives. Vanelle Records was hosting a showcase for their artists at my Uncle Jack's restaurant. Zoe's sound was on the lines of Norah Jones but unique in her own right. Of course, she knocked it out of the park and ultimately paved the path that would change my parents' lives.

After she finished her set, the crowd erupted with applause. Little did they know that a scouting rep from Dax Records happened to be in the audience and listened intently to Zoe. Dax Records was a subdivision of Sony Entertainment; the rep knew raw talent when he heard it.

As they say, the rest is history. My parents were on their way to California to further build on the success they found in Chicago. With the label behind them, they could focus on their songwriting. Once they were approached by Paramount to write the score for their upcoming action movie, they decided California was the best place to be.

I didn't hear my dad behind me as he took a seat beside me. He let out a breath and reached for one of my hands.

"I hate it when we fight. I'm hopeful that you have calmed down sitting out here and we can come to an understanding," he said.

I rolled my eyes toward my father, knowing I was just being a brat at this point. The momentary truce was now over. He sighed and told me that I had hurt his feelings, and I was continuing to do so by behaving this way.

"You know, Uncle Jack always said that if he saved a nickel for every time you rolled your eyes, he would be an extremely rich man. Do you remember the jar he kept for every time you rolled your eyes? He would add a nickel to it. It's probably filled to the rim by now," he chuckled to himself, making me smile along with him.

"I guess I tend to roll my eyes a lot, don't I?"

"Yes, that's putting it mildly."

"Daddy, I'm sorry for not being supportive of the move and all these changes. I just don't believe I can be happy here."

He pulled me into a hug and then said, "You feel that way because you haven't given it a chance. Please come to the party with us today. Talk and introduce yourself. Many kids your age will be there with their parents. You have to try, Nicolette. Please, for me?"

"Okay, daddy, I will try. Can I wear what I want?" I asked kidding around, knowing my mother was now in ear shot of our conversation.

"Absolutely not!" she yelled.

Yup, she heard me. My father just shook his head at me but smiled too.

Deciding to not back down, I said, "I am not wearing the dress you picked out for me. I am fully capable of choosing my own outfit, thank you very much."

"You will wear exactly what I have chosen for you, along with the strappy sandals that match perfectly. End of discussion!" she bellowed. *Wow, they sure loved throwing out that phrase a hell of a lot.*

She went back inside with a look of satisfaction on her face. My father followed but not before telling me to get a move on.

Why does she always get her way? Can't I win once in a while? Yeah, fat chance of that happening. You're the kid, right? I rolled my eyes and deeply sighed as I pulled my feet out of the warm pool water.

Three hours later, I was finally ready to go. I had officially been remodeled into what could only be described as a California Barbie doll. My mom pulled out all the stops. I got a manicure and pedicure. My usual out of control waves were trimmed and styled into long layers instead of a pile of hair on top of my head. She didn't understand how it was easier to just throw it in a bun and not give a crap about what it looked like. I didn't know anyone out here anyway, so impressing anyone was not high on my to-do list.

Not to give her too much credit, but mom sure knew her stuff. I wore a Zac Posen sundress fitted perfectly to my small frame. Mom completed my ensemble with a new wristlet for me to carry. She always thought of everything. I took one last glance in the mirror before joining my parents.

"Yes, you are a brat, but a stylish one. You can do this. Remember what Uncle Jack told you: find the good in any situation."

My parents had their game faces on as we arrived at the St. Clair home. We were not poor, but this was just obscene money. An assistant to the event planner greeted us, and we all received our name badges. She escorted us to the main tent, where the party was in full swing. I looked around and refrained from rolling my eyes. I knew my father was watching me, and once I showed him that I was trying, he smiled and leaned in to kiss my cheek.

"Thank you, Nicolette. I love you."

"I love you too."

Michael

"Tell me again why I'm here? This garden party is going to pale in comparison to what I had planned today with my friends. I'd rather be on my boat having a good time with people I actually want to associate with. I wanted to celebrate the holiday out on the ocean."

"Michael, you are here today, for one reason and one reason only. I want you to stand beside me and..."

"What, father? Show a united front? Make a perfect impression? Me, the golden boy, and you, who we all know is not the perfect example of a suitable parent. I love how we have to pretend in public."

"That's enough from you. You will be the perfect son today, as we both know you are not. You represent me out there, and you will engage in conversation with our guests. Oh, and son..."

"Yes?"

"Don't forget to smile."

"I understand. You wish for me to fake it?"

"You are exasperating at times, Michael."

"So, I can leave then?"

"No, you may not!"

As my father droned on about my responsibilities, I caught a glance over the balcony as my eyes found the fountain below and the beauty standing beside it. I had never seen such a beautiful girl in my life. I was mesmerized by her. Surely, I would have remembered if I had met her before. Now that my curiosity was piqued, I asked my father who she was.

He huffed. "Honestly, Michael," my father grunted and looked down below at the girl who had caught my attention.

"That would be Nicolette Vanelle. She's the daughter of the new songwriting team we just hired to write the score for *No Surrender*."

"Well, maybe the day is looking up. I'd say now is the perfect time to go work the crowd, and she is just the person I intend to dazzle with my charm first."

"Listen, Michael, she is younger than you. You behave, and keep your hands to yourself."

"Don't I always?" I replied with a smirk.

Nicolette

I was left on my own while my parents were chatting with their colleagues. I was lost in thought by this enormous fountain when someone tapped on my shoulder to get my attention. Startled, I turned around to see piercing brown eyes staring back at me.

"Hello, Nicolette," he said with a cool manner to his tone, sending an uneasy feeling up my spine. His eyes perused over my body and then landed on my name badge before he said, "I'm Michael St. Clair. Welcome to our home, and thank you for joining us for our Fourth of July celebration. I do hope you will stay for all the festivities."

I was not sure what to make of him; he sure acted the "player" quite well. I would definitely sum him up as a guy Uncle Jack would have no problem setting straight. As uncomfortable as he made me feel, I tried to be polite.

"Nice to meet you, Michael," I replied.

"Will you do me the honor of dancing with me? I love the song the band is playing."

I was a little unsure, unsettled by his bold attentiveness would be a more accurate description, but I did promise my parents I would try to fit in. I felt his eyes staring back at me, waiting for an answer to his question.

"Please, Nicolette, just one dance? I will be a perfect gentleman."

He extended his hand toward mine, and all I thought was, *Sure you will.* Michael confirmed my suspicions with a wink in return.

"Okay," I said as I accepted his hand, and he took the dance he asked for.

"So, what's your deal, Nicolette? For such a beautiful girl, why the sour face?" Michael asked as he continued to twirl me around and make me the center of attention. I was not comfortable being here with him. I felt as if all eyes were staring at us.

"Not to be rude, Michael, but I didn't want to be here today."

"Why ever not?" he questioned. "It's a party with lots of fascinating people, good food, and of course, yours truly."

So, the player has a sense of humor. I couldn't believe he actually got me to laugh.

"Now that our awkward moment has passed, tell me about yourself."

I sighed. "What do you want to know?"

"Anything you're willing to tell me."

I was fighting an internal battle within myself. I honestly didn't feel like giving Michael, a complete stranger, a play-by-play on my life. I bet he would argue that we were friends by now, but I still tried to keep it as uncomplicated as I could manage.

"I'm seventeen. I will begin my senior year at a new high school. The best part, I will not know a single person."

"Starting over is not so terrible. I'm sure you will meet new friends sooner than you think. You already know me, and I'm awesome."

"Wow! Confident much? If your head gets any bigger, it may not fit through the door."

Now I knew that may be perceived as rude, but he looked like he could take it. He actually laughed and smiled brightly back at me.

"Well, what can I say? It's in the California water, and we only drink the best out here."

I ignored his last comment and asked, "What's your story, Michael? Tell me about you."

"I'm nineteen and ready to begin my sophomore year at Stanford University," he proudly told me.

The song ended, and he thanked me for the dance but not before placing a kiss down to my hand. I excused myself from Michael's company and walked over to the bar for some water. Michael was quickly by my side again.

"Would you like something stronger than water?"

"No, thank you. I don't drink."

He asked again, "How about some champagne? One glass is not going to hurt you."

"I'll stick to water, but thank you." *Take the hint already.*

"Okay. Fair enough. I will get myself a glass and be right back. Please wait here, understand?"

I managed to half smile back at him before answering, "I'll be around, Michael."

"Oh, I hope so, Nicolette."

Thank goodness, he left. I wasn't in the mood to wait around for a guy I had just met. The beach down below looked inviting, and I decided to take a walk. Living in Chicago all my life, I didn't have too many opportunities to take in the beautiful ocean. Yes, the ocean out here was a "pro" on my list of likes and dislikes.

Simon

"Sam, I can't believe I let you talk me into this."

"Will you stop complaining? Since when do you miss an opportunity to mess with that jerk-off St. Clair?"

"Whom are you referring to, Sam?"

"Ha! I knew you couldn't resist. Dude, get your ass up here now and take a look."

I grabbed the binoculars and scanned the crowd. Of course, the usual blondes were in attendance. No one that I wanted to take a second glance at. I recognized Alexis and Bailey, twin sisters. I scoffed and then continued on to the many mindless beauties.

"Simon, don't you think it's time to saddle up again? Get back into the game?"

I looked over to my friend and raised an eyebrow. "The last time I checked, I wasn't a cowboy, Sam."

He laughed in return, but said, "Hey, just stating the obvious, dude. It's been months since the accident. Simon, don't you think it's time to move on with your life? I'm sorry, man, but Jennifer is gone."

"It's not like I have forgotten, but thank you for the reminder. She was my first real girlfriend here in California, and I cared about her. That is something that you just don't forget. I wouldn't be telling you that I was okay if I wasn't."

"Okay, fair enough. Now get back to scanning the crowd. I'm sure there has to be someone who appeals to you."

I took back the binoculars and looked again. I was ready to give up when my eyes found someone who wasn't familiar to me. For some odd reason, I felt drawn to her. *What the hell?* That never happened to me before, not even with Jennifer.

"Sam, do you know that girl?" I asked as I handed him the binoculars to take a look at the mystery girl walking along the shoreline.

"Nope, never seen her before."

I scaled down the wall and jumped down to the sand. Sam called out for me as I began to take off running.

"Hey! Where are you going?"

I sprinted off to meet the beauty that I could not seem to take my eyes off of, as I screamed back to my friend, "To meet someone new!"

Nicolette

The warm sun and breeze coming off the ocean felt so good on my face. I removed my sandals and buried my feet deep into the sand. I leaned back on my elbows and took in the beautiful beach, almost missing the hot guy walking over to me. I was trying not to stare, but he was shirtless, and his stomach was ripped with muscles. His sexy, beach-tousled hair was blowing in the breeze; perfect hair I easily could rake my fingers through.

Where did that come from? Okay, take a breath before you hyperventilate. This is not the first good-looking guy you have met. No, I'm wrong. He is definitely the best-looking guy I have even seen this up close. I looked up and covered my eyes from the sun as he got closer to where I was sitting.

"Hi, how are you?" he asked with a smile showing off his kissable mouth.

Okay, now you lost it. Breathe, Nicolette.

Playing it cool, I responded, "I'm okay. How are you?"

The flirtatious stranger smiled again and said, "Lucky."

"Why lucky?" I asked.

"I'm lucky because I picked the right time to walk on the beach."

I giggled, and now my cheeks were probably red from the blushing I knew I was doing. I said, "Hey, wasn't that a line from a movie?"

"Yup, and it worked!" He smiled again and laughed. Extending his hand, he said, "I'm Simon…Simon Paulson."

"I'm Nicolette Vanelle. Nice to meet you."

As if he was reading my mind, he answered my unspoken question.

"I'm a party crasher if you must know. My friend lives on the other side of that retaining wall. If you sit on top of it, you can see everything that is happening over here at the St. Clair estate."

"Oh, I see. Not sure if you are a peeping tom or just nosy. Do you know them?" I questioned.

"Unfortunately, I do, but I try to keep my distance."

"Why? Is there a reason why you don't get along with them?"

"Too complicated and too long to explain," he replied.

"You know, it's not my business. I didn't mean to pry. I guess I was the nosy one."

"More like curious, but that's okay. I would rather just sit here and get to know you then talk about the uptight St. Clair's."

"Oh, so you have met Michael?"

He laughed in response to my question and said, "Yeah, you can say that. So, if you don't mind me asking, what brings you here today? Not that I'm complaining."

There was something in his voice that gave me a safe and comfortable feeling.

"I'm here with my parents. They are new to working with Mr. St. Clair."

"Do they work at Paramount?" Simon asked.

"No, they don't. My parents are songwriters and are writing the score for Paramount's new movie."

"Wow, writing songs sounds cool."

I shrugged my shoulders. "I guess it is. They love what they do."

"You don't seem too enthused about it."

"I'm sorry. Don't get me wrong, I'm happy for my parents. It's just taking me time to get used to living out here. Being a transplant kind of sucks."

"Yeah, I understand that more than you know. Where are you from?"

"Chicago. I just moved here about six months ago."

"That explains it then."

I was confused by his comment. "Explains what?"

"I knew you couldn't be from around here, not with that accent of yours and the color of your hair."

"Wow! You figured all of that out with just two deductions. One: The color of my hair. Two: The tone of my voice."

His happy expression had fallen, and I knew I had to tell him that I was teasing him.

He said, "Sorry, I didn't mean to offend you. Most of the girls around here either have naturally blonde hair, or they color it blonde. Your hair is just gorgeous and natural. You don't see that too often living out here."

I believed I may have blushed with his flattery as my skin heated. He was quite the flirt.

"Well, thank goodness for being different. I wouldn't want to look like everyone else, now would I?"

"I don't think you could, Nicolette. You are already a standout in the crowd."

And there he goes flirting with me again. He gave me a sexy wink, and I felt the heat rising again in my cheeks. I was having a great time talking with Simon and enjoying his company until Michael unexpectedly interrupted us. I didn't miss the daggers that Simon shot over to Michael as he got a bit too close for my liking.

"I've been looking all over for you, Nicolette. I asked you to wait for me," he said with an annoyed undertone to his voice.

I didn't even know this guy, and here he was behaving as if I belonged to him or something. I quickly glanced over to Simon, who remained quiet.

"I wanted to walk on the beach," I simply said.

Michael looked at me like I had just slapped him across his face. He quickly schooled his features and reached for my hand.

"Oh, well my father's parties can be on the boring side," he said as he tried playing off his foul mood.

"Oh, really? I thought you said his parties are pretty awesome," I joked, getting Simon to laugh at my snarky comment.

He ignored my jab and said, "Anyway, I see you met Simon." He gestured over in Simon's direction. "Come to think of it, I don't remember seeing your name on the guest list."

"Hmm, I'm sure you must have forgotten to add me," Simon gave it right back to him, earning a soft chuckle from me."

Michael wasn't impressed. "How did you get in here?" he demanded.

"Here's the funny thing, Michael. I used my two feet. Relax, I was just leaving anyway."

Simon

I leaned over to Nicolette and kissed her on her cheek, promising to see her soon. She smiled in return and gave me that beautiful blush again, one I definitely wanted to see again. I jogged down the beach with the thoughts of Nicolette running through my mind. She was so beautiful, not like anyone I have ever met. I felt my heart beat faster around her. Sam was waiting for me by the wall.

"Hey, how did it go?" he asked.

"Have you been here the entire time?"

"Um, yeah. I came down to get a better look at what sent you racing off. Who's the girl, Simon?"

"Her name is Nicolette Vanelle, and she may just be the future Mrs. Simon Paulson, my friend."

"I'm happy for you, buddy. Find me a girlfriend too, and maybe my senior year won't completely suck."

"I'll see what I can do. Let's grab the boards and get some surfing in before we totally lose the day."

I glanced back toward the St. Clair home and thought of her. *Oh yes, I will be seeing Nicolette again.*

Nicolette

Just as Michael began to speak, my cell phone buzzed with an incoming text. *Whew! Saved by mom!* I texted back as I began walking away from him.

"Where are you going?" asked Michael.

"My mom wants me to join her and my father inside."

"Nicolette, I thought maybe we could take some time and get to know one another better."

"Sorry, another time. My parents are waiting for me."

I picked up my sandals and sprinted away from him. I stopped before entering the tent to put my shoes back on. Sure enough, my father was waiting for me.

"Hey, having fun?"

"I am. Turns out today wasn't so bad after all." I smiled.

"That's wonderful. Come over here with me. I want you to say hello to our host. Clayton, do you remember my beautiful daughter, Nicolette?"

"Of course, I do. How are you, dear? Are you enjoying yourself?"

"I'm fine, sir. Yes, it's been a great day."

"Have you had a chance to meet my son, Michael? I'm sure he's around here."

Oh, you mean God's gift to the world son? I wanted to say, but my father gave me a raised eyebrow gesture to be nice.

"I have, sir. We met earlier."

I stood quietly and listened to my parents talk with Mr. St. Clair about the new songs they planned on writing. After a while, I excused myself and mingled throughout the tent. I met some girls that were trying to get John Mayer's attention, but he was clearly ignoring them. I smiled at the fact that my family was actually close to John and we were on a first name basis. I used that as my way of breaking the ice with the girls.

"Hi, I'm Nicolette Vanelle, and you are?" I asked.

"Hi, I'm Alexis Hamilton, and this is my sister, Bailey."

"It's a pleasure to meet you."

They replied in unison, "Likewise."

The girls were smiling and looked me over with curiosity. I took a chance on what I thought the two sisters were trying to do before I walked over.

"So, do you know John?" I gestured over to where he was standing. They both looked at me with surprise, knowing I had just busted them.

Alexis spat out, "No, but we would like to."

"Well, let's see what I can do about that." I gave them a sly smile and a confident wink.

"Um, what are you doing?" Alexis asked. They were holding onto each other, very surprised at my bold statement.

I stood on my toes and waved my hands above my head as I called out to John. He turned around and smiled warmly at me while waving back. I just giggled to myself knowing how I just shocked the girls. I guess I should have let on how I knew John, but I was having too much fun, and wasn't my father the one that asked me to try and make the best out of today? John came over, and my new friends melted like sugar in the rain.

"John, I would like you to meet Alexis and Bailey Hamilton." I then turned my attention back to the nervous girls beside me. "Ladies, this is John Mayer."

"Nice to meet you. You better watch out for Nicolette," he said, as he bumped my arm with his elbow.

Swatting him in return I said, "What's that supposed to mean? I'm a nice person." I stuck my bottom lip out like a pouty two-year-old.

"I always did know how to rile you up, didn't I?" he said as he pulled me into a hug.

John was really a nice guy, despite what all the gossip magazines said about him. He was down-to-earth and liked to have fun. I hadn't seen him in several months. He still looked the same, wearing his old jeans and a signature white t-shirt. Obviously, dress codes for famous musicians were optional at an event like this one. I knew the twins would die if they didn't get an autograph or, better yet, a photo.

"Hey, John, can we get a photo with you?" I said in my most annoying giddy fan voice.

He shook his head. "They can. You, I'm not so sure about."

He laughed again as he pulled me back into his arms for a hug. He signaled over to a waiter who was close by. He asked him if he would take a few shots of us. I was standing in front of John as the twins were on either side.

John leaned in and whispered, "Are you enjoying yourself, Nickel?"

I smiled and said, "Yes, but that's a private nickname between me and my uncle. You swore to keep it a secret."

The girls were still in fangirl heaven and continued to stare at us while John and I continued on with our lively conversation.

John said, "Sorry, but it kind of stuck with me after your uncle called you that."

"It's okay. You're forgiven."

"How do you like living in California?"

"I'm planning my escape after my birthday."

"Nicolette, just give California a chance. You never know...you may fall in love with it."

John hinted that maybe I was being a bit stubborn for my own good and too hard on my parents by fighting with them. We were interrupted by someone telling John that he needed to get moving and meet so and so.

John didn't look too interested but said to me before he left, "Nicolette, think about what I said. You might just change your mind about things."

"Doubtful," I said while giving him one of my famous eye rolls.

"There's that gesture that I love."

"I did it just for you."

"I loved it. Okay, I have to get going. Ladies, it was a pleasure meeting you. Have fun, Nicolette. You're only young once."

In my most dramatic attempt, I grabbed his arm, "Please don't leave me here."

He laughed again. "Don't quit your day job."

We always had the best time to play around with each other any time he visited Chicago. He actually developed a close relationship with my parents and Uncle Jack. He leaned down and kissed my cheek before turning to leave and rejoin his entourage. As he faded back into the crowd, I continued with my theatrics.

I finally stopped reminiscing and refocused my attention back to the twins. They were both staring at me with their mouths wide open in shock.

"What?" I said as innocently as possible.

"You're messing with us, right?" They said in unison which was beginning to creep me out a little. It was as if they couldn't speak without the other.

"We are definitely going to be best friends," Bailey squealed. Alexis nodded and agreed with her sister.

I giggled at them. I guess I found it funny they were so fangirling over John Mayer, the famous musician. I just viewed him as my friend. I guess I should have mentioned how I knew him, but that was for me to keep to myself. Back in Chicago, I attended parties like this all the time, so meeting a celebrity was no big deal to me, but to Alexis and Bailey, it probably was the coolest thing that ever happened to them. Knowing that made this day so worth it.

My stomach was rumbling something fierce since I hadn't eaten since breakfast, and that was just a muffin. I walked over to the buffet table that was set up near the bar. I leaned over to examine my choices, and Michael grabbed me unexpectedly.

"There you are," he whispered close to my ear. "How about that drink now?" he asked as he began to stroke his fingers up along the side of my face.

I stepped back and felt alarmed with his bold intrusiveness. "Sorry, I can't. I need to find my parents."

He smiled at my obvious ruse to get away from him. "Nicolette, your parents are talking it up with my father. Why don't you relax and have a good time? We can watch the firework display together." He was quite determined to change my mind, but I wasn't taking the bait. He then said, "I don't usually hear the word 'no,' but you are definitely worth the effort."

I pulled my hands out from his grasp, clearly angry. I stared at him and said, "I don't appreciate you putting your hands on me!"

He clearly looked affronted. "I'm sorry, I was just messing around."

"I wasn't. Where I come from, your version of messing around will get your preppy ass kicked. Please do not put your hands on me again."

After meeting, someone as fabulous as Simon, I was just annoyed at this point. It was definitely time to go.

"Look, I'm sorry if I offended you. Will you please accept my apology?" he asked and once again turned on the charm of the rich frat boy.

"I have to go, Michael. Take care."

Michael

I watched Nicolette as she walked back into the main tent only to be swept up by her father. Seth, my friend, joined me after she walked away from me.

"What's up, Michael? You have trouble closing the deal?"

"No, nothing like that, but I will. You know how I hate to be told *no*."

Nicolette

"**R**eady to go, sweetheart?" my mom asked.

"Yes, I am so ready to leave."

"Did you have a good time today?"

"Actually, I did. The party was fun." I was thinking of Simon when I answered her question. "I even met some girls, who announced they will be my best friends." I laughed at that. "I also spent some time catching up with John."

"That's great, honey; I was hoping you would get the chance to talk to him. He asked about you when he was talking with your father." My mom winked as she looked at my father.

"What are you hiding from me now?" I asked.

"Oh, well, we do have some good news to report."

Jumping up, I screamed, "Sweet! We're moving back to Chicago?"

"Nicolette, really?"

"Come on, mom. Can't you take a joke?"

"I can. So, do you care to know or not?"

"Of course. Go on."

"Well, a certain someone—John—wants us to produce two new songs for him."

"That's great. I am so happy for you, mom."

"Also, they will be on the movie soundtrack we are collaborating on with Paramount!"

"That's exciting news."

I was truly happy for my parents, and the perfect day they obviously had. I was thinking that it was time to ease up on them and try to accept my new life here. I felt exhausted and needed a hot bath to fall into. My angel of a housekeeper, Gracie, must have read my mind. She had everything ready for me when I walked into my bathroom.

"You are the best. Thank you so much. And you filled it with my favorite bath oil." I hugged Gracie in appreciation for her kindness.

"Relax and enjoy your bath. Afterwards, I have a surprise for you."

"Gracie, what surprise?"

"You have my homemade gelato waiting for you in the freezer."

I hugged Gracie tightly. I relaxed and enjoyed the sweet smell of lavender, as I soaked and listened to Norah Jones sing "Don't Know Why." I was in heaven.

Nicolette

I felt relaxed after my heavenly bath. I couldn't get Simon out of my mind. I kicked myself for not getting his phone number.

Maybe I would have if it weren't for Michael interrupting us. He did say he would see me again, but how? I quickly sent a few e-mails to some friends back home when my phone alerted me that I had a text message.

I looked down to my phone and saw four messages, all from Michael. How did he get my number? I was annoyed at the fact on how pushy he was. I was going to tell him exactly that when yet another message came through.

Michael: *Hi, Nicolette. I am calling you now. Please pick up your phone.*

I almost shut my phone off. *Who does he think he is?* This guy was extremely arrogant. By the fourth ring, I answered the call. In my most nonchalant voice, I said hello. Michael was not amused.

He was almost shouting at me, "I texted you five times. Didn't you read them?"

"Michael, how do you have my number?"

"I have my ways." He laughed. "At this point, I feel as though I am being led on, and I do not like it."

I scoffed at his ridiculous statement. "You can't be serious right now. Explain to me how I'm leading you on? I only met you this afternoon. You don't even know me."

"I want to get to know you. Allow me to take you out."

"I don't think so."

"Why not? How about we start with dinner and a movie?"

"Don't take this the wrong way, but why me? I'm in high school, and you are in college, Stanford by the way. How can you be interested in me when you could probably date anyone you want?"

"Nicolette, this isn't a big deal. One date is all I'm asking. Don't overthink it."

"I'm not overthinking anything, I'm just not into you. I'm not sure how you got my number, but I don't like it."

He snickered. "I have my sources."

"Okay, now I'm freaked out."

"Listen, it's nothing to get upset over. I have friends in high places. I usually can get anything I want, so a phone number was no big deal. Come on, I'm joking around. You have no reason to be nervous. It's one date. What are you waiting for? We could end up having a good time."

I hesitated. "As friends?" I asked, hoping he understood that I wasn't looking for anything else.

"Yes, as friends. Besides, I spoke to your parents."

"You did what? Did you say that you…"? I was now up and off my bed. He was really beginning to piss me off. What was I thinking ever even considering going out with him?

"Yes, I asked their permission to ask you out. They thought it was a great idea."

I was beyond angry at this point. What a pompous jerk to use my parents to get to me. I wasn't sure who to be mad at more, my parents or Michael. I chose both.

"Thank you, Michael, for asking for my parents' approval, but it's mine you need, not theirs. I'm a big girl who is perfectly capable of deciding whom she wishes to go out with, and right now, you are not high on my list. Have a good night, Michael. Don't call me again."

I snapped my phone shut without giving him a chance to respond. What an asshole! I was pissed. Where did Michael get off trying to suck up to my parents? Did he just assume because he's rich that I would just drop at his feet and go out with him?

My phone beeped again with more text messages from him. I just shut it off and completely ignored him. I should have just gone to bed, but instead, I decided to confront my parents. I was so done with them making decisions for me. I was going to be eighteen in a few months, and they treated me as if I were still a child.

Without as much as a simple hello, I exclaimed, "How could you give Michael St. Clair permission to date me?"

By the look on their stunned faces, I quickly regretted my outburst. I practically shouted and realized my tone was louder than it should have been. I bit my bottom lip to stop myself from saying anything more.

My father looked at me and gave me his full attention. "Excuse me, Nicolette? What has gotten into you? And, more importantly, why are you shouting at us?"

"I'm sorry, but I'm angry. I just got off the phone with Michael, and he told me that he asked you for permission to date me, and you said yes."

"Yes, we spoke to the boy when we were introduced to him at his father's party."

"So, it's true? How could you do this to me?"

"Slow down, Nicolette. It's clear you have been misinformed. We did not give him or anyone else permission to date you," my father stated.

"But…"

"But what? You really believe we would just hand off our only daughter to a complete stranger? We barely said five words to him."

Now feeling very foolish, I said, "No, but you know his father. He said he asked you."

"He lied then. For whatever reason, he lied to you. Yes, we know his father. Clayton St. Clair is simply a business associate of ours. We have a working relationship with the man. As far as being friends with the guy, that's a bit premature at this juncture. Furthermore, regardless of whom I know, neither your mother nor I would ever force you to date, anyone, you were not comfortable with. That is *your* choice."

"I'm so sorry, daddy, for accusing you of something I know in my heart you would never do. Please forgive me for not trusting you."

"Already forgotten."

He walked over to me to give me a hug. I always felt protected in his loving arms.

"Why would Michael just lie to me? I don't understand him at all."

"Because he's a rich, spoiled, young man who probably gets everything he wants, and that includes the girls."

"Daddy! I can't believe you just said that."

"Why? Is it not true? Do you have a different opinion of him, Nicolette?"

"No," I answered, "I knew who he was from the minute we met. The only reason I even talked to him was that you asked me to 'mingle' and 'get to know the other kids' at the party. Right?"

"Yes, we did. However, he's in college, and you are still in high school. You are far too young and impressionable for a guy like that. He has no business of any kind with my high school-aged daughter."

"Only by two years, daddy, but I do agree with you."

"Okay, let's change the subject on overbearing rich California boys. Did you happen to meet anyone else at the party?"

I smiled. Mom looked over at me suspiciously. I felt my face warming just thinking of Simon.

I said, "Well, now that you ask, I did meet someone. I took a walk on the beach to enjoy the beautiful view when he just appeared out of nowhere."

My father raised his eyebrows as he listened to me.

I gleefully responded, "His name is Simon Paulson, and I enjoyed his company."

"How much did you enjoy with Simon?" my father asked.

"Enough to want to see him again, and I'm hoping I will."

"How old is this boy?" asked mom.

"I guess around my age. The subject didn't come up."

"Two suitors in one day…I guess today wasn't as unpleasant for you as you thought it would be."

"You were right, both of you. I had a great day. It didn't suck after all."

"That's wonderful to hear. Nicolette, we want you to like it here. This is our home now."

Rolling my eyes, I understood exactly what my father was saying; loud and clear.

The rest of July flew by. Day by day, I was getting used to living out in California, but I still missed Chicago and Uncle Jack so much. I was invited to many parties by Alexis and Bailey. They were right: we became close friends.

The girls had a cabana at a private beach club their parents owned. It was the size of a small apartment. They hosted many parties while their parents were out of town. It was considered the hot spot. At one party, I did meet some cool people. One of them was Jameson, who was known around school as the in-house party coordinator, a title he shared with Bailey. I also met Sam, best friend to Simon.

I was hopeful in seeing Simon again, but he never showed up. I wasn't going to pretend that I wasn't disappointed, but I went on to have a good time with my friends. Sam told me that parties weren't Simon's thing. I wondered if Simon would be interested to know that it wasn't mine either.

It was the last weekend of July, and I couldn't believe school would be starting soon. The Beach Club was hosting a volleyball tournament, and I was invited to go with Alexis and Bailey. Mom and dad were out of town on a quick trip, so I stayed over with the girls. We were up all night talking.

They were early risers, where I just wanted to stay in bed. Alexis put an end to that quickly by blasting Lady Gaga and jumping on my bed. *Should I tell them that I am not a morning person?* Bailey dragged my tired ass out of bed and shoved coffee into my hand.

"Come on, Nicolette! Time is wasting, and we have some hot guys to meet."

Bailey practically pushed me into the bathroom. I took a quick shower and got dressed.

I began to say that I was ready when Alexis put her hands up and said, "Hell no, Nicolette. What are you wearing? I think we can do better than that."

I looked at my appearance and asked, "What's wrong with what I have on?"

"Nothing…if you don't want to attract any attention today. You are so wearing a bikini. I heard it on good authority from my sources that Simon will be down at the beach today."

My eyes lit up. "Where did you hear that?"

"Sam, of course."

I let out a gasp of excitement. Finally, I was going to see Simon. As I was jumping up and down with Bailey, Alexis ran down to the surf shop. She returned with three bikinis in hand. I took one of the suits from her to try on. I almost fainted when my eyes zeroed in on the price tag. *Oh shit...*

Alexis just laughed. "Daddy won't mind."

I hesitated. "Alexis, I'm not sure—"

"Of course, you are. Think of it like this. Whatever you don't like, I'll just keep. It's our gift to you for introducing us to John Mayer. As you can see, we have a poster-size picture of all of us hanging up right over there. I love it on that wall. Don't you, Bailey?"

"I do. Now, go change."

The suits were beautiful. I hugged both girls and chose the champagne color bikini. It really complemented my skin tone. It showed just enough skin to attract a certain boy's attention. I was hoping that boy would be Simon.

The event got under way, and there was still no sign of Simon. Following the volleyball game, I was getting restless with the mindless chatter and constant bobbing of my head back and forth. I told Alexis and Bailey that I needed a break and was going down by the water. They weren't interested in joining me, so I went alone.

I grabbed a towel and a water, telling them I'd be back in a bit. I picked the perfect spot near the shore. I laid my towel out and fell onto my back, closing my eyes and soaking up the sun. I was not sure how long I was out there.

I felt a chill come off from the water as the clouds briefly blocked the sunshine. I slowly opened my eyes and then quickly closed them again. I hadn't noticed him. I took a few deep breaths and opened my eyes to see Simon smiling back at me. My breathing felt erratic. He had been watching me, and the thrill of knowing that excited me.

He leaned in and whispered in my ear, "Hello, Nicolette."

It was so sexy rolling off his tongue.

He was breathtakingly good looking. It took everything in me not to just kiss him. I never felt this way before, and my body's reaction to Simon surprised me. I didn't know what came over me, but I started to raise my right hand to run my fingers through his beach-tousled hair. *Get a grip, Nicolette!* I put my arm down.

"Hello back. I was wondering when you'd get here." *Shit! Did I just say that out loud? What is it with me and my runaway mouth?*

"Really? So, you were expecting me to show up today?" Simon asked.

I smiled. "I have to be honest with you. I may have heard from a reliable source that you liked beach volleyball."

"And, let me guess, could your source be Alexis, Bailey, or Jameson?"

Leaning closer to him with our mouths inches apart, I slowly turned my head to whisper back, "All of the above."

The electricity between us was strong and intense. It was an invisible force that pulled us forward with no anchor to hold us back. Simon leaned in and skimmed my lips with his. I felt my heart race as he continued to tease my mouth. In that moment with Simon, with him gazing back into my eyes, I was just lost in his.

"Do you want to take a walk with me?" he asked.

I didn't answer. I just grabbed a hold of his hand as we stood close together. We walked along the shore with our hands linked together. We talked about everything; no subject was off limits. It was so easy talking to Simon.

Thank you, Mom! I silently mouthed the words as I looked up to the sky. She and my father repeatedly told me to be patient and to give California a chance. Come to think of it, everyone who cared about me told me the same thing, including John and especially Uncle Jack.

Speaking of the parents, I blurted out, "Oh crap!"

"What's wrong?" Simon asked.

"Nothing. Do you mind if I call my parents for a quick sec? I was supposed to check in with them."

Looking relieved, Simon said, "Sure. No problem."

My conversation with my parents was short. I told them I was fine and having a great time with my friends. I wasn't specific as to which friends, but I figured that conversation would wait for another time. I took to the motto, "If they don't ask, I won't volunteer the information."

I completely forgot about the tournament and the twins. I was having too much fun with Simon. We walked hand in hand until almost dusk, where we found ourselves back at the club, huddled around the huge bonfire. He had his arm around my shoulder and pulled me close to his side as we watched the fireworks light up the sky.

My phone was going off non-stop with text message alerts. I was silently praying for it to just stop, fearing I knew who it was. When I finally took it out of my pocket to shut it off, Simon grabbed it from my hand. He surprised me, but I wasn't upset.

I simply said, "I'll just turn it off."

He took a quick glance at it and said, "No need. It was just a solicitor," as he handed me back my phone. "Nicolette, will you excuse me for a minute? I have to take care of something."

"Of course. Are you okay? May I join you?"

"Yeah, I'm fine. I won't be long. Stay here, and save my seat?"

"Of course. Hurry back."

He looked at me as if he just caught his breath, as he inhaled sharply. He winked at me and then took off.

I couldn't believe I just said that. *Yeah, I can.* I spent the most wonderful day with the sexiest boy on the beach.

Simon

I had it bad. When Nicolette smiled at me, she literally had the power to take my breath away. When I saw who was texting her and the lewd messages that followed, I was fucking pissed.

I cursed under my breath as I made my way over to the St. Clair's cabana. No one answered the door. I went around to the deck to find Michael, Seth, and a few girls I recognized from school.

With his voice slurred, clearly drunk, Michael asked, "Paulson, what the hell are you doing at my party?"

"Don't worry, asshole. I'm not staying. I was just wondering why you were texting Nicolette?"

"I would have thought for a smart guy like yourself that it would be obvious," Michael said, again slurring his words. "I wanted to invite Nicolette and her friends over here to party with us."

"No thanks. Nicolette has all the friends she needs and respectively declines your invitation."

"Is that coming from Nicolette or from you?" Michael asked, now suddenly sober and ready to come at me over Nicolette.

"It's coming from *me*, so stay away from her. Do you really want to go down this road again with me? I mean it, Michael. Back the fuck off!"

Michael bravely said, "Hey Simon! What if I don't? What are you going to do about it?"

What the fuck! He really doesn't get it.

I turned around and simply replied, "You don't want to know the answer to that."

Nicolette

What could be taking him so long to return? I decided to go look for Simon. I walked around for a bit and still saw no sign of him. I was about to walk back to the bonfire when I walked into a solid chest of muscle.

Without looking up, I said "Finally, you're back. I was getting lonely without you."

I suddenly realized I wasn't in Simon's arms, as I was getting dizzy from the smell of liquor coming from his breath. It was Michael.

"What the hell!" I screamed and tried to step back.

His arms got increasingly tighter around me. He licked his lips and smirked. "If I knew you missed me, I would have been here sooner."

The scent of him was making me sick, and just his touch was creeping me out. I finally used the defensive techniques my Uncle Jack taught me and managed to push him off me.

I stepped backward and found my voice. "Fuck you! Step the hell back, asshole. You're drunk, and it's not you who I missed."

Michael didn't flinch. He just stood there as his eyes roamed up and down my body. I wrapped my arms around my waist. I felt exposed and wanted to shield my body from him. Jameson walked over and pulled me to his side, sending Michael a clear message to back the hell away. I was so thankful for the help.

What happened next, I couldn't believe. I was startled by the sudden movement of Michael being slammed by Simon. *Where did he even come from?* Sam was following close behind, as Jameson pulled me closer to protect me from getting in the middle of two guys wrestling on the sand.

Simon was back on his feet and shouted at Michael. "What the hell, St. Clair! I told you to stay the hell away from Nicolette."

Michael was now up on his feet and pushed Simon backward, but he was too quick and remained standing. I was shaking as the twins showed up and made their way over to me. They didn't seem surprised about seeing fists being thrown around.

I stepped around Jameson and asked Simon, "What the hell is going on?"

Michael remained quiet, but once again his eyes were locked down on my body and then stopped at my breasts. His obvious staring sent shivers down my spine.

"Don't look at her, you prick!" shouted Simon as he lunged for Michael again.

Sam pulled him back, and I yelled, "I've had enough of this bullshit!" My perfect afternoon with Simon and our friends was now ruined. I began walking away with Simon now by my side.

"Please, Nicolette, wait," Simon called out.

"No. I just want to go home. I don't know what that was back there, but I can tell you that I didn't like it one bit. I didn't come here today for this, and I don't appreciate watching two guys go to blows over me. See you around, Simon."

I turned away from him and walked faster back to the cabana. I heard Simon call out for me, but I kept going but not before hearing him shout at Michael not to come near me or he would be eating sand again.

"Please, Nicolette. Can I explain myself and clear this up before it totally ruins our night?" Simon pleaded with me.

I finally stopped and turned to face him. "It already feels ruined. What was that back there with Michael?"

Simon bent down to place his hands on his knees and take in a deep breath. "Please, just give me a sec to catch my breath, and then I will tell you."

"Okay," I replied, crossing my arms over my chest.

"He and I know each other, that much you know. We have history, and not the good kind. We are not friends and never will be. I like you, okay. I genuinely care about you, but when I saw who texted you, I just couldn't see straight. I was angry and jealous."

"Why? What was on there?"

"I guess you never looked at them when I gave you back your phone?"

"Why would I? I believed you when you told me it was just a solicitor. I had no reason not to trust your answer, and honestly, I was having too much of a good time to care."

Simon was now smiling and stepped closer to me, asking permission with his eyes to touch me. I softened my stance and stepped forward. Once I was in his arms, he breathed in a calming breath.

He said, "I really am sorry. Once I saw his crude messages, I just knew he was probably drunk. All I wanted to do was shut him up. I'm sorry I chose my fists to do that. I didn't mean to scare you. I'm not that guy, Nicolette, but I am that guy that would protect his girl."

His girl? Yes, I heard him right.

I reached for his hand and looked deeply into his eyes. "I believe you, Simon, and I know you wouldn't hurt me. I'm a big girl who can take care of herself, especially with guys like Michael."

"I get that, but why should you have to when you have me around to protect you?"

I was feeling weak in my knees and desperately wanted Simon to kiss me. I decided to be brave and just go for it.

"Simon, can I ask you a question?"

He smiled and pulled me closer to his chest. He was tall and lean with his body lined with toned muscles. He smelled like the ocean, and his eyes were so blue you could see your reflection in them.

I asked him, "Will you kiss me?"

"I was hoping you would say that," he whispered as he leaned into my mouth and crushed his lips onto mine, making my lips numb and my legs turn to jelly. Simon was first to pull away, breaking his tight hold on me. "Aside from the brief interruption, today has been amazing. Nicolette, can I see you again?" he shyly asked.

"Um, isn't it obvious? Didn't our kiss convince you that I like you, Simon?"

"I guess you have to tell me again because I didn't quite get it the first time."

I moved my hand to the back of his neck, as I pulled him down to me. I kissed him hard as our mouths connected. He stepped back and almost looked dizzy.

"Convinced yet?" I giggled.

"Yes, that did the trick. So, I guess that kiss was a 'yes' to my question?"

"It was. Simon, you most certainly can see me again."

He swept me up and off my feet into a spinning hug. I felt amazing in his arms and didn't want this feeling to end. We missed the rest of the fireworks, as we were having some of our own. I was where I wanted to be, right here with Simon.

I did not want our time to end, but it was late and I promised my parents I would go home after the beach party. Sure, I could have stayed at the cabana with the girls, but I didn't want to push my luck with my parents, nor my curfew.

Simon drove me home, and he didn't want our night to end either. Thirty minutes later, we were in my driveway making out a little before he jumped out and opened my door. I smiled and thanked the universe for bringing Simon into my life. He took my hand in his and walked me to my front door.

"Can I kiss you one more time before I say goodnight?" he asked.

His face was flushed, waiting for me to answer him. I reached up to his cheeks and kissed him first. He wrapped his long arms around my waist and kissed me back. He halted our kiss and took in a deep breath.

"I wasn't expecting that, Nicolette, but I'm not complaining either."

"Thank you for a wonderful day and an amazing evening," I said as I gave him one more hug and then stepped inside.

"Nicolette," he asked quietly. "Please tell me that I will see you again?"

"I promise, Simon. Yes."

I felt my cheeks heat up as I watched Simon walk back to his Jeep. I leaned up against the door and smiled happily. I was so in over my head with Simon Paulson, but I didn't care.

I whispered silently to myself, "California is beginning to look up for me."

Three

Nicolette

The bright sunshine and my loud alarm woke me up on what I predicted would be an amazing September day, the first day of my senior year. After enjoying the best summer of my life, thanks to Simon and my new friends, I was ready for today. More importantly, I couldn't wait to be in Simon's arms again.

I leaped out of bed with happy butterflies dancing around in my stomach. I couldn't believe how happy I was, no longer the sullen teenager from when I first arrived a few months ago. Alexis and Bailey made my first summer in California a memorable one.

We were thick as thieves. These girls were non-stop fun. To begin at a new school was difficult enough, but now that I knew they would be there helped make the change that much easier. Jameson, Sam, and of course, Simon, would be there too.

I tore into my closet and examined all the new purchases mom and I had chosen for my wardrobe. I wanted the perfect outfit for today. Thanks to the shopping spree I enjoyed with my mom and then the girls, I had so many selections to choose from. I kept it simple. I decided on a denim mini skirt, a camisole top, and a light sweater. My ensemble was completed with my favorite Doc Marten boots. I kept my hair down and applied some light mascara and lip gloss. My cheeks blushed with thoughts of seeing Simon this morning. With one last glance in the mirror, I was ready to go.

I greeted Gracie with a good morning hug, and she had my breakfast ready for me. Gracie knew how I was always nervous on the first day of school, but I told her, "Not today. I am more than ready. I'm looking forward to going."

Gracie raised her eyebrows up at me with that curious look of hers.

"What?" I asked.

"You look happy, that's all. It's nice to see it, and I am guessing Simon has something to do with it?"

Did she have a secret radar to my thoughts?

"Yes, Simon is one of the reasons why I am so happy today."

"Never mind," she said. "Eat your breakfast before it gets cold."

I could easily forget my name when I thought of Simon. He was just so handsome, and I couldn't wait until I could wrap my arms around him. I gathered my things, and then I noticed flowers on the table that weren't there last night.

"These are beautiful. Dad has great taste," I said to Gracie.

"Those are not for your mom, but for you."

I looked at Gracie with wide eyes. "Yeah, right, who would send me flowers?"

I read the card:

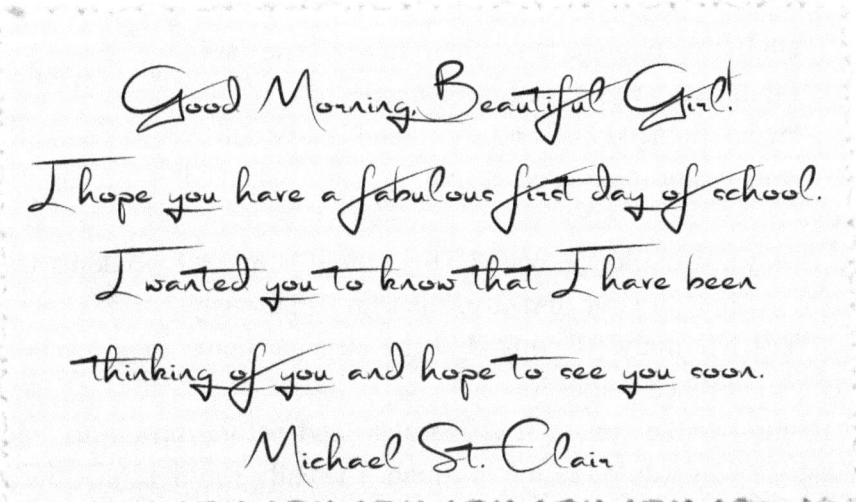

Good Morning Beautiful Girl!
I hope you have a fabulous first day of school.
I wanted you to know that I have been
thinking of you and hope to see you soon.
Michael St. Clair

I placed the card down as if it burnt my hand. How bizarre for Michael to send me flowers. After the fight, he had with Simon and how I told him off, it was incredibly strange for him to do this. I didn't have time to give this anymore thought. I had to get to school…and to Simon.

"Bye, Gracie, see you later," I called out as I pulled out of my driveway.

I was driving my new baby blue Volkswagen bug, courtesy of mom and dad. I loved my car; it was so me.

As I pulled up to the quad, I saw the girls waiting for me. They ran over and started chatting away. Simon pulled up next, but this morning he was on his motorcycle. My eyes lit up like a Christmas tree just at the sight of him. He saw the excitement in my eyes and walked over.

"Good morning," he said. He gave me a kiss on my lips and pulled back. I wanted more, but he gave me a wink and whispered, "I'll kiss you the way I want to…later."

He caught up to Sam, as Alexis walked up and laughed at the sight of the two of us.

"Shut up." I giggled.

"God! You two are fantastic together," she said.

"I think so. Let's hope Simon agrees too."

"He would need his head examined if he didn't."

I was going to say something in return when Simon came over to us.

"May I walk you to class? This school is huge. I wouldn't want you to get lost on your first day," he said flirtatiously.

"Yes, you may." I winked at the girls as Simon took my hand. "See you at lunch, ladies."

Simon walked me to my first class and before turning to leave, he said, "You won't see me at lunch. I usually run the track during that period."

"Maybe I'll skip lunch and watch you run sometime."

"Hell yeah! I would love that!" Simon picked me up and soundly kissed me goodbye.

"O-M-G, Simon, everyone is looking at us." I held onto him before he put me down.

"Yeah, that's what I wanted. Now the other guys will know that you are very taken."

He ran off and left me to enter my class, along with my reddened cheeks that so easily gave me away. I had completely fallen for Simon Paulson.

My first day had been amazing so far, with my morning flying by. I liked all my classes, and the teachers were pretty cool. I wished my friends were in more of them, but at least I got to have English with Simon. By the time I reached the quad for lunch, Alexis practically dragged me down to the grass, begging me for details about Simon. She was so curious and asked me question after question.

I took a deep breath and looked over to my friends, who eagerly waited for the 4-1-1 on Simon, but I wasn't the type of girl to kiss and tell. What I had with Simon was pretty special, and I didn't want to complicate it with gossip.

"Girls, there is nothing new to report," I said and then began eating my lunch.

"Come on, Nicolette! You're holding out on us."

"Seriously, I'm not. I like him a lot, and I hope he likes me too. After this morning, and the very public display of affection in front of my first class, it is clear that we are more than friends, but Simon hasn't officially said the words yet."

"What does that mean?" asked Bailey. "Are you a couple? Or just friends with benefits?"

"It hasn't gotten that far yet. Seriously, get your mind out of the gutter. Okay, I would think after he said that I was 'taken' this morning, I would say we are together and I was his girlfriend. However, until he actually confirms it with words, I will remain hopeful. Is that good enough for you?"

"Yeah, 'hopeful' with a lot of making out in-between! Nicolette, who are you kidding? You are so his, but okay, play the friend card for a little while longer," Alexis said as her sister agreed with her.

"Nicolette, what you might not know is that Simon is probably considered the most popular guy here at school. He's dated a bit, but he's been single since the winter formal. I've seen him at parties with tons of girls all around him, but no one has been able to land him since Jennifer Williams."

That caught my attention. "Who's Jennifer Williams?"

The twins glanced at each other and looked regretful that they may have said too much.

Bailey said, "Jennifer was his girlfriend from the start of the junior year until February."

"What happened?" I asked.

"She died in a car accident on the night of the formal," Bailey explained.

"Oh my God! That's terrible. Poor Simon. I can't imagine how he felt losing someone that was close to him."

"They were beginning to fade out anyway," Bailey said without any emotion or regret.

"Are you fucking kidding me, Bailey? What is wrong with you? No matter what they had during their relationship, she still died. What a horrible tragedy for her family to have gone through, and for Simon too. Knowing him for the few months I have already, I can only imagine how much he cared for her."

I was disgusted with Bailey and her lack of empathy when telling me about Simon's former girlfriend. I also felt very sad for Simon and just had a strong need to see him. I threw out my lunch, having lost my appetite. The girls were surprised at my reaction and called out for me, but I ignored them and left to find Simon.

I rushed over to the track and watched him run and leap hurdles. He was so strong and athletic. I leaned up against the fence and watched him round the last corner. He smiled when he saw me. He slowed and walked over to me, trying to catch his breath.

"Hey, have you decided..." He stopped and must have noticed my tear-stained face. "You've been crying. What's wrong, Nicolette?" he asked softly as he brought me in for a kiss. "Your lips are so soft. Please, don't cry. Tell me what's wrong."

"I'm sorry. I just needed to see you. I'm better now."

"You don't lie very well. You've seen me. Now tell me what has gotten you so upset."

"It's nothing, really. You looked fantastic out there."

"Nicolette, you can talk to me. Please?" he asked again.

I was feeling foolish for crying and showing him this emotional side of me, but I was hurt for him. How could I tell him that?

"I was at lunch with the girls, and while talking with Bailey and Alexis, they mentioned that you had a girlfriend here who passed away. They said some things, and let's just say I didn't have a great reaction to hearing it. They acted as if it wasn't a big deal, but to me it was."

"I can see that." He leaned in to wipe the rest of my tears away.

I welcomed his touch and reached out to his perfectly tousled hair, gently combing my fingers through it until he finally looked up at me.

He said, "It's true. She was smart and very pretty. Unfortunately, she made an extremely foolish decision one night, and it ended her life."

"Do you want to talk about it? I'll understand if you don't."

"It's okay, it's not like it's a secret. I took Jennifer to a party after the winter formal. I wasn't one for going to them, but she really wanted to meet up with her friends. She was drinking quite a bit and smoked some pot. When I saw Jennifer and how she was acting, I got angry. I told her to stop, or I would break-up with her. Jennifer laughed it off and didn't take me at my word. You see, she was book smart and always got straight A's, but her parents were very strict. They kept her close and never really allowed her to venture too far off her academic path. On the weekends, away from their watchful eyes, she liked to let loose and forget about being the perfect daughter and just be a silly teenager."

"I understand the silly teenager part but drinking and doing drugs? That's not a good thing, Simon."

"I know that, and that's why I threatened to end things with her. I wasn't into that kind of lifestyle and certainly didn't want my girlfriend to be either. She took it too far when she got drunk and stoned. She was acting foolish, dancing crazily with guys, and being irresponsible. I had enough of the floor show. I called a cab and gave specific instructions to the driver to take her straight home. The next day, I received a call from her brother. He explained that she had been killed in a car accident. The days following her accident, I had discovered that Jennifer drove her car back to the party. She was still drunk and high. Jennifer ran a stoplight and smacked right into a semi-trailer. I heard from reports that she never saw him coming. She was pronounced dead at the scene."

"I'm so sorry, Simon." All I wanted to do was hold him, so I did exactly that.

"Thank you, Nicolette, but I'm okay. Her parents never held any resentment toward me, and they appreciated the fact that I did try to get her home. Jennifer was the one who decided not to stay home. It hurt like hell for a while, but my parents had me talk to someone about it. My family was amazing throughout all of it. I'm doing much better with it now."

"I'm sorry you had to go through something so horrible. Thank you for trusting me with your story. I will always keep it between us. You have my word."

"I trust you. You are so easy to talk to. I'm comfortable and feel like I can tell you anything. Do you think that's weird?"

"No, not at all. I feel the same way about you."

Our conversation then shifted from words to actions. He cupped my face with his hands and kissed me softly.

He said, "There goes the second bell. I guess lunch is over. Since you missed it because of me, how about I take you somewhere after school?" He smiled as he waited for my answer.

"That would be perfect. I'll call my mom to ask her, but I'm sure it shouldn't be a problem."

"I will follow you to your house, and then we can go on my bike. You're not afraid of motorcycles, are you?"

I shook my head no. The thought of being on the back of Simon's bike with my arms wrapped around him thrilled me. I called my mom but reached her voicemail. I left her a message and told her about my after school plans.

He kissed me one last time before leaving the track. "Okay, get to class before you are late. I am smelly and in need of a shower."

"You smell perfect to me." *Yes, I actually just said that.*

Simon didn't say anything in reply. He just smiled and looked happy as he walked toward the gym.

After the sound of the last bell, I was beyond excited to take a ride on Simon's bike. It was a shiny, cherry red Harley-Davidson Road King Classic. Simon's motorcycle didn't blend in with the typical sporty bikes here in L.A. My heart accelerated at the sight of him sitting on it while waiting for me.

Simon jumped off his motorcycle, and the look on his face told me exactly what he was thinking. He wanted to kiss me. I ran up to him and once again, he swept me up off my feet and into his arms. This was the best place to be. I welcomed his kiss, and then he gestured over to Bailey, who was trying to get my attention.

"I won't be a minute. Let me talk to her," I said.

Simon glared over at Bailey. He was clearly annoyed with her. She apologized for her insensitive behavior at lunch. I accepted her apology and turned back to Simon. He stroked my cheek and kissed me again. My body felt on fire, and all I wanted was to kiss him again and again, but I hesitated. He was putting out all the signals that he wanted me as his girlfriend but still hadn't said the words.

We left school, with him following me home. I quickly parked my car into the garage and ran over to Simon. He picked me up and placed me on the back of his bike.

Good thing I remembered to slip on my shorts underneath my skirt or Simon would have seen a lot more of me. *Not that I would complain about that, but I will keep that little thought to myself.*

We arrived at the restaurant, and Simon parked his bike. He easily lifted me up into his arms and kissed me before placing me down.

"You know, I could have gotten off all by myself," I told him.

"You could have, but what fun would that have been?" He winked and then placed his hand on the small of my back as he led me into the restaurant.

I almost bit my lip, realizing the innuendo in what we just said to each other and what it implied. It was hard not to run away with my mouth around Simon. All these new feelings I was experiencing with him felt amazing, like the way he asked me to hold on tight to him and how his hands grazed the inside of my thighs when he placed me on his bike. The best was when I was pressed hard against his leather jacket when he told me to lean into him while taking the turns. He didn't have to ask me twice.

We had chosen a booth toward the back for privacy. The waitress handed me a menu, and I began looking through it.

I started, "So, this is the Juice Bar. I've never been here before, but everyone at school said it was a popular hot spot."

"Yeah, I don't know about that. I just like the food, and now the company," he said and went back to looking at the menu. "So, why did Bailey apologize to you?"

I didn't want to have this conversation with him right now. Having to hear it from the girls and then Simon was hard enough, and I didn't want to upset him over Bailey and her insensitive comments.

"Nicolette, please look at me." He gently lifted my chin so he could look directly at me. My body trembled under his touch as his fingers grazed my chin.

"Simon, do you seriously want to discuss Bailey, of all people, right now? Let's just enjoy our date." I was hopeful that he would agree with me and change the subject.

"No, not really, but I do want to know why you were so upset back at school. What happened to Jennifer was no secret. The entire school and faculty are well-aware on what happened the night she lost her life, but I also know how some people can be cruel when talking about it. Is that it? Did Bailey say something hurtful?"

I hesitated at first, which just made Simon more determined to know the truth. "No, not exactly hurtful, but more like insensitive. The girls didn't exactly hold back when they were talking about Jennifer and my reaction to hearing it was reactive. I was upset. No matter what, she was a daughter, a friend, a classmate, a girlfriend, and a sister. I can't even begin to imagine how you felt losing her and how her family dealt with their loss."

"It's amazing to me how you can go on about someone you never knew and have so much compassion for, and then you have the friends who can talk about her as if she was just a distant memory."

"Thank you, Simon. But I am not special by having compassion, I am just human."

"I would beg to differ on that. You are amazing. I haven't stopped thanking fate for putting me on the same beach as you on the very day we met."

I had to catch my breath after hearing Simon say those beautiful words to me. My eyes glazed over, and I felt as if I were floating on air. He finally snapped his fingers to stop me from daydreaming.

"Nicolette, are you okay?"

"Yes, I'm fine. You just caught me off guard. I kind of feel as if the conversation has just shifted. My head is spinning right now, and I am finding it hard to form words."

He leaned in to kiss me and then said, "You are adorable. Perfect in every way. Let's order some food, and then we can talk some more."

Simon made it clear that he didn't want to talk about Alexis or Bailey. He felt they could be superficial at times and warned me to be careful on what I chose to tell them. I was a little taken back by his comments, but since he was the subject of our lunch conversation, he had every right to be angry with them. I defended them and asked Simon to give them another chance. People could surprise you and end up being your closest friends for life.

I was starving by the time the waitress brought out our food. No one could make a burger like my aunt back home, so I went with a grilled vegetable panini. Simon's plate was overloaded with protein and carbs. I grimaced at all the calories, but he just took a huge bite out of his sandwich and winked over at me.

After we finished our meal, we sat back and shared a dessert. I told Simon that I was usually guarded with new people but found it easy to talk to him. He said he felt the same way about me.

"Okay, let's recap," I said. "I told you about Chicago. We covered our favorite music. Likes and dislikes, and of course, my Uncle Jack and his amazing restaurant. If you ever find a reason to visit the city, you must try my aunt's specialty burger. It's a hit on the menu."

"Sounds like a plan, but only if we go together. You can be my tour guide of the Windy City."

I smiled at Simon's casualness as if we were going to be together long enough to be able to take a trip like that. I asked, "What's it like having three older brothers, and them being triplets?"

"My brothers are very cool, but as the youngest, sometimes they tended to tease me a bit too much. They always have my back, though, and I am lucky to have them. I would love for you to meet them when they visit on their school break."

"I would love that, but as long as they don't sandwich me like they do to you."

"Um, sorry, I can't promise that."

We both laughed knowing his brawny brothers would do exactly that. After enjoying another ride on the back of his motorcycle, we were back home at my house. Simon walked me to my front door, smiling all the way.

"I had a really good time today, Nicolette."

He was about to kiss me good night when my front door suddenly swung open, and staring back at me was my father, not happy one bit.

"Hey, daddy, I was just saying goodbye to Simon. I'll be right in."

He totally ignored me as he looked over to Simon, kind of sizing him up. I loved the protective side to my dad, but he didn't have to be when it came to Simon. I totally trusted him. My father extended his hand out and introduced himself.

"I'm Mason Vanelle, Nicolette's father."

"Pleasure to meet you. I'm Simon Paulson," he replied and shook his hand in return.

My dad accepted his greeting and then rubbed his chin. "Have we met before?"

"Yes, we did, sir," Simon replied. "We met over the summer at the Beach Club."

I gave my father a look to not embarrass me in front of my boyfriend, at least I hoped he was. Simon stood tall and accepted my father's invitation to come inside. Simon reluctantly took a seat that dad gestured to him, and I sat beside him. My stomach felt nervous, but Simon appeared to be calm.

My dad gave Simon a serious expression and then said, "You seem like a responsible young man, but here's the thing. School ended at 2:15. It is now after seven. The way I see it, you have spent more than four hours with my daughter, and I don't know that much about you to justify that length of time." *OMG! Yup, he went there.* The words that followed that were not what I was expecting. "Are you dating my daughter?"

"Daddy!" I screeched.

My father glared back at me. "What? Is that not what is happening here? It's a fair question and one I would like an answer to."

"I care about your daughter. As far as officially dating, we haven't discussed that yet," he answered and nervously looked back over to me.

I suddenly wanted to remove myself from this conversation and call it a night. Here was Simon being honest, but after all the time we spent together, I would have thought it was obvious that we were a couple and he was my boyfriend. Throwing out statements that all pointed to a relationship, and now to sit here and somewhat deny it, had me confused. We had a strong connection between us. I knew he felt it too just in the way he touched, kissed, and hugged me. The entire school knew our status better than we did. How did he not know what we were?

Dad continued, "You see, Simon, we are new to California, and this is Nicolette's last year in high school. I want her to meet many new friends and get acclimated to her new school."

Hello! I'm still in the room.

"I understand that, Mr. Vanelle. I have only lived in California for two years now. My family are transplants from Colorado."

"What? Really?" I questioned and was quite surprised upon hearing that.

Simon patted my thigh and then said, "You didn't ask. You *assumed* I was a surfer dude from Cali."

I smirked at him.

"What brought your family to California?" dad asked.

"My mom was offered her dream job and accepted the offer to be dean of students at California State University."

"That's quite impressive."

My jaw dropped a little, and my father just smiled. My dad had high standards for me, and now knowing what his mom does, Simon earned some brownie points in the boyfriend department.

My dad wasn't finished yet. "What does your father do?"

"My dad is a lawyer and practices in the private sector."

"Well, seeing how you've been raised by a lawyer, I think I'm done with my cross-examination." They both laughed and seemed relaxed around each other. "Nicolette is our only daughter. Her mother and I do not wish her to socialize with just anyone, but you seem like a level-headed young man."

"Thank you, sir. I am," he said confidently.

"Simon, we are hosting a party here in a few weeks. The guest list will mostly include business associates, but we are hoping for friends as well. Please consider this as my invitation to you and your parents. You are more than welcomed to join us."

My head snapped up, and I looked at my father back to Simon. *Party? Here? The Paulson's are invited? ...And I still don't know if he's my boyfriend yet?*

"Thank you, sir. I will pass along your invitation to my parents."

"Sounds great. I am happy we had a chance to get to know one another better. Nicolette will see you out."

Dad turned to say just one more thing to me as if I could not sink any further into embarrassment. "Not too much longer. It's a school night, and I am sure you have homework to do." He kissed me on my forehead and left us on our own.

"Simon, are you okay?" I nervously asked him. *Yup! It was nice knowing you.*

"I'm okay. No worries. Is your dad always like this? He was a bit forward, but I understand where his protectiveness comes from."

"He can be protective, but his intentions always come from a good place."

Simon shook his head and laughed. "Jennifer's mom was the same way. Her dad was the softy. She was my first serious girl-friend. So, I am not that experienced when it comes to nervous fathers."

"Simon, I wasn't thinking that at all, I was just..." he cut me off and shrugged off what I might say.

"It's cool. Relax. I have to get home myself. I will see you to-morrow at school."

As I stood and watched Simon drive off on his motorcycle, I could not help but feel hurt by the way he just left. *Thank you, dad. You just scared away someone I cared about.*

Once back inside, I hurried up to my room and slammed my door for effect. *Simon just got up and left. No kiss goodbye, not even a pat on the back. "It's cool. Relax. See you at school tomorrow?" What the hell just happened?*

A few minutes later, I heard a knock on my bedroom door.

"Leave. Me. Alone." I shouted. "You. Ruined. Everything." I didn't care how harsh I sounded, nor did I care if I hurt his feelings. Just like he didn't care about mine, or Simon's, for that matter. *After the way Simon left, he probably won't want to see me again.*

The knocking continued. "Please, honey. Can we talk?"

"Don't you think you've done enough talking for one night? Go away!" I shouted at my closed door.

I buried my tear-stained face in my pillow and blocked my father out. Just then, a softer voice called out for me. It was my mom this time.

"Nicolette, may I come in? I promise not to let your father follow," she said. I opened my locked door to her and began to cry again. She hugged me back with my head on her shoulder.

"Shhh, it's okay, baby." She stroked my hair and tried to calm me down. "Why don't we sit down and you tell me all about it?"

I hugged my pillow and sobbed again.

"It's daddy. He completely humiliated me tonight in front of Simon. His behavior was over the top, and for what? Because I came home late? Mom, it was only a little past seven. I stayed out later than that back in Chicago."

"Nicolette, did you ever think that maybe dad was just being a dad? You never had a problem with your father and his protectiveness before. And what about Uncle Jack? He's worse. He literally held a baseball bat when boys would come to our door."

I laughed at that memory because mom was spot on with her description of Uncle Jack.

"Okay, mom, I see your point, but don't you get it? It was you and daddy that wanted me to meet new friends and love California. Love my new life. So, when something good happens to me, like meeting a wonderful guy like Simon, he goes all warden-like and scares him off? Tonight, was different. He didn't need to behave like that toward Simon. You should have seen him, mom. Simon couldn't get away fast enough."

My mother just sighed. "Nicolette, I believe you are getting upset over nothing. If this boy is all that you say he is, then give him the benefit of the doubt before you convince yourself that whatever this is between you is over. As for your father, go downstairs and talk to him. He loves you more than life itself. You need to give him a bit of a learning curve when it comes to his only daughter and the fact that you are growing up. And now we have dating to add to the mix. I am sure it's quite evident not only to your father but to me as well that you are falling in love."

I looked at my mom, "Is that what this is? Am I falling in love with Simon Paulson?"

She smiled lovingly at me, "Sweetheart, you tell me."

I then hugged my mom with the strongest hug I could manage. "We shall see. I'll keep you posted. I love you, mom. I'm going to go talk with daddy now."

"I love you too. Your father is in his office."

"Don't let it go to your head or anything, but you were right. Dad was just doing his thing. I'm very lucky."

She responded, "Am I hearing things? You did just say that, right?"

I laughed and made my way downstairs. Mom looked as if she had just won the lottery. Yes, we had our fair share of fashion battles and a test of wills, but she was my mom and she loved me.

Once I reached my father's office door, he opened it with his arms wide open for me.

"I'm sorry, daddy, but you surprised me. I didn't know what to think of it."

"Nicolette, the last thing I want to do is upset or make you angry with me. I love you, and I just don't want you moving too fast. We are far from what we are used to, and as much as I want you to meet friends and make positive connections, I'm also trying to remain protective of you."

"I understand that, but you have always taught me that I need to learn how to walk before I run. I have always known where your heart is when it comes to me. I'm not a little girl. I'm almost eighteen, and you raised me right. I would never willingly do anything to disappoint you or mom. I'm just trying to adjust to this new life you moved me into, and Simon may be a part of it. At least, I am hoping he still wants to be. Please, trust me."

My father hugged me once more, and I thought I saw tears in his eyes. "I love you. And I do trust you. You are amazing."

By the time my head hit the pillow, I was completely drained. Despite my father and his meet-and-greet with Simon, it was a pretty amazing day. Yes, I learned some sad things too, but the time I spent with Simon was fantastic.

I didn't like how he left here tonight, though. My head was beginning to ache just thinking about it. *Simon cares about me, he said it himself. I know it, and he does too. His physical reaction when he touches me excites us both. I get dizzy in every kiss we share. So why did he leave? Or why hasn't he called me by now? Is he that freaked out over a few questions from my father?*

You know what, Nicolette? Go. To. Sleep! I do have a terrible habit of overthinking the crazy scenarios that run through my mind. All this worrying will be forgotten by tomorrow, and it will not even matter, I hope.

Four

Nicolette

I arrived at school with a few minutes to spare. I jumped out of my car and ran for my first class. I made it to my math class with less than two minutes before the bell rang. I wasn't in the mood to listen to my teacher drone on for the next ninety minutes, but if I had gotten enough sleep the night before, then I wouldn't be so cranky this morning.

And...success! I didn't fall asleep in the world's most boring class. I was in need of strong coffee and maybe some chocolate too. Chocolate cured all, right? I had a fifteen-minute break before my next class. One thing I did love about this campus was the enormous palm trees planted all over. I sat down under one and began to look over my study notes. I was focused on what I was reading when Michael walked out from behind the tree.

"Hey!" he shouted.

I yelled, "What the hell? You scared me! What are you doing sneaking up on me like that? And, better yet, why are you here and not at Stanford?"

Michael put his hands up as if he were surrendering. He looked all too happy at my expense.

"That's a lot of questions to my simple hello," he said as he sat across from me.

"Um, Michael, you do realize where you are?" I asked him.

"Paranoid much? Geez, Nicolette, relax."

"You know, you are the second person to tell me to relax within twenty-four hours, and I don't like it," I spat out.

"Sorry. I was here on another matter, and I simply saw you sitting there. I figured I would say hello, but clearly, by your warm welcome, I am not wanted."

He got up and began to walk away. I felt like a total bitch. This wasn't me. I was just projecting some misplaced anger toward him.

"Hey, Michael," I called out as he stopped and then turned around. "I'm sorry. I didn't mean to run you off. It's been a rough morning."

"Apology accepted. Do you have a few minutes then?"

I looked around with no one in sight, especially Simon. I took a glance at my phone and told Michael I had a few minutes left before I needed to leave for my next class.

"Did you receive the flowers I sent?"

"I did. Thank you. It was very thoughtful, although I'm curious to why you would send them at all?"

"Call it a peace offering. I get that I was a total jerk the last time we were together. So, what better way to apologize to your girl than to say it with flowers."

"Let me be clear. I am not your girl. The last time you saw me, I was with Simon, not you."

"Damn, you certainly know how to kick a guy when he's down. I was just trying to be nice."

"I see that, but why are you coming on so strong? Especially when, if you haven't figured it out already, I am interested in someone else."

"Relax. Sorry, you don't like that word. I like you. I don't see the problem here."

"I'm flattered, but whatever you think is going to happen here, it's not. I have feelings for someone else."

"Simon Paulson…is he the one you are into?" he calmly asked.

"Michael, I don't think that's any of your business."

He stepped closer, a bit too close for my personal space. "It is my business if he's the one standing in my way to you."

"One last time. Michael, the only person standing in your way is me. I decide who gets my time. I don't appreciate being lied to, and I hate guys that play games. Stay away from me. And do not ever try to use my parents' working relationship with your father to get close to me."

I gathered up my backpack and threw my coffee out.

"Nicolette, I was only playing around. It doesn't change how I feel. Can we just start over? One date is all that I ask. I promise you that you will have fun."

I began walking away. "I don't think so."

He caught up to me and blocked my path. "Why not? Give me one valid reason."

"God! You are making it really difficult to be nice here. We don't have anything in common. You're in college. Why do you want to hang out with a girl in high school? Don't you have a frat party to get to? Please, take the hint. I like someone else." *I just need Simon to tell me that he wants me too.*

"Okay, wait. The fact that you are in high school will not stop me from pursuing you. It's not a big deal. Is it too ridiculous to believe that I just might like you? All I am asking is for a date. Come on, give me a chance. Think about it, and give me a call."

Before I could respond to him, he leaned in and kissed me on my cheek. I was still in a daze when the final bell rang. Shit! I was late.

Simon

What the fuck? I couldn't believe the exchange I just witnessed between Michael and Nicolette. I wanted to punch something, and his face was my intended target. *What the hell does he think he is doing?*

Michael is still trying to take my girl out from under me, and after I have warned him over and over again to back the fuck off. I cursed at myself because I knew I had no right to be mad, especially after leaving her last night. I didn't even call her, which was stupid. I didn't have any claim to her, not a real one of any kind. This was entirely my fault for not making her mine sooner. It was clear to me after I left that Nicolette wanted more. Wanted me. So, what the hell was my problem? If I didn't tell Nicolette, how I felt about her, I might as well push her into Michael's arms, and fuck that if I will ever allow that to happen.

I followed him to where he parked his car, away from prying eyes. I didn't need a suspension right now for beating his ass down. My coach or teammates wouldn't be too happy if that happened.

When I was in reach, I called out to him. "Hey, what are you doing here?"

"Hey, Simon. Always a pleasure seeing you."

"Fuck you and your fake pleasantries. I saw you with Nicolette. I told you to stay away from her. She is off limits."

"Why? Because you said so? I think based on the conversation I just had with her, she is single and very available," he enunciated slowly. He knew I was ready to pounce. "Again, she's fair game. If I want to pursue her, I will. And, Simon, there is not a damn thing you could do about it. Surely, you have learned already from the past that when I want something, I usually get it."

I saw red. The fucker had the balls to bring up the past. I lunged forward but pulled back my fist. This piece of shit was not worth it.

"Be careful, Simon. You don't want to go there again with me."

"I think I do, and I will, you motherfucker!"

I lunged forward to hit him when I was pulled back by Sam.

"Dude, chill the hell out. He's not worth it. You have too much to lose over hitting this piece of shit."

I wrestled out from Sam's hold and got into Michael's face.

"Stay out of this, Sam. This is between us."

"Yeah, Sam, I think the golden boy can fight his own battles. Can't you, Simon?"

"You know that I can. I will have no problem taking you down. Stay away from her. This will be the last time I warn you."

"Sure, Simon, whatever you say." He laughed as he stepped into his Mercedes and drove off.

"Sam! What the hell? I didn't need your help back there. I can handle Michael just fine on my own. That sonofabitch was with Nicolette again! She's *my* girlfriend!" I shouted as loud as I could, not caring who heard me.

"Does she know that?" asked Sam.

I was trying to catch my breath. I was so angry. "Know what?" I shouted back.

"Your girlfriend...does she know that she is? Look, Simon, I'm your friend, and I am telling you straight. If you don't tell her soon, then you will lose her. What the hell do I know? I'm not even seeing anyone at the moment, but if I had a girl like Nicolette, then I would certainly have enough guts to tell her how I feel. But, since you are too much of an ass, to be honest with her, then St. Clair is right. She is very available."

"The hell she is, Sam! I love her." *Oh shit! Did I just say that out loud?*

"What was that, Simon? I don't think I heard you. You...what?"

"Shut up, Sam. I love her. I love Nicolette, and no one, especially Michael St. fucking Clair, is going to take her away from me. She is mine. I'm going to tell her exactly how I feel about her today."

"Good for you, man, but you need to get your shit together when it comes to Michael. He is the only one that has the ability to get under your skin. And you let him every single time."

"I love her, Sam."

"Yes, you've said that. Now, tell it to her."

"You're right. I am an ass. What have I been waiting for?"

"Hey, girls will do that to you. Go find Nicolette, and talk to her."

"Believe me, Sam, I want to. I want to hold her in my arms so much right now, but I'm afraid I will scare her off. I'm not ready yet. I think I will blow off my next class and go run the track for a bit. I need to clear my head before seeing her again. I will catch up to her at lunch, and by that time, I would have burned off all of this tension."

"Whatever you say. Good luck."

"Yeah, thanks, man."

I ran five miles and grabbed a quick shower. My coach caught the tail end of my run and was happy to see that I was practicing. If he only knew the real reason I was here today. By the time I reached the quad, lunch was nearly over. I texted Nicolette a few times but didn't get any response back. I walked up to her usual table, and she was missing.

"Hey, do you know where Nicolette is?" I asked the girls.

"She texted me that she was skipping lunch to go to the library," said Bailey.

"Seriously? On the second day of school? Come on, Bailey. Where is she really?"

"I don't know, Simon. Here, I'll show you the text." She handed me her phone, and sure enough, Bailey was telling the truth.

"Okay, thanks. I guess my girl is a bookworm."

"Your girl? Does she know that?" asked Alexis.

I turned around to answer her and made it clear to everyone in our group once and for all about our status. Nicolette was officially off the market and mine. "She will after I tell her. She's mine, Alexis."

"It's about time," The girls said in unison.

Yeah, I know it is. Once I reached the library, I walked around the entire room, and there was no sign of Nicolette. *Where is she?* I was frustrated that she wasn't answering my texts. I guess I had no choice but to wait until I saw her in English.

I tapped my fingers on my desk and still no sign of Nicolette. The final bell rang, and our teacher closed the door. *What the hell? Where is she?* I was too frustrated to stick around. I grabbed my backpack and walked out. I called over my shoulder that I was feeling sick. Not a lie technically, since I actually was sick from not knowing the whereabouts of my girl.

Her usual parking spot was empty. She had to have cut out for the day. I did the same. I pulled my bike out and headed right for Nicolette's home. If she wouldn't answer her phone, then she was going to answer her door.

Once I got to her house, I was just getting off my bike when I saw her walking toward me. She looked tired, and it was clear she had been crying. This was my fault. I only prayed she would give me a second chance to make it right.

Nicolette

"Hi, what are you doing here?"

"I could ask you the same thing, but we both know we should be in English right now. I didn't take you for a girl who cuts school, especially on the second day."

"I'm not, but I didn't want to be there today."

"Is that because of me?"

"Does it matter? I think you made it clear how you felt last night, or how you don't feel about me."

"That's not true. Please, Nicolette, can I explain?" He looked hopeful. His eyes were crystal blue, like the ocean. I already felt lost in them.

"Okay, let's go sit down under the gazebo."

"You see my bike. Can we go for a ride? Down by the beach?"

"No, I don't think so. It's been a long day, and I would rather just stay here."

"Okay, whatever you want, Nicolette."

I want you. I silently wished to myself.

He said, "You missed lunch today, and you didn't respond to any of my messages."

"I know. After last night, I thought you wouldn't want to see me again, and it was easier to just avoid you today. You know, protect my heart. I'm sorry for shutting you out. It was childish, but you gave me a reason to. I mean, you didn't even call me last night or this morning. What was I supposed to think?"

"You're right. We should always talk to one another, and I'm sorry too. Before another word is spoken, can I do what I wanted to do last night before your father interrupted us?"

71

"What's that?"

He didn't let me continue. He pulled me onto his lap and kissed me. First, it was hard, and then it was gentle. He held me with his hands wrapped around my body, and I enjoyed his lips on mine. He broke our kiss but held my face in his hands.

"Nicolette, I want you to be my girlfriend. I want you to be mine. I care about you, and I know you care about me too. Am I wrong?"

My head began to spin. He just told me that he wanted me. I was such an idiot! If I would have just talked to him today, then all this misery could have been avoided.

"No, Simon, you're not wrong. I would love to be yours."

He hugged me again and kept me close to his body. He smelled amazing with the mix of his body wash and salt water in his hair. He must have gone surfing this morning.

I said, "I'm sorry about my dad and his questions."

"It's no big deal. I was wrong not to have called you once I got home. If I had been honest about my feelings from the very beginning, then you would have never had to deal with Michael today."

Michael? How does Simon know that I saw him today? Just then my phone buzzed in my pocket. "Sorry, it's probably my mom." I looked at the number and declined the call. It was Michael again. I didn't want Simon to see it, but it was too late.

He loosened his hold and shifted me off him. He looked upset. He paced the patio and ran his fingers through his blonde hair. "Michael, right?"

"Yes, it's him. He was also on campus today. I tried to tell him again that I wasn't interested, but he will not take no for an answer." I was praying Simon would believe me. I didn't want to lose him after he just told me that he wanted me as his girlfriend.

"Was that before he kissed you?"

"Simon, it's obvious you saw it. And it was before. I told him repeatedly that I was not interested, and the only guy I have feelings for is you."

Simon let out a breath and rejoined me on the couch. He held my hands in his and placed a kiss down onto them. "Nicolette, I am so very sorry for not being honest with you sooner about my feelings. I hated the fact that you hid from me today and what Michael did. I looked all over for you, and when I finally found you, I saw him with you. Once you had left, I confronted him. He is all about playing games, especially when it comes to me. He will use you, Nicolette, anyway he can to hurt me. He's done it before and will do it again. He needs to know that you are unavailable."

"Simon, if you would have stuck around, then you would have heard me tell him that I am not interested in him. I said it several times, and he just wouldn't take a hint. No matter what I said, it didn't faze him one bit. He still asked me out and told me to think about it, to call him when I was ready."

"Well, you're not calling him, and if he comes anywhere near you again, then I need to know about it, okay?"

"What is it between the two of you? Why do you hate each other so much? Whatever it is, you can trust me with it, Simon. You do know that, right?"

"Of course, I do, baby. I just don't trust Michael, and I want you to stay away from him. I need you to promise me. If he comes around again, you need to tell me."

"Simon, you're starting to scare me."

"I'm sorry. I don't mean to. I already told you that I have a history with Michael, and it's a long and complicated one. I don't want to talk about it."

"Simon, I have only seen Michael a few times since first meeting him on the same day I met you. He has sent flowers to the house, wishing me well on my first day of school. The second was at the beach party with you, and now today."

"Nicolette, don't you see? That's way too much already. He's a jerk, and he needs to get a fucking clue to whom you belong to. You are mine, and I will never allow him to get in reach of you again. I almost punched him today, but Sam stopped me before I could."

"I see that you are hurting. Why can't you talk to me? Tell me why you dislike him so much."

"Can't you just agree not to see him, and leave it at that?"

"Not until you give me a valid enough reason."

Simon pulled me into his chest and slammed his lips onto mine. I felt the adrenaline vibrating through him. He couldn't stop touching me, and I didn't want him to. He calmed his kiss and then held my face, leaning our foreheads close to the other. He kissed me again and again and then said, "There's your reason. I have to go, but I'll call you later."

Simon walked out from my yard and toward his motorcycle. I ran my fingers across my swollen lips and still felt his kiss.

I didn't understand him, not at all, but I knew someone who might be able to help me. I texted Bailey and asked her to come to my house on the way home from school. I was determined to find out the truth.

Jumping up and down, Bailey couldn't hold back her happiness after I told her my news. "Yay! You two are finally official! I am so happy for you, but can I say that I knew this way before you did? We all did. It's about time he came to his senses. Oh, I can't wait to tell Alexis! Let me call her right now. She's shopping with Jameson. Oh my God, he's going to just freak out."

"Bailey, pump the breaks. Although this news is awesome, it is not why I asked you over."

"Come on, Nicolette, this is big news." She began typing away on her phone.

"Stop! Bailey, you can text your heart out later. Right now, I want to ask you something."

"Fine! What's up?"

"Why do Simon and Michael hate each other?"

Her smile dropped.

I pleaded, "Please, I know you know the reason."

"Yes, I know. Everyone knows, but Nicolette, it's not something we talk about. I shouldn't have even mentioned what I told you yesterday. It's none of my business, and you were right to call me out on it."

"Okay, so then it's about Jennifer, Simon's girlfriend."

"Ugh! If you want to know so bad, just ask Simon."

"I can't. Whatever it is, he won't share it with me. When I pushed him earlier, he practically shoved his tongue down my throat to shut me up. Not that I minded, his kisses are amazing. Anyway, that's beside the point. I want to know the whole story."

"You pretty much know it, but what you don't know is this. After the formal, we all attended a party at the Beach Club. You know Jennifer was drinking heavily and getting stoned. After her fight with Simon, she left our group and joined Michael's. He was there with his friends, partying just as hard. They began dancing and putting on quite the floor show. Simon was sickened by it, and we did everything we could to calm him down."

"Now, this is beginning to make sense to me. Simon hates Michael all because he was involved with Jennifer."

"It's a little more complicated than that."

"How so?"

"It wasn't pretty, Nicolette. Simon was so angry and embarrassed by how she was behaving. She was so wasted and all over Michael, you know what I'm saying?"

"Yes, I am beginning to."

"What a scene they were making! They didn't care that everyone just stopped and stared at them. He licked her neck, and his hands were all over her body. When he finally lost his shit, Simon pulled Michael off Jennifer, and then they began punching each other. They both flew over a table and landed on the floor. Michael managed to get Simon off him, and then he landed one good punch to his face. It was a mess. By the time it was over, Michael and Simon both were bloodied and banged up pretty good. Jennifer was throwing up the entire time in the bathroom. Simon had no idea that after he finally sent Jennifer home that she would go back to the party. It's been something he has had to live with since placing her in that cab. In the beginning, he did blame himself for not driving her home personally, but he was so hurt and betrayed by her that the best he could do was call a cab. Most guys wouldn't have even done that, but he's too honorable."

"I understand it now. Why would Simon ever want to relive this? It will always be with him. He doesn't need to explain it to every girl he meets."

"It's still painful for him. He says he has moved on from it, but how could you? We still feel he blames himself, at least in a small way."

"Bailey, Jennifer was the one that made the decision to drive, get drunk, and do drugs. Simon did the best he could do for her. This is not his fault."

"We know that, and we have told him that, but maybe you will be the one to make him believe it."

"Was Jennifer cheating on Simon with Michael?"

"There had been rumors that circulated around school, pretty bad ones too. Simon never knew the truth, even after she died. Who knows if he believed the rumors? What you don't know is that Simon and Michael never got along with each other, even before Jennifer came into the picture. Michael was a senior when Simon transferred to our school. Simon was a hit from the minute he stepped onto our campus, and with his athletic abilities, he became popular right away. And, Michael wasn't having that."

"Wow! What do you think I should do? Do I try to talk to him about it?"

"It's up to you. This is Simon's story to tell. You need to have patience and understanding. He will tell you when he is ready. That is my best advice."

"Thank you, friend. I know that was hard for you, but I love you for sharing it with me."

"You're welcome, and I am so very happy for you two. He's an amazing guy, and if any girl was going to win his heart, I am glad it was you."

Five

Nicolette

*I*ce cream cures all, right? That's what I told myself as I helped myself to a heaping bowl of chocolate fudge brownie while waiting for mom and dad to come home. I hadn't heard from Simon yet, and I tried not to call him. I remembered what Bailey told me about patience, and this was me giving him space until he was ready.

I had gotten into the habit of screening my calls since Michael would not leave me alone. When my phone went off again, I thought it was him, but to my surprise, it was Uncle Jack.

I brightened right up. "Hey, Uncle Jack, what's up?"

"Hello, Nickel, not too much. I had a few minutes and wanted to check in on my favorite niece."

"I'm your only niece."

"Well, that's why you're my favorite. So, tell me what's new in your life? How is the first week of school going?"

"I'm only two days into it, but I'm doing well. You will be happy to know that I have chilled out on my complaining about California. I've met some new friends, and I have a…"

"You have a…what? Nicolette?"

"Okay, twist my arm. I have a boyfriend! He's wonderful. You would love him. His name is Simon, and he is just amazing."

"Well, he better be, because you deserve someone special. As long as he treats you right, we will never have a problem."

I rolled my eyes and took in a deep breath. I was happy he couldn't see me doing that, but he probably knew. I had already gone through the big inquisition with my father, and I wasn't ready to have Uncle Jack grill me too.

"How are your parents doing?"

"All good. You know how they roll once they begin writing new material. I hardly see them, but they should be home soon."

Uncle Jack groaned on the line. I'm sure he wasn't all too happy with my slip of the tongue regarding my parents' presence.

"Nicolette, are you alone often? Because I was assured that would not happen. Didn't your father install a recording studio in your home?"

"Please, Uncle Jack, don't get upset. The studio is still under construction, and it's not like I'm abandoned. They go to work every day, just like I go to school. They're a little late tonight but that's not all the time, so don't worry. Okay?"

"I can't help it. You are too far away, and it wasn't like that when you all lived here in Chicago."

"Okay, I hear you. I love you. Please, don't worry. I'm fine."

"You better be, because if I hear different, I will be on the first flight out there and wring your father's neck."

Poor Uncle Jack and his blood pressure. Why do I always open mouth, insert foot?

While talking to my uncle, I received a few text messages, all from Michael.

"Hey, Uncle Jack, I have to go."

"Is everything okay? Nicolette, are you still there?"

"What? Oh yeah, I'm here. Sorry, I just have to take care of something. Can I call you over the weekend?"

"You know you can, day or night. If you need me, I'm there for you."

"I know, and thank you. I love you, Uncle Jack. We will talk soon."

I read the messages after I ended my call, and they were all the same. *Call him. When are we going out? Blah, blah, blah.* What is it with this guy?

After hearing more about their past, I had a better understanding what was driving Michael and his determination to win me over. It was about topping Simon, and the hell with that. I told Michael that I didn't play games, nor did I appreciate the guys that played them. I needed to tell him that I was with Simon, and this constant calling, texting, and sudden appearances had to stop.

I must have written ten messages explaining why it would not work out with Michael, but after scrapping them all, I just went with simple and to the point.

Me: *It's not going to happen. I have a boyfriend. Take care.*

I hit the send button and I waited. My message was blunt, but it needed to be. My phone pinged back with his reply.

Michael: *Boyfriend? Since when?*

My phone started to ring. *Okay, so much for being blunt. Now, what do I do?* I didn't have to look at my phone to know who was calling me. I reluctantly picked up.

"So, you're available this morning when I asked you out, and now tonight, you have a boyfriend? Wow! You move fast, don't you?"

"Really? You need to get your hearing checked if you believe that I said that I was available. I didn't say that I was. I told you that I had feelings for Simon. You just chose not to hear me, because you are too busy talking over me. I am so done with this. Just leave me alone."

"You want me to leave you alone? Then why agree to go out with me? You didn't push me away when I kissed you, now did you, Nicolette?"

"You caught me off guard, and I wasn't thinking about anything beyond my next class. And as for the kiss? That was more like a peck on the cheek that I would have given to my grandmother. You need to stop making things bigger than they really are."

"You need to stop denying what is going on between us. You feel it, I know you do. Here's my theory on the boyfriend. I think your boy, Simon, knew that I had a chance with you, and he swooped in and got to you first by delivering exactly what you wanted to hear. Now, with just a few words, you're his girlfriend. He knows I am the better man and has no chance at beating me. This is just a temporary interference. I will win in the end."

"Seriously, Michael, that's what you believe? That Simon had this diabolical plan to steal me away from you? I can't be stolen if I was never yours, to begin with. I'm not sure what world of rational thinking you are living in, but in my world, I have a boyfriend, and I will never go out with you. I hate to break it to you, but you give Simon too much credit. He's not thinking of you at all."

"Ouch, that one hurt. You surprise me, Nicolette. I love when you pull the claws out when you are heated. Do me a favor? Sharpen the claws, so when I fuck you, you can write your initials on my back. Then everyone will know who you belong to, especially Simon."

"You are disgusting. I don't need anyone to help me prove my point here. I can easily sharpen my boots and kick your ass all by myself. You are such a pompous prick. Keep on dreaming if you believe I would ever give you the time of day after what you just said to me. I tried to be nice to you. Our parents work together, and I didn't want things to be awkward between us, but you just won't see reason."

"Go out with me, and your parents will still have a job in the morning. You know, I can be very persuasive when it comes to my father. This is the movie business. Things change in a heartbeat. Scenes get cut, musicians get replaced...you know, that sort of thing."

"Are you threatening me?"

"Just stating the facts, baby. Friday night, I'll pick you up."

"No, you can go fuck yourself." I ended my call and threw my phone.

What an asshole! Trying to bully me into going out with him, or he will have my parents fired? No way would I allow that to happen. *Just stay calm, Nicolette. He's just messing with your mind. You pegged him from the start, and you were right not to trust him.* He's a spoiled rich kid that didn't like not getting what he wanted. He was not the first person to ever believe this, and I am sure would not be the last. But he sure was forward!

My skin was crawling when he talked about us having sex. He's a pig. I just had to ignore him and not allow him to get under my skin. My parents worked too hard and to come this far in their careers. I would not allow this jerk to jeopardize that. It would blow over. It had to.

I finished my homework and took a shower to calm down after my fight with Michael. I heard the garage open and knew my parents were home. I had great news to share with them about Simon, and I wasn't going to let what happened with Michael to sour my mood.

"Nicolette, we're home," Dad called out as I was just walking out from my room. He waited for me to get downstairs and then enveloped me into a hug.

How did he know this was exactly what I needed?

He asked, "Hi, honey, how was your day?"

"Better, now that you're home. I missed you today."

"Well, that's a nice thing to say. Your mom and I miss you every day. Come, dinner's ready, and I'm starved."

"Hi mom," I said, as I began passing the dishes around the table.

"How was your day, Nicolette? We want to hear all about it," she said as she took a sip of wine.

Focus on Simon and not Michael. They look happy tonight. No need to make them worry.

"I have news," I said as they both looked up at me. "Simon asked me to be his girlfriend, and I said yes."

They both looked at each other, and mom looked like she was ready to say something, but dad beat her to it.

"Nicolette, don't you think you may be rushing into things with this boy? He's very nice, don't get me wrong, but you've only known him a short time. Attaching a label to yourselves so soon may be premature."

I was going to be calm and not react negatively. "Dad, it's not a short time. I've known him since July, and I believe that's enough time to decide if I like him, and I do. He cares about me too, maybe even loves me."

My father nearly choked on his wine, but then I turned to my mom. She knew how I felt about Simon, and I think would be more understanding out of the two.

"Mom, he is wonderful. He's the star of the track team. Simon is popular, an A student… he's the real deal. Out of all the girls in our school, he wants me for his girlfriend."

"Okay, take a breath. He would have to be blind not to see how just amazing you are, Nicolette. I believe your father would agree with me. As long as Simon continues to treat you well and makes you happy, we are fine with you having a boyfriend. Just take it slow, and don't make him the center of your universe. We want more for you, you know that. This move can be an amazing adventure if you take advantage of all the new opportunities you have been given. A boyfriend is just an added bonus. Do you understand?"

"I do, but no worries. I have it covered." I got up to hug my mom, and I knew she was on board. I turned back to my father, who was uncharacteristically quiet.

"Dad?"

"As long as he behaves himself, I don't have a problem with you dating Simon. If he steps out of line with you, he will have me to deal with. You'd better reiterate that to your boyfriend."

If only my father knew that I'm the one that can't keep my hands off of him.

"Daddy, you don't have to worry about Simon. He has been perfect."

"That's good to hear. I don't want another incident like the one we had to deal with back in Chicago."

"I can't believe you are comparing what happened in Chicago to what I have here with Simon. Two very different guys and it was a big misunderstanding."

"I can't believe I am hearing this!" My father dropped his silverware down to his plate and took a sip of his wine. "You call a drunk boy coming to our home and pinning you down on the couch a misunderstanding? He's lucky he still has legs to walk on. If he would have hurt you, I don't know what I would have done."

"You overreacted then, as you are right now. Can we drop this?"

"No, we can't. He had his hands all over you. I'm thankful we came home when we did. You are too trusting. Sometimes teenage boys are not always thinking with their brains but with something else. Be careful. I would have thought you would have learned your lesson. This is why we want you to focus on school, friends, and not boyfriends."

"Thank you for the reminder. And lesson? Yeah, I learned the hard way. I was practically shunned at school after you nearly choked Jason to death."

"Remember this, Nicolette. That boy was lucky that it wasn't Uncle Jack who walked in and saw him on top of you."

"Mason…" Mom interrupted my father's rant and looked a little pale at the mention of Uncle Jack's name. "Let's drop this."

"Mom? Is everything okay?" I asked.

"Yes, I'm fine. What your father is trying to say is that he is protective, and Uncle Jack is the same way. We just love you so much. Sometimes we can get carried away, that's all. Right, Mason?"

He cleared his throat and silently nodded.

What was that all about? I asked to be excused and went upstairs. I was done with this conversation and too exhausted to argue with my father. I was holding my phone in my hand and wanted to text Simon when my mom knocked on my door.

"Are you okay, honey?" she asked.

"Yeah, I'm fine. Is daddy mad?"

"No, he's fine too. He's just dad and never wants you to be hurt. We both approve of Simon, so no worries."

"Mom, can I tell you something?"

"Yes, you can tell me anything."

"Michael St. Clair…"

"What about him?"

"He's been around. He's been calling, texting, and the flowers that arrived a few days ago, well, they were from him. He showed up at school today and asked me again to date him. I keep telling him that I am not interested and I have a boyfriend, but he's not really hearing me."

"Nicolette, if this boy is harassing you, then I will be having a conversation with his father. I will put an end to this."

"No, mom, please don't. You and daddy work with Mr. St. Clair, and I don't want to come between your relationship with him just because I am not getting along with Michael."

"Yes, it complicates matters, but you are our daughter, first and foremost. Everything comes second to you. I hope you know that."

"I do, and that's why I don't want you to say anything. We had a fight tonight over the phone. He said some things, and I said some things, and then I hung up on him. I don't believe I will be hearing from him again. I mean, he's in college. I think this was just him trying to prove something, but I'm okay."

"You will tell me if you are not, right? I know we are super busy right now, but we always have time for you. You can always talk to me or daddy. We love you so much."

"I know, and I love you too. There's one more thing."

"What's that?"

"Michael and Simon have some history between them, and it's not good. Simon has asked me to stay away from Michael."

"Why don't they like each other?"

"Simon hasn't told me everything yet. What I do know, I heard from Bailey."

"Okay, listen. I trust your judgment when it comes to your decision who to be friends with and who you are comfortable dating. Whatever is going on with Michael, I am sure he will get over it. It's not like you will have any more interactions with him. I'm sure he will focus his attention on someone else. You just concentrate on what makes you happy."

I hugged my mother and didn't want to let go. This was what I needed.

She said, "Oh, baby, I wish I could tell you that things will get easier, but it's all part of growing up. The teen years are complicated ones, but they can also be the best times of your young life. This is the time to have fun with your friends, think about the prom, and not take life too seriously. You only have that small window before you have to consider college and taking on the world, you know?"

Before going to bed, I sent a text to Simon.

Me: *Just wanted to say good night. See you tomorrow at school, my boyfriend!*

Simon: *I can't wait. Dream of me, my girlfriend!*

The next few weeks were spent with Simon and the rest of our gang. Simon took me for a ride on his motorcycle practically every day when the weather permitted. My dad was nervous about me riding on it, but Simon was an experienced rider and protected me. Things with Michael calmed down too. I didn't hear from him again since the night of our fight. I was taking that as a good sign. The subject of Jennifer never came up. I wasn't going to pressure him to share any more of his past with me. I was having too much fun just being with him.

One night, Simon invited me over to his house to meet his parents. They accepted my parents' invitation to attend our party, and Simon wanted me to get to know them before that. I was nervous, but Simon said not to be and they would love me. Ted and Marina Paulson welcomed me into their home and shared many embarrassing stories of Simon and his brothers. My boyfriend's face turned red a few times during the evening, but you could hear in his dad's voice how much he was loved.

"I had a great time tonight. Thank you for inviting me over. Your parents are great," I said.

"Yeah, they are. You know, you are pretty special too. You charmed the pants off them. I told you they would love you."

Yeah, but do you *love me? I wanted to say, but I remained quiet.*

"I better get inside before my dad comes out. I'll see you tomorrow." I kissed him goodnight and made my way upstairs. I already missed him. I was in love with Simon Paulson and fell asleep dreaming about him.

When I woke up the next morning and went downstairs for coffee, my house was buzzing with chaos. Gracie had her hands full with delivery people who were setting up for tonight's party. Hosting a huge party like this was not out of the norm for my parents, but this was not Chicago, and I knew it was important to my parents to make a good impression tonight. Many important guests would be here this evening, and it was going to be completely wine, dine, and impress.

"Come on, Nicolette, we are going to be late for our appointment," Mom shouted up the stairs. *We seriously needed to get an intercom. No, scratch that. Bad idea.*

She and I had another spa day, but this time I was looking forward to it. Just thinking of Simon and how he will react to seeing me all made up made me excited. I left my hair down in loose waves that cascaded over my shoulders. I was wearing a fabulous dress, and my makeup looked flawless.

Guests began to arrive, and I was patiently waiting for my boyfriend. Jameson, Sam, and the girls all arrived in one car. The girls looked hot and were hoping some available guys would be here tonight. Jameson was hoping for that too. I didn't want to burst anyone's bubble, but I doubted that would happen tonight. The gang took a look around and helped themselves to drinks while I sent Simon a text.

Me: *Where are you?*

Simon: *Sorry, baby, running late in traffic. Be there soon. Save a dance for me.*

Simon could have all my dances! I squealed with giggles and made my way outside to join my friends. We had a dance floor set up in the backyard, and Jameson pulled me onto it. He twirled me around the floor as he did his best moves. We were all having a great time when I felt strong arms wrap themselves around my waist. Yes! Simon was finally here.

I turned around to hug him back, and it was Michael who was holding me. His eyes traveled up and down my body as if he was picturing me naked. We'd been here before, and I was not going to do this again with him, not at my parent's party.

"What the hell, Michael? Keep your hands off me." I gritted my teeth.

"What? Can't a friend dance with another friend?"

"Not like that, and you know it. I have a boyfriend. I have made that quite clear to you, and one that will not be happy to see your hands on me, again!"

"I see no boyfriend here, so, let's dance." Just as he was about to grab me again, Sam rescued me by pulling me to his side.

"Michael, she said no, so take a hike. We don't want any trouble here tonight."

"Sure, Sam, we wouldn't want to upset Simon, now would we?"

He walked away and took his smug attitude with him. I hugged Sam and thanked him for the save.

"You're my hero. Thank you," I told him.

"No, that job is reserved for someone else, and he is walking this way," Sam said as I turned around to see Simon approaching.

I immediately prayed that he didn't see what happened with Michael.

"Hey, baby, sorry I'm late." After saying hello to Sam, he reached for my hand and slowly pulled me into him. He kissed me twice but never took his eyes too far from Michael. He was sending him a warning and then led me away, where we could be alone.

"Before you say anything…" I said, as I was silenced with more kisses and was relieved to know that he wasn't angry after seeing Michael.

"Hi," he whispered in my ear with more kisses that he slowly ran down my neck. "You look beautiful."

"Back there with Michael, I thought it was you, and then I turned around…"

"Shhh, I'm not upset. Sam handled it just fine. I am not going to allow Michael or anyone else spoil our evening. I am with the most beautiful girl in the room, and I want to dance with my girlfriend." He extended his arm out to me and escorted me back to the dance floor. "Have I told you how beautiful you look tonight? I know you probably spent hours at the salon, but I am dying to run my fingers through your gorgeous hair. You are breathtaking, Nicolette."

"Thank you, Simon. You don't look too bad either."

Just then, he grabbed the edges of his suit jacket. He opened and closed it as he did his best modelesque pose. My guy was hot, and all mine. I giggled at his silliness as I drank in his amazing abs pressing against his body clinging shirt. I couldn't help but run my tongue over my lips, wishing I could touch him right now. He was just so good looking, and if he had the power to read minds, he would know I was wanting to run my tongue all over his tight stomach.

I think he knew. He cupped my face in his hands and kissed me senseless. I swirled my tongue around in his mouth, not wanting to break our connection. We both needed to come up for air. He took my hand and led me back into the house. We spotted his parents and mine talking. After a short conversation, we were back with our friends.

Alexis was first to give me a hug, followed by Bailey. "Your home is gorgeous. Thank you for inviting us. We have a great idea. How about we stick around for another hour, and then hit a club that Jameson wants to take us to?"

I responded, "Sounds great, but I have to pass. You all go and have a great time."

"Come on, Nicolette. Live a little," Bailey chimed in.

"Girls, have you looked at my boyfriend lately? Believe me, I have everything I need. Now go and dance your asses off."

The girls and Jameson did stay for the hour they promised and then left to go clubbing. They had a hired limo for the night, and I was sure the mini bar was well-stocked.

"Hey, Sam, no clubbing for you tonight?" I asked.

Simon just laughed and wrapped his arms around my waist.

"I don't dance, Nicolette. I will leave that to Jameson."

Simon said, "Don't worry. I can't dance like them either. Those girls have me beat. Besides, slow dancing with my girl wins out every single time."

I said, "You are too much. Will you excuse me for a minute? I'm going to go upstairs to use the restroom and check my makeup."

"You look beautiful, Nicolette. You don't have to fix anything. But hurry back, okay?"

"I will." I kissed him back, as he playfully swatted my ass.

"You are driving me wild. Go, before I take you somewhere more private."

"Promise?"

"Count on it," he said.

I couldn't stop smiling. *I love you, Simon Paulson, and just maybe I will tell you tonight.*

Simon

S am said to me, "I have to say...dude, you surprised me back there with your restraint. I thought St. Clair was going down."

"Sam, I'm not about to hit Michael, especially at Nicolette's home, and in front of her parents. I will admit, the thought crossed my mind, but I saw that you had everything under control. He never changes, always trying to get a rise out of me. I had already known he would be here tonight with his father, and I promised Nicolette that I wouldn't allow him to ruin our night. Believe me, Sam, I won't be so easily blinded again. He will not come between what I have with Nicolette."

"Happy to hear that. I didn't mean to bring up the past."

"You didn't. I meant what I said about Michael. This time around, I will see him coming, and I will make sure he stays far away from Nicolette."

"Don't hit me for saying this, but it wasn't entirely his fault."

"What are you referring to?"

He sighed. "Jennifer. She was cheating on you. We all knew it, but you didn't want to believe it. Did it really matter who she was cheating on you with?"

I tried to keep my voice low, but I wasn't happy where this conversation was leading to. "What the fuck, Sam? You are supposed to be my friend, my best friend. Whose side are you on?"

"Yours, you know that. I will always have your back, but Simon, you have carried the burden of blame for too long now. You hate Michael, that much is clear. You blame him for taking your girl, but you never include Jennifer and her part in all of this. Why is that?"

"She's dead. Why talk about something that I will never be able to change? I tried hating her for cheating on me, and with that piece of shit, but I always return to the fact that she is gone. So, no matter what happened in our relationship, I can forgive her."

"I hear the words, but then I see the actions. Why continue to hate on Michael? They are both to blame for what happened that night. He knew you and Jennifer were together, but he went after her anyway. Yeah, he was wrong to do that. Did she stop him? No, she didn't. Jennifer may have been the smart bookworm we knew her to be, but there was something inside of her that was drawing her to Michael, and that mistake should be on her. You did all you could for her that night, and she still made the decision to get behind the wheel. I was there after she died. I saw the mental beating you put yourself through. You need to let it go."

"I have, Sam. I love Nicolette. I can't explain the depths of my feelings for her. I just know I was meant to be on that beach on that day that brought me into her life. I have never felt this way about anyone. What I had or I thought I had with Jennifer was not real. This connection with Nicolette is real. I am going to tell Nicolette exactly how I feel about her."

"Good for you, man. Since you practiced on me, I guess it's about time you tell her. She loves you, Simon, and has been waiting to hear the same three words from you."

"I plan on it. Now, time to find my girl."

Nicolette

"You look hot, Nicolette. Your man is waiting for you," I said to myself as I took one last look in the mirror. My lips were still tingly from Simon's kiss. Damn, he had the ability to do wild things to me with only his tongue. I wanted to make love with him; it's all that I'd been dreaming about. I knew he was the one. I wanted Simon Paulson to be my first, my everything.

I reached the top of the landing, only to be stopped by Michael. *Not again!*

"Hey, beautiful."

I stepped back, putting enough distance between us. "Don't call me that." I tried to step around him, but he blocked me.

"What are you doing?" I raised my voice, not caring who heard me.

"Can we talk for a few minutes?"

"No, not now, not ever. Leave me alone. I have to get back to the party, and you are in my way."

"Roadblocks can be removed. I'm right here, Nicolette, and if you would stop fighting me at every turn, you would see how good we can be together."

"I am so over playing this game with you." I tried to shove him, but he didn't move.

He held me in place and then looked directly into my eyes, sending cold shivers down my spine. "This is not a game. I want you. I have wanted you from the first moment I saw you. You are all I think about."

Trying to be brave, I tried again. "You may believe you can just snap your fingers and win me over, but not this time. You will not be getting me. I have a boyfriend, and he is the only one that I see and want. Now, let me pass or I will scream the roof off this house."

He stepped back, and I thought I was in the clear.

"We're not done talking, Nicolette."

"Yes, we are!"

He suddenly grabbed my wrist and pulled me back away from the stair landing. He tugged me back so hard, twisting my wrist. I ignored the pain. With the adrenaline and anger flowing through me, I swung around and raised my knee up to his balls. Uncle Jack taught me well, and no fucking guy was going to touch me without my permission. He went down easily and whimpered in pain. My wrist was already beginning to swell. Michael was in a fetal position on the floor.

I leaned in to say, "Don't ever think of touching me again. I have had enough of this shit, and you. Stay. Away. From. Me! Or the next time, I will be introducing you to my Uncle Jack and his favorite baseball bat."

I quickly ran to my closet to grab a sweater. It was the only thing I could think of to hide my now injured wrist. I took the back staircase that led to the kitchen, swallowed down two Advil, and found Simon.

He stopped his conversation with Sam and opened his arms for me. I smiled as best as I could and walked into the safety of his embrace.

Six

Michael

"*D*on't you ever touch me again. I have had enough of this shit, and you.*"

I woke up in a cold sweat, as my mind replayed what happened with Nicolette the night before. Fuck! Why did I push so hard? What made me such a bastard? I liked this girl, and I just wanted to know her better. She freaked out and then kneed me in the balls, where I still felt the pain from her assault.

I'd never had to put in so much effort to get a girl. Yes, I put my hands on her, but I didn't mean to hurt her. If she didn't jerk her body back in the way she did, her wrist wouldn't have twisted. Now, I had to go downstairs to explain what happened to my father. I was sure Nicolette told her parents about last night, and now I had to tell him. He may not even care, but I guessed I would find out.

"Father, can I talk to you for a minute?" I asked as I entered his office.

He was in a meeting with his lawyer. He looked up from his stack of papers with disgust, clearly annoyed with my interruption.

"What is it, Michael? I'm very busy."

I scoffed. What else is new? I stiffened my back and raised my voice. "As I said, I need to speak with you."

"John, leave us, please. My son obviously has something on his mind." His lawyer stepped out and closed the door. "Okay, Michael, you managed to clear the room. What is it?"

"Gee, dad, thanks a lot."

"Michael, I don't have time to play games right now. Either you tell me what you want me to know, or get the hell out of my office."

"Fine! Something happened last night at the Vanelle's party."

"I'm listening."

"I was speaking with Nicolette, and things got out of hand. She tried to leave before I was done talking. I grabbed her wrist, and then she completely freaked out."

"You did what? What the fuck, Michael! You know better than that. What were you thinking, putting your hands on that girl—an underage girl, I might add?"

"Give me a small break. Don't twist my words and make it worse than it was. All I wanted was a few minutes of her time, and she freaked out. If she would have just talked with me, all of this could have been avoided. I didn't mean to hurt her wrist. You know what I got in return? A knee to my balls."

"I don't know what in the hell has gotten into you, Michael, but you need to forget about this girl. I told you to stay away from her, but did you listen? No, you didn't. She is seventeen years old, and you are almost twenty. Go sow your oats up at school, and stop wasting your time with a high school girl who clearly does not want you."

"It doesn't matter. I love her. I want her."

"Did I hear you correctly? You love her? Michael, for the love of God, you don't even know her. What is this? Another repeat from last year? You know how badly that turned out for you."

"I know what I want. I'm not going to stop trying to make her mine. I just have to make her see that."

My father charged me from behind his desk and grabbed me by my collar. "Now, you listen to me, son. You have to stop this obsession you have with this girl. If she said she is not interested in you, then you must accept that. Do you understand me, Michael?"

"If I say no, then what then? You will send me away again?"

"That's not fair, Michael, and you know it." He released me and walked over to his bar for a drink. "What is unfolding now before my eyes is not the same situation you had last year with that girl. She came to you with her own volition. You had no way of knowing what she was going to do."

I clutched the sides of my father's desk, watching the color change in my hands. The anger was boiling inside of me. "That girl meant nothing to me! Nothing at all. She was just a piece of ass that gave it up to me. She meant nothing."

"Michael, she was someone's daughter. How could you be so cold? For the life of me, I don't know what the hell is wrong with you."

"I'm fine. It is not my fault that Jennifer is dead, but you sure blamed me enough times for it. I am so over taking the heat for this. She was the fool that got behind the wheel when she was too fucked up to drive. Yeah, we had fun, but that's all it was. I didn't put a gun to her head to fuck me. She did that all on her own. The night of the party, I practically ignored her all night until she asked me to dance with her. I'm over it. From you down to golden boy Paulson, I'm done taking the blame over some slut that was fucking us both."

Slap! Right across my cheek. *Yeah, should have seen that coming. Dear old dad never liked hearing the truth.*

98

"That is about enough from you. You will stay away from Nicolette, or I will strike at you anyway I can. You do not want to push me on this. Grow the hell up, and be a man. Not this weak version who whines when he doesn't get his way."

"Fuck you. I am what you made me. This is what you get when you abandon your only son."

"Not this again, Michael. What? I didn't give you enough attention? I was working for Christ's sake."

"It's more than that. You have been a ghost around here since mother died. You left me alone to be raised by the servants. I needed a fucking father! Not this pale version of a man standing before me. If you don't like how I turned out, then that's just tough shit!"

I slammed my way out of his office, regretting why I ever chose to go to him in the first place. He never listened to me anyway.

I picked up my mother's picture and ran my fingers over her beautiful face. I whispered, "Sorry."

I tossed and turned the entire night. I was such an idiot for fighting with Michael. I should have just screamed when I threatened to, but no, that would have been too simple. Was my father, right? Was I too trusting?

I pulled out my arm from under the covers and examined it in the light. I had some bruising, and you could see the outline of Michael's thumbprint. I kept it hidden from Simon and my parents last night, which was not easy. Simon kept trying to hold my hand, and I had to jerk away from him at least once. He gave me a look after that, and I just played it off. *Yeah, real cool, Nicolette.*

Simon wanted to see me today. How would he react when I tell him what happened? And of course, I still had to deal with the parents. I let out a huff and hid under my covers. I heard knocking coming from outside my door.

I called out, "Go away, I'm sleeping."

Of course, do they listen? Nope, not in this house. It was Gracie, who walked in and pulled the covers off me. "Good morning. I say you have about sixty seconds to get downstairs before your father comes up to get you himself."

"I love you, Gracie, and thank you for the warning, but tell them I am sleeping."

"Now, why would she do that when clearly you are wide awake?" my father said as he made his way into my bedroom. Gracie made her exit, and then daddy opened all the drapes in my room. "Good morning, sweetheart. Rise and shine." He was too chipper for a Sunday morning.

I rubbed my eyes and sat up against my headboard, discreetly hiding my arm. "What has you in such a good mood?" I asked, still yawning.

"Why not be in a good mood? Our party was a success. You have two amazing and very talented parents. The networking paid off, and we made some great contacts. We already have new projects lined up for next year. Isn't that great?"

"It's wonderful. I am so happy for you."

"Happy for *us*, Nicolette. We win as a family, remember that. Now, get up!" He playfully tossed a pillow at my head.

"Daddy, I'm tired. I just want to sleep in. Is that okay?" I prayed he would take the hint but the look of concern was in his eyes.

He leaned in to feel my forehead. "Nope, no fever. Just checking."

"Sleep. I want to sleep."

"Fine. You have one more hour, and then I would like you to join us downstairs for brunch, okay?"

"Thanks, daddy."

He closed the door behind him, and I just cried. He looked so happy, and I didn't have the heart to tell him about Michael. I knew they would not take too kindly knowing that he hurt me and I kept it from them. I was right to be quiet. Just the look on my father's face convinced me that I did the right thing. If I had told him last night during the party, they would have gone after Michael, and then his father would have gotten involved. No, I did the right thing.

There was no sleeping for me, not with all that was on my mind. I brushed my teeth and tossed my hair in a messy bun. I might as well join my family downstairs, and I was hungry.

Brunch had been arranged out on the patio. I was about to walk outside to say hello to my mom when I heard my name and decided to hang back and listen.

"Is Nicolette joining us?"

"She's still in bed. Let's give her a little more time. I thought she may have been coming down with something, but she didn't have a fever. She didn't seem herself," I heard my dad tell my mom.

"She's probably tired. She was up pretty late last night. The Paulson's were the last to leave, and she looked pretty cozy dancing with Simon. They are a cute couple, don't you think?"

"Yes, they are just fabulous."

My mom laughed. "Oh, Mason, don't be like that. Our baby is in love, and he clearly only has eyes for her. Anyway, while you are in a good mood, did I tell you that I was talking with Marina last night? She has offered to give us a tour of the campus."

"Christina, don't you think that's a bit premature? Nicolette is finally beginning to acclimate to her new high school and living here. Touring a college campus, I think, is a bit much. We should leave that up to her."

"Mason, it's not a big deal. What will it hurt to take a look?"

"Did you forget that Northwestern is still her first choice?"

"I haven't forgotten, but that was then, and this is now. She didn't have a California boyfriend last year when she made that decision. Kids change their minds all the time, and I have a feeling that Nicolette will change hers."

"Yes, that may be true, but I want our daughter to choose what's right for her, and not make decisions based on her love life."

I had about enough of eavesdropping on their conversation. "Planning my life again, mom?" I said as I walked out to join them.

"Good morning, or should I say, good afternoon? Don't be snarky, honey. We were just talking. Can I fix you a plate? You must be hungry after all that dancing last night." Just the thought of food made my stomach roll over. I knew I had to tell them.

"Mom, Dad, we need to talk."

Their happy faces had gone from smiles to worry.

"Nicolette, what is it?" Mom stood up and rounded the table to come over to me.

She reached for my arm, and I pulled it behind me. Tears were beginning to fall, and I began to tremble. My nerves were getting the best of me, and I could not hold back any longer.

"Baby, what's wrong? Talk to me. Why are you hiding your arm?" My dad was now by my side, and as soon as they saw the tears, they both wrapped their arms around me.

I couldn't talk, so I just showed them. They didn't take it well.

"Oh, Nicolette, what happened? Your wrist is black and blue," my mom shrieked, with dad looking just as upset.

"It doesn't hurt." I lied.

She took a closer look and began pressing down on it, causing me to wince. "Yeah, right. Who are you trying to convince? This is swollen, and I am taking you to a doctor to have it checked out."

"Mom, that's not necessary. It's a little tender, but I took Advil after it happened."

"Nicolette, what exactly happened to cause this injury to your wrist?" my father asked. "Look at me when I am talking to you. What happened to your wrist? Did Simon do something to you?"

"No!" I shouted back at him. "Simon would never hurt me. I love him, daddy."

"Okay, I had to ask. I'm sorry. Please, explain to me what happened. I will not ask again."

"It was Michael St. Clair. He did this to me."

"I'll kill him! How dare that boy put his hands on you!" my dad screamed.

"Mason, please calm down. Nicolette, why didn't you come to us with this last night?"

"You were having such a great time at the party, I didn't want to bother you. I thought I could handle it on my own."

"You could never be a bother to us. You are our daughter. And to know that our daughter got assaulted in our own home, I just feel sick over this."

I looked over to my father, who wasn't saying too much, and I said, "Daddy, I am so sorry."

He rushed over to me and brought me in for a hug. "Nicolette, I need to know what happened with Michael," he calmly asked me. I looked over to my mom for help, but her eyes widened knowing it was time to tell my father.

"I'm waiting," he said.

"I can't do this right now. I got into a fight with Michael. I tried to walk away from him, and he didn't like it. He grabbed my wrist to make me stay, and then I kicked him in his balls. I told him if he came near me again, I would have Uncle Jack introduce his bat to his preppy ass."

"That's just fucking great! Bring Uncle Jack into the mix. What about us, Nicolette? I am your father! And I had a right to know what the hell was going on with my own daughter."

"I told mom that you always do this! You always react this way, and every time I mention Uncle Jack, you get so defensive. Why is that? He's my uncle. If he hadn't taught me how to protect myself, I may have been hurt more than just a bruised wrist."

I knocked back my chair and got up to leave. My father slammed his fist down to the table, making some of the dishes fall and shatter.

"Do not take that tone with me, Nicolette. And let's leave your uncle out of this. I know you would like to just put this behind you, but the fact remains that this boy hurt you last night and in our damn home. I need to know everything, and you are not leaving this god-damned table until I do!"

"Mason, may I have a word with you back inside?"

"No, you may not. Christina, why are you trying to pacify her? This is not like our daughter to keep things from us, and now I come to find out you've been doing the same thing? Are you her confidant now? I get to just remain in the dark?"

"Will you please calm down?" my mother pleaded, but he wasn't having it.

"No! I will not calm down until someone tells me what the fuck is going on!"

I had never seen my father so angry before. I was crying uncontrollably and could not stop my tears from falling. This was all my fault. My father threw his hands up in the air and followed my mom back inside the house. I pulled my knees to my chest and buried my face.

Gracie came out to check on me, but I didn't want to be consoled right now. I just wanted to go back upstairs and forget I even said anything. Time ticked on by, and finally, my parents came back to the patio.

My father wrapped his arms around me and whispered through his tears, "I'm sorry. Having to see bruises on my child does not sit well with me. I want to hurt him as much as he hurt you, but I know I can't do that, not really. Please, talk to me. Mom filled me in, but I need to hear from you that you are okay."

"If you talked to mom, then you pretty much know the story. What happened last night is what I already told you. I tried, daddy. I really did try to be civil with Michael for the sake of the business dealings that you have with his father. But Michael made it impossible to do that."

"What does our working with his father have anything to do with what happened here last night?"

"If I didn't agree to go on a date with Michael, then he was going to have you and mom fired from the movie."

"What? That little shit. Nicolette, he lied to you. Don't you see that? He manipulated you into believing that he had the power to fire us. Even if he did, we would never use our daughter to further our career. We do not need this job or any other job that bad to ever put you in harm's way."

"I'm sorry."

"Stop saying that. You have done nothing wrong. He is the one that should be sorry. Did you tell Simon about this?"

"No, I can't. He would go after Michael, and I can't risk Simon getting in trouble. They have already fought more than once over me, and if I had just told you the truth from the beginning, then none of this would have happened."

"You don't know that. Guys like Michael and where they come from, well, they feel entitled. I want you to stop blaming yourself. He is in the wrong. Let me take a look, please?"

I moved my arm around and followed his instructions as my father examined my wrist. "Okay, I believe it's just a sprain. Let me speak with your mother while you go upstairs to wash your face and get dressed. When you finish, come back downstairs, and I will wrap your wrist."

"So, no emergency room?"

"No, that's not necessary. I love you. Now, go on."

I did as he asked, and went upstairs. My face was blotchy and red from crying. I looked awful and was in no shape for anyone to see me right now, especially Simon. As I came back downstairs, I heard loud voices coming from the kitchen. I remained behind and just listened to the mess that I was responsible for.

"Mason, please talk to me."

"Why? You don't talk to me."

"That's not fair."

"You're right, none of this is fair. The minute our daughter confided in you about Michael, you should have told me. When did that change? This boy comes into our home and assaults our daughter, right under our noses, and I'm not supposed to be angry about it? And then I have to hear how our daughter idolizes my brother and his way of handling things. What the fuck! He is the last person I would go to for help, and you know why that is."

Again, with Uncle Jack? Why is my father so defensive when it comes to him? He was never like this when we all lived in Chicago.

106

"Mason, I didn't say that. You have every right to be angry, and I am sorry that I kept something so important from you."

"Come here. I'm sorry too. But, baby, what do you expect me to do? We have to deal with this situation, and it has to happen right now."

I watched my parents hug one another, and I just about lost it. I felt responsible for their stress.

"I'm sorry. I'm sorry, daddy."

"Hey, stop that right now. Nicolette, I promise you everything will be okay. You did nothing wrong. This is all on him. I see that you already wrapped your wrist."

"Yeah, Gracie took care of it for me."

"Thank goodness for Gracie. Okay, we're all going over to speak with Clayton about his son."

"Well, I'm not going." I raised my voice.

Cupping my face, he said, "Nicolette, you don't have a choice. This has gone on long enough. This nonsense with Michael ends to-day. Now, let's go."

My stomach was in knots the entire drive over to the St. Clair home. I was trying to focus on the music I was listening to when my phone chimed with a text. I knew it was from Simon since I selected a special alert tone just for him.

Simon: *Hey! How's my girl doing?*

Me: *Good.*

Simon: *Just good? I think we can do better than that.*

Me: *What did you have in mind?*

Simon: *You, on the back of my bike. Legs wrapped around mine, holding on tight.*

Me: *Sounds perfect, but I can't.*

Simon: *Why not?*

Me: *Out with the parents. Can I text you when I'm home?*

Simon: *Yes, but hurry!*

That was fun. At least I found a reason to smile today.

We were just reaching the St. Clair's home when my phone rang. It was Michael. I handed my phone to mom, who looked enraged that he had the nerve to call me.

My mother hit the accept button and placed it on speaker for my father to listen. I wanted to puke. It didn't register with him that I never said a word once the call connected.

"Hey, Nicolette. I want to apologize for my behavior last night."

"What behavior is that, Michael? The way you have been stalking my daughter? Or the way you assaulted her by putting your hands on her?" My stomach rolled again, as I listened to my father yell at Michael.

Silence.

"Hello? Are you still on the line?" my father asked.

"I'm here, sir."

"You have nothing to say?"

"I'm so sorry for hurting Nicolette. I never meant to cause her any harm. I will be forever regretful for doing that to her."

"So, you admit it?"

"Yes, sir. I'm very sorry."

"You should be. Not only did you assault my daughter, but you have constantly harassed her. What the hell is wrong with you?" my father shouted. "Michael, this conversation is not over. Tell your father that I am on my way over."

He ended the call without waiting for a response. He looked at me through the rearview mirror and gave me a reassuring smile.

"Don't worry, baby. Everything will be okay."

The security guard waved us in. My father parked the car and helped me out.

"Mom, I feel sick. I can't do this."

"Nicolette, you have nothing to be afraid of. We will be with you the entire time."

I didn't say anything more, just silently nodded in agreement with my mom.

Seven

Nicolette

Once invited in, a housekeeper led us into the library to wait for Mr. St. Clair. I had a creepy feeling that we were being watched. Something about this house did not sit well with me. It was so cold.

My father paced the room and looked down to his watch. He never liked to be kept waiting. My mother was quiet, and I just felt sick. Mr. St. Clair entered with a man who was introduced to my parents as his personal lawyer. My father scowled and shook his hand.

"Clayton, you must know why we are here. Look at my daughter's wrist. Your son is responsible for this."

"Mason, before this gets out of hand, I want to apologize on the behalf of my son. Michael is regrettably sorry for his behavior toward Nicolette. He never meant to hurt her. When their friendly conversation shifted to a more serious one, that's when things spiraled out of control. For Michael's part in their argument, I am truly sorry for any stress this has caused for not only Nicolette but to you as well."

"Friendly, you say? Clayton, I don't see it that way at all. Not sure what your son has told you, but according to our daughter, your son forced her into a conversation she did not want to have, and then when she wanted to leave, he blocked her from doing so. That is not a friendly conversation."

"Look, Christina, Mason, we have an exceptionally good working relationship. I would be displeased to have it compromised over this misunderstanding that I am hoping we can resolve privately. You have my word that this will never happen again. I have spoken with Michael, and he has given me his promise that he will not bother your daughter again. I, for one, would like to move on from this unfortunate incident and put it behind us. Wouldn't you agree?"

"Is that why you have a lawyer here? To move on?" my mother questioned.

"John was already here on another matter, so I found nothing wrong with asking him to join us."

"Where is your son, Clayton? He must be here since he phoned Nicolette while we were driving over here."

Judging by the look on Mr. St. Clair's face, he wasn't expecting my father to say that. "He's not at home. I felt it was best if I am the one to speak with you today." Turning his attention to me, he said, "Nicolette, I am sure you shared with your parents your most honest version of what transpired between you and my son last night. Michael did the same with me. Surely, you will take some responsibility for the part you played in this? After all, you did assault him as well?"

Did I hear him, right? He actually turned it around on me?

My father was barely hanging on, and now to sit here and listen to Michael's father defend him and blame me just pushed him over the edge. He shoved his chair back, knocking it to the floor.

111

"You didn't just say that, Clayton? You have to be out of your fucking mind to believe we are going to just sit here and listen to you pass the blame onto our daughter. Your son is lucky that I am not at the police station pressing charges against him, or better yet, beating him within an inch of his life."

"Mason," mom tried to interrupt, but my father just raised his hand up to her. He was livid.

"What did you expect her to do? She defended herself against your piece of shit son. Yes, I said it, and I damn well mean it. I'd say your son got off easy. I want Michael to stay away from my daughter. No calls. No messages. No flower deliveries. No contact whatsoever. If he tries to ignore this warning and contacts Nicolette in any manner, I will get a restraining order, but not before he and I have a conversation. And I am sure it will not end well for him. Do I make myself clear on this matter?"

"Yes."

"Good. Now, as far as our business relationship goes, we don't have one, at least not with you. We are the song writers. We may be writing and producing songs, but we are not on your payroll. Our relationships are with John Mayer and the other musicians collaborating on this movie. We can walk away at any time. At this point, I don't give a shit about your movie, your soundtrack, or your son."

"Okay, I have listened to you, and now you will listen to me. Is that what you want? To break our contract?"

"If that's what it will take to keep my daughter safe. Yes, I will."

"Mason, I don't believe you fully understand what is at stake here. You are involving a personal matter and allowing it to cross over into our business. No matter what you believe, you signed a contract with Paramount Studios to write and produce our movie score, as well as songs for our movie's soundtrack. You would be in breach, and furthermore, blacklisted in Hollywood. If you walk away from one of the biggest movie studios in the world, what does that say about your work ethic? Think about it, Mason. This is business, and you must separate the two because they are not the same."

I had to do something before my parents lost everything they worked for. "Daddy, please, I'm okay. This is your career, and I would never forgive myself if it was in jeopardy over what happened between Michael and me. Let's just go home."

"Nicolette, are you sure? Not one thing in this world is as important when it comes to you."

"I'm sure. Please continue your work, and finish what you started."

My parents were conflicted, but not Mr. St. Clair. He looked like the Cheshire Cat, smug and enjoying the victory he just won over my parents. My father deeply sighed and then turned back to Mr. St. Clair.

"As long as we understand each other when it comes to Michael. He needs to stay away from my daughter. If he does that, then we will continue our work."

"You have my word, Mason. He is truly sorry, and will not bother you again."

I literally felt sick to my stomach. My legs felt weak and I was a bit shaky from not eating. I just wanted to go home. After all that was said and done, Mr. St. Clair got what he wanted, and Michael was absolved from his actions.

My parents walked out first, and then I felt a chill roll down my back. I looked up to the staircase landing, and that's when I saw him. Michael had been here the entire time. He mouthed something to me that I couldn't make out. I practically tripped over my feet walking out of the door.

Michael

"You can come down now, Michael. I take it you were listening?" my father said to me.

"I tried, but with the door closed, it was difficult."

"Michael, you dodged a bullet today with the Vanelles. I barely managed to hold back her father, he was so enraged. You have to stay away from their daughter. I gave them my word. Please, do not go near Nicolette."

"Father, you had no right to make that promise. I have apologized to her. What crime did I commit? All I wanted to do was take her out on a date, but instead, I am being treated as if I were a criminal."

"Michael, moving forward, you will get yourself back to school, concentrate on your studies, go to all your classes that I pay for, and socialize with your own circle of friends. With enough distance and time, they will be able to put this behind them and move on. Your actions nearly cost us our writing team, which would have resulted in a huge financial loss for Paramount."

"Sorry, we wouldn't want that to happen," I said, sarcastically.

"That's enough out of you. You don't have a clue, do you, Michael? I should seriously think of cutting you off. Maybe then you will get one. You just can't manhandle an innocent girl to get what you want. Her father could have forced my hand here today and pushed for a restraining order, which would have been a matter of public record. I refuse to be embarrassed by this. Take charge of your life, and get the hell back on track. Forget about this girl, and find another warm body to keep you cozy at night. Anyone but Nicolette Vanelle. She is off limits."

"She'll come around. I just need to give her more time. I messed up last night, and I own that mistake."

"Michael, you haven't heard a single word I said, have you? STAY. AWAY. FROM. THAT. GIRL! Have I made myself clear enough for you?"

"Oh, yeah, crystal."

My father said nothing more and slammed his way out from the library.

I could still smell her perfume in here. I took in a deep breath and exhaled slowly, committing everything about Nicolette to memory.

She'll come around...I'll just have to up my game.

Nicolette

I texted Simon as we drove away from the St. Clair's home. I needed him so much and just wanted him to hold me.

Me: *Hey!*

Simon: *Are you home yet?*

Me: *No, but will you meet me at the Juice Bar?*

Simon: *Yes! Be there in 20.*

Me: *I miss you.*

Simon: *Miss you more.*

"Hey, daddy, drop me off at the Juice Bar. Simon is meeting me there."

My mom turned around and asked me if my wrist was still bothering me.

"It's fine, mom. It's just a little sore."

"You haven't eaten anything today. Please, Nicolette, order something more than an iced coffee."

"I will, I promise."

I made it to the restaurant before Simon and sent him a text that I was waiting for him.

Me: *I'm here.*

Simon: *On my way!*

Me: *I'll be in our booth.*

Simon: *I'll find you.*

I was way past the point of hunger. I ordered some food while waiting for Simon. If I could, I would totally avoid telling Simon about Michael. I had already retold the story twice now, and I was too tired to do it again, but he had a right to know.

This was why meeting in a public place was a good thing. Anytime Michael was involved, Simon lost it. This way, if he got angry, he may not make too much of a scene. The bell chimed on the door, and in walked my boyfriend. Simon was dressed in board shorts and his usual white t-shirt that clung to his body in all the right places. He was so hot, all I wanted to do was to jump into his arms. I got out from the booth and walked right into his welcoming embrace, burying my face into his chest. He returned my hug, but it felt off. He pulled away, and his eyes focused on my hand.

"Hey, I missed you," he said.

"I missed you more. I've had the worst day."

"Why is that? And why is your wrist wrapped? What happened?"

I wanted to play it off and not give my wrist too much attention, but Simon was not taking his eyes off me.

"Can you sit, please? I'll explain."

Simon had his arm around my shoulders as we got comfortable in the booth. I was making small talk until he asked again. Before I could answer him, the waitress delivered my food and asked Simon if he wanted anything. He just ordered a Coke and picked on my fries.

"I'm waiting, Nicolette. How did you injure your wrist?"

"Simon, before I explain, will you promise me something?"

"Anything, just tell me." A look of concern was all over his face.

How will he react once I tell him about Michael? I said, "You have to promise not to overreact. Please, just let me get it all out."

He huffed in frustration. "Okay, I promise. Why are you stalling? Just tell me."

My mouth felt suddenly dry. I picked up my water and drank it all down. I was so nervous, and the way Simon was staring at me wasn't making what I had to tell him any easier.

"The reason why my wrist is wrapped up is that it's sprained."

"And? How did you sprain it? When did you sprain it? Did this happen today? Or last night? Because I was with you the entire night."

I put my head down in shame, and then whispered, "Not the entire night."

"What?"

"Do you remember me stepping away to go upstairs to use the restroom? Remember, you were talking with Sam?"

"Yes."

"Well, when I was coming out from the bathroom, Michael was there. He was waiting for me outside in the hallway. We were alone at the top of the landing, and as much as I tried to leave and return to the party, he blocked me. We argued it got ugly, and then he grabbed my wrist, twisted it, and now it's sprained."

"What the hell! Nicolette, why am I just hearing about this now?"

"Shhh, Simon, keep your voice down," I whispered.

"I will not keep my voice down. Is this why you asked me to meet you here? Because you knew I would have this reaction? What the fuck? Why didn't you tell me this last night? I don't fucking believe this!" Simon was shouting and cursing loud enough for the entire restaurant to hear him. All eyes were on us.

"Simon, people are staring at us. You promised to hear me out. Please calm down and let me talk."

"I don't care. Let them look."

"Well, I care. If you don't calm down, I'm going to go home."

He inhaled a few deep breaths and pulled me into him. "I'm sorry. I'm sorry. This is not me, not by a long shot. Just the mention of his name, and the fact that he's responsible for hurting you, I just want to beat the shit out of him."

"Get in line. That's exactly what my father wanted to do."

"Please, tell me what happened with St. Clair."

"Okay, do you remember when you and I decided to be together? I mean, as a couple?"

"Um, yes, it was the happiest day of my life."

Okay, swooning over here. "It was also the day Michael was at school to talk to me. You already know how he wanted me to go out with him, and I said no. Well, he called me later that night after I sent him a text telling him that I was with you and we would not be going out."

"I asked you to stay away from him, Nicolette. Why did you have to call him?"

"Simon, I didn't call him. I texted him. He called me in response to my text. He said the only reason why you asked me to be your girlfriend was that you knew he wanted me, and you just beat him to it. I was so pissed off after that and I argued with him, but he still went on to accuse me of leading him on, and then said uglier words to me. I just was over it and hung up on him. That was the last time I heard from him, up until last night at my parents' party."

Now with some distance between us, Simon was clearly pissed off. "Is that what you think? I only asked you to be my girlfriend because I didn't want St. Clair to top me? What he said is so far from the truth, and it is just another malicious act that Michael is known for. I knew he would do something like this. I just had a feeling deep inside, but I trusted you to tell me the truth if he bothered you again, and you didn't, Nicolette. You should have told me."

"I'm sorry. I don't know how many more ways I can say it. I have retold this story to my parents and have shed more tears than I have ever done before. I'm sorry that I hurt you but look at it from my side. He not only physically hurt me, but he threatened me as well. He said that my parents' relationship with his father would be in jeopardy if I didn't go out with him. He basically said he had all intentions of fucking me. He made me sick. I fought him and kicked him so hard in his balls for ever believing he could just touch me so freely. I didn't know if he had the power to actually have my parents fired, but I still fought back. I had no choice but to handle it the best way I knew at the time. Last night was too important to my parents, and I wasn't going to be the one to mess it all up for them. Are you angry with me?"

"Yes, but I'm angrier with him. This is why I wanted you to stay away from him, and now, he put his hands on my girlfriend. I am going to kick his ass all over Beverly Hills."

"No, you're not. My parents handled it. Please, Simon, I'm sorry. You need to let this go. I have."

"Let this go?" Simon looked at me as if I had grown two heads. "How can I, babe? He hurts my girlfriend, and you just want me to do nothing?"

"Exactly! He's not worth it, and I would never forgive myself if you got into trouble because of me. Let it go."

"I wish it were that easy. Nicolette, you don't know him like I do. Michael St. Clair is not a good guy. He used and hurt someone that I cared about once, and I don't want the same thing to happen to you."

"Jennifer?" I whispered.

"You know, don't you?"

"Yes, I know, and you don't know how sorry I am that you ever had to go through something so horrible like that."

"I replayed that night over and over in my mind. If I would have driven her home myself instead of the cab, maybe she would still be alive today."

"She was determined to get back to that party and to Michael. You have to forgive Jennifer for hurting you, and then you have to forgive yourself."

"You're right. Everyone is, but it still hurts. Her family was torn apart after losing her. They will never be the same without her."

After talking about Michael and then Jennifer, a wall was suddenly between us, or at least, that's what it felt like.

"Are you speaking to me?" I asked him.

"Yes, I'm just processing all of it. I'm upset that you were hurt."

"I'm already over it. How about this for a cover story? You took me surfing, and a hard wave crashed into us, sending me flying into the surf. I tried to grab the board, and then that's how my wrist got twisted."

"Creative, but the truth always sounds better."

"Not in this case. Besides, our friends will love it."

We left the Juice Bar and took a ride down to the beach with me on the back of his bike. Our hands were linked the entire time we walked along the water.

He had shared so much of his personal pain with me, I felt it was time to share a piece of my past with him. "Simon, you're not the only one who had some misfortune your junior year."

"I'm sorry, what did you say?" My words finally dragged him out of his haze, and he focused his attention back on me.

"I had a boyfriend last year. Jason, star of the football team. We were so different. He was popular, not that I wasn't, but we didn't have a lot in common. I had my friends. He had his friends. He loved to party and hang with cheerleaders. I preferred the coffee house and art museums."

"Why were you with him?"

"Good question. I guess the times we were together, we had fun. One night, I skipped the usual keg party and stayed home. They had just won the championship, and he wanted to go out to celebrate. My parents were out for the evening, and I was catching up on homework. A very drunk Jason showed up on my doorstep, and I let him come inside to sleep it off. I made him some coffee, and when I returned to the living room, he appeared to be sleeping. I placed the hot coffee down, and that's when he grabbed me and flipped me to my back."

"What an asshole! Please tell me he didn't hurt you."

"He didn't. At first, I thought he was joking around, but then he pinned me down and didn't allow me to move. That's when I fought back. He called me a cock tease and told me it was time to give it up. I screamed and tried to wrestle from beneath him, but he was too strong. I didn't hear my front door open. Before I could even blink, my father had him off me and into a choke hold. It was so scary. I really thought my father was going to kill him. Today with Michael, I thought the same. Long story short, we broke up. I survived the rumor mill at school, and then months later, I moved here."

"And met me." He kissed me soundly on my lips.

"Yes, I met you. The best day of my life."

"I respect your father, and now understand why he is so protective of you. I guess if I had a sister, I would be the same way."

"Are we okay?"

"Yes, more than okay. Please, if anything else happens with Michael, you'll tell me, right?"

"I promise. I doubt he will be bothering me again."

We watched the sun set over the ocean, and he drove me home.

He said, "Don't oversleep tomorrow. I'll be driving you to school."

Catching me off guard, I asked, "Don't you run in the mornings?"

"I do, but I can push it off until lunch."

"I would love that." I stood on my toes and kissed my boyfriend good night and was happy I still had one.

After passing out when I got home, I woke up refreshed and excited to see Simon. I picked out an awesome outfit and made my way downstairs to see Simon already here and having breakfast with my mom.

"Good morning, Nicolette," he winked at me.

"Good morning," I replied back. Oh, that sexy smile of his. It gets me every time. "I didn't expect to see you this early and in my kitchen." I completely ignored my mom.

"Good surprise?"

"Yes, absolutely." I kissed him on his cheek, with my mom clearing her throat.

Totally interrupting the flirting with my boyfriend, she asked, "Good morning, Nicolette. How did you sleep?"

"I'm good, and my wrist feels much better."

"Good. Keep it wrapped for one more day. I need to run. I'm late. Your father is already at the studio. I love you. Have a good day at school. Simon, be careful driving."

"I will." After she left, he said to me, "Now that the coast is clear, may I give you a proper hello and kiss?"

"Yes, you may. I thought you forgot."

"No chance of that happening."

Simon stood up and cupped my face with his hands. He tenderly kissed me. I groaned in between breaths and felt a surge of electricity flow through my body. I wanted him so much. I wanted him to touch me.

Ugh! Remembering we had to leave for school, I stepped back to see him smiling. *Good to know I wasn't the only one having naughty thoughts this morning.* We arrived at school and joined Alexis, Bailey, and Sam on the quad before our first class.

"Where's Jameson?" asked Simon.

"He took a mental health day. He said he was going to the spa," replied Sam.

"It's only October, so I guess he's starting early?" Bailey chimed in and explained that he occasionally needed a day to himself. She went on to explain that after they left my party, they went clubbing and Jameson ran into an ex-boyfriend. They got into a fight and then left.

"Is he okay? Did anyone talk to Jameson on Sunday?" asked Simon.

Bailey said, "Yeah, I did. He's fine. I took him shopping. I gave my daddy's Amex a workout, and his short-lived heartbreak was forgotten."

We all laughed. Yeah, shopping on Rodeo Drive cured all.

Simon walked me to class and whispered something naughty in my ear. He made me blush crimson and then left a kiss on my neck. My boyfriend was quite the tease. I watched him sprint off until he disappeared out of sight.

I dropped off my backpack in my locker and saw one long-stemmed rose taped to the front of it. How romantic of Simon to leave this for me. I inhaled the sweet-smelling flower and opened my locker to find a note fall to the floor. It wasn't from Simon, but Michael. How did he manage to do this?

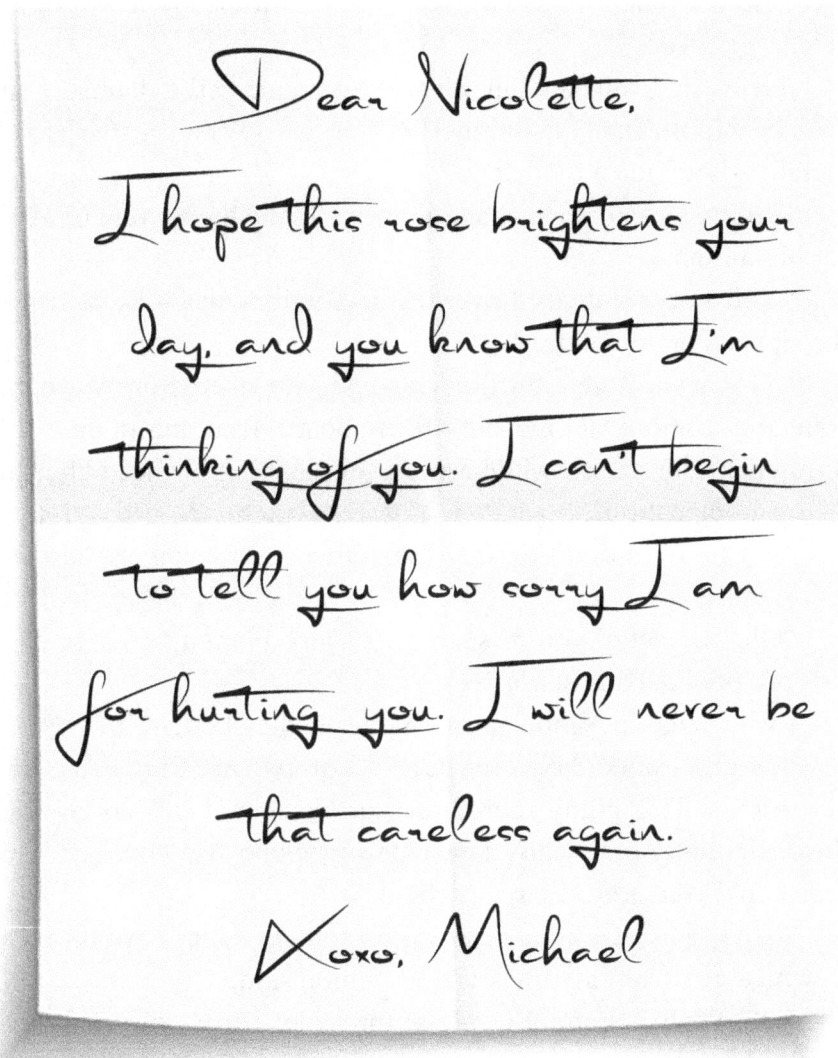

Dear Nicolette,

I hope this rose brightens your day, and you know that I'm thinking of you. I can't begin to tell you how sorry I am for hurting you. I will never be that careless again.

xoxo, Michael

I looked over my shoulder and scanned the hallway. Was Michael here? Watching me? I threw the rose away but kept the note. I shoved it in my purse and left to meet our friends for lunch. Simon texted me that he would skip his workout and join me. He saw me first and got up to take my tray from me.

"Hey, boyfriend! Thank you, but I'm not helpless."

"I know, but why should you carry anything when your man is here to help you?"

Alexis interrupted, "Oh, please! Someone call a dentist, I am in need of a root canal. Damn, the sweetness between the two of you is literally giving me a toothache."

I shot a look to Alexis, and then she made the gesture of zipping her big mouth.

"You never did say how you hurt your wrist?" Bailey said as she sipped her smoothie.

"You never asked. Surfing accident. My instructor over here," I pointed to Simon, "let me slip off my board, resulting in this." I lifted my hand for effect, while Simon was shaking his head after hearing my explanation.

"It's funny. I don't exactly remember it how you are describing it."

"Oh, Nicolette, you're such a city girl, blaming your boyfriend for your poor surfing skills."

I whispered in Simon's ear, "You see, they bought it."

The girls rolled their eyes at us. "You two are truly nauseating," said Alexis. This is my fourth year at this school and no boyfriend. You, Nicolette, practically land one on your very first day, and of course, he's the hottest guy in school."

"Now, don't be a hater, Alexis. I told you that I would fix you up with a guy from my track team," Simon said.

"Oh, yeah...Jimmy? Don't remind me. Have you seen the car that he drives?"

Simon leaned into me and whispered, "You see, what did I tell you? Superficial."

"Excuse me, what was that, Simon?" Alexis shouted.

"Oh, nothing. I have to go and workout with my lowly teammates who don't measure up to your standards. See you around, Princess. Baby, I will text you when I'm done."

Smiling back at him, I said, "I can't wait."

He lifted me into his arms and slammed his mouth down to mine. I loved how he kissed me, and he gave me one more on my nose before jogging away.

"What was that about? Am I a snob?" I felt bad for Alexis, and how she doubted herself. I would have to remind Simon later that he had hurt her feelings. "It's no crime for liking nice things, is it?" asked Alexis.

"No, it's not, but you need to take people for who they are, not what they have."

She scoffed. "Where did you hear that from? A Hallmark card?" snickered Alexis.

"I guess I was raised differently. And not from a Hallmark card, but from my Uncle Jack." I'll admit, I was a bit short with her. "I'm sorry. Ignore what Simon said. You are perfect, just the way you are."

"Okay, I'll go out with Jimmy. Besides, his body is hot."

"Yay! That's the girl I love." I hugged my friend.

"Okay, if you two can focus on me for a second, that would be great," Bailey said. "We have covered boyfriends, surfing accidents, and snobby girls. No offense, Alexis. I love you. Now, I have some news of my own to share. I met a guy a while back, and I recently bumped into him again a few weeks ago. We started talking, and he asked me to a college party this weekend!" Bailey clapped her hands in excitement.

"Wow! That's awesome. Who is he?" asked Alexis.

"His name is Seth. You remember him, right? We talked to him at the St. Clair's party."

"Oh, yeah, he was cute. I'm so happy for you, sis."

"I'm happy for you too, Bailey," I said but cringed inside. If I remember correctly, he was a friend of Michael's, and that could complicate things if he and Bailey got serious. And any friend of Michael's is concerning to me. "What college does he attend?" I asked, already knowing the answer. My gut was screaming to be careful. Something wasn't right about this.

"He goes to Stanford. The party is going to be at his fraternity house." *Bingo! I knew it.*

"I told him I would only go if I could bring my two best girls with me. Please say yes. Are you in?"

Alexis said, "Yes, I will be there. Wow! I have to go shopping. What will I wear to a college party?"

While the sisters celebrated, my stomach was rolling over. "I'm sorry, Bailey, I can't go. My parents are not going to give me permission to go to a college party."

"You can just say you're sleeping over at our house, and they will never know."

"Well, I will know. And what about Simon? I don't think he would appreciate his girlfriend going to a college party surrounded by other guys. Sorry, but count me out."

Bailey continued to pressure me into going to the party with them, but I was firm on my decision. It was all too coincidental that a mutual friend of Michael's was now suddenly interested in one of my friends. I was hoping she would take the hint and just let it go. I didn't want to be at odds with my friends, but I also couldn't tell them about Michael.

The rest of the week, I avoided Bailey, and by Friday, she was annoyed and avoided me. I wasn't going to change my mind, nor ever mention it to Simon. I planned on skipping lunch to watch Simon practice down at the track.

When I was walking across the parking lot that led to the field, Bailey called out to me. "Hey, glad I caught you. This was in front of your locker." She handed me a wrapped box with a note attached to it.

"It's not mine."

"Well, it has your name on it." She handed it to me, and I just tossed it in my bag without opening it. "Hey, the party is this weekend. Have you thought about it? Will you go with us? I already have a date lined up for Alexis, and I'll be with Seth."

I decided to change tactics to prove my theory was right. "Okay, Bailey, you win. Simon and I will see you at the party."

"Um, that won't work, Nicolette. You have to come on your own."

"Why?" I questioned. It was all adding up. Piece by piece. I didn't want Bailey to believe I didn't trust her, but I knew Michael had to be behind this. And now mystery packages are showing up at my locker? How convenient. "I'll ask you one more time, Bailey. Why is it so important for me to come alone? And why can't I bring Simon with me?"

She groaned. "Seth has a friend he wants you to meet. I already told him that you would be there. What is the big deal? Support a friend. I would do this for you."

"Wow, I never would believe that you would try to trick me like this. How could you do this to me, Bailey?"

"What is your problem? No one is saying you have to do anything with the guy. All you have to do is hang out with us, and that way, everyone is matched up. You don't want me to look like a liar to Seth, now, do you?"

"I don't care how you look. What you did is not acceptable. Friends don't deceive one another. I don't know what game your guy, Seth, is trying to play here, but leave me out of it. You lied to me. And I refuse to be friends with someone I can't trust."

"Nicolette! You can't be serious. You'll stop being my friend because I want you to come to one party with me?"

"You are missing the point here. You kept the real reason why you wanted me to go, and I don't play games with people, especially my friends. Friends don't lie to each other, and that's exactly what you did. I have to go. Don't follow me."

"Nicolette, I'm sorry! Don't go," she shouted out, as I ignored her and walked off.

I didn't go to the track to meet Simon. I ran to my car. I needed time to think. I felt so betrayed. I was angry with Bailey, Seth, and Michael. Why couldn't he just leave me alone? And now, to use my friend to get to me? The mystery box was sticking out from my bag. I should have just thrown it away, but curiosity won out, and I opened the note first.

Hey Beautiful,

I miss you so much.

Are you thinking of me?

I'm giving you this time to move on

from what happened with us.

I'm hoping that we can start over

and be friends again.

Please tell me you want that too?

You know my number. Use it, please.

xoxo, Michael

My hands were shaking. My entire body was shaking. Why was he doing this to me? When I opened the box, I found a heart necklace inside. I threw it down to the floor of my car and gripped the steering wheel. How was he getting these packages to me? I didn't know what to do. Should I tell my parents? Tell Simon? No, I couldn't do that. He would go after Michael, and then it would be Simon getting into trouble. I couldn't risk that.

"Hey!"

I screamed. "Holy shit! Simon, you scared me!"

Simon laughed, as he put his hands up. "I'm sorry, baby. I didn't mean to. Wait for me while I go and take a quick shower."

"Sure, no problem. I'll just do homework while I wait."

"I'll hurry. See you soon." Simon leaned in to kiss me and ran back to the gym.

I was thankful he didn't notice the box. I stuffed the note and necklace back into my bag, and then caught him in my rearview mirror. Michael was here, and he was watching me from his car. I froze. I put my head down. When I lifted it, he was gone.

The following week was quiet. The package deliveries stopped, and I didn't see him lurking around. I was jumpy but tried my best to hide my fear from Simon. I never told him or my parents. I just wanted to forget. My parents were nearly finished with writing the songs and the score for the movie. Everything was working out for them, and I didn't want to cause any stress for my parents or their working relationships.

Not seeing Bailey at all the following week was beginning to weigh heavily on my mind. I was beginning to believe that Simon was right about superficial friends. How could I have been so wrong about her?

"Hey, beautiful." I jumped at hearing those words. "Hey, don't be scared, it's only me," Jameson said as he wrapped his arm around my shoulder. "Geez, Nicolette, you look like you've seen a ghost. Why do you look so sad?"

"I'm fine. Just wondering where the girls are. I haven't seen much of them."

"Well, thank goodness you have me around for the latest scoop. Bailey cut today. She said she had errands to run. And our girl, Alexis, is watching Jimmy run and sweat all over the track as we speak."

"Ha! I thought she didn't like him."

"I guess she changed her mind because she has been there every day this week."

"I'm happy for her. I guess that explains why I haven't seen her, but what's up with Bailey?" *I guess I already knew. After our fight, I practically shunned her after that.*

"No worries, beautiful. You know how girls get when they have boyfriends. Speaking of which, here comes yours now. Come on, Nicolette, let's make him jealous. Put your hand on my leg." For the first time all week, I laughed. God, I loved Jameson.

"You are too much. What a flirt you are."

"Yeah? Then why am I still single?"

"The right guy is out there for you, I just know it," I told him.

"Okay, in the meantime, can we share Simon?"

"No! he's mine."

We both laughed.

Simon called out, "Hands off my girl." Smiling at his friend, he made his way over to us. "Baby! I missed you. Get over here, and kiss me."

Jameson jokingly stood up. "Okay, lover, I'm on my way."

I swatted him away. "I think he was talking to me."

"Damn, you get to have all the fun. Enjoy your man, Nicolette. I have a spa appointment to get to."

"Bye, Jameson." I waved him off and then turned back to Simon, who was waiting for his kiss. I gave him more than that, as I hugged him tightly and squeezed his butt. His sexiness was too much for me on most days.

"So, let's talk about this weekend. How are we celebrating your birthday?" Simon asked.

"Quiet, Simon. I haven't really broadcasted to the world. I would prefer just quiet time with my boyfriend. Is that okay with you?"

"Birthday? Did I hear you right?" I turned around, and Jameson was back.

"I thought you had an appointment. Where did you just come from?" I asked.

"I do, but as you can see, I forgot my messenger bag. This is a Gucci, and this hot coochie doesn't leave his Gucci behind."

"I love it. That was a good one." Simon said.

"I know what to do. You only turn eighteen once. Let's put out a mass Twitter alert and have a party down at the Beach Club. My parents are away, and their cabana is free for me to use. It has a huge deck that leads down to the beach. We can do a bonfire, booze…the works. What do you say, beautiful girl? Are you in?"

"Calm down, Jameson. I already have plans to take my girl out, and they don't include your Twitter followers."

"We have plans?" I asked in surprise.

"Yes, we sure do. I was just testing the waters with you before I sprung my surprise on you." He kissed me soundly and went back to talking with Jameson.

"You always take my fun away, Simon. Party, party, party!" he chanted.

"No, another time."

He pouted. "It won't count if it's after your birthday."

"Sorry, take it or leave it."

"Fine! I seriously need to get a boyfriend. You straight couples are killing me."

"We love you too!" Simon called out to Jameson's retreating back. Simon hugged me tighter after Jameson left. "I don't want you to worry. I have your birthday covered. We will have an amazing night, I promise you. Do you have to be home anytime soon?"

"No, my parents are working late, and they know I am with you."

"Perfect. Let's take a ride down to the beach. The sky has been clear all day, so you know it will be an amazing sunset. Will you watch it with me?"

"Yes, lead the way."

We stopped at the Juice Bar for some dinner and brought it with us to picnic on the beach. He placed a blanket down, and we quietly ate our sandwiches, or at least, I did. Simon was going on about his upcoming track meets and how well Jimmy has been doing.

I just kind of stared out to the ocean. I had so much on my mind. Keeping secrets will do that to you. I felt as if I was breaking Simon's trust by not being upfront with him about Michael. But I knew I had to protect him, so I remained quiet and just allowed the guilt to weigh me down.

After a while, the silence became too much for Simon. "Hey, Nicolette, care to tell me what's wrong? You haven't said two words to me since we left school. Are you mad at me?"

"No, don't be silly. I just have a few things on my mind, that's all."

"You can tell me anything. You know that, right?"

I just nodded and tried not to cry. Simon was so good at reading my body language and knew when something was off with me. I thought I was doing pretty well at hiding it from him.

"Can we take a walk down by the water?" I asked.

He grabbed the blanket, and we walked down the beach until we were far away from the docks. We found a secluded spot that was past the dunes. He placed the blanket down and pulled me down with him.

"Whatever is bothering you, you can tell me. I'm here for you," he said as he kissed the top of my head.

"I know. Can you just hold me?"

"Always."

I was resting on my elbows when Simon leaned in and began to kiss me behind my ear. He then trailed a path of kisses down my neck. With each kiss was a tickle until he reached my lips.

I moved and wrapped myself around him. I wanted him so much. I loved him so much. I returned his kiss and ran my fingers through his thick, messy hair.

He placed his one hand behind my neck and the other under my blouse. When he slid his fingers over my lacy bra, I began to tremble. As he continued to explore my body, I warmed under his touch. Without ever taking his eyes away from mine, he unclasped my bra.

I felt an overwhelming surge of excitement that was building inside of my body. I didn't quite understand all the feelings I felt, but I knew I didn't want him to stop.

He looked into my eyes and wanted permission to go further. I blinked my response and let out soft moans, as he began to suck on my nipple and twisted the other between his fingers.

The feeling was intense as I gripped the blanket. Just when I thought I was going to explode from within and scream out his name, he whispered, "Let go for me."

I felt as if I was floating above my body and exhilarated all at the same time. I had never experienced anything like this before. I wanted to give everything to Simon. He kissed and kissed me, and then covered me up. I had goose bumps that lined my skin. He warmed me with his body. When I opened my eyes to look at him, I had never felt safer and protected. I was embarrassed to actually say the word, but he could read me like a book and did it for me.

He whispered, "Yes, baby, that was an orgasm. I hate to ask, but was that the first one you've had? Please, say yes, or I may have to beat the shit out of someone."

I laughed. "Simon, that was incredible. Yes, it was my first. You are my first," I whispered.

He pulled me on top of him and wrapped his arms around my back as he kissed me. I breathed him in as I felt his hard erection press into me. I had never done anything with a boy, other than kissing. Not even with Jason. Simon was truly my first that I allowed to touch me in such an intimate way. I loved and trusted him. With Simon, it was so much more than I can ever begin to describe. It just felt right. When we finally came up for air, he broke me out of my trance and said the words I had been waiting to hear.

"You are amazing, Nicolette. I love you so much." He held my face and waited for my response. My eyes should have said it all, but my tears came first. He wiped them away with his thumbs and continued to kiss me.

Breathlessly, I said, "I love you, Simon. I have since we met."

He let out a breath and folded me into him. He kissed and kissed me and professed his love for me. I couldn't believe that I would turn eighteen tomorrow, and my boyfriend just gave me the best present. He loved me. I had never been happier.

Eight

Nicolette

I closed my front door behind me and leaned against it with the happiest smile on my face. I was in love. My mind was in a blissed-out haze that I didn't see my father standing in the entryway. It was obvious he was waiting for me.

Not even my dad could spoil this night for me. "Hi, daddy."

"Hi, daddy? I believe you owe me a little more than two words. Do you know what time it is?" he asked with his arms crossed over his chest.

"Yes, and I know I am late, but I have a very good reason."

"And what might that be?"

"Simon loves me!" I practically shouted. I was so happy.

He didn't look too surprised at that and just smiled back at me. "Wow! That's major."

"Daddy, before you give me the lecture on how young we are and I should take my time, I'm going to tell you, thank you, but no thank you. Simon, he's the real deal and makes me incredibly happy."

Taking me by surprise, he opened his arms and invited me in for a hug, a reaction that was so unlike him. He kissed the top of my head and said, "I'm happy for you, Nicolette. To see my daughter this happy, and to smile the way you do, is all we have ever wanted for you."

"So, no lecture?"

"Nope, not tonight. It's your birthday tomorrow, and we are giving you a free pass, but don't make it a habit of breaking curfew."

"I won't. I love you, daddy."

"I love you more. Now, go to bed."

I thought about how my life had changed so much in so little time since we moved here. I was adamant about leaving Chicago and fought my parents all the way. I convinced myself that I would never be happy again and mourned the loss of my beloved Chicago, friends, and Uncle Jack, who I never wanted to leave behind.

Now, five months later, I had an amazing group of friends, a boyfriend who loved me, and this new life that I loved. Yes, I had never been happier, and those feelings sent me into the most peaceful sleep.

I was jolted out of the best dream ever when the celebrating trio barged into my room with noise makers. Gracie was carrying a small birthday cake with eighteen candles lit and waiting for me to make a wish. I placed my hand on my heart and held back my happy tears. This was a tradition with mom and dad. They always woke me up early on my birthday and sang to me. It didn't matter what my plans were for my special day, they were the first to share it with me, and I loved them so much for it. I moved forward and hugged my parents with a group hug.

"Happy Birthday, Nicolette!" all three shouted together.

I leaned forward, with mom pulling my long hair back. I closed my eyes and blew out the candles. They cheered me on, and then mom asked me if I made a wish. I told her that it had already come true last night with Simon. Of course, I did not tell her that he gave me my first orgasm on the beach. *Yeah, I will keep that to myself.*

Gracie gave me a hug and then sliced up the cake. It was my favorite, strawberry shortcake.

As I savored every bite, my dad said, "Close your eyes, Nicolette. You know what's coming next."

Present time! He always was so excited when we got to this part. All three did the countdown. When I opened my eyes, my bed was full of presents.

Gracie asked if she could go first. Her smile was infectious. I pulled back the layers of tissue paper and found a beautiful handmade patchwork quilt made especially for me by Gracie.

I told her, "This is beautiful. I will always cherish it. Thank you."

With tears in her eyes, she said, "Happy Birthday, Nicolette. I love you as if you were my own."

It was mom's turn to cry, and she did. My poor father, he was outnumbered with all the hormones in this house.

My parents gave me CDs, clothes, and spa certificates. I received a package from Uncle Jack and Aunt Sara, and I was asked not to open it until my birthday. No reason to wait now. My father handed me their gift, and I opened the wrapped box, only to find a small Tiffany box. Inside was a platinum bracelet with an inscription on the inside: *Happy 18th Birthday, Nickel.*

Mom clasped it on my wrist and then hugged me. I loved it. Uncle Jack had chosen a gift with his special nickname for me engraved on it. His thoughtful gift meant the world to me. "I miss him, daddy, and Aunt Sara too."

"I know, honey. You'll see them soon."

I tried to smile, but unless I was going back to Chicago, I had no idea when I would see my precious Uncle Jack again. The start of my birthday had been perfect. I received text messages from new and old friends, but the best one yet was from Simon.

Simon: *Good morning, baby! Happy Birthday. How were your dreams last night? Mine were all about you, and a bit naughty too! I can't wait until you are back in my arms tonight. Have an amazing day. I love you, Nicolette.*

Me: *Who is this? I think you have the wrong number.*

Simon: *Smart ass! You're lucky that I love you.*

Me: *...Love?*

Simon: *With all my heart.*

Me: *I love you too.*

That was fun. The rest of my day was spent with mom. We went to lunch and then to the spa for some birthday pampering. I only got a manicure and pedicure, wanting to do my own makeup and hair. I regretted my decision once I was undecided on what to do with my long locks. I played around with styles, and then after a couple of hours, it was perfect. I was twirling around in front of the floor-length mirror. I felt like a princess, and I knew my prince would arrive at any moment to sweep me off my feet. I was still in my dressing room when mom knocked and asked to come in.

When I walked out, she gasped and covered her mouth with her hand. "Oh, baby, you look so beautiful." I showed her my best vogue moves as she clapped her hands. "You just look perfect. I can't believe you are eighteen years old."

"And that would make you..."

"Um, don't even think about finishing that sentence. We don't discuss *my* age, thank you very much."

She came in to tell me that Simon was waiting for me downstairs. I practically sprinted to the door. Mom called me back for a quick hug and then walked me back over to the mirror. She stood behind me and wrapped her arms around me. Sometimes we had a crazy relationship, never agreeing on much, but I knew she loved me.

"Take your time, Nicolette. He will wait for you." Mom winked at me and then walked out of my room. I got the feeling that was mom's way of sending me a message about sex, without actually voicing the words.

I let out a breath and made my way downstairs. As I descended the stairs, Simon was waiting for me with his hand outreached to me. He looked incredible, dressed in black pants and a matching jacket, with an open-collared white shirt. Beyond sexy, I thought. I didn't care what he planned for us tonight, I just wanted to kiss him and be only with him. He drank me in with desire in his eyes.

"You are so beautiful, Nicolette. Happy Birthday." He brought my hand up to his lips and kissed it. He placed a beautiful corsage designed with white roses on my wrist. I felt like a princess. "Do you want your present? Now or later?"

I squealed with anticipation, I happily said, "Now. Please."

"Close your eyes, baby." I closed them tightly, but when I peeked, he waved his index finger at me. "No present until you close your eyes." I behaved.

He stroked my neck with his fingers and kissed me behind my ear. I felt him taking my earrings out and replace them. *Simon bought me earrings for my birthday.*

I was so excited to see them. He took my hand and led me over to a mirror.

He whispered, "Open your eyes." He stood behind me, as we continued to look at one another in the mirror. He had given me diamond encrusted earrings in the shape of a rose. "I knew they would look perfect on your very kissable earlobes," he said as he nipped at each one. "Do you like them?"

I was speechless when I saw them. "I love them. How can I not when you were so thoughtful to choose something so beautiful for me. Thank you, Simon."

"Not as beautiful as you. I love you. Happy Birthday. Are you ready to have some fun?"

"I don't know how it can get any better than this moment right here with you. My day has been perfect. You're perfect."

"Well, your night is going to get better, just wait and see. Let's go." Simon placed his hand on the small of my back and walked me out to a waiting car.

"You hired a limo?"

"Only the best for you." He kissed me.

"Are you going to tell me where we are going?"

"Nope. It's a surprise. And you need to stop asking. As we drove along, he never stopped kissing my hand, and then the inside of my wrist. My insides were on fire with every kiss he placed on me.

"Okay, now for the fun part." He asked me to humor him by wearing a mask that he placed down in my hand. He wanted me to be completely surprised. I complied, but the anticipation was killing me.

"We're here," he said, as he helped me from the car and into his arms.

"Simon, can I please take this blindfold off?"

"Just a few more steps, and then you can." He held my hand the entire time he walked us to wherever we were. "Okay, I'm going to remove the blindfold now. Keep your eyes closed until I say you can open them." It was so quiet, you could hear a pin drop. I was kissed on my cheek, and then my boyfriend whispered in my ear, "Open your eyes, baby."

"SURPRISE!"

I was in the middle of my very own surprise birthday party. One by one, I was greeted with hugs and happy birthday wishes. I tried so hard not to cry. Simon could not stop smiling and then asked me to turn around for my next surprise.

"Uncle Jack!" I shouted out, as I jumped into his arms and he spun me around. Best birthday ever.

"Happy birthday, Nickel! You didn't really believe I would have missed out on seeing you turn eighteen?" I couldn't stop the happy tears from falling. Mom handed me a wad of Kleenex. I lifted my wrist to show him that I was wearing his lovely gift.

I inquired, "Where's Aunt Sara?"

"I'm sorry, but she just couldn't get away. She asked me to give you a big hug and tell you that she will be visiting soon."

"That's okay, I understand. I just can't believe that you all pulled this off, and without me suspecting a thing."

"Uncle Jack, how long are you able to stay?"

"I fly home tomorrow evening, but we will have the entire day tomorrow. Now, go have fun with your friends." I hugged him tightly and then rejoined my boyfriend.

He held me in his arms as he twirled me around the dance floor. I was in heaven. "How did you manage all of this, Simon?"

"I had lots and lots of help, especially from the girls and Jameson. He sure played it off well."

"Yes, he did. I never knew." I scanned the room again and spotted Bailey with Jameson, smiling back at me. Now I knew they were the secret party planners who helped out Simon. I had a twinge of guilt for not trusting Bailey and doubting our friendship.

"Good, that was the plan. I just wanted to give you the best birthday party you have ever seen. I'm just sorry some of your old Chicago friends couldn't make it. I tried."

"And I love you for that. It's okay. All the people I love are all right here in this room. I grabbed his face and pulled him down to me for a change, kissing him with all of the love that felt for him. I wanted to show Simon how much I appreciated and loved him. He made me so happy, especially tonight with his thoughtful surprise.

"I love you, Nicolette. Are you ready to have some fun?"

"Lead the way, boyfriend."

On cue, Jameson ran up and scooped me up into a hug.

"Put me down!" I laughed

"Do you love it? You little minx."

"Yes, I do. Thank you so much." I hugged him back.

We danced for hours, and my feet were killing me, but it was so very worth it. Slow dancing with my hot boyfriend made me forget about the ache in my feet. He held me as close as two people could be, which made me forget my own name. He never stopped kissing me. I didn't believe anything could top this night with Simon, my family, and our friends. The dancing made me thirsty. We were enjoying some refreshing punch when Bailey interrupted us.

"Happy birthday, Nicolette."

"Thank you, Bailey. Everything looks amazing."

"It was my pleasure to help out. Hey, can we talk? It will only take a minute."

"Don't be long. We still have a few dances in us before the night comes to an end," Simon said as he kissed me and gave us some privacy.

She asked, "Are we still friends?"

"Yes, we are. I'm sorry that I have shut you out, but I had my reasons. Now, you did all of this for me? I was completely blown away by it. Thank you."

"I owed it to you. Nicolette, I'm sorry for not hearing what you were trying to tell me. I should have respected your feelings and not have pressured you into changing your mind about the party. I was wrong, and I hope you can forgive me."

"It's forgotten, but why was it so necessary to have me there?" I knew the reason. I just wanted to hear her say it.

"Nicolette, Seth asked me to bring you along because he had a friend he wanted you to meet. He warned me that if I didn't show up with you, then he didn't want me there either."

"Wow! What an asshole. You didn't go, did you?"

"No, and neither did Alexis. Jimmy had invited her to a movie, and she preferred that over a college party. She told me she was taking your advice and giving him a chance. As you can see, her blossoming romance with Jimmy is going well."

"Come on, let's go to the restroom. We can finish our talk in there," I said as Bailey followed. Once I checked my makeup, we sat down to finish our talk. "Bailey, if I may, do you know the friend whom Seth wanted me to meet? Please, I need the truth."

Her lip quivered before answering and then she said the one name I feared. "Michael St. Clair. He has been behind this from the beginning."

I stood up and almost felt dizzy with her revelation. I gripped the sink for support. I knew it. I had always felt it but needed to hear her say it, and now I had. The reality of it felt like a knife in my back. Bailey was my friend, and I felt betrayed by her and the lies she told.

"Michael?" I said, gritting my teeth. I backed her into a corner with my arms that caged her in. She looked so ashamed, but I wasn't about to feel sorry for her. "I can't believe you did this. Why, Bailey? You knew how I felt about Simon. How could you make a promise that I would go?" I was angry and hurt, and I turned away from her.

"Nicolette, I was confused. I believed that Seth cared about me. I was ready to sleep with him. He was just using me to help Michael get to you."

I'd never shared with my friend the history that I had with Michael nor his attempts to stalk me. Now I felt bad for being so angry with her. This wasn't entirely her fault. She had been manipulated by

Seth, and then Michael. As my friend, she should have been honest with me, and that's what hurt.

"Please say that you forgive me, Nicolette? I don't want to lose you."

"Bailey, I'm not angry, but more like disappointed. I wish you would have come to me from the very beginning and not have taken it as far as you did. I have questions, but this is not the place to ask them. I have to get back to Simon." Just as I said it, my phone pinged.

Simon: *Boyfriend misses you.*

Me: *I'll be right out.*

I took a moment to steady my breathing. What started out as an easy conversation with my friend quickly turned into something so much bigger. I made my way back to the great room when I was blocked by no other than Michael.

"Happy birthday, Nicolette."

He reached for my hand, but I quickly pulled it away. I tried to step aside, but there he remained and continued to block my path. Here I was, alone with him again! With no help in sight, I was on my own. I wanted Simon to rescue me. Where was he?

"Nicolette, I'm not going to hurt you."

"Michael, the last time you said those words to me, I ended up with a sprained wrist. I don't know why you are here, but I need you to move."

"I don't want any trouble. I was already here having dinner with friends, and then I saw you. I thought it may have been fate. I just wanted to say hello."

"Just leave me alone. Stop with the gifts, flowers, and notes. Stop using my friends to get to me. Yes, I know what you did to Bailey. You are such an asshole. If you don't stop harassing me, I will tell my father."

His lips twitched as if my telling him off was getting him excited. He made my skin crawl. "Nicolette, why are you fighting it? We can be so good together."

"In your dreams. I will never be yours. Leave me alone."

"So, let me ask you a question. If you really believed I was harassing you, then why hasn't your father already paid me a visit? Here's what I think. You love the attention I'm giving you. It excites you. You know the truth, don't you? That's why you haven't told anyone yet, and that includes your precious boyfriend. How is Simon?"

"You leave him alone. You leave me alone."

"I can't, and I won't, not when he is the one standing in my way to you. I love you, and I want you. Stop fighting your feelings, and just be with me. Dump that loser, and be with me."

He was certifiable. This couldn't be happening. My phone pinged with probably more messages from Simon, but, where was he? Michael grabbed my hand and prevented me from reaching my phone.

"You will realize that he is not right for you, and you will come to me. Fighting the inevitable is just making me want you more. I'll play it your way... for now."

"Michael, you are out of your mind if you think I will ever be yours and leave Simon. It will never happen for you and me. You need to accept it. Now, let me go."

He didn't. He gripped both of my arms, not to the point of pain, but a clear message that I wasn't going anywhere. He slammed his mouth down to mine as I struggled to break free. I had so much rage inside of me that I managed to step back and slap him across his face. He jerked his head back as if he enjoyed what I just did.

"I love you, Nicolette. I will see you soon. You can count on that."

MARY WASOWSKI

My chest was heaving. I couldn't breathe. Just then, Bailey came looking for me. "Hey, Nicolette, Simon is getting pretty impatient out there on the dance floor. Hey, are you..."

I ran off into the ladies' bathroom and rushed to the nearest stall. My stomach heaved, and I began to forcibly vomit. I wanted his touch off me. My entire body was shaking, and I tried to get it back under control.

"Nicolette, are you okay? I'll get Simon."

"No! Don't you dare! Give me a minute," I called out. I must have looked a mess. My lipstick had been smeared over my lips, and my skin was red from throwing up.

"Nicolette, what just happened? Can I do anything for you?"

"No, you have done quite enough." I didn't mean to be curt with her, but I just couldn't do this right now. "Just forget what you just saw. Go back out there and tell Simon that something didn't agree with me, and I am settling my stomach. I'm going to clean up, and then I will be out."

"But Nicolette..."

"But nothing! Go!"

I turned away from her and washed practically all my makeup off my face. There was no point in covering it up, I knew what I looked like. The best I could do was fix my lipstick and touch up my hair.

I took a few calming breaths and then left to go find Simon. I saw him pacing near the dance floor. The guys were with him, but he looked angry.

"There you are! Where have you been?" he practically shouted at me.

I played it off. "Didn't Bailey find you?"

"No, I haven't seen Bailey since you two walked off and talked."

"Okay, I'm sorry. I ate something that made me sick, and I've been in the bathroom this entire time." *Another lie.*

"Oh, baby, I am so sorry. I should have tried to find you, but whatever was going on with you and Bailey looked pretty serious. Are you okay? Should I take you home?"

"No, I'm much better. Let's dance."

"Okay, as long as you promise me no more girl talks tonight."

"Don't worry. That's the last thing I wish to do. I just want to be with my amazing boyfriend. Thank you for the best birthday ever, Simon."

"You are most welcome, Nicolette. I love you. Have I told you how beautiful you look tonight?"

"You have, but not sure that still applies."

"Never, you are gorgeous. Sick or not."

We danced to a few more songs, and then my night came to an end. Simon walked me to my door, always the gentleman. He cupped my face and gazed into my eyes. "I love you. I'm going to make you very happy."

I nearly cried. "You already have."

"In you go. I'll call you tomorrow." Without another word or kiss, he sprinted back to the limo.

Tomorrow will be the day I will spend time with Uncle Jack and then finally tell my parents about Michael, but with a few minutes still left on my birthday, I was going to forget about him and dream of Simon, the one who loved me.

Nine

Michael

The days that followed my confrontation with Nicolette were hard on me. I couldn't eat. I didn't sleep. I scared her again by coming on too strong. I just wanted to be close to her, but she rejected me again, and then I got angry and pushed for more. I rubbed my tired eyes, I needed to sleep, but I was too wired replaying all that happened at her party. When I finally crashed, all my dreams were of her.

I thought I was going to stop breathing when my eyes found hers. She was stunning, and all made up looking absolutely gorgeous. I remained out of sight, as I watched her dance with that fucker Simon Paulson, a thorn in my side for far too long now. I hated to see how he touched her, and the sight of her eyes sparkling when she looked into his. I wanted those eyes on mine. She had me all twisted and fucked up in the head like no other girl I had ever known.

"Michael, you need to let go of this fucked up obsession you have for this girl. It's not healthy, and you are going to get yourself into a hell of a lot of trouble that you do not need," Seth shouted, breaking me out from my dazed and confused thoughts.

"Oh, please! If you mean Simon Paulson, I can handle him. I've done it before, and I can do it again."

"Yes, he's part of it, but what about your father? Do you really want to continue to push him? Did you forget last year? He had you packed and on his company jet within hours after hearing about Jennifer's death. You were so strung out on drugs that night, and when you woke up, you were in the fucking psych ward in a private facility far from here. Is this girl worth taking that risk again? Everything you have done since meeting this girl has not made any sense. Come on, you are one of the most popular guys at our frat house. You have your pick. Any girl, any night, to fuck as much as you want. Tell me, Michael, what makes this one different? Make me understand, so I can help you."

"I can't explain it. She's not like anyone I have ever met before. I refuse to let her go."

"You are seriously beginning to freak me out. We live in California. You mean to tell me that out of all the hot girls, a high school girl from Chicago does it for you? You're not thinking clearly, and going days without sleep is fucking with your mind. Let this go, and move on."

"Why are you here, Seth? I didn't ask for your help, nor do I want your advice on whom to fuck. I have heard all the lectures I can stomach from my father, I don't need to hear them from you too."

"I think you do. Michael, I'm your friend. I want to help you and make you see that what you are doing is not right. You have been warned by your father, her father, and let's not forget Simon, her boyfriend." The way he enunciated the word *boyfriend* made me sick.

He continued, "Think about what you are doing. No good will come from it. Don't you see that? She doesn't want you and has made her feelings about it quite clear."

I held my head to drown out his voice. Seth didn't know what the hell he was talking about, none of them did.

"I need more time with her. If she would only talk with me for a few minutes, and without anyone coming between us, then I know I can make her see how good we could be together."

"Michael, shall I remind you what happened the last time you tried to force her to talk to you? You nearly broke her hand. Then, like some crazy stalker, you track her to her birthday party and confront her again. What the hell is wrong with you? All you are doing is scaring and pushing her further away. You are out of control. You need help."

"Oh, I need help? That's a bunch of bullshit, and you know it. Exaggerate much? For the last time, all I did was reach for her hand. Nicolette was the one that overreacted, but I'm the one that got blamed. She's made me out to be an abuser, a stalker when all I want to do is love her. She has been brainwashed by Simon that I am this evil person who just wants to do her harm, but it's not true. I love her. I love her, Seth! Why doesn't anyone understand that!"

My head was spinning as I staggered over to my father's bar. The amber liquid burned my throat, but I welcomed it. Anything to numb my mind. I was going crazy over thinking about Nicolette and arguing with Seth.

I swallowed another shot and then turned to Seth. "You must listen to me. I never meant to cause even the slightest measure of pain for her. You know me, Seth. I didn't mean it. I just lost control for a brief moment, and it is something I will not do again. You know this, right?"

"Are you sure about that, Michael? Because I'm not. Remember, I was there when you spiraled out of control the last time you obsessed over a girl. I don't know if I can go through that again with you."

"Oh, fucking hell! This again? What happened to Jennifer was not my fucking fault. I am so tired of beating a dead horse. She came to me, remember? You talk about letting shit go…what about you, Seth? You're the one that is messed up, throwing my past in my face. That's not cool."

"If you would just listen to me, you would know that I am not talking about Jennifer and her accident. I'm talking about what happened after her death. You were out of control. I covered for you so many times with your father, I lost count. Please, Michael, I am asking you as your best friend. Let this girl go. It's not worth it. The next time you are on that edge, I may not be there to pull you back."

"Good! I won't fall." I shoved past him and opened the entryway door. "Get the fuck out, and don't come back here. This conversation is over."

"No!" shouted Seth. "It's not. Let me help you."

I grabbed him by his throat and shoved him out the door. "I said, get out! Don't come back here."

"You are making a mistake, one that will not end well for you," he said as he coughed in between breaths.

"The only mistake I made today was to invite you in. I don't need, nor do I want your help. Go away, and don't come back here." I slammed the door in his face and never looked back.

I woke up with the resolve to not think of Michael and all the bullshit he had been putting me through. Instead, I focused on having a great day sightseeing with Uncle Jack. We stopped at all the touristy places and ended our tour on the Hollywood Walk of Fame. This was his favorite place. He snapped photo after photo of the famous blocks of actresses that he loved. He looked so happy and carefree. I wish I could have said the same, but I felt buried under my guilt for not being honest with my father or Uncle Jack. I never had a problem talking to him about anything, but this was different. Other people were involved that could get hurt, and that was the last thing I wanted to happen.

"Hey, Nickel, you're awfully quiet. What's on your mind?" he asked, as we slowly walked back to the parking lot.

"I'm fine, just sad that I have to drive you to the airport. I wish we could have had more time, that's all."

He smiled at me, but I wasn't sure if he believed me. "Nicolette, I will always be here for you, no matter what. I love you so much, and I would do anything for you. You have always had your own mind and very good judgment. If you say that you are okay, then I am going to believe you. Having said that, I want you to know that you can tell me anything."

"I know, and Uncle Jack, you don't have to worry about me. I have everything under control, I promise."

I was thankful for small miracles when my phone buzzed with a reminder to leave for the airport. My dad wanted to drive, but I insisted taking Uncle Jack. I didn't want to waste one minute of time spent with him, not when he lived so far away. He grabbed his carry-on from the backseat and rounded the front to give me a hug. I tried not to cry, but it was impossible. There were so many reasons why I needed to let the tears fall, and not just because he was leaving.

"Oh, my sweet Nickel, don't cry. I can't get on that plane knowing you are so sad. I promise you that I will bring Aunt Sara back out here for a visit and soon, okay? Now, dry those tears, or I am not leaving."

"Yeah, okay. I'm sure Aunt Sara would have a problem with that when you didn't show up at passenger pickup. Don't worry, I'm fine. Give Aunt Sara and Tommy a hug from me. I love you so much."

"I love you more. More than you will ever know."

My heart ached as I watched my uncle walk into the airport terminal. I didn't look away until he was out of sight. Once I returned home, I declined dinner and went to bed. I shut my phone off and just prayed that I would be able to find a resolution to all my problems with Michael. Of course, I chickened out and didn't talk to mom or dad. I was too exhausted.

I had plenty of time on my hands with the Thanksgiving holiday approaching. The girls invited me to go shopping on our half-day off from school. Simon, Sam, and Jameson spent the rest of the day down at the beach surfing. Alexis must have bought out half the store and the same jeans in multiple colors. Over coffees and a shared dessert, we gossiped about our guys.

"What does Jimmy like you to wear?" Not sure why I asked, but I thought I had noticed lingerie in one of her bags.

"Nothing," she teasingly replied. "Okay, maybe a thong, but that's even pushing it."

My mouth dropped open, and both Alexis and Bailey laughed in hysterics.

"I thought that might catch your attention, Nicolette."

"You slept with Jimmy?"

"Yes, and it was hot as hell. My man has moves, and not just on the track. Don't look so surprised, Nicolette. You haven't done the deed with Simon yet?" she asked.

I buried my face in my hands. She had no filter when it came to talking about sex, and I was afraid someone might have overheard her.

She said, "Wait a minute, seriously? You two can't keep your hands off each other."

"Alexis, leave her alone. I think you're making her uncomfortable," Bailey said as she gave me a knowing look that spoke volumes.

"I'm sorry. You know I was just joking around, but really, I'm just surprised. Just the way he looks at you, it's like something more, you know? Simon is serious and is so committed. He's not playing around with your heart. You can trust him."

I replied, "I know I can. As for sex, it hasn't gotten that far yet, but to say I haven't considered it would be a lie. Just the thought of what it would be like to make love with him makes my stomach flip, and in a good way."

"It will happen for you two, there's no rush. All I can say is that I have you to thank for helping me see the light. Jimmy is amazing."

"Was it your first time?"

"No, it wasn't, but it felt as if it was. He was gentle, kind, and loving throughout the entire time. My first time was in the back of some stupid jock's car after a pep rally. Yeah, that's a memory I wish I could forget. I know I tease you a lot, but if you want to wait, then that's what you should do. Simon is not going anywhere. He loves you. We all see it."

I hugged my friend and agreed. After we dropped Alexis home, Bailey wanted to hang back and talk for a while. I had been avoiding the subject of Michael, but Bailey kept my secret, and it was time to share it with her.

"Are you okay, Nicolette? I mean, really okay? You were so upset that night, and you shut me out from helping you."

"Bailey, are you okay? I mean, after all, that Seth did?"

"I'm trying. I guess you are not the only one that has been keeping a secret. Not even Alexis knows. He's not a bad guy. I think he found himself in a situation with Michael, and because he was his best friend, he probably didn't see the harm in helping him out. I get the feeling that Seth never knew the real reason behind Michael's manipulations, but maybe he does now. I had been avoiding him since your party, and after what Michael did to you, I didn't want anything to do with Seth, especially if he's like his friend. He called me repeatedly after our fight, but I told him that I didn't want to see him again, and I think he finally got the message. Okay, your turn."

"I'm sorry he hurt you. Falling for the wrong guy sucks. My problem is that I have the right guy who loves me, and another who won't leave me alone. You have to promise not to say anything to anyone, especially Alexis. Can I trust you?"

"You know that you can."

"He's stalking me, Bailey. Michael will not leave me alone. It's been happening since the party at the beach, and he will not go away. It doesn't matter what I say or do, he doesn't get it. Then with the packages at school, flowers to my house, and suddenly showing up at my birthday party...he always seems to know where I am, at all times. How is he doing it?"

"Nicolette, will you wake up? He's rich and uses his father's connections at his disposal. He could have paid off a random student to leave those things for you. He's dangerous, and this entire situation has gotten out of hand. It's time to tell someone. You need to tell your parents so they can help you."

"I will. I just need to pick the right time to do so. I am so ashamed. You don't know how hard this has been for me."

"I think I do and so does Michael. He is doing everything he can to break you down. You have to fight back, Nicolette, and not allow him to intimidate you. I have a bad feeling about this. Please, promise me you will go to your parents."

"Okay, I promise."

Her words weighed heavily on my mind. I knew my family would protect me, but I didn't understand why I hesitated to ask for their help. Deep down, I knew why. My parents have given everything to me, and I knew how hard they worked for their success. One word from me, and that success would be placed in jeopardy, and snakes like Mr. St. Clair would not hesitate to pull the rug out from under them. No, I wasn't going to risk it. Things had been quiet again. Michael hasn't bothered me.

We joined our hands in prayer, as my father said his Thanksgiving blessing. I was so thankful for so many wonderful things I had in my life, and the guy to the right of me, holding my hand, was one of them. Simon joined us for the holiday after declining to go out to visit his brothers. He said he didn't want to miss our first of many holidays we would spend together. He speaks with dreams in his eyes, as if he knew something wonderful about our future that he hadn't let me in on yet.

"Thank you for sharing today with me, Simon. I loved that you were here."

"Right here in your arms was the only place I wanted to be. I love you so much, and if I have my way, we will be spending all our holidays together. What would you say to the idea of driving up to Big Bear for some skiing over school break?"

"I would love that, but I have a problem."

"Whatever it is, I can fix it."

"Okay, remember what you just said when you are teaching me to ski."

"Ha! I guess living in Chicago didn't give you any time on the slopes."

"Nope. The biggest winter activity I did was ice skating."

"Okay, I promise to be patient and only take you on the trail for beginners. Deal?"

"Or, we can skip skiing altogether, and just make-out in front of the fire."

"Yeah, your plan sounds better."

He winked, and then took me in his arms to kiss me madly before leaving. I knew I had to let him go, knowing dear old dad was probably watching us from the window.

I told him, "I love you. This has been the best day ever."

"I love you more, and you haven't seen the best yet."

Ten

Nicolette

nother day, another text from Michael. I read his messages as I paced my room. I had made up my mind about Michael and my decision to handle him on my own. I reasoned with myself that I was now an adult and could make my own decisions. I believed the first one would be to change my phone number.

I was about to send Michael, a big "fuck-off" text when my phone rang with a number I didn't know. It was Seth McCarter, Michael's friend, and Bailey's ex. I was about to hang up on him, and then he asked me to meet him down at the Juice Bar, just to talk. I wasn't sure if he was setting me up for another surprise meeting with Michael, but he promised it would only be him. So, like the idiot that I am, I agreed to go.

When I walked into the restaurant and saw where Seth was waiting for me, I immediately felt regret. He was in my booth, the one I shared with Simon. I should have just turned around and left, but I was curious to what Seth would say, and I stayed. I kept the pleasantries to a minimum and got right to the point to why I was requested here.

Seth went on to explain a little about Michael's past to me and why he may be doing the things he's doing. He was only fourteen when he lost his mother to cancer. They were very close. Seth believed that when his mom died, she took a piece of Michael with her. His father ignored him and left him to be cared for by staff.

Yeah, where had I heard that before? I didn't want to be a bitch, but it was so cliché. The rich kids drove the fancy cars and were afforded everything their hearts desired, and pretty much were left on their own by neglectful parents. For Michael, it was his father who couldn't give him the time of day. It was a sad story, but after hearing it, it still didn't sway me to feel sorry for him.

What Michael had been doing to me was cruel and selfish. He was playing games and doing a great job with messing with my mind. He was a classic manipulator and had all the signs leading to a young sociopath.

"Nicolette, thank you for listening. I just felt if I shared a few things about Michael, then maybe you would be able to understand him better."

"Seth, I can't imagine how he felt losing a parent at such a young age. It had to be awful for him, but that doesn't give him a free pass to traumatize me. He says he loves me? Why does he love me? He doesn't even know me. No, no matter what you say, I believe it was his ego that took a beating when I said I wouldn't go out with him."

I continued, "Michael is spoiled, entitled, and believes that everything he wants, he is within rights to have it. That may work for material items but not for people. He hurt me. He scares me. I just want him to leave me alone. You don't know how hard it has been to keep him away and not get my family or my boyfriend involved.

He's caused enough trouble for me, and I can't bring this to my family. He needs to move on."

"He's intense, Nicolette, but I don't believe he would ever hurt you."

"He already has, and more than once. Don't you see? He is hurting me daily by harassing me the way he has. If you are truly his friend, then help him. Make him see that he's wrong."

"I have tried, I swear that I have. Like you, I just don't know what to do."

I held my head in my hands and just sighed in frustration. This was a waste of my time. Sure, Seth had been sincere when talking about Michael, but like him, he just didn't realize the severity of this situation. When I got up to leave, I didn't notice Simon was standing in front of our booth, not looking too happy.

"Hey, what are you doing here? I thought you had to study?" he asked with annoyance to his tone. "And was that Seth McCarter I saw you talking to?" *Yup! Not only did he sound annoyed with me, but jealous too.*

Any other time, I would have been loving the fact that Simon was jealous, but not today. My head was pounding with a headache, and I wasn't up for a big explanation to why I was here instead of at home where I said I would be. Simon wanted to spend the day together, but I texted him the night before telling him another time. My mom had given me the speech about not planning your entire life around your boyfriend, and to focus on myself once in a while. I was trying, but every time I did, Michael would mess it up for me.

"Yes, it was Seth. I finished up with my pre-math test, and after finishing my errands, I stopped by here for a juice. What you saw was just Seth saying hello." *Another lie that so easily rolled off my tongue.*

He seemed satisfied with my answer and slid into the booth to sit beside me. "I'm sorry, baby, I didn't mean to accuse you of anything, but I didn't think you knew him that well."

"I don't. It was just two people being in the same place at the same time."

He crushed his mouth down to mine as if he was hungry for a taste of me. I was beginning to feel a bit embarrassed by his very public display of affection, but he didn't care who was watching. When I looked into Simon's eyes, after realizing he saw me with Seth, something had shifted from love to possession. I knew Simon probably had some hidden feelings about losing Jennifer to Michael, so I understood how he might have felt seeing me with another guy, but he never had to worry. I was in love with him, and I would never knowingly do anything to hurt Simon.

Just like that, he pulled me out from the booth and right into his arms. "You're here, and I'm here, so let's go down to the beach. I have my bike right outside." He was leading me out of the Juice Bar when I pulled back on his hand.

"Simon, wait a minute."

"What's up?"

"I have my car here. Why don't you follow me home, and we can hang out? The beach can wait." I wanted so much to tell him the truth, but again I held back.

He let go of my hand and ran his fingers through his hair. He was frustrated, and I knew it was from me pulling away from him. He had already been disappointed that I didn't want to see him today, and then he found me with Seth.

"Listen, if we go back to your house, then I can't be with you the way I want to, not with your parents around. We have already lost half the day. Let's leave your car here and bring back some food to my family's cabana down at the Beach Club. I have the key, and we can be alone."

"I would rather drive my car, and I will follow you to the Beach Club, okay?"

"Yeah, whatever." His muscles tightened in his jaw. He wasn't my happy boyfriend at the moment, but that was my fault.

Once we settled into the cabana, he asked, "Dance with me?" after plugging in his iPod. "I'm sorry for how I acted back there at the Juice Bar. I was jealous that you were talking to Seth. I was mad that you hadn't been with me, and I was mad that I couldn't take you for a ride on my bike."

"Sounds like you were mad." I winked.

"Smart ass! Yeah, I was, but not anymore. I'm sorry. You are the last person I ever want to be a jerk to. Forgive me?"

"Yes, and I love you too!"

We danced to a couple of songs, and then he lit a fire after I placed a blanket down in front of the fireplace. Simon devoured two burgers in just a few bites, while I hardly touched my food. I was holding back again, and I was so afraid to tell him about Michael. He moved the bags aside and pulled me on top of his lap.

"You are so quiet, baby. What's on your mind? And please do not tell me its nothing. I see it in your eyes. What's wrong?"

"What you see is someone who loves you. I'm happy. You always make me feel safe and protected."

"Nicolette, you are so special to me. I can't even begin to show you how much I love and want you." He kissed me slowly down the inside of my neck, sending shivers down my spine. He held me as close as he could as he continued to kiss me. He didn't need to say the words aloud for me to figure out that he wanted to make love to me. I felt it every time he touched me, and I wanted him too.

I knew he loved me. That was the one true thing in my life that I never doubted. I wanted Simon to be my first.

With the remote in his pocket, he changed the music to Norah Jones, one of my favorites. He was so strong, and with me still in his arms, he stood with no effort at all, holding me close to his chest, swaying back and forth, kissing, and loving me. I closed my eyes, and I was lost in him. I was practically floating on air and savored every feeling I felt with the stroke of his tongue on my heated skin.

164

My heart began to accelerate, as Simon now carried me over to the couch.

"Open your eyes, Nicolette. Do you trust me?"

I breathed out, "Yes, with everything I have."

Without another word spoken, he began to unbutton my top and remove me from it. He tossed it to the floor and leaned in to kiss my lace-covered breasts. "You are so beautiful," he whispered, as he removed my bra next and tossed it to join my top on the floor. My upper body was bare and completely exposed to him. "Nicolette, we don't have to do anything you're not ready for. I just want to see and touch what's mine."

I sat up and pulled him down and on top of me, kissing and teasing his mouth with my tongue, as I felt his hard erection rub against me. My underpants were soaked, as my body spoke for me. I wanted him, all of him, but could I, knowing that I kept a secret from him? I ignored my guilty conscience and lost myself again and again with Simon. He sat up on his knees, quickly tugged off his t-shirt, and exposed his muscled, tanned skin. I wanted to touch and kiss every delicious inch of him, but he stopped me.

"No, baby. Tonight is for you. Let me love you. He slowly and sensually pushed me back to the couch, as I lifted my pelvis for Simon to slide my shorts down, followed by my panties. He placed his hands on my knees and parted my legs. He moved forward to kiss me, and then he kissed me somewhere else. "Keep your eyes open for me. I want you to watch me as I make you come."

I felt dizzy, high, and breathless with anticipation. I trusted Simon with my body, heart, and soul. I had been fantasizing about this moment ever since he told me that he loved me, maybe even before that.

"Lie still." He dropped his head down between my legs, as he entered my slick folds with his tongue. He slowly slid his finger inside of me, as my body came undone. I gripped the sides of his head, as I encouraged him to take me deeper. I was in a blinded state of sensation. With another flick of his tongue, I felt the intense sensation of my orgasm erupt within my body, as I shouted Simon's name. It was indescribable, and never before had I felt so amazing.

He held me close to his body and placed his forehead down to mine. He never once took his eyes away from mine. He was beautiful. "Thank you, baby, for sharing your beautiful body with me. I love how it responds to me, and to my touch. You can't imagine how much it meant for me to do that with you. I can't wait to make love to you, but I'll wait forever if I have to. I will never pressure you. Just being with you here is enough. I love you so much, and I thank God for bringing us together on that day down the beach. Some things in life are just meant to be. We are meant to be."

It was almost impossible to hold back my tears. He didn't say anything more, just held me, while we simply loved each other. His erection was still hard, and I thought I should try to do something to please him, but when my hand got closer, he held it in place.

"No, not tonight. I just want to hold you, Nicolette."

As he drifted off into a blissful sleep, my mind was racked with worry. I wanted to make love to him, to give myself to Simon in every way that matters, but he settled for holding me instead.

Without a doubt, he had shown how much he loved and wanted me every single day since we decided to be together. I owed him so much more than I had given him. I was riddled with guilt for lying to him and keeping secrets. I wanted to run, as, in that very moment, I felt undeserving of his love. I tried to move out from under his heavy arms, but his eyes blinked open. He noticed the tears in my eyes, as I took in his panicked expression.

"What's wrong, baby?" he asked as he wrapped his arms around me. "Do you regret it? What we did?" he asked. His muscles had tensed up, as did the muscles in his jaw.

When I shook my head, he visibly relaxed. "Okay, then what's wrong? Why the tears? We talked about this. I don't ever want to pressure you into sex, especially if you are not ready. I felt if we tried this first and you were comfortable with it, then we could move forward to making love." Once he said the words, he looked regretful. He moved me under him and got off the couch.

He nervously paced in front of the fireplace, and then said, "God! I must sound like a dick! This is not coming out right. I'm sorry, Nicolette."

"You didn't do anything wrong, especially nothing I didn't want. I loved what we shared, and very much I might add. When can we do that again?" I asked, causing him to rush back over to the couch to hold me.

"Oh, thank fuck! You had me worried when I saw you crying." He held me as my face was nestled onto his naked chest. The more he held me, the more he relaxed. After kissing me again, he then got up to change the music. With his back turned, I quickly gathered my clothes and began to dress.

"What are you doing?" he asked. "Okay, Nicolette, how much longer are we going to dance around this? I know you and I feel it every time I touch you. Something is wrong, and you are hiding it from me. You need to talk to me and tell me what has you so upset. If it's not me, then what is it? We have come so far, I'm not going to allow you to just pull away from me."

"I have my reasons, Simon, and I don't want to hurt you with them."

He sighed and then cupped my face. "The only way you can hurt me is by leaving me. Whatever it is, we can work it out. Please, tell me what's wrong?"

Eleven

Nicolette

"**M**ichael. It's Michael St. Clair."

Just the mere mention of his name, his body went rigid and his facial expression changed from concern to anger. He gave me an incredulous look as if I just punched him in his stomach. I already felt regret and just wanted to forget that I ever said anything.

"Simon, there are some things you don't know, and if you give me a chance to explain, I will tell you everything. You don't know how hard it has been for me to keep this from you."

"Nicolette, there shouldn't be anything you have to tell me about St. Clair because you gave me your word that you wouldn't speak or see him ever again," he shouted.

"Simon, please let me explain."

"Nicolette, have you had any contact with him or not? Tell me, now!"

"It's complicated."

"No, it's not. Just a straightforward answer. Yes or no? What is it?" he asked again. This was what I was afraid of. He was angry and frustrated with me, turning his back to me and walking over to the fireplace. He gripped the mantle and hung his head low. "You lied to me. The question is, why? I asked you repeatedly to stay away from him and to tell me if he made any attempts. Don't even bother lying to me. I see it written all over your face."

"How long have you been seeing him behind my back? I bet he loves this. God! I feel so fucking betrayed." *No! This was the last thing I wanted to happen and for Simon to believe.*

"Simon, you're wrong. Please, will you listen? You said that you would," I pleaded.

"Yeah, I did say that, but that was before I ever believed that you were lying to me."

"Stop it, Simon. You are turning my words around. I know you are hurt and confused, but if you would allow me to explain it to you, I know you will understand. I would never hurt you. I haven't betrayed you, and I would never cheat on you. How could you ever believe that? I have done everything I can to convince Michael that I am in love with you. He has this sick belief that we are like two destined souls that belong to one another. The only one that I want and will ever want, is you. On the night of my birthday party, he was there, Simon, lurking in the shadows and watching me and you. He was angry how you were touching me when we were dancing. He listed it word for word. He made me violently ill with how he spoke to me. I tried to get back to you, but he blocked me, and I had no choice. I was alone again with him. Do you think that was fun for me? He grabbed, caged me in, and prevented me from moving. I feel as if I have been under attack, and I am begging for my freedom from this nightmare. Please, Simon, I am begging you. Believe me, please. I love you, only you."

I waited for Simon to calm down, and then he turned around to face me, not looking any better from the first time he turned away. "If that's true, then why keep this from me? Your birthday was weeks ago."

Has he heard a single word that I said?

"But, you didn't come to me, did you, Nicolette? Did you tell anyone? By telling Michael that you loved me, did you honestly believe that would stop a guy like him? No, what you did by not coming to me with the truth was further encourage him. There is something really wrong with him, and this is not the first time I have seen it. This is why I asked you—no, begged you—to stay away from him and to be honest with me. Okay, if you were so afraid of my reaction, then what about your parents? The police? I don't understand you. I can't wrap my mind around this."

"I couldn't tell you. I was confused and scared. I was afraid for my parents and their deal with Mr. St. Clair. He had already threatened them once, and I wasn't going to be the one to ruin their career. They have worked too hard for it. Please believe me when I say that I truly believed if I ignored him, he would eventually just give up and move on to someone else."

"Has he moved on? Because I will tell you this. The Michael I know is relentless. He stops at nothing to get what he wants, and he doesn't care who he hurts along the way to get it."

"Simon, don't you see? He's lost. He can play his manipulative games. He can send me all the flowers and gifts in the world, and it wouldn't change one damn thing, certainly not the way I feel about you. I love you. He knows that, and you know that. You must believe me. You are all that I want. What we have is real, a real love that is so undeniably strong, that no matter how much he tries, he will never be able to break us. Please, please, Simon, look at me. Show me with your beautiful oceanic blue eyes that you believe me. You love me too, and we will get through this."

I was drained and all cried out. He just stood there in silence. *This can't be happening. Please come back to me, I silently prayed.*

"I'm sorry, Nicolette, but I will not go through this again. I won't have another Jennifer in my life."

Crushed!

"I can't believe you just said that. Why Simon? How could you be so cruel?"

"Easy, you did it. And it's totally true. You lied to me and behaved exactly the way I feared you would. You played right into his hands. He basically said that you would on the night of the bonfire party. It was just a matter of when, and now, it's happened. I trusted you, Nicolette. I fucking trusted you with everything I had, and all I ever wanted in return was honesty and your love in return. I can't believe I am here again."

He wasn't the only one that could shout out his pain. I poured my heart out to him, and he threw every single word back in my face. And he wasn't even sorry for it. I shoved at him, forcing him to turn around to face me. If this was the end for us, then he was going to look at me when he broke my heart.

"Simon, I trusted you too. You promised to love me. I trusted you tonight with my body. Do you even know what a gift that is? And this is what I get in return? Coldness. Anger. Rejection. You promised to listen, but I guess it was too hard for you to hear it. Well, it hasn't been easy for me, either. I've been living with this daily torment from him, and all I have wanted was for him to stop. I never asked for this, and I sure as hell didn't want Michael's attention. I just didn't know what else to do without hurting you, or my parents."

With his hands on his hips, the coldness still there, he said, "How's that working out for you?"

I was done. I wasn't going to stand here and defend myself any longer. I cried and poured my heart out to Simon, the one who said he loved me. The one who said he would listen to me. The one who said he would never hurt me.

So then...why did he?

I grabbed my purse and stopped at the door, leaning my head against it. I prayed that he would stop me from leaving and tell me that we would be okay, but he never moved, just remained quiet and looked at me as if I was a stranger. I felt numb. With the last of my courage, I turned around to look at the beautiful guy who just a few hours ago was my entire world.

"Simon, I know you may never forgive me for hurting you, but you hurt me too, and in a way, that is literally crushing my soul. You promised that I could trust you and you would listen to anything I had to say. You said you would fix whatever it was that was hurting me, but you didn't do any of those things. Instead, you compared me to someone who hurt you so deeply that the love you had for me has now been replaced with anger. I never believed you were capable of being so cruel." With my unstoppable tears now falling, I whispered, "Goodbye, Simon."

He never came to me, not that I thought he would. I didn't know how I even made it home. The drive was just a blur.

My house was quiet, and I was thankful my parents were upstairs asleep. I climbed into bed and cried into my pillow until I crashed over the devastation this night had become. A few hours ago, I was blissfully in love with Simon Paulson. Now, because I kept a secret from him, he hated me. Would I wake in the morning to find a break-up message on my phone? The thought of losing him forever made my stomach roll. I felt sick.

The next morning, I rolled over to hit my alarm. I wanted to throw it out of the window. When I was finally able to move and sit up, my head was dizzy and my heart was broken. I looked down to my phone and had no messages. *Yeah, he hates you now. What did you expect?*

My parents already left for work by the time I got downstairs. I knew they would be in the studio all this week finalizing the tracks for the movie. I knew John Mayer was in town to do some voiceover work for a commercial he was involved in, and my parents were also on that project as well. It was all for the best anyway that they weren't home because I was saved from having them see me look so distraught over my fight with Simon last night.

I declined breakfast from Gracie, and I grabbed a piece of fruit on my way out the door.

"Shit, my phone is now dead," I groaned. I leaned my head back to my seat and just re-played the same words that Simon had shouted at me last night.

"I trusted you, Nicolette. I fucking trusted you."

I couldn't do school today, nor could I face anyone, especially Simon. I drove down to the beach and parked my car in the marina parking lot. Breathing in the salt air and watching the boats sail by was calming for my wretched soul. I had been down here all morning and watched the fisherman haul in their morning catches. I had a headache, and the absence of food was making me feel worse.

My phone should be charged by now. While I was driving down here, I remembered I had a spare battery charger in my car. I turned it back on, and my phone came to life with multiple text messages from the girls, and one from Jameson asking me to go shopping with him. Oh, I loved them, but what I didn't see were any from Simon. But I did have two voicemails. *Do I listen to them? And risk my heart any more pain? I have cried all day, and I could barely see with how swollen my eyes were. Okay, why not? You already feel like shit. What's another punch to the gut?*

I heard a deep sigh before his words:

"Nicolette, please call me when you get this message. You didn't come to school today. You're not at your house. No one has heard from you. Where are you? I love you. Those are the three words I should have said, but I was stupid, jealous, and angry. I am

so sorry, but even more than that, I feel ashamed. I have never felt sicker in all my life than the way I felt last night when I watched you walk out the door. I should have never let you leave, but I was angry and I didn't trust myself. You had every right..."

As my tears rolled down my cheek, his message cut off. I hit the next message, and it was Simon again.

"You don't know how much I wish I was saying these words in front of you, but I guess this will have to do for now. You had every right to call me out and tell me off. I was cruel and heartless, and I hate myself for it. It was Michael, he was the one that I hated, never you. Turning my back to you was the biggest mistake of my life, and it should have been my love to make you stay, not drive you away. Please, forgive me, baby, and call me. I couldn't deal with school, and I left to search for you. I have been everywhere, and still no sign of my beautiful girl. If you're still mad at me, that's fine. Just call me back, and let me know that you are safe. I promise you, we will be okay. I love you, and I will never lose my faith in you or us again. Please let me know where you are, and I will come to you."

Simon

S hit! Voicemail, again! What do I do? Where do I look? I had been driving around for most of the morning and now afternoon. I wanted my girl back and to beat the hell out of Michael St. Clair. My anger was driving all my emotions at this point and led me right to his door…Clayton St. Clair. I rushed past his secretary, who was calling out to me to stop, but I was too fast and rushed inside his office.

"What is the meaning of this?" he shouted from over his laptop.

"Sir, I tried to stop him," the secretary called out.

He waved her off and looked back over to me. "You have five minutes, Simon, and then I will have security throw you out."

"That's okay, I won't be here for that long."

"Okay, you have my attention. What's on your mind?"

"Michael. He's the one who brought me here today. He's been harassing my girlfriend for months, and if you don't reign him in, then I will."

"And how will you manage to do that? Another brawl? Maybe it's you who needs to be controlled, not my son. You don't come into my office and threaten me. Who the hell do you think you are?"

"I'm someone who loves his girlfriend very much, and I need to protect her from that psychopath you have for a son. He has completely lost his mind and believes that he has a future with Nicolette. Well, I am here to tell you that will never happen. He is scaring her, and he needs help."

"Let me be clear, Simon. Tokens of affection do not warrant restraining orders or violence. What are you afraid of? That maybe, just maybe, Nicolette, may actually like my son and choose him over you?"

Is he fucking serious? He was just as arrogant as his son, maybe even worse.

"Okay, Mr. St. Clair, you hear me," I said without backing down. "I will do whatever it takes to keep your fucked-up son away from my girl. From here, I am going to Mr. Vanelle, and then my father, who is a pretty good lawyer. This harassment is going to end, and that means today."

"Are you threatening me, Simon? I have lawyers too."

"No threats, sir, just delivering a promise. You tell your son to stay the hell away from my girl, because if he dares to go near her again, then don't say you weren't warned." I slammed out of his office and left him stunned into silence.

Fuck him, and the hell with his son. I called Mr. Vanelle and was told he was recording and could not be disturbed. I told the secretary that it was a matter of life and death, and it involved his daughter. I waited for a minute, and then he got on the line and nervously asked what was wrong.

I couldn't do this over the phone. I asked him to meet me downstairs in the lobby, where I was waiting for him. The line disconnected, and within a couple of minutes, Mr. Vanelle stepped off the elevator and rushed over to me.

"Simon, where's Nicolette? Has she been harmed?" he asked.

"I don't know, sir. She didn't come to school today, and I have been looking all over for her. We got into a bad fight last night and I haven't heard from her since."

"Okay, calm down. I am sure she's fine, maybe just taking some time to cool off."

"For her sake, I hope you're right."

"Okay, let's start from the beginning. What the hell is going on?"

"Michael St. Clair."

"Clayton's son? What about him?"

"It's a long story, and I don't have the time to explain it all. I only found out last night, but he's been stalking her, and all the warnings we have given him has not stopped him from going after your daughter. He's dangerous and needs to be stopped. When she finally told me last night, well, I am ashamed to say that I didn't have the best reaction. We argued, and she left. I need to find her."

I watched her father pinch the bridge of his nose. He schooled his features, but I knew he was just as surprised as I was. "I didn't see her last night when she got home, nor this morning. We have been so busy with our work, and too oblivious to notice that our daughter was in trouble. I promise you, Simon, I will take care of this today. Let's go."

Michael

"I'm going…where?" I screamed at my father.

"You heard me, Michael. You have created quite the problematic situation with the Vanelles. Just another mess that I have to clean up. The jet is fueled and ready to go. You will be away for as long as you need to be for me to set this right. Dammit, Michael! I warned you." My father shouted at me, as our housekeeper zipped up my bag.

I shouted, "Stop packing my things, and get the hell out of my room." She scurried off, and then I turned back to my father. "Why do I have to leave? I have done nothing wrong."

"Yes, you have. You know exactly what you have done. You just couldn't leave well enough alone. You had to go after that girl after I specifically told you not to. Now, get your shit, and go down to the car. You have a plane to catch, and I don't want to hear another word about it."

"The hell I am. I am not going anywhere and certainly not without Nicolette."

"Do you hear yourself? She is not yours. She never was, nor will she ever be. You have crossed the line, and so far, I have not been able to save you from yourself, but I am going to try. You are still my son, and you are in need of help. These delusions are going to break you, Michael, and I will not allow that to happen."

My head was spinning. I was not going to that facility, not again. So, they can dope me up? No! I will never be locked up again.

"Stay away from my girlfriend. I am not yours. I love Simon. She is not yours. She loves Simon. I love Simon. I love Simon. I love Simon."

"Shut up! Shut up!" I shouted as I held my head. "You don't know anything."

"Michael, what has gotten into you?" My father stepped closer to me, as I shoved him away. He stumbled backward and slammed his head against my wardrobe. My hands were shaking. I had never been so angry in all my life. I crawled over to where he was unconscious. I felt for a pulse and was relieved he was still breathing. I was ready to dial 911, and then I heard the voices again.

"I love Simon. I love Simon. I love Simon." It was her voice. She was taunting me.

"No!" I shouted, and then looked back to my father.

"You're wrong, Father. You all are. You don't know how I feel about her, and neither does she, but she soon will. You have left me no choice. Tonight, Nicolette Vanelle will know exactly how much I love her."

I left him and his home in search of Nicolette.

Nicolette

I listened to Simon's message on repeat before calling him back. After all that I had put myself through, I was relieved to know that Simon still loved me. He sounded devastated and broken on my voicemail. He loved and wanted me, and his feelings hadn't changed. I dialed him right away and didn't want to waste another minute without him.

"Simon," I said, as I sniffled through my tears.

"Oh, thank God," he said. "Where are you?" he nervously asked.

"Beach. I'm parked down by the marina."

"Of course, you are. I should have looked there first. Are you okay?"

"No, but I'm better since I listened to your messages."

"Nicolette, I am so sorry. I have been searching all over for you. Please stay where you are, and wait for me. We are on our way."

On our *way? Who is Simon with?*

"You're not coming alone?"

"No, I'm with your father, and he wants to talk to you."

"Nicolette, I love you. I have been so worried about you." I heard the concern in my father's voice. I felt foolish and filled with regret over not trusting them to help me. "Sweetheart, don't cry. We are on our way. I promise, we are going to right this wrong, and you will never have to deal with Michael St. Clair again. Stay where you are, and we will see you soon."

"I love you. Daddy, please hurry."

"We are. Simon has my permission to run every red light. If it brings us closer to you, then that's all that matters."

I felt relieved for the first time today. We were going to be okay, and Simon still loved me.

The temperature by the water began to drop and caused me to shiver. I had forgotten my jacket over by the benches and stepped out of my car to get it. I put it on and felt the warmth from the fleeced material. I leaned over the railing and breathed in the cool salted air. The breeze swept over my skin, and for the first time to-day, I actually smiled. I felt peace and believed that my days of wor-rying over Michael had come to an end.

His ringtone was playing from my jeans pocket, "Your Body is a Wonderland," my favorite from John Mayer, and our song.

"Hello," I answered.

"Nicolette, we hit some traffic. I'm going to have to take the de-tour and go around. Where are you?"

"I'm still down by the boats."

"Okay, listen to me. We want you to go back to your car and lock yourself in. It's late, and you shouldn't be down there by your-self."

"Okay, I will. I'm fine, Simon, so much better."

"I'm happy to hear that, but I would feel better knowing you were safe in your car. Please, go now. I am driving as fast as I can."

"Okay, I love you."

"I love you more. See you soon."

And I did. Simon was my everything, and I couldn't wait to be back in his arms. I walked up the path that led to the parking lot, and as I turned the last corner, I was grabbed from behind.

"DO. NOT. SCREAM."

I could do nothing but to obey my unknown assailant. My body was dragged down the same path I had just taken. I was picked up and forced onto a boat named Lydia's Joy.

Two hands on my back shoved me forward. It was with such a force that I stumbled and lost my balance. I hit my head down on the hardwood floor, making me catch my breath. I managed to open my eyes to find it was Michael hovering over me. His breathing was heavy, and his dark eyes glared back at me.

I could not form any words. I was shocked, scared, and confused to why he was doing this to me. Without warning, he picked me up and slammed me back up against the wall, as if I were a child's rag doll. Another blow to my head, but this was to the back of my skull. I was still awake, but barely. He was a frightening blur as he leaned over where my body was lying motionless on the floor. I had never been so terrified in all my life.

"Oh, Nicolette, how I have waited for this moment. You running away from me stops now. I have tried everything to show you how much I love you. We are meant to be together. Don't you know that by now? All that I have done has been for you. I have loved you from the first moment I saw you standing by the fountain. You looked so beautiful then, as you do right now. I've hated being rejected by you. I told you repeatedly how much I loved you, and what did you do with my words? You shunned me, again and again. You ripped my heart out and stomped all over it."

I was so dizzy and nauseous. His voice was cold and menacing.

"You even had your precious Simon tell me to stay away. Why did you do that? Do you know how much that hurt me? To be discarded like nothing? I am no fool, and no one makes me look like one. You run off to him, every chance you got when you should have been with me. Tonight, my love, I'm going to make sure you never run from me again. Tonight, my sweet and beautiful Nicolette, I make you…mine."

PART
TWO

A life changed...

Twelve

Nicolette

As my body was laid out onto the cold and hardwood floor, Michael continued to hover over me like a wild animal about to kill his prey. It felt exactly like that. Was I going to die tonight? And by his hand? He was sweating. His mannerisms grew more erratic as he continued to taunt me.

This was unimaginable. *Think, Nicolette. You have to fight him, but with what? And how? He's holding you down to the floor and using the weight of his body to do it.*

"Please, Michael, not like this. I'm begging you. Please don't hurt me." I began to cry harder which angered him more.

"Shut up! Don't make me gag you. This is your fault. You drove me to this point, Nicolette. You say you don't want me to hurt you, well, what about all the times you hurt me? Rejection followed by rejection, and then you unleash your father on me. As if he could really have stopped me. You were the only one who had the power to, don't you realize that? All you had to do was go out with me, but you refused me. Simon was in my way, always in the way. Do you see your beloved now? No, he won't find you, and if he does, he's going to know what you gave me tonight, and only to me."

"No! Please, I can't have my first time like this. We can talk it out, please. Michael, let me go. I promise I will not tell anyone what happened here tonight, not to anyone. Just let me go. I want to go home." I cried.

He grabbed me hard by my chin, forcing me to look at him. "Now you want to talk? What about all the times that I wanted to talk to you? You never gave me a chance, but you will now. Don't be scared, I'm not going to hurt you. I'm going to show you how much I love you, and I promise, Nicolette, you are going to love every bit of me as I take and make you mine."

They say in the direst of circumstances, you can have a strength you didn't know you had. Here with Michael, I found mine. I wrestled from beneath him, as he smirked at me. His hand slipped, and that's when I bit him as hard as I could. He shouted in pain and called me obscenities as I tried to escape. I was still dizzy from hitting my head, but I had to try.

I nearly made it to the cabin door when he grabbed and pulled me back down to the floor. I clawed. I kicked. I screamed at him to stop, but he was every bit the animal I feared him to be, and then he hit me across my cheek. My lip was split open as my mouth filled with the metallic taste of blood. I tried to reach for anything I could use to hit him with, but his hands restrained me to the floor.

"Yes, Nicolette, I love it! Let me hear you," he taunted, as I continued to fight him. "Stop it, Nicolette! You want this here with me. I know you do."

Michael straddled my body as he tore open my top, shredding it into torn pieces. With one hard tug, he ripped my bra from my body, as if it was nothing. I was bare, exposed, and I wanted to die knowing what he was going to do to me. I tried to break free, but he was just too strong. He moved just enough to pull my jeans down, followed by my panties. I was naked and tired, with no strength left to fight him. This was a nightmare. I prayed that it was just a horrible dream and at any moment, I was going to wake up, but it wasn't. This was very real. I begged him to stop and told him *no* over and over.

My voice was hoarse from screaming. I had no tears left to shed. This was my nightmare. This was happening. I had no means of escape.

I shut my eyes and prayed for my father and Simon to rescue me, but they didn't come. I was alone with him and the harsh truth of what was about to happen.

Michael St. Clair was about to rape me.

He held me down and savagely kissed me to silence my cries. I smelled the liquor seeping from his pores, mixed with sweat that was now all over me. He layered my skin with his poison. All over my neck, chest, and between my naked breasts.

"This is it, Nicolette. The moment that you become mine. This is the moment that I have been dreaming about, and now you will know just how much I love you."

I squeezed my eyes closed and escaped him in my mind as I was transported to another time when I felt safe and loved, a time when I was with Simon.

Please, God, save me.

He entered my fragile womb as a surge of pain ripped through my body, tearing and destroying my insides. My spirit had been shattered. Michael St. Clair changed my life with his act of brutality. My entire world and the life I knew up until an hour ago had been changed.

A life changed forever.

He showed no mercy. Delirium had taken over his mind. I saw two soulless eyes staring back at me, as he continued to push his hard length inside of me. The smell of spilled blood was in the air.

The pain was excruciating. He pushed harder, faster, deeper, all at the same time, breaking me apart, piece by piece.

"I'm going to come so hard for you. I love fucking you, and I'm so turned on knowing that I'm the only one who has been here. The only one that will be here. Nicolette, I love you." He shouted at the top of his lungs as he reached his climax, further shattering me like broken glass.

I want to die.

He pulled out of me, as I winced in pain. He lay next to me with his sounds of grunts and erratic breaths. He rolled over and shifted his body back onto mine. He kissed my forehead and once again said how much he loved me.

This was not love. This was masochism.

My body began to uncontrollably shake. I was cold, so cold. He stood and refastened his pants. I didn't believe I could move my limbs. I hurt everywhere. When my legs finally moved, I pulled my knees up to my chest to cover myself up. I was curled up into a ball and silently begged him not to touch me.

He kneeled down and whispered sinisterly to my ear, "This will teach you to never run from me again. You are mine, Nicolette, and I am yours. It's best to remember that."

Still, on the floor with no strength left, his threatening words echoed through my mind. I was shaking to the point of freezing. It was December, and we were on the water. He was a monster and didn't care that I laid there frozen, naked, and bleeding from his savagery.

I wanted my father to save me. He ignored me and walked over to the bar to pour himself a drink. Was he toasting his victory over me? Did he believe that he actually won?

Hell, no! As much as I wanted to just crawl up and die, I knew I still had some fight left inside of me that he couldn't take. I had my will. I heard all the voices of the people that loved me. My parents.

Uncle Jack. He was screaming out for me to remember. To remember what to do in the event you were in danger.

I tried, Uncle Jack. I fought so hard.

I tried to focus and looked to my surroundings. His back was still turned and completely oblivious to me. My eyes found a trophy that sat on a shelf just above me. I slowly moved and managed to get up from off the floor with shaky legs. I tried to scream out as the mixture of blood and semen trickled out and down the insides of my thighs. With all the courage and strength, I had in my soul and body, I reached for that trophy and lunged forward at Michael.

I struck him in the back of his head, and the trophy broke into two pieces, but not before Michael stumbled over the bar stool. I wanted to run, and then he tried to grab me again, but I was ready this time. I grabbed the scotch bottle from the bar and hit him again, this time knocking him unconscious.

I began screaming, screaming as loud as I could until my head felt it was going to explode from the pain surging through it. I cursed at Michael and shouted in rage for what he did to me.

"You bastard! You filthy, disgusting pig! You will never touch me again. I hate you. I hate you. I hate you." I began to kick him in his ribs and then dropped to my knees to punch his back.

"You monster. I hate you. I'll kill you," I continued to scream at his still form.

I didn't hear the cabin door open, as I continued hitting Michael. Strong and familiar arms pulled me up onto my feet and into safety. The room began to spin as pain pierced through every inch of my body. "Simon," I said, through my blurred vision. "I'm sorr…"

I was saved. He found me. Thoughts of happier times with Simon flooded my memory as I felt my body float away. I never felt freer.

He was shouting at me to stay awake. "Nicolette! Stay with me, baby. Help is on the way."

I want to stay, Simon, but I'm so tired, so very tired.

With nothing left, my eyes closed as the darkness consumed me.

I'd watched bedside vigils play out in mushy and over the top movies. We loved to watch them. Never without fail, I always cried, and mom did too. She held my hand as the hero took the bullet to save the woman he loved, and then slowly died as she cried over his lifeless body. Yeah, that's how I felt at the moment. I heard familiar voices all around me. They were muffled, but one I could make out without even trying was my mom. She was crying and asking why I wasn't awake yet. My father was comforting her by saying that I would be okay, that I had to be okay.

I tried to listen for Simon. Was he here with me? And then I remembered how he found me on Michael's boat and then hearing him beg me to stay with him. I would never forget the horrified look on his face when he took in the scene before him. I was naked and beating Michael's still and bloodied body. I didn't want to stop. I wanted to hurt him, as he hurt me. I didn't have to focus on Simon's voice because I felt his warm hand fold into mine as he shuffled his chair closer to my bed. I wanted to open my eyes, but my eyelids grew heavier and I could do nothing to get them to cooperate. I knew it was him. Simon had not abandoned me. He loved me.

The pain was felt throughout my entire body, I was so exhausted. I was willing myself to move a limb, anything to show my family that I was here with them, but all I could do was lay there in pain and rest until my body caught up with my brain. Simon was here, talking to me. My hands were held in his as I heard him beg for me to come back to him. This was torturous to be powerless to my body and not be able to show that I was fighting my way back to him.

"Nicolette, please, wake up. You need to open your eyes and come back to me. I love you so much, and I am so sorry for not protecting you. Maybe deep down inside you blame me for what happened to you, no more than I blame myself. This is my fault. If I hadn't let you go that night, you would have been with me today, instead of alone and believing as if I didn't love you anymore. I wish

I could take all your pain away. To go back in time and prevent that animal from hurting you. I'm so sorry. Forgive me, Nicolette. I need you."

No, Simon, it's not your fault. It's mine. I should have told you about Michael and all he was doing to me, but I allowed the fear of hurting the ones I loved to make me silent and afraid.

The sound of his cries and devastated tone to his voice had further hurt my broken heart. Did I have anything left? I wanted to comfort him, but the darkness continued to consume me, preventing me from returning to my waiting family and Simon.

The sounds of our song filled my hospital room. It was our song, "Your Body is a Wonderland." John was my favorite singer, not because we were friends, but because his music spoke to me. I loved to hear him play his guitar, and sometimes he would even debut new material just for me before the rest of the world heard it. He was amazing, and so was Simon for playing the music my heart needed to hear. I knew what he was doing. He was willing me to come back to him.

I felt wetness on my cheeks, as his tears fell on my face. He placed soft kisses and then pleaded with me to wake for him.

"Nicolette, please, open your eyes. I love you. Everyone loves you. Your parents are waiting, and so am I. Alexis, Bailey, Jameson, and Sam have been camping outside your room and taking shifts to sit with you. I didn't want to leave your side for even a second, but when I couldn't be here, they were. I'm here now and doing everything I can to bring you back to me. Just open one eye at a time, or move a finger. Give me a sign, anything that tells me you are on your way back. I love you. I love you with everything I have and all that I am. I promise to never fail you again. Just wake up so I can prove it to you."

I'm trying, Simon. I want to see you too.

How long had I been here? It felt like days. My eyes were sore. The pain that pulsated through them felt like gritty sand. I failed and failed to open them, but with all my effort, they finally did. They immediately burned from the light above me. It was so bright. I had to blink several times for my eyes to adjust. I tested my limbs. I wiggled my fingers and toes and shifted my legs and feet from under the covers.

I could see him. I had never seen him with hair on his face. Clearly, he needed a shave. To look at my handsome boyfriend for even the briefest of moments made me forget why I was here. He looked so tired. Had he slept at all?

His hands were wrapped around my arm, the one that didn't have an IV connected to it. I moved my fingers to the top of his overgrown and shaggy hair, gently tugging on the long strands to get his attention. He startled awake and let out a deep sigh of relief when he realized I was too. Tears fell down his face as he leaned in closer to me and whispered, "Thank you, God."

I half-smiled at him, not knowing if this was a miracle or a punishment. Yes, I was awake, but my memory was intact to relive every single moment of my brutal attack. I still felt Michael on me. The smell of his stale drunk breath attached to me as if it was a second skin. I felt dirty and in need of a shower.

My parents came rushing in. My mom, not knowing where she could touch me, just held my hand and kissed it, with my father doing the same. I ached everywhere, especially in my heart.

"Thank God, you're awake. I have—no, *we* have—never been so scared. You came back to us, Nicolette," mom cried.

A tall slender woman walked in a few minutes later and introduced herself as Dr. Jonas. She spoke with a Swedish accent.

"Welcome back. Can you tell me where you are?"

I replied, hospital, and sighed.

"How are you feeling? Can you describe your pain level to me? On a scale from 1 to 10?"

I shook my head. My mouth was dry, and I wasn't ready to do this.

"It's okay, Nicolette. I can see for myself. You have been through an incredible ordeal. Just lay still while I check your vitals." She was kind and gentle with me. She cleared the room, all except for my mom, who refused to leave my side. She didn't let go of my hand as Dr. Jonas continued with her exam.

"Am I okay to get out of bed? I need to use the bathroom, and I want to shower."

"Not yet. You were dehydrated and still have a catheter. I want you to finish the bag of fluids you have before I disconnect your IVs. It's been nearly 48 hours since you were admitted. Are you able to share anything with me?"

Yes, I can remember how I ended up here and the person responsible for it. I was raped! I was shouting at the top of my lungs in my head, but instead of voicing aloud my frustrations, I simply answered the doctor's question. "I remember everything."

"Good, your head is healing and faculties are in check. Nicolette, you have a concussion as a result of taking blows to the back of your head. You have quite the bump, but no brain swelling. You have skin abrasions and bruising, along with trauma to your uterine wall. We repaired a tear with stitches that will dissolve on their own. For the next few days, you may experience some discomfort, for which I can give you something to help alleviate the soreness."

Mom interrupted her. "Doctor, can this wait? She's in no condition to go through this right now. She's just awakened and is in pain. You disclosing every detail of her injuries is not helping right now."

"Mom, please, I can take it."

"Yes, I'm sure you can, but why should you have to? Please, Nicolette, this is not the time to be stubborn."

"Mrs. Vanelle, I sympathize with you, and for all that Nicolette has gone through, but she's an adult, and it is my job to make her aware of her condition and the treatment plan I put in place from the minute she was admitted and became my patient."

"Well, she's my daughter, and all I am asking for is some sensitivity."

Hello! I'm in the room. "Mom, it's fine. Please allow the doctor to finish."

"Thank you, Nicolette. Now, what I am about to say will be difficult for you to hear, and I understand why your mother would want to shield you from it, but as your doctor, I am not only obligated by the oath I took as a doctor, but also a responsibility to the law. A crime has been committed against you, and I had to take the necessary steps to collect as much evidence I could for your case. I'm so sorry."

"Just get on with it. I want out of this bed, and I want to shower."

"Fair enough. My findings through the rape kit were collected and handed over to the police. The detectives in charge have asked to speak with you whenever you are ready. You don't have to do anything you are not prepared for, and as your attending physician, I will close off this room until you tell me otherwise."

"I want to shower," I repeated.

"Okay, I see I can't convince you to rest a bit longer. Just stay where you are and I will send my nurse in to disconnect you, and then she can assist you with bathing."

"No, I'm her mother. I'll help my daughter."

Oh, mom, not today. She's just trying to help, and I know you are too, but I don't have the strength to fight anyone right now. All I want to do is to take a shower and not have a fucking debate over it.

My mom continued to hover over me, as the nurse came in to help. She disconnected my IVs first and then wiped the area clean. "Okay, Nicolette, I'm going to remove the catheter now. This may sting for a moment. Can you take a deep breath for me?" I nodded and then closed my eyes until it was over. Just the thought of someone touching me down there made me want to scream. "Do you think you can stand on your own?" the nurse asked.

"I think so."

"That's fine. We will take it slow," she said softly.

"I'll help her." Mom stepped beside me.

"Mom! I got it, back off," I shouted. Fuck!

I let out a breath and then told the nurse I was fine and would be with my mom. She took that as her cue to leave, and then without another word said, my mom had her arms wrapped around me. She wasn't doing anything wrong. She was being a mother who cared. She needed to help me, and I needed to let her.

She helped me into the bathroom and closed the door behind us. I was in a hospital gown, but just the thought of removing it from my body terrified me. Memories of the rape were there, so vividly clear. Visions of Michael and the way he tore my clothes away from my body sent cold shivers through me.

Oh my God! And Simon. He saw me naked after the attack. Oh, my God. Oh, my God. My heart began to race, as my body continued to shake.

"Nicolette, it's okay. Mommy's here..."

My eyes snapped open, and I was on the floor, in her arms.

"Did I just pass out?" I asked.

"Yes, you must have gotten dizzy, and then you literally passed out in my arms. Oh, my sweet girl, you're exhausted. Let's get you back into bed. You can shower when you're stronger and have eaten something."

"No! What I want is a damn shower. I don't want to eat. I don't want to sleep. I just want to get clean. Leave me alone!" I shouted as I gripped the sides of my head in pain.

My mother's beautiful face went ashen with fright. She didn't push, just asked me if I could stand. I told her that I would be fine by myself and would hit the call button if I needed help. She seemed to be satisfied with my answer and left me be.

"I'll be right outside if you need me."

"Just go, please. I want to be alone."

I felt sick for pushing her away, but I didn't want mom, of all people, to see me right now, nor anyone, for that matter. I knew this was her way of not feeling completely helpless, but I wasn't ready. I closed the door and let out a sigh of relief. I couldn't lock it just in case I did need help.

I gave myself a few words of encouragement before removing my hospital gown. I was now naked and standing in front of the mirror, taking in the sight of my injuries. I had bruises lining my arms, stomach, ribs, and on the insides of my thighs. Bruises on top of bruises marred my pale skin. I looked over my shoulder and took in the road map of black and blue marks that lined my shoulders and back. I now knew why I ached all over my body. The evidence of my attack was clear as day. Michael shoved me with great force.

My cuticles were bloodied. A few of my nail beds looked torn. I looked again to the mirror and the grotesque image that stared back at me. Why did this happen to me? My body surrendered into an uncontrollable fit of tears and rage. I grabbed the soap and turned on the hot water until it nearly scalded my skin. I felt so dirty, scrubbing my skin until it bled. I didn't feel the pain I was inflicting on myself. I needed to wash him off me. I felt him on me, in me, and I just wanted to die. I had no strength left. I dropped the soap and slid down the tiled wall, holding my knees to my chest and crying out my pain.

"Nicolette..." I heard my name. It was Simon. No, he couldn't find me like this. I couldn't speak. I didn't move as the hot water had now turned cold. When he found me, I was still sitting in the shower stall, cold and shaking from the...what? The change in temperature? Or just the fear of Simon touching me? He leaned in, turned the water off, and slowly kneeled down in front of me.

"It's just me, baby. Don't be scared. I'm going to lift you into my arms and carry you back to your bed. Can you put your arms around my neck?" he asked so softly.

I shook my head, and that was good enough for him. He covered me with my robe as I buried my face into the soft material of his shirt. I cried and cried but wasn't afraid. Never of Simon.

My mother had left a bag of toiletries and a night gown. I was still covered with my robe when he asked to lift my bruised arms. I did with no fight. He managed to dress me without exposing my body to him. He was the last person I wanted to see my beaten body. Well, that actually wasn't true.

Thoughts went to my Uncle Jack. How would he ever be able to understand what happened to me? He was so protective, even more so than my own father. I knew my Uncle Jack had a bad ass way about him. You easily saw it in the way he carried himself and ran his bar. He was tough, this I knew, and he always wanted me to be the same. He taught me how to fight and defend myself. I used everything I had when fighting Michael, but even with all that training, he still managed to hurt me.

"Okay, you're dressed. I'm just going to comb out your hair for you. Is that okay?"

I nodded in agreement, and then Simon began to gently brush the tangles out of my thick and wavy hair. He was so careful of me, so aware of my head injury. I hardly felt the brush combing through my hair. I declined the hair dryer. I was so tired and just wanted to go to sleep. Once he was done with the brushing, he simply twisted my long strands into a loose braid and tied off the end with a hair tie.

"Not bad, Paulson," I whispered.

He was so gentle and treated me as if I was made of glass that was at risk of shattering. Did he know that's exactly how I felt? He placed me under the covers, and I hardly felt him lift me. I was exhausted. Simon didn't appear to look any better. Had he slept at all? I slowly drifted off to sleep as he held my hand and told me that he would be here when I woke up, but not before he told me how much he loved me.

Thirteen

Nicolette

Memories of my shower meltdown flashed through my mind, making my head hurt, and then I saw him. Simon was still here. He never left my side. He had his head against the recliner and his arm stretched out to hold my hand. He must have been so uncomfortable sitting upright, and for who knew how many hours? I didn't want him to leave, but I knew him staying here at the hospital was not healthy for him. And what about school? He had commitments. His teammates needed and were depending on him. His coach must have been so pissed off with him. The list went on, but instead of further tormenting myself, I felt it was just best to wake him. I would never be able to thank him for all he had done. He was so tender taking care of me yesterday. God! I was such a mess. And so much more than he probably bargained for.

"Simon, wake up," I quietly said.

He didn't stir right away until I moved my hand. He looked around the room and then back to me. He brought the chair closer and leaned in to kiss my forehead.

"Hey, dumb question, but how did you sleep?" he asked.

I tried to sit up, but I felt as if a truck had run me over, and my body still ached. He sensed it right away and helped me into a better sitting position.

"I slept well. That sedative the night nurse gave really knocked me out. I guess I needed it."

"You did, and I'm happy you were able to get some rest. You've been through so much the past few days, but I have to warn you, it might get worse before it gets better."

"Why? The unimaginable already happened." Once I said the words, I immediately regretted them. The look on Simon's face was guilt-stricken. "I'm sorry. I shouldn't have said that. I don't know how to act anymore. How to just be normal again."

"Don't you ever apologize. You didn't do anything wrong. You say whatever is on your mind, and to hell with everyone that has a problem with it."

"That's just it, Simon. I didn't speak my mind when I should have. When it would have made a difference to prevent what happened to me. We're going to have to talk about it, sooner rather than later."

"I know, but let me just have these last few minutes with you before they come in to speak with you."

"Who?"

"The two detectives working your case. Dr. Jonas and your parents have held them back, but now you are out of time. They want to interview you about what happened with Michael and what he did to you."

"Simon, you can't even say the words, can you?" I said.

He looked tormented and unsure. I didn't want to push him and was going to tell him that if he wanted to go home for a while, it would be okay, but my family arriving prevented me from doing so.

"Oh, my sweet girl. How are you this morning?" daddy asked as he came closer to give me a hug. My mom joined him, and then while in my group hug, I glanced over their shoulders to see the detectives by the door.

"Um, Mom?" I said, and then she turned around and gestured to them.

"Nicolette, these detectives are here to ask you a few questions. Baby, if you are not ready, we will ask them to go away until you are."

Mom was interrupted by the male who stepped up to introduce himself to me, followed by his partner. "Mrs. Vanelle, that's not recommended. It is vital that we speak with Nicolette and not put this off any longer than we already have." He then turned back to me. "Nicolette, I am detective James Westphall, and this is my partner, Amy Lewis. I can't even begin to know how difficult this has been for you, but if you would just fill in some of the blanks, then we can continue on with our investigation."

I looked back and forth between my parents and then to Simon, who had stepped away and was leaning against the wall. He gave me a small smile of encouragement, and then I agreed to speak with the detectives. My parents didn't look happy, but they joined hands and moved to one side, while the detectives were on the other.

Detective Lewis went first. "Okay, Nicolette, we have taken statements from your father and boyfriend on their accounts that led to Michael St. Clair raping you on his father's yacht that is housed down at the Beach Club Marina." I shuddered at the sound of his name, but it's been said, and we had to deal with it.

"Where is he now? Is he in jail?" I questioned.

Detective Westphall answered, "No, he had to be hospitalized due to the injuries he sustained, but I can assure you that he is nowhere near you and is under guard by my orders. He can't hurt you anymore, certainly not with the beating you gave him."

"I wanted him to suffer, just like the way he made me suffer. He hurt me so much, and not just that night on the boat, but for months now."

"Why don't you tell us about it?" Detective Lewis asked.

"I met Michael St. Clair back in July at his father's annual mixer. I was there with my parents, who were invited to attend. He introduced himself to me, and we shared a dance. From the beginning, I felt like he came on very strong with me. He was demanding of my time and aggressive in the words he spoke. He left me on my own for a while, and then I went to take a walk on the beach, where I met Simon Paulson, now my boyfriend."

"That must have been exciting for you. Did you see Michael when you returned to the party?"

"He found us on the beach. I was just talking with Simon, and he appeared to be hostile and annoyed with me. I had just met Michael, and he behaved as if he had staked a claim on me. This was how it was for months. All the while, it was me telling him that I was not interested in dating him, but he pushed and pushed with deliveries of flowers, gifts, unexpected visits. He would not leave me alone. We would go through episodes of silence, where I felt he may have moved on, and then it would start up again."

"Did you tell anyone in your life that this was happening to you?"

"Be careful, detective," my father warned.

"Mr. Vanelle, I'm sorry for the questions, and I know they are hard to hear, but the timeline has to be established. Okay, Nicolette, we know about the two physical encounters you had with Michael. One was at your home back in October, where he was in attendance at a party with his father. The second was your birthday party at the Beach Club in November. Is this correct?"

"Yes, it is."

My father looked angry and stunned to hear all this, while I kept it from them.

"Okay, we have enough for the stalking charges. Now, it gets really hard. In your words, we need a detailed account of the day in question, December 12th, 2008, and all the events that led to Michael St. Clair kidnapping and raping you on the yacht named Lydia's Joy."

"That's enough, all of you, get out!" my father screamed. "This is my daughter, our daughter, and the way you are speaking to her, it's sickening to me. She didn't have her car stolen, she had her life stolen from that animal. I wish she would have killed him on that boat! The world would be a better place for it."

"Mason!" my mom shrieked and tried to calm him, but he wasn't having it.

"Mr. Vanelle, if I have to, I will have you removed from this room. Now, although it is a tragedy what happened to your daughter, it is also a crime that needs to be investigated. Your daughter is an adult and the victim. We need to finish questioning her and without any more interruptions from you and Mrs. Vanelle."

I was holding my head in pain. This was a nightmare. I looked over to where Simon was standing. He wiped away a few of his tears and then tried to look as if hearing all that didn't have an effect on him. I calmed my father and told him that I was okay to continue. He didn't like it. Neither did I, but it all had to be told if I was going to see any justice for what Michael did to me.

I drank some cool water and asked my parents to rejoin me and gave the option to Simon to leave if he wanted. He shook his head and then came over to sit beside me. I moved over so he could sit on my bed. I needed him beside me to hold me, to make me feel loved and safe. It would be the only way I could continue. Once the room calmed, I looked over to Detectives Westphall and Lewis.

"I did not go to school that day, and I drove down to the marina. I had gotten into a fight with Simon the night before and needed time to think."

"What was the fight about?" asked Detective Lewis.

"It was about Michael. I had been so afraid to tell Simon about Michael. They argued before over me, and I didn't want my boyfriend to get into trouble by going after him. Nor did I want my parents' working relationship be compromised because of me. I thought I could handle it all on my own, but I was wrong. I told Simon everything, and he was hurt and angry. I can't say I really blamed him, but it still hurt. I left and went home. By the time I had come downstairs, I was told by our housekeeper that my parents were already at work. I couldn't do school, not when I was nursing a broken heart. That's why I was down by the marina. I spent the entire day watching the boats and the day catches from the fisherman. My phone had been off while it charged on a spare battery pack I used. I just sat there all day and didn't know that Simon was looking for me. I felt alone and hurt and just wanted some time for myself at a place that made me happy."

"We can understand that, Nicolette. What changed that made you want to get in touch with Mr. Paulson?"

"I got back into my car, not really knowing what to do. I turned on my phone and saw that he had texted and left me two voice mails. Once I listened to them, I knew I had to call him. Once I did, he told me he was with my father and asked me where I was. After I told Simon my location, they were on their way to the marina. I was scared, knowing my father knew the truth, but he assured me that Michael wasn't going to hurt me anymore. That he would put a stop to it. I felt relieved."

"And then? What happened?" Detective Westphall questioned.

"The unthinkable. If I only stayed in my car like they asked me to, but I didn't."

"Why, Nicolette? What led you to go back down to the docks?"

"My jacket. I left it on the bench and wanted to go get it. It was a favorite of mine and I didn't see any harm in doing so. I had no way of knowing what would happen. Michael was there. He was always watching me. Most times, I never knew. The night he raped me was just another moment that he waited in the shadows for me, and with this time, striking."

My mother was in tears, my father's face had hardened, and Simon's hand tightened in mine. This was unbearable, but I went on.

"I was grabbed from behind and dragged down the same path I had come from. He told me not to scream, and I didn't. I was picked up and taken down below to the living room cabin. It looked like a trophy room of some sort. There were couches all around with a bar off to the side."

"Is that where the attack took place?"

"Yes, Detective Lewis, it was. He threw me down, and I hit my head on the hardwood floor. I was lightheaded from not eating all day, and then the blow to my head made it worse. He revealed himself to me, and then began tearing my clothes. I fought so hard and used everything I knew to stop him from hurting me, but he was just too strong. Deranged, drunk, and filled with hate, he raped me. I begged him to stop, as my insides tore. The pain was horrific, and I kept wishing for him to kill me so it would be over. He showed no mercy. After he finished, he left me on the floor while he got up to pour himself a drink."

"I looked around for something to hit him with, and then I saw the trophy. It looked heavy enough to at least give me enough time to escape. His back was still turned when I hit him the first time. I almost got away from him, and then he grabbed me again, but then that's when I grabbed a bottle off the bar and hit him again. Michael had been knocked out, and I was free. When the blood poured out from my broken body, I just snapped. The smell was turning my stomach, that and his scent on me. I hit him again and again with my fists, and I kicked his ribs in. I stepped out of myself and fought and fought until Simon pulled me away from him. I remember only a few words after that, and then I woke up here in the hospital."

They were satisfied with my explanation and said their goodbyes with adding that Michael will never be able to hurt me again.

Their case was strong, along with all the physical evidence that was collected. My father was silent. He walked the detectives out and told me he would be back soon, but not before saying how brave and strong I am. I didn't feel like either of those things but said nothing in return as they made their way out.

Throughout the entire time of retelling my story, Simon remained by my side. He wasn't saying much, so I just asked him. "Do you want out? Because I would not blame you if you did." He shifted off the bed, and I thought I had my answer. When he didn't leave, I was surprised.

"Nicolette, I love you, probably more now than I ever thought was possible. You are incredible, and your strength astounds me. With all that you have been through, you sat here calmly and retold your story without even blinking. I am so proud of you, and no matter what has happened, it changes nothing, at least not for me."

"Simon, I want nothing more than to be with you, but I am just afraid this is going to be too much for you. You deserve better, and I want that for you."

"I deserve you, and you deserve me. We love each other, and that's all that matters. The rest of it, well, we will figure it out, okay?"

"Okay."

A food tray was brought in for me, and my stomach rolled. Nothing about hospital food was good. Simon smiled and told me that he would run down to the Juice Bar and bring me back something better. He kissed me goodbye, and I tried to close my eyes until he returned.

I fell asleep and was plagued with memories of Michael raping me. I kept hearing his voice over and over again, *"You're mine, Nicolette."* I squeezed my eyes tight and prayed for him to go away.

When I woke from my nap, Simon wasn't back yet, and I didn't know where my parents were. I called the nurses station and asked for someone to come into my room. My nurse from the night shift

205

returned and asked what she could do for me. I was going stir crazy in bed, and my muscles were so sore. I asked if I could take a small walk around the hall, thinking it would make me feel better.

She checked my chart for any notes from Dr. Jonas, and although I was disconnected from my IVs, I still had a concussion. She told me that I needed to stay in bed and continue to rest. I agreed to appease her, and then when she left my room, I tried to get up. I took it slow and managed to get out from my bed and at least walk around the room. It was a private room with only my bed in it, so I had room to move around. On my second pass, I heard voices from outside my room and waited for whoever it was to come in, but they never did. I opened my door just a little to see who it was, and I was relieved to see it was mom and dad. I was going to call out to them, but then I heard them arguing over me. It was hard to go unseen and listen at the same time. I left it open just ajar and stepped behind the door.

"Mason, don't you think it's time we call Jack? He has a right to know what has happened to Nicolette."

"Absolutely not! We are not calling my brother, Christina! He is the last person I want finding out about Nicolette."

Why would my father say that? And why did he sound so angry? It's Uncle Jack; I adored him. Why couldn't he know about me? I'd call him myself if I knew where my phone was. I then realized what day it was and how I missed my weekly scheduled call with him. He was probably worried, but that didn't explain why my father was so angry.

"Mason, please calm down. Jack loves Nicolette, and you know if he doesn't hear from her, he will worry. I bet he already is going crazy. Have you checked your messages? Or the ones at home? He's been calling all our phones. I imagine he's tried Nicolette's phone too."

"Christina, I'm sure he has, but I can't deal with him right now, and you know why that is. He was just beginning to accept our decision to move here. You saw how at peace he was when he was here for the party. Who knows? Maybe it was all for Nicolette's benefit, but we had no issues and I was happy for it. The minute Jack finds out about what happened to Nicolette, he will go insane, and you know what he is capable of. No, we can't tell Jack about Nicolette. Promise me, no calling my brother."

What he's capable of? What the hell is going on? Something was not right, and I just wanted to crash their little hallway pow wow but remained quiet and continued to listen. This was the only way I found out anything. My parents were not the best communicators when it came to me, always claiming to have my best interest at heart and not leaving me much to say about it.

Mom said, "What about Nicolette? Do you not care what she wants? Because I do. I know Nicolette, and I know she is going to want to speak with him. They are very close, and she will never understand why she can't talk to him. How will you explain it? She will fight you, you know she will, and where will that leave her? She's been through hell and will want to not only talk with Jack but want to see him too! And Sara."

"I don't know, Christina. I just don't know. I didn't know that some sick fucker was stalking our baby, and then he fucking rapes her? I want to kill him and make him pay for what he did to her, but that's not me. No, that's reserved for Jack. I've seen it before, and when my brother is pushed too far, he is more dangerous than I will ever be able to explain to you. No, we have to protect our daughter and Jack from himself."

My head was beginning to hurt, and I felt dizzy all of a sudden. I held onto the door for support and tried to listen to my parents. What they were saying did not make any sense to me. All those things about Uncle Jack and what they feared he would do if he found out about me. I almost closed the door, and then what I heard next stopped me.

I peered through the blinds to watch my father take my mother in his arms. She was crying on his shoulder, and then she looked directly into my father's eyes and said, "Mason, she's his daughter too. We have to call him. It's the right thing to do."

I was frozen in place. No, it can't be true. It can't be. The room began to spin, as my stomach wretched. I tried to move as fast as I could, but the bathroom was too far away, and I vomited all over the floor. It just kept coming up until I had nothing left. My parents must have heard me and came rushing into the room.

"Nicolette! Oh my God! Mason, call for a nurse." She called out for my father who asked a nurse to come into my room. I felt so faint, but before I could fall, my father lifted me into his arms and carried me over to the bed.

"Oh, my baby girl, what were you thinking? You need to stay in bed. Can you sip this for me?" he asked as he handed me some water.

The nurse told him that electrolytes were better, and she would bring some Gatorade in for me. They didn't know that I hadn't eaten yet, and after hearing my parents argue, that must have triggered my already sensitive stomach. After examining me, the nurse didn't like my color and paged Dr. Jonas. She soon arrived and examined me.

"You are dehydrated, again. Nicolette, if you don't follow my orders, I will be forced to put you back on an IV and administer the fluids that way. I see you did not eat your breakfast or lunch. Your body needs nutrients and fluids. Without them, you are at risk for becoming weaker and prolonging your stay here. Now, is this what you want?"

I said, "No, I just want to go home."

"That's what I want for you too, but not yet. I need to get your dehydration under control first, and then I want to see you eat."

"I promise, I will. My boyfriend is bringing me back something."

"Well, in the meantime, I am going to order some broth for you. I want you to finish the entire serving and then drink all twenty ounces of this beverage, okay?"

"Okay, I will."

"Don't worry doctor, I will make sure she finishes all of it," mom said.

"Thank you. I will check in with you later. Get some rest."

My room had been cleaned, and mom helped me wash up and change. I was so tired from the entire day and just wanted to sleep. After I finished my soup, my eyes began to grow heavy.

Simon called my mom and told her that he had gotten a flat tire on the way to the Juice Bar. He had no spare, or he would have changed the tire himself. It was already late, and he had to wait for the mechanic to fix his Jeep. I was disappointed, but I knew he would come back as soon as he was able.

My father came back and read to me for a while, while my mom sat quietly, holding my hand. My sleeping pill was beginning to work, and I was slowly drifting, but not completely out like the previous doses they gave me. Dr. Jonas said this was lighter but effective. My father kissed me goodnight and asked my mom if she was ready to go home yet.

She had said no, and wanted to be with me a little longer. He nodded and then told mom that he was going to take a walk and would return soon.

Mom asked, "Nicolette, are you feeling any better?"

"I am. The soup helped. Not a big fan of the Gatorade, but I drank it all down."

"Good, your body needs it. Get some rest and I'll be back soon."

"Where are you going?" I sleepily asked.

"Not far, just outside to make a call. You'll be alright?" she asked.

"Yes, I'll be fine. Go make your call."

I had seen the look in her eyes when I said the words. She was relieved as if she was waiting for me to tell her that it was okay. Was she going to call my uncle? And defy my father? I was too tired to think about it and drifted off to sleep.

Christina

I knew I was doing the right thing. I felt as if I was betraying my daughter's trust by not telling the one person I knew she would want to be by her side. I only had a short window of time before Mason would return. I knew he would be angry, but this was the way it had to be. I had a sinking feeling that if I didn't reach out to Jack, then he would come out here and make matters worse. No, I'm doing the right thing. This is what Nicolette would want, and it's about time I put her first.

"Thank you for calling The Neighborhood Bar and Grille, this is Tommy."

"Hi, Tommy, Christina Vanelle here."

"Well, hello beautiful, how are you? How's life treating you out in California? We sure do miss you guys around here."

"Thank you, Tommy. We're fine."

"Just fine? I would think you would be on top of the world."

"It's been a rough day. Anyway, I don't have long to chat. May I speak with Jack?"

"Sure, let me get him for you."

I heard Tommy call out his name over the loud sounds coming from the big screens. No doubt, a big game was on.

Jack's tone was short and curt with me. He was angry. I can't say that I blamed him. We kept him at arm's length since we left Chicago, and with the news, I would tell him, I hadn't even begun to hear angry yet.

He shouted, "So, your phones do work. I was beginning to think you might be avoiding me. Sure, I can see Massimo doing that, but not my Nickel. She missed our call this week, and come to think about it, I haven't heard much from her since her birthday. Now tell me, what the hell is going on?"

"I'm sorry, Jack, you don't know how much. I know we've hurt you, but that was never our intention, especially after all that you have done for us."

"Oh, hell! I'm sorry. I'm sure I am overreacting, but I just miss you all so much, especially my girl. Talk to me, what's going on?" he asked again.

I braced myself for what I would say next.

"Jack, this call is difficult. I have been trying to find the right words to say this to you, but there aren't any, not for what I have to tell you."

"Damn it! Woman, you are scaring the hell out of me. Just say it," he demanded.

"It's Nicolette. She's in the hospital."

"Hospital? Is she okay? Was she involved in an accident? OMG! That damn motorcycle. I warned that Simon to be careful with my girl. Was she badly hurt? What's her condition?"

With all the assumptions and questions that followed, I was beginning to regret my decision to call him. Mason was right. As soon as he heard the reason why she'd been hospitalized, he was going to lose his mind. Hell hath no fury when it came to Jack Vanelle.

"Christina? Hello?"

"She was raped." Just three words I knew would change Jack forever. I heard rustling coming from his end and then the sounds of shattering glass. I was shaking and barely hanging on.

"I'm on my way."

The line went dead. I clutched my phone to my chest and cried. What did I just do?

Fourteen

Michael

My head pounded. Sharp pangs of pain shot through the back of my head and down my neck with pierced pins and needles. *What the hell?* I struggled to open my eyes, but when I did, my vision was blurred. I tried to make out the two figures standing by my bed, but I didn't know who they were. *My bed…where the fuck am I? This is not my bed.* I also took stock of my right hand, which was handcuffed to the bed rail. *What the hell is going on?*

"Well, you're awake. That's good. If she would have hit you any harder, you'd been worm food by now," the unknown female said as she smirked at me, and in not the friendliest manner.

"Hello, Michael, before I leave you with these two detectives here, I would like to examine you. I'm Dr. Donaldson."

I answered weakly, "My head hurts."

"I'm sure it does. You suffered two blows to the back of your skull that resulted in you having a serious concussion. You have twelve stitches in total. Your ribs have been bruised, not broken, although they may feel as if they are. Expect the ribs to be tender for the next several weeks."

"Anything else?" I asked him.

"No, that pretty much sums it up. I will leave you to your company."

"Enjoy your nap?" the guy asked with his mocking tone.

"Well, according to you, I should be happy it wasn't a dirt nap, right?" I said.

"You got lucky, son."

"Yeah, I don't feel so lucky. Okay, I get why I'm in a hospital, but why am I restrained? Do you even know who my father is? His lawyers eat cops like you for breakfast. Get me out of this, now!"

"Are you referring to Clayton St. Clair?"

"Yeah, that's right."

"Yes, it's coming back to me now. He's the same father whom you assaulted before leaving to kidnap and rape Nicolette Vanelle. It's crazy how the mind works. How sometimes you believe one thing to be true, but really, it's just all made up in one's mind. Kind of like your sick obsession over that poor girl."

I shuttered at the mention of her name. *No, I didn't do the things he said I did. Did I?*

"Before we get to the fun part of my job, allow me to make the introductions. I'm Detective Westphall, and this is my partner, Detective Lewis. And you, Michael St. Clair, are under arrest for the kidnapping and sexual assault of Nicolette Elizabeth Vanelle and the physical assault on Clayton St. Clair. You have the right to remain silent. Anything you say can and will be used against you in a court of law. You have the right to an attorney. If you cannot afford an attorney, one will be provided for you. Michael St. Clair, do you understand the rights I have just read to you?"

"Yes," I replied.

"With these rights in mind, do you wish to speak to us?"

I closed my eyes and squeezed them tightly. *No, this is wrong. Why is this happening to me? I've done nothing wrong. I love Nicolette and would never hurt her. I remembered arguing with my father. He was trying to send me away, and I fought him. I shoved him hard, and he fell and hit his head. No, I didn't mean it. I was angry with him, but like Nicolette, I would have never knowingly hurt him.*

"Mr. St. Clair, I will ask you again. With these rights in mind, do you wish to speak with us? We can talk now or down at the station."

I looked at them and answered, "I understand. I will talk with you now."

The male detective began to question me but was interrupted by my father's lawyer.

"Do not say another word, Michael. My client will not be answering any questions today. I need to see the warrant," he barked, as the detective handed the paper over to him. With my unrestrained hand, I rubbed my temples as the sensation of pins and needles radiated through my head. The detectives and my lawyer bickered back and forth with each other, which made me feel worse than I already did.

"It's okay, John. I'll cooperate with them. I don't have anything to hide."

"Michael, you don't understand what you are agreeing to right now. You need to rest."

"I'm not a child! And, yes, I do understand. John, once I explain this misunderstanding, everything will be straightened out."

"I believe it's a little more complicated than that, Mr. St. Clair." Detective Lewis said as she stepped up close to my bed. "You are being charged with sexual assault, not to mention the list of various charges against you, and that includes stalking. We will get to all of that, but first the matter at hand. The rape of Nicolette Vanelle on the evening of December 12th, 2008."

"I didn't hurt Nicolette. I love her. She's my life. I would never hurt her for anything in the world."

"Well, you certainly have quite the different narrative on what you believe to be love, Mr. St. Clair. Your victim, Ms. Vanelle, has given a different account of the events that took place on the yacht, Lydia's Joy. Here, see for yourself the evidence of your love, and then tell me if you believe it's the same as Ms. Vanelle's."

She handed me an envelope with picture after picture of body shots of Nicolette. Her beautiful porcelain skin was painted with shades of blues, purples, and yellowish tones. Hand marks on her upper arms, neck, and even under her chin were visible and clear enough to be seen in these photos. I pushed them away, as I couldn't look at them any longer. I felt sick.

I began to tug at my handcuffed wrist. "John, do something. Have them release me, now!" I shouted and made my demands.

"I'm sorry, Michael. I can't do that. You will be discharged first thing in the morning and taken downtown to be processed. Your case is in the hands of the prosecutor, and I will try to delay if I can, but they want you in front of the judge as soon as possible to be arraigned."

"No, I didn't do anything. It was a misunderstanding. Let me explain," I cried out.

Detective Lewis slammed her hand down to the bed rail and vehemently glared at me. "You call raping a young and innocent girl a misunderstanding? She suffered a skull fracture due to your version of love. There is not one part of her body that is not covered in bruises. She has been torn from the inside out. You are one sick sonofabitch!"

"Amy, that's enough." Detective Westphall said as he pulled her back.

"No, Jim, I'm just getting started."

"Let's go. We're done here. Get some rest, St. Clair, because once you arrive down at county lockup, you'll have to sleep with one eye open. Word gets out that they have a rapist in their midst, and there's no telling what will happen to you. They don't take kindly to spineless rich boys that prey and rape young women."

"Fuck you! Fuck you both. You can all go to fucking hell! You don't know anything. I love her. I love her," I continued to shout as they walked out from my room with my doctor returning. He injected something into my IV, and I drifted off to sleep.

Nicolette

I had been here for several days now and wanted to be home and in my own bed. Simon was amazing. He'd been here as much as he could manage between school and track practice. No matter how much of a brave face he put on for me, I knew having to see me like this, and in a hospital, really messed him up. He was angry at Michael and probably with himself for how we argued the night before I was attacked. I told him repeatedly that I would never allow him to blame himself for what happened to me. I knew it would be too much for me to bear if he did that. He promised me that he wouldn't, but I still saw the pain in his eyes every time he looked at me, no matter how hard he tried to hide it.

I tried not to think of Michael, but it was hard not to. He was here somewhere in this hospital, and I was afraid. I knew the police had been posted outside of his door, but that didn't stop my mind from worrying.

My parents were quiet, not saying too much to me, and the subject of Uncle Jack did not come up again. My phone was still missing, and I never did find out if my suspicions were correct about mom and if she called him. *Why not?* I wondered and made a mental note to ask her about it once I was home.

The hot shower soothed my sore muscles. This time, I didn't scrub off all my skin. I just wanted to feel clean again and wash away what he did to me. I finished drying my hair when Dr. Jonas knocked on my door.

"Good morning, Nicolette, how are you feeling today?" she asked with hope in her voice.

I sighed and shrugged my shoulders. "Still a little sore, but the showers are helping." Any other answer would have been a lie. My heart was broken, and my mind still reeled from all that happened to me.

She sat down at the table and gestured for me to join her. She placed down what I assumed to be my chart and then said, "It will take a few weeks, maybe more, before all the tenderness subsides. I don't want you to push your recovery. Nicolette, your body suffered through an immense physical trauma, and the injuries you sustained will need time to heal."

"Yes, I know that!" I snapped at her. "I'm sorry. It's just hard being reminded about this ordeal all the time."

"I understand that, but if you're feeling up for a talk, I would like to go over some things with you."

"You're here, might as well."

"As you know, we collected many samples from you on the night you were admitted to the hospital. Along with those collections were blood and semen. Your fingernails had D.N.A. from Mr. St. Clair under them, along with hair and skin fibers."

I remained quiet and listened to Dr. Jonas deliver a detailed report of my rape as if it was the most natural choice of conversation to discuss.

"Nicolette, he didn't wear a condom. You've been tested for various STDs, which came back negative, but I recommend repeating those tests in six months from now. What's important now is a pregnancy test. Do you remember when your last menstrual period was?"

My mind drew a blank. "I'm not sure, around Thanksgiving?"

"Nicolette, I have to make you aware that if you were ovulating around that time, there is a chance you could be pregnant. It's too early to test now. At your next appointment, we can run the test then, just to be sure. I also would like to put you in contact with the Rape Abuse and Incest National Network, also known as R.A.I.N.N. You would be able to get help and support through their staff of counselors. Have you ever heard of this organization? Or know anyone familiar with it?"

"Yes, I've heard of it, and no, I guess I would be the first one out of my friends to use it. I can't honestly say that I'm thrilled about it."

"Do you have any questions you'd like me to answer?" she asked. I couldn't speak, and if she didn't leave soon, I was going to fall apart in front of her.

"I'm sorry, Nicolette. I'll leave you to get some rest."

She gave me a sympathetic smile. I took the information packets she had handed me and tossed them across the room. I began to silently cry. How did I get here? A few days ago, I was blissfully happy with Simon. And now? I'm in the hospital being handed STD pamphlets and helpful info, all because some animal raped me.

"You motherfucker!" I shouted out. "Why did you do this to me?" It felt good to scream. It meant that I still had a life inside of me, something that I wasn't going to allow Michael St. Clair to take from me.

Mason

"You did what!?" I had never shouted so loudly in my life.

"Mason, I had to call him. He had a right to know," she responded.

I held my head, not believing how my wife would betray me like this. I begged her not to call my brother, but she went against my wishes and did it anyway.

"Christina, you can't imagine what you have just unleashed by calling my brother. The hell that will rain down upon us will be catastrophic. He is going to be out of his mind if he isn't already.

"Mason, you're scaring me. Do you honestly believe this about Jack? Your own brother? The one who gave us our greatest gift and a chance at becoming parents? No, I won't believe it. He loves us and Nicolette."

"Okay, Christina, some things have to be seen in order to be proven. Let's see if I'm right," I said, as I watched the tall, dark figure step off the elevator and walk right toward me.

"What? What are you sa...?" And before my wife could finish her question, the beast emerged.

Jack lunged and had me forcibly pinned up and against the wall. He shoved me so hard, I felt the sheetrock crack. I could not move, nor could I speak. He gripped me by my throat and hit me with just a taste of his anger.

"How could you let this happen to my girl?" Jack's tone was menacing. I continued to struggle beneath his hold, but my efforts were futile against his bear-like brawny arms.

"Jack, get your hands off him. You're killing him. Let him go!" Christina's words finally registered with my brother and he finally let go, as I slid down to the floor to gasp for air. Security was alerted, and always the mediator, my wife explained that this was just a misunderstanding between family, and we would not cause any more disturbances.

"Mason, are you alright? Oh my God, Jack, if I knew you were going to react this way, I would have never called you. How could you do this?"

After a few minutes of coughing and guzzling down a bottle of water, I was able to finally speak, but he shot me a look not to. Jack was behaving in every way that I feared he would. He gripped the back of his neck, and then turned to look at Christina and completely ignored me.

"How did you expect me to be, Christina? You all go out of your way to avoid my calls for days, and then when you finally do call, I'm told that my beautiful girl has been raped by some animal. How the hell did you think I was going to react? You should know me better than that!" He then glared at me and said, "Isn't that right, Massimo? I protect what's mine. Always have. Always will."

"Oh, Jack, I didn't want to believe you could do this," Christina cried.

"If you believed I was going to be anything else but enraged about this, then you don't know me at all, woman. I love that girl more than my own life. She's a part of me, Christina. Whether you like it or not, she is of my blood. And now that her blood has been spilled, I want the fucker who is responsible for it."

I was on my feet and tried to make sense of Jack's arrival and what it would mean to Nicolette, knowing he had come for her. I knew it was just a matter of time before she would ask for him, and now that he was here, I had run out of time.

"Massimo, I need to see her. Take me to my girl now," he demanded through gritted teeth.

This wasn't my first time witnessing my brother unravel and lose control, and it probably wouldn't be the last, but I wasn't going to stand here and take another hit like the one he delivered when he arrived. Like Nicolette, Christina loved Jack. The four of us were always very close. Despite our differences in personality, he was always my brother first. He was upset, and rightfully so, but now he was just being spiteful and directing all of his anger toward me.

I said, "Jack, it's clear by your actions that you are in no state of mind to see Nicolette at this time, especially after the scene you just caused. You need to calm down and let us take care of our daughter."

"I don't think so, and hell will freeze over if you think for one second that I am leaving. Nickel is my daughter, just as much as she is yours, or have you forgotten that? I have abided by the agreement we had in place all these years. I never stood in your way, nor Christina's. All I ever wanted was a place in her life, to love her, and to be there for Nicolette every single day of her life. I kept my word, as my hands were tied the day you made the decision to leave Chicago and move to California. You took her from me! All I could do was watch that poor girl cry as she waved goodbye to me."

"Jack, be reasonable. You know that's not the way it happened. We discussed it as a family and made a mutual decision that was best for my family. I thought you understood that."

"No! I never understood it, but it didn't matter, now did it, Mason? You wouldn't have cared about my feelings, nor how it affected Nicolette."

"That's not true, and you know it. Stop trying to play the martyr here. Jack, you act as if you are the wounded party when Nicolette is the one we should all be concerned about."

"Oh, believe me, she is the only one that I am thinking about right now. I have always put her first and should have never agreed to let you take here to this place. She would have been fine and unharmed if she had stayed with me. You promised me! You swore that you would always protect her."

"Jack, she has been protected from the first moment we held her in our arms. What happened to Nicolette was beyond my control. I had just found out all that was going on with her on the night she was raped."

After I said the words, I knew my brother was teetering on the edge of whatever control he had left. He never looked at me with such malice before, and I feared he may never look at me in any other way again. He paced the hall and continued to grab the back of his neck. Christina was crying, and I didn't know what else to say to him but that I was sorry.

"You know, Mason..." He enunciated my name as it made him sick to voice it. He never got over me changing it, and he knew I hated it when he addressed me using my real name. "This is bullshit. Let me ask you something: where the hell were you? Where? Because you weren't with Nicolette when you should have been. How could you be so oblivious to what was going on in her life? 'Beyond my control?' No, my brother, that should have been the first thing to have, especially over a young and impressionable girl. She needed you. You failed her. You're her father, and yet, you did nothing! Why? Explain it to me. Too busy with your career?" he continued to spew hate with his cold mocking tone.

Christina cut in. "Please, Jack, stop this. Blaming Mason will not change what has happened to Nicolette. I am begging you to keep the promise you made to us all those years ago. She has been put through hell and is way too fragile right now. Please give us more time."

"No, you have had nothing but time. I will not wait any longer. Once she knows the truth, she will want to be with me and Sara. Now, where is she? I am going to see our daughter, and then I will take care of the animal that did this to her. He will not see me coming, and I will enjoy every minute of pain that I inflict on him, just as he did to our precious girl. I will get justice for her, and it will be done in the only way I know how…my way."

"No! Jack, don't go after Michael. How will that help any of us if you're in jail? And what about Nicolette?"

"Don't worry about me, Christina. I can take care of myself. I will do whatever it takes to right this wrong for my daughter. You sure as hell can count on that."

Fuck! Not again. I walked over to Jack and made him look at me.

I said, "After all these years, that is still your answer for everything. Right, Jack? Hit first, ask questions later. Stay out of it. The police are taking care of Michael. You want to help? Fine. I can't stop you from seeing Nicolette, but if you go anywhere near Michael St. Clair, I will go to the police myself and have you arrested. Do you hear me, big brother? Stay out of it."

No emotion. Not one twitch of his eye. This was when he was the most dangerous when he shut down and went silent. You never knew what he was thinking because he showed nothing to give you a clue. He turned and walked away from me. I let out a sigh of relief, and then he stopped. I held my breath, not knowing what he was going to do. And then so quietly, he walked back over to me and whispered these words for only me to hear.

"Remember who you are, brother. Papa may have changed our names, but that doesn't change who we are and where we come from. You, Massimo Anthony Vanelli, make me sick. Stop running. Stop hiding. Remember who you are! Il sangue è più spessa dell'acqua, ed è stratificata sulle mie mani e radicata nella mia anima. Tutto in nome della famiglia. La nostra famiglia."

Chills layered my spine as he pushed in the last inch of his "metaphorical knife" into my back. I said nothing more to my brother and watched him walk away and not look back. I didn't just fail Nicolette, I failed him.

"Mason, what was that all about? What did Jack say to you?" Christina asked. I held my chest and tried to take a few calming breaths. My neck was still pulsating from where he nearly choked the life out of me. I took my wife's hand and pulled her to me. I didn't know what to do. "Please, you can tell me. What did he say?" she asked again.

"He said: blood is thicker than water, and it is layered on my hands and ingrained in my soul. All in the name of the family. Our family. Remember who you are."

She looked incredulously at me. "What does that mean? I don't understand."

"You don't want to know. I need to find my brother. Please go sit with our daughter. I'll be along soon."

"Are you sure that is a good idea? He's so angry, Mason. I'm scared."

"You should be. We all should. I need you to leave."

"Come with me, please."

"No! You were the one that called him here, and now I have to deal with it. I warned you, and you chose not to listen to me. Nicolette, getting raped? That is just the beginning of our nightmare. If I don't try to stop Jack, the family we believed we had will be destroyed. Now, go to our daughter."

I couldn't say another word to my wife, nor try to comfort her after her tears fell. I had to find my brother. I searched the hospital grounds and was about to give up when I spotted my brother leaning up against a wall, taking long drags of his cigarette. I slowly walked over to him, as if he was a wounded animal. In a way, that's exactly how I would describe him.

"I thought you quit?" I asked and pointed to the cigarette still in his hand.

"I did. I guess hearing how my daughter was brutally attacked made me want to start up again. You know, tough habit to break. Cigars are my thing, but this is not the time I want to just kick back and enjoy a fine cigar, right?"

"Jack, can we talk? Please, like brothers."

"I don't want to hear it. There is nothing you can say to me right now that will make me change my mind. That fucker has to die."

"What about Sara?"

Glaring at me with daggers, he said, "What *about* Sara?"

"Do I have to really say it? I more than anyone understand your first instinct is to want justice for Nicolette, and the only way to do that is by ending the life of her rapist. You are not thinking clearly, and you're allowing your anger to make decisions for you. Please, Jack, remember who you are. You are not that man anymore, not the man who is standing before me now. The 'hit first and ask questions later' approach may have been your way in the past, but you let that go a long time ago. Please don't let what happened with Nicolette bring you back into the world that you never belonged in. Please, I am begging you."

He hit the brick wall with his fist, barely causing a scratch to his thick, calloused hands. He slid down to the ground and covered his face.

"What do you know about my old life? You were just a kid."

"I know enough, and I know you got caught up in a life that you didn't want, but you lived it until you saw your chance and broke free from it. You met Sara, and she changed you. You fell in love. You became better for her."

"That's low, Mason, even for you."

"Yeah, and spouting off Italian quotes on family loyalty isn't? You knew that was low, but you said it anyway."

"I will not apologize to you, nor to anyone about the sacrifices I had to make when it came to our family. I couldn't stand how hard mama and papa worked. You were so little, you could do nothing but make them smile with the beautiful music you played. I did what I had to do and will never regret those choices."

"Yeah, but you do. I know you do. You just won't admit it. If it was just about deliveries and making some fast money, that would have been okay, but it was so much more than that. You can play it off as much as you want, but I knew you were the muscle in Johnny's organization. If a lesson had to be delivered, they called you. And before you try to deny it, I saw you."

"What the hell are you talking about?" He was now on his feet and backing me against the hard brick wall to my back.

"You know exactly what I am talking about. It was the night of my school concert. Mama was sick, and papa was working late. You promised them that you would take me, but you never showed up. When you finally did come home, I saw your bloodied knuckles and how hard you tried to hide your hands from mama and papa. They knew Jack, and so did I. I hated you at that moment because I knew you were responsible for Mikey Marino never walking again. All because you did a 'favor' for Johnny."

I continued, "You say you have blood on your hands? Yes, you do. I am begging you as your brother to not spill any more blood. It's not who you are. You are a better man than that, and maybe I didn't see it growing up, but I do now. You are my big brother. I love you. You always protected our family, and still do today, but I'm afraid for you. Don't allow what happened with Nicolette to bring you back to those dark days. Think of Sara, who loves you. She needs you, and you need her."

"Stop it, Mason. Now, you're just hating, and it's low, even for you."

"Don't you see? I'm not trying to hurt you. I am trying with everything I have to save you. To hold onto my brother. I can't lose you, and neither can Nicolette, nor Sara. We need you to be strong, stronger than you have ever been, and fight those demons inside of you. I can feel your need of revenge radiating off you. It's so strong, but you have to be stronger."

I continued, "Don't you know that I want to rip that boy apart for what he did? But I can't, not without causing more pain for our family. Hurting Michael will not change what happened to Nicolette. The only thing it will prove is more blood on your hands. For the last time, I am begging you in the name of our family, on the blood, sweat, and tears of mama and papa, and their hopes and dreams for their sons to have a better life: Don't do it. Don't go back there again and retreat to a place that none of us can go with you. Remember where you've been, and what it took to be here now. I love you, Jack. Remember who you are."

I could count on one hand all the times I witnessed my brother cry. The first was when he sat by our mother's deathbed and prayed for her survival. The second time was when he prayed for God to save his beloved Sara from cancer. The third time was when Nicolette was born and he held her for the first time, promising to love her forever and to always keep her safe. And now, today.

A few tears fell down his tormented face, as I asked him to make one more promise, a promise I wasn't sure if he would ever be able to keep, but I had to try.

This time, it was me who walked away. I didn't look back at the broken man who wept against his personal battle of right and wrong: my brother.

Fifteen

Simon

I wanted to crash on my bed, but sleep was not in the cards for me. I would grab a shower and a quick bite to eat before heading back over to the hospital. It was hard leaving her today, but my coach was breathing down my neck, and I knew not showing up would have meant disaster for my teammates. I had a good relationship with the coach, but I was also the captain. He depended on me to lead my team, especially with the championships coming up.

The sprays from the hot shower soothed my tight and overworked muscles. I ran too many miles to count today while my mind replayed the horrific images of Nicolette's naked and bloodied body beating down on Michael. I blamed myself for her attack, although she didn't. I couldn't help it. The images were too graphic, and every time I closed my eyes, I saw them.

That day, I was blinded by my hatred of Michael, and then I was angry with Nicolette for lying to me. The look on her face when I rejected her love was just another image that I would never forget. I wanted her to leave because I didn't trust my temper if she stayed. I knew she wanted me to run after her, and that's what my brain was telling me to do, but it was my heart that needed to catch up. By the time it did, she was gone, and our future was uncertain.

To witness the love of my life in that condition made me ache for her. I had never been so scared in all my life. I had no time to react. She was in need of medical attention. I thanked God for a father's instinct. He said he had a terrible feeling about Nicolette, and he called the police en route to the marina. But we were too late.

On my way out to the hospital, my father asked me to stay and talk with him for a few minutes. When I called over my shoulder that I had some place to be, he called me back.

"Simon, ten minutes is all that I am asking, and it's not a request. My study...now." He gestured with his hand and pointed to his office. I never argued with my father and didn't want to choose now to do so, but my girl needed me.

I took a seat and asked, "What's up?"

"I think you know. We're worried about you and how Nicolette's assault is affecting you."

"I'm fine. You don't have to worry about me."

"Like we didn't have to worry when you lost Jennifer? That kind of worry, son?"

"Dad, I can't believe you choose now to hit me with this. Jennifer has nothing to do with Nicolette, and the situations are not the same."

"The pain is. I see it when I look into your eyes. Son, we are here for you and so are your brothers. You just need to allow us to help you."

"I appreciate it, but I'm fine. I have to go, dad. Thanks for the talk."

"Simon, I wasn't finished."

I let out a frustrated sigh and sat back down. I didn't have time to have this argument with my father. I knew he cared and was worried, but he didn't have to be.

"Son, no matter how many assurances you give to me and to your mother, it will not lessen our worry for you. It broke our hearts after we found out about Nicolette, and we will never be able to put into words how sorry we feel for not only her but her parents. No parent ever wants their child to be hurt, especially in a manner such as the brutal attack she endured. Having said that, you are our son, and that means we have to put you and your feelings first. You've missed school. You've missed going to practice. You're not eating well or sleeping. We are well within our rights to be concerned."

"I'm fine, and if you're not able to accept the answer that I have given to you, then that's not my issue, it's yours."

"That's not fair, and if you were in the right frame of mind now, you would know that what I am telling you right now comes from the love we have for you. All that I am asking is for you to take some time."

"No, you're not. You're asking me to walk away from Nicolette, aren't you?"

He looked down to the floor and let out a breath before focusing back on me. "Yes, that's exactly what I am asking."

"Dad, I know you and mom love me, but I am asking you to back off. I have always admired and respected you, but for the first time in my life, I stand here in disappointment. How could you ever expect me to just give up on her? What is she now, damaged goods? Yes, what happened to Nicolette was horrific, and I don't believe I will ever forget how I found her, but I will try for her. I can't just flip a switch and turn off my feelings. Let me be clear so there are no misunderstandings when it comes to my relationship with Nicolette. I love her. I know what I am doing. Please trust my judgment, and do not ever compare what happened with Jennifer to what is happening with Nicolette. You hurt me tonight. I never believed my own

father could ever do that to me, but I guess that's just one more lesson I will have to come to terms with. I mean no disrespect, but that
works both ways. I'm a man. I'm still the same man you raised me to
be, and to ask me to just give up on the woman I love is not who I
am, nor will I ever be. If the roles were reversed, you would never
walk away from mom. You're not built that way, none of us Paulson's are. I love you, dad. I know what I want, and she is waiting for
me to return to her."

I grabbed my keys and walked out of his office. He followed me
to the entryway but made no more attempts to stop me from leaving.
I saw my mother as she waved to me from the top of the stairs with
tears and sadness in her eyes. I hated to hurt them, but I knew where
I needed to be. I felt him at my back as I kept walking toward my
Jeep, knowing he stood in the doorway, watching me go.

Nicolette

I received a text from Simon, telling me that he was on his way. I was nervous about seeing him again, and I knew why. We hadn't discussed my rape, and what would happen to us once I was discharged and back at home?

"Will you listen to yourself, Nicolette? You act as if 'your rape' was a tangible object you could physically hold. I guess in a way, it was," I said aloud and then cursed myself for even bringing it up.

I'd had enough already with my parents and Dr. Jonas as if I would ever forget. That was my problem: I would never forget. I remembered every detail of that night and feared that memory would be attached to me for the rest of my life. Michael St. Clair left an everlasting imprint on my soul, and no matter how many showers I took, I would never be able to wash away what he did.

"You, stupid girl! What the hell were you thinking? Why didn't you trust the ones that loved you? I was so concerned about everyone else's feelings, that I didn't care about my own, and now I have to carry the burden of those choices for the rest of my life. How could Simon ever want to be with someone like me? I'm dirty and disgusting. No! I have to end it before I hurt him any more than I already have," I shouted out to my empty room, where I felt the walls begin to close in around me. Bile rose up in my throat, and then I felt sick to my stomach. Michael was here, and he was going to hurt me again. I screamed at him, but he kept coming toward me.

"Leave me alone! I hate you. Go away!" I continued to shout, and then I closed my eyes and pulled the blanket up to my neck. I pulled at my hair to the point of pain. My scalp was burning, but I didn't care. I wanted this pain so I would never forget. I continued to pull at my long strands and then let out piercing cries as I saw his face again. *"I love you, Nicolette. You're mine. You will always be mine. I'm going to show you just how much I love you."*

"No! Help! Someone help me, please." I was screaming at the top of my lungs and felt so small because I felt I had hit rock bottom and could not fall any further. I was thrashing beneath my blankets with hot beads of sweat soaking my skin.

"Help me!" I cried and shouted as loud as I could until I felt the stick of a needle pierce my arm.

"Nicolette, it's okay. You're safe. I'm here to help you."

I slowly opened my eyes and saw Dr. Jonas, and then my eyes found Simon's devastated ones. Simon was here, watching from the doorway, holding a bouquet of flowers. Tears were streaming down his face, as my wrists were bound to my bed rails, and then the drugs took over and I drifted off to sleep.

Simon

My poor girl. She looked like a cornered animal. Her doctor had no choice but to restrain her. She was hurting herself. The tips of her fingernails were bloodied, just like when I found her on the night on Michael's boat. She was in so much pain and finally hit her breaking point.

After the nurses cleaned her scalp and wiped down her hands, I sat beside her for a few minutes. Her parents had gone home for the evening, and I expected to see them anytime now. Dr. Jonas said that she was going to call them. I placed her flowers down and pulled up a chair to sit with her. I placed her delicate hands on mine and kissed each one of her fingers. She was so small but so strong in spirit. My girl was fighting, just as she did that night. She fought Michael, and now she's fighting through her pain. I hate that she hurt herself and now has to be restrained, but Dr. Jonas said that it was best for her safety.

The injection she received would keep her sleeping for the rest of the night, and hopefully, by morning, she would wake up with a calmer mind. I hated to see her like this. I leaned over her and placed a kiss on her forehead.

"I love you, Nicolette." I kissed her again and then turned to see her father standing at the door to her room. I followed him out to the hall.

"How is she?" he asked.

"She's sleeping. They had to give her something to calm her down."

"Yes, I know. How are you doing?" he looked at me just as my father had done earlier.

"I'm fine, Mr. Vanelle."

"Simon, you are far from fine, and so is my daughter. You have been here around the clock, and now with this happening with Nicolette, I think you should just go home and leave her be. She needs rest. Once we bring her home, we will have to focus as a family to help her recover."

"Mr. Vanelle, I am not walking away from Nicolette, let's get that straight. You are the second person tonight who has asked me to do that, and my answer is no. I love that girl in there. She needs me, and I need her."

He didn't say anything more to me, there was no point. I wasn't going to allow anyone to come between us, not ever again. I stayed out in the waiting room and gave him privacy to his daughter. He sat and read quietly while I paced outside the room. All I wanted was to spend some time with Nicolette tonight and make her feel better. I brought new music, books, and her favorite muffin from the Juice Bar, which was now crushed in my backpack.

"Simon, you can go in now," Mr. Vanelle said.

"Thank you." I grabbed my bag and began walking toward her room.

"Simon," he called out. "I'm sorry. I wasn't trying to push you away. I know how much you love my daughter. I just don't know what tomorrow is going to bring, for any of us."

I didn't respond. I simply nodded and walked toward her room. I texted my father and told him not to expect me home tonight, and I would see him tomorrow. He texted back, asking me where I was planning to sleep, and I lied by telling him Sam's house. I would have said anything to spare his feelings, but knowing my father, he probably already knew where I would be. I wasn't leaving her, and I wanted to be the first person she would see when she woke up. I had to be here.

Her hands were still bound, but I managed to hold one of hers in mine. I placed my head down and tried to close my eyes. I wasn't sure how long I was out for until the sun began to light up her room. I slowly lifted my head and saw the most beautiful eyes looking back at me.

"Hey, there's my beautiful girl. Welcome back," I whispered softly and then kissed her hand. "Are you thirsty? Can I bring you anything?" I kept rambling on until I saw the first tear fall. More and more fell, as each one had the power to further break my heart. "Baby, don't cry. Talk to me."

"I'm sorry, Simon. I'm so sorry."

"You don't have anything to be sorry for. You scared me last night, but I was more scared for you. Can you tell me about it?"

"I guess I just freaked out for a moment and couldn't shake the bad memories. Every time I closed my eyes, he was there. It felt so real. I heard his voice and felt his touch."

I knew exactly how she felt, but I could never share that with her. She'd been through enough and didn't need to worry about me too. I held her hand and just listened.

"Dr. Jonas visited me earlier and gave me all sorts of help pamphlets. She wants me to see a therapist, attend group meetings, whatever. It just felt so overwhelming that this is what my life has come to. I tried to sleep, but then I was too wired and kept replaying everything in my mind. His voice is still there, Simon. He mocks me and won't leave me alone. I just want him to leave me alone."

"Nicolette, he is never going to hurt you again. He's going from here to jail. I promise you, he will never hurt you again."

"Simon, I have to tell you something."

"Okay, I'm listening." I sat as close as I could on her bed and wiped away her tears.

"I think we should break-up. It's for the best. We can't see each other anymore."

"What? No! You don't mean that."

"Simon, you deserve better, so much more than a girl like me. I just can't give you what you want. I am a complete mess. Part of my breakdown last night was worrying about you. I know we haven't really had a chance to talk about it yet, but that doesn't mean that I don't know and feel what you are thinking. I see the pain in your eyes, just as much as you see it in mine. I was raped, beaten, and nearly killed by Michael. When you found me that night, I was praying for death, because after he raped me, that's how I felt. I didn't believe I had anything left inside of me, but then when I knocked him out, I just wanted him to die. Do you understand that? I wanted him to die for what he did to me, and then you were there. You saw how I looked. I don't ever expect you to just be okay with this when even I don't believe I will ever be."

"Nicolette, we are going to get through this, and no one is walking away from each other. I love you too much to ever just leave you behind. The day I told you that I loved you was the day I sealed my heart with yours. I'm fine, Nicolette, and I am not going anywhere."

"Simon..."

"No, this conversation is over, but not us. Not ever."

She didn't look at me, but I prayed she believed me. Dr. Jonas arrived, followed by her parents. I stepped aside to give her doctor some room to examine her. Her father patted me on my back, with her mom giving me a compassionate smile.

Dr. Jonas greeted her, "Good morning, Nicolette. How are you feeling?"

"Alive."

"Anything else?"

"Hungry."

"Okay, how about in here." She touched the side of her head and then directed her attention to her heart. "Nicolette, I believe you know what I am asking. Before I remove these restraints, I need to hear your answer."

"I'm not going to hurt myself."

"What about last night? Can you tell me about it?"

"Last night was last night. What do you want from me? I am not suicidal if that's what you are thinking. I was angry and in pain. In pain over what has happened to me. I was in pain believing that I had disappointed my parents. I was in pain thinking about Simon, and then I was in pain over me. I was angry with myself for giving Michael chance after chance to do the right thing. All I wanted was for him to leave me alone, but he didn't, and now look at me. I am lying in a hospital bed and tied to it. I'm not crazy. I fought him, daddy, I swear I did," she said, as she once again tugged on her wrist restraints. I watched her father rush over to her and kiss her forehead.

"I know you did, baby. You were so brave. Nicolette, we love you." He angrily turned around to face her doctor and then demanded Dr. Jonas to remove the restraints.

"My daughter doesn't need these to be safe. What she needs is to be home with her family, and that happens today. Remove these restraints, and discharge my daughter," he stated, with his tone getting louder.

"Mr. Vanelle, the restraints were necessary at the time. She is my patient. I had to put her safety first above anything else." He didn't say anything else to her doctor and waited while she unfastened her wrists. Once she was free, her father pulled her up into a hug. Her mother joined them, as I waited for my turn.

"We love you. I'm going to go with Dr. Jonas to begin the paperwork for your discharge. No more tears, okay? Let mom help you get ready, and then we can bring you home."

"Okay, I will."

She looked over to her mom and asked if she could have a few minutes with me. Her mom gave us the time and waited outside.

"Simon, I..."

I put my hands up and then walked over to my girl. She looked so sad and broken. "No more tears, and no more talks about breaking up. We have a lot to figure out, and we will once you are home. I just need to know that you will not shut me out. I promise you that I am not walking away from you, not ever. I love you, Nicolette."

"I love you, Simon. I'm sorry for hurting you. You are the last person I ever want to hurt. I just didn't know what else to do."

"Why don't you let someone else do the worrying, and you concentrate on getting well? I have to go but just know that I am going to be thinking about you every second until I see you again."

I wanted to hold her but wouldn't push until I knew I would be welcomed. She gave me a small smile and then allowed me to give her a hug. I placed one more kiss to her head, and then I left her with her mom.

Sixteen

Michael

I was freed from my handcuffs to shave and shower before I was to be discharged and taken down to be processed. John, my father's lawyer had been with me for most of the morning and went over all that would happen today. Once I was ready, the guard handcuffed my wrist back to my bed. I wanted to scream at him but was advised to keep my mouth shut.

My father hadn't arrived yet, not that I expected him to. John told me that I was lucky he was helping at all after I hurt him. My father took six stitches to the back of his head and suffered a mild concussion.

While John shuffled papers into his briefcase, all my thoughts were of Nicolette. No one would tell me anything about her. Was she okay? Did she hate me? I had to know.

"John, I need to see Nicolette."

He looked at me with shock but didn't answer me.

My father did as he entered my room. "Did I hear you right? You would think after two blunt trauma hits to the back of your skull, some sense would have been knocked in. There is no way in hell you are getting anywhere near that girl...not ever. Do you see where you are? You are bound to your hospital bed. You have two uniformed police officers standing guard outside of your room. Yeah, like walking out of here on your own is going to happen. Your freedom and your wants ended the minute you hurt and raped Nicolette Vanelle."

"Dad, please, help me. I need to explain to her how sorry I am, and I never meant to hurt her. I forgive her for hurting me."

"Clayton, if I may?" His lawyer stepped in front of my father and pulled a chair to sit beside my bed. I could do nothing but listen, since I was restrained. "Michael, if you are not going to listen to your father, then listen to me. I know the law, and if you were anyone else, you would have been examined and taken into custody days ago, but it was this man's influence and my skills that have kept you safe in this bed and not locked up in a cell. The facts are not disputable. You will be charged for the sexual assault of Nicolette Vanelle. For the time being, I have done all that I can. Once you are released, you will be arraigned and go before the judge to give your plea."

"I'm not guilty. I love that girl."

"No, you raped that girl," John said, his voice laced with annoyance.

No, it's not true. They're wrong. All of them.

"Michael, you are lucky that I am helping you at all. You need to shut your mouth and listen to John. No more delusional thinking about that girl. Do you hear me?"

"If you hate me so much, dad, then there's the door. Don't stick around on my account because of all the times you didn't."

"Yeah, that's right. I'm a terrible father. Poor, sad Michael. Abandoned by his mother who died and a father who worked day-in and day-out to provide the life you now have. I'm sorry your mother died and you never felt that I loved you, but you're wrong. I'm done justifying myself to you. You have bigger problems than some daddy issues. Do what John says and keep your mouth shut. You may still believe that you are king of the world, but in truth, we are all you've got, and you better start coming to terms with that."

John said nothing more as he followed my father out of my room, leaving me alone to think about all they said.

Mason

I reached his voicemail again as I tried to get in contact with my brother. He dropped out of sight after our fight yesterday. I had his room made up for him back at the house, but he never showed up. I was beginning to really worry, and I feared he might have come back here to see Nicolette, but I wasn't sure.

"Any luck?" Christina asked.

"Nope, not one call or text returned. I'm worried."

"About Jack?"

"Who else? Not knowing where he is, or what's going through his mind is beginning to make me nervous. It's the unknown. Jack has dropped off the grid before, but this situation with Nicolette has him on the edge of rational thinking. I can't imagine him going far, but he hasn't called Sara, which is disturbing. He wouldn't have left without visiting with Nicolette. For all we know, he may have last night."

"Yes, but Simon was with her. Don't you think he would have told us if he saw him?"

"Not if he was asleep at the time. Did you take a close look at him this morning? That boy is exhausted. His father called me. Ted wanted me to try to persuade him to go home, but Simon took it completely wrong. He was hurt thinking that I was pushing him away when it was just out of concern for him and Nicolette. They are so young, and to have to go through something like this is way too much to handle for either one of them."

"He loves her. What did you expect?"

"I love her too." We were both taken by surprise to see Jack standing behind us.

"We know," I said to my brother. "I've been calling you all night. Where have you been?"

"As if you really care."

"Jack, what happened yesterday was my fault. I shouldn't have attacked you the way that I did. I just wanted to reason with you in regards to Nicolette."

"You mean, our daughter? Yes, we will certainly have time to discuss Nicolette, but first I need to grab a cup of coffee and clean myself up. I'll be back in a few minutes."

"Jack, where were you?"

"Why? Afraid I might have done something bad?" he mocked.

"Stop it. I was just concerned."

"I spent the night down by the beach. Kind of morbid, don't you think? Returning to the scene of the crime. The one place that changed my daughter's life forever."

"Oh, Jack, why would you put yourself through that? You could have stayed with us."

"I have my reasons. How is Nicolette? Is she coming home today?"

Christina always had a soft spot for my brother and never could disappoint him. She turned away, which only incensed my brother.

"Woman, don't make me ask twice. What happened?" he yelled.

I yelled back, "Don't call my wife 'woman.' She has a name."

He talked right over me and placed his hands on his hips, demanding an answer from my wife.

Christina responded, "She had a rough night but is better this morning. I don't want to get into it right now. Here comes her doctor."

"Fine. I'll be back in ten minutes."

Thank God for small miracles and sending us Dr. Jonas right at that moment. Telling Jack about Nicolette would make him completely lose it. He was barely hanging on as it is.

245

"Mr. and Mrs. Vanelle, here are your daughter's discharge papers. I just left her and went over instructions for her post-op care. First and foremost, she needs rest. Her scans showed no active bleeds from the head trauma she endured, which is great news. You will have to bring her back for her suture removal, and it can be on the same day as her first therapy session. Per our conversation and with your permission, I have gone ahead and scheduled that appointment. Everything you need is here in this folder."

"Thank you so much for taking care of our daughter."

"It was my pleasure. She is an incredibly brave young woman. She's going to need a lot of time and patience from you as she heals and tries to make sense of this terrible tragedy. Sadly, she's not my first patient to have gone through this. Some were not so fortunate. Give yourselves some time to heal as a family."

"Thank you," we both said. My wife appeared so tired, as I welcomed her in for a hug. I told her, "We will make it through this. We just have to...What the fuck?" I shouted over her shoulder.

"Mason? What's wrong?"

"You have a lot of nerve showing up here. You need to leave," I shouted at Clayton, who casually walked over to us as if it was the most natural thing to do.

I looked around the hallway for any sign of Jack, but we were alone here.

"Mason, I just want a few minutes of your time. I'm truly sorry and heartbroken over what happened to Nicolette. There will never be enough words to express how deeply sorry I am, and to have to live with knowing my son is responsible for her pain."

"Clayton, there are not enough apologies in the world to make up for what your son did. It was incomprehensible, and I will not rest until he is punished for the crimes he has committed against my daughter."

"Mason, I see that you are upset, but I came here today in hopes of trying to reason with you and hope to find a resolution to this unfortunate circumstance."

"Unfuckingbelievable! He fucking raped my daughter!" I lost it. I did the one act that I always judged my brother for. I pulled my fist back and in a rage punched Clayton St. Clair straight in the mouth. He stumbled backward but caught his footing.

"Mason! Stop this. Haven't we suffered enough? You are just going to make a bad situation worse," my wife pleaded.

"Really? Because I think our daughter being raped and having to live with her new reality is pretty bad. I don't think things can get any worse."

"Sure, they can. He hasn't met me yet," Jack interjected. We stepped back and watched in horror as Jack backed Clayton up against the wall and caged him in. *Fucking A! Jack is back. And for once, I would agree with him.* "So, this is Clayton St. Clair, whom I've heard so much about."

He tried not to look intimidated by Jack, but who was he kidding? Jack had the power to make you shit yourself with just a cold glare on a good day.

"Yes, that would be me. Who the hell are you?" he asked, and then he pulled a handkerchief from his pocket to wipe his bloody lip that I was responsible for.

"My name is Jack Vanelle, Mason's brother. I'm also the uncle of the most precious and wonderful girl in the world, Nicolette. You know her, right? She is the innocent girl that your pig of a son raped, which makes you that piece of shit's father. Isn't that right, Mason?" he said, sending me one of his cold glares.

Clayton managed to shove off the wall and away from Jack. "I don't have to listen to this. I came here today on good faith, trying to make amends."

Hearing those words made Jack see red. He put his hands up to me and then focused all his energy back on Clayton. "Amends? The only amends that I will ever be able to live with is knowing your pig of a son is dead."

"What? Get out of my way!" We watched him try to move past Jack, but my brother shoved him back against the wall and held him in place.

"I wasn't finished. You are not going anywhere until I am done," he said through gritted teeth. "Your son committed an act of violence against my niece. He took her innocence against her will. Do you have any idea how that makes me feel? To know that he put his dirty hands on my girl! One way or another, your boy will pay and suffer for what he has done. I will not rest until he gets everything he deserves, and I will enjoy every minute of his suffering."

"I don't care who you are. I will not yield to your threats, and I don't scare easily. My son will be dealt with for his actions."

"Oh, you're right about that, St. Clair. He *will* be dealt with."

With one last shove, Jack released him and left. Clayton cleared his throat and fixed his tie. He tried to play it off, but we knew different. He never gave us a second glance and left through the same doors Jack did.

"Well, that was scary and intense. Mason, are you okay?"

"Scary doesn't even begin to describe what just happened here. He's untouchable, Christina, and that's when he is most dangerous. Come, let's take our daughter home."

Michael

John reviewed everything with me. "Okay, I think that covers everything. I will meet you down at processing, and it is my hope that we can expedite your arraignment, but with this case in the hands of Prosecutor Jennings, it's highly unlikely. He's going to want you to sweat it out for the night. Let's take it one step at a time. Michael, you keep your eyes open and don't turn your back on anything or anyone."

"Yeah, thanks for the tip," I said.

"I mean it, watch your back."

I looked up at the clock and watched the minutes tick by until it was time to go. I closed my eyes and leaned back on my pillow to calm my nerves. His words worked on me, and I was beginning to feel nervous. The door opened, and a man entered my room. He was a big dude, probably around 6'3" in height, maybe taller. He didn't look too friendly, and as I went to hit my call button, he lunged forward and snatched it away from me.

"Who the hell are you?" I demanded to know. "Where is my guard?" He placed a piece of tape over my mouth, and I was now silenced. I was trapped with nowhere to run.

"Now that I have your attention, asking me who I am is not important. Did you think you could just rape my beautiful girl and not expect to be punished for it? Think again, rich boy, because what's coming for you will be nothing like the pain you inflicted on that poor, defenseless young girl. You are a pig, and do you want to know what happens to pigs? Hmmm?"

My eyes widened as I watched the scary stranger pull a blade from his pocket. He taunted me with it as he placed the cold metal against my cheek, and then down my neck, where he stopped at the base of my throat. I felt the heaviness of the blade and the pressure against my skin, not knowing what he would do next.

"Pigs get slaughtered. No one will be able to save you. Not your rich daddy or his money. You are lucky to still be breathing. Had I known of you sooner, you wouldn't be."

He continued to glide the blade back and forth on my neck until he dropped it and grabbed my throat, restricting my airway.

He leaned in as close as he could and whispered in the coldest tone I had ever heard, "Michael St. Clair, you will suffer greatly for what you did to my Nicolette, just not today."

He released my throat and slapped my face, as he ripped the tape from my mouth. I coughed and struggled to breathe as he walked out from my room.

Nicolette

My mom helped me pack my things and then arranged for my flowers to be delivered to all the patients throughout my floor. The only bouquet I kept was the one from Simon. I missed him so much, though it had only been a few hours since he left. I promised I would call him once I was home and settled. I reserved the usual eye roll and snarky comment because I didn't have a clue on how I would be once I walked through my front door. I just knew I wanted to get out of this hospital and never come back here again.

My father pushed my wheelchair, with my mom walking alongside us. We waited for the elevator, and then I heard my mother gasp. I looked up to see what was wrong, and then I knew. My father seethed with anger as we watched Michael come down the hall, accompanied by Detective Westphall and a uniformed police officer. Dad let go of my chair and charged at Michael, but he was restrained by another police officer who arrived just in time to stop my father from hitting Michael.

"That's enough, Mr. Vanelle. I know you want your pound of flesh, but this is not the way. I promise you, he will not be able to get near your daughter again. Take her home and concentrate on your family."

"It's easy for you to say. It wasn't your baby girl he raped."

"Mason, let's go." My mother took his hand and led him into the elevator.

I tried to keep my eyes down, not wanting to look at Michael, but that didn't stop him from calling out to me.

He said, "Nicolette, I love you!" Before my father could respond, the doors closed, and then he was gone.

"Mason, what were you thinking? Don't we have enough to worry about with Jack, and now you going around hitting people is going to make a bad situation worse."

"Christina!" he shouted.

I asked, "What is going on? What are you not telling me? And what does Uncle Jack have to do with this?"

"I'm sorry, baby, so sorry," he said as he knelt down in front of me, showing me so much emotion. He was crying, and it broke my heart to see him in so much pain. He placed his head down and continued to cry out. "I failed you, Nicolette, and I don't know how to come to terms with that."

"Daddy, you didn't. Don't you know how much I love you? Let's just go home and try to pick up the pieces."

He said nothing more, nor did he answer my questions about Uncle Jack. I knew we would have to talk about what was troubling my father, but for now, it would have to wait.

My father carried my bag, and mom insisted to help me inside. She looped her arm around mine, and we walked in together. I didn't need it, but this was me allowing her to help.

Once inside, Gracie hurried over but was cautious not to crowd me. She had tears in her eyes, and I wasn't going to deny her a hug. I walked forward, and then she pulled me in. I knew she was another one in my life who loved and silently cried for me.

"I'm okay, Gracie," I whispered.

"Okay, Gracie, let her come up for air. Nicolette is tired and needs to rest. Is her room ready?"

"Yes, Mr. Vanelle."

"Perfect. Please bring her things upstairs to her room, and we will be up shortly."

"Dad, I can manage just fine. If you continue to treat me like a fragile piece of glass, then I will for sure shatter. Let's try to find our normal, okay?"

He smiled, "Okay."

I was just about to follow Gracie upstairs, and that's when he popped out from the living room.

"Uncle Jack!" I shouted. Without hesitation, I ran and jumped right into his strong arms. Uncle Jack held me as tight as he could, and I didn't want him to let me go. I missed him so much, and having him here was what I wanted most but was afraid to ask because of my father and what I overheard.

"Oh, my sweet girl. Let me look at you." He put me down but didn't let go of my hands. He had tears in his eyes as he looked me over, and when his eyes found the faint marks that were visible, his features hardened. He held my face and pulled me back in, kissing my forehead. "I need to know, are you okay?"

"No, I'm not, but I will be. Are you staying with me?"

"Is that a serious question? There is no place I'd rather be, nor is anything more important than you. I will stay for as long as you need me to."

I cried on his shoulders, as he held me. I told him that I wanted him to stay forever. I didn't miss the worried glances between my father and mother.

"Listen, you just got home, and I'm not going anywhere. Why don't you go upstairs and rest? We will have plenty of time to talk when you're feeling up to it."

I didn't want to leave him, but I sensed that whatever was going on between my parents and him was not for me to know.

Mason

I waited until I was sure our daughter was in her room before I tackled yet another hard conversation with my brother. He fixed himself a drink and wore his usual hardened expression anytime we were at odds. I took a deep breath and tried my best to assure my wife that we could have an amicable conversation, especially with Nicolette right upstairs.

"Jack, where did you go after you left the hospital?"

He downed his drink and poured another. "Mason, it's of no importance to you. Don't worry about my whereabouts, and that goes for you too, Christina."

"That's just it, I do need to worry about it. Did you go after Michael St. Clair?"

"I think you need to be more specific."

"Don't play with me, Jack. You know exactly what I am asking. Did you hurt him?"

"Concerned about our daughter's rapist? That's great. Where was your concern for our daughter when that animal stalked her for months? Hmmm, Mason? I would really like to know."

"Dammit, Jack! Enough already. I will not stand here in my home and defend my love for Nicolette. Just answer my fucking question. Did you go after him?"

"Yes, I did. He's still alive if that's your next question."

"We know. We saw him as we were leaving the hospital. He tried to talk to Nicolette."

After I said the words, the look on my brother's face changed from hardened to complete rage. The glass that he tightened his hand around shattered, spreading broken glass all over the top of the bar.

"Jack! Your hand. Let me see." Christina rushed over to help him, but he refused her and grabbed a towel off the counter.

"I'm fine," he said through gritted teeth. He was anything but fine.

"Jack, she's okay. He didn't get close today, but I did. I caused another scene, but this time it was in front of Nicolette. I broke down in the elevator. I had never felt so helpless in all my life, but we've been assured that he will not get bail. No doubt, I'm sure there is probably a plan in place to get him out of the country, but he would have to be released first. He's locked up, and she's safe."

"It doesn't matter, Mason. Whether he's locked up or not, he will never be able to hurt her again. I will never allow it to happen. I have people in place to make sure of it."

"We won't either, Jack. You can call off the dogs. You need to allow the justice system to work."

"Yeah, right! I'll take my chances protecting her my way," he said and then poured one more shot.

"Jack, do you remember our conversation at all?"

"I do, Mason. I heard every word of it."

"But…did you listen? Because the way you are acting right now tells me that you didn't. I need to know that you will not do anything else. Let the courts handle this."

He completely ignored what I said and as usual talked right over me. "I need to call Sara. I want her to join me here, so we can both be close to Nickel."

Christina gave me a concerned look, and then I felt my stomach drop. This was the last thing we needed right now.

"What about the restaurant? You just can't up and leave your business."

"It's handled. I have plenty of trusted employees that are more than capable of looking out for my interests. My main concern is Nicolette, and I don't give a fuck about anything else."

I then turned to my wife. "Christina, would you mind giving me some time alone with Jack?"

"Sure, I'll go check on dinner. Jack, are you staying?" Christina directed her attention over to my brooding brother, who softened when he answered her.

"I would love to, but I'll leave that up to my brother after we finished talking."

"Jack, we love you. Please remember that."

"Look, before you ask me to leave, you can forget it. I am not leaving Nicolette. If you don't want me to share your home, that's fine. I'll make other arrangements, but I will not be too far away. One more thing, do not ask me to go home. I will not just bend at your will and leave her again. Do you understand? Massimo?"

"Do not call me by that name, Jack. Call me Mason, for fuck's sake!"

"Why, Massimo? Are you ashamed of it?"

"Your words, not mine. We may be brothers, but we lead and live very different lives. All that I am asking of you is to respect that, especially with my daughter."

"*Our* daughter! Isn't that what you meant to say? I have always respected you, brother, but it was you who disrespected me and my wishes. Had you left Nicolette with me and Sara, then this nightmare we are all living now would not have happened. My precious girl is upstairs beaten and broken, not just physically, but emotionally too. And all you can say is to not call you by the name you were given at birth? Get over yourself! Because I will address you any fucking way that I want."

This was going nowhere and getting worse by the minute. "Our only concern is our daughter. I will not continue to argue or justify my reasons for anything with you. I am done, Jack, and whether you want to admit this or not, I know what's best for her."

"Which is what…keeping the truth from her? She's my daughter just as much as she is yours. You took her from me, and I had no choice but to let you. You destroyed me, brother. I love that girl more than life itself, and you took her from me so you could move out here. And for what? Tell me."

"Stop it, Jack." I never sounded so defeated.

"The hell I will. You had an extraordinary life back in Chicago. You were already successful, but you got greedy and wanted to play with the big boys. Look around, Massimo." He gestured around the room with his hands in the air. "This is what you've got. A broken home and a broken child. Our precious girl. Our beautiful girl that you neglected and didn't protect!"

"Uncle Jack?" she shakily said. We both turned around and were stunned to see that Nicolette was standing there. I went to her, but she put her hands up to stop me. I looked over my shoulder and glared at my brother.

"Nicolette, please?" I begged. I just wanted to hold her, but she stepped back and it felt as if there was this huge wall between us. She had never heard us arguing, at least not like this. I only prayed she didn't hear the truth that I tried so hard to protect her from.

"I heard you screaming at each other. What the hell is going on between you two? This is supposed to be my safe place, remember? I don't feel very safe at the moment, especially when the two men who I love most in the world are at odds with one another. I know I am the reason behind it, and I'm so sorry for that, but I just can't deal with anything else. Please stop fighting, and work out whatever differences you have. I love and need you both," she said through her tears and then turned away from us.

I called out for her, but she went back to her room, adding one hard slam of her door, effectively blocking us out.

Seventeen

Nicolette

"**H**ey beautiful, I was hoping to hear from you." Just the sound of Simon's voice calmed me. He called me "beautiful" as if I would ever feel that way again. I tried hard to bite back the tears after he said the words that always made me feel special.

"Simon, I miss you," I whispered, as I was on the verge of tears.

"Say the word, and I will leave my house right now to see you."

"I wish, but I can't. Everything is a mess. My Uncle Jack is here, and any other time, I would be over the moon, but he's fighting with my father. I just want them to stop."

"Do you have your iPod with you?"

"I do."

"Okay, scroll through the playlists, and you will find one that's marked, 'Simon loves Nicolette.' I added a song for all the times that I missed you."

"Simon…110 songs? You are too much."

"I guess I missed you a lot."

"I missed you too, and I want to see you."

"You will. Just take some time tonight to rest and be with your family. Whatever is going on with your father and uncle, I'm sure they will figure it out. You just concentrate on getting well. The gang is dying to see you, especially the girls." He hesitated. "Um, Nicolette?"

"What's wrong?"

"I told them about the rape. There was no way I could hide it from them. Please don't be upset with me."

"I'm not upset, nor could I ever be. I love you and our crazy mix of friends. They've been calling, but I'm just not ready to talk. I wouldn't know where to begin."

"They understand. They wanted me to tell you how much they miss and love you. They'll be here when you're ready." *Ready? Will I ever be?* "I can't think about school right now, not with Michael's arraignment coming up. I haven't heard anything, so I'm assuming it will be tomorrow. After tomorrow, everyone will know what happened to me."

"Nicolette, I wish I could hold you right now and tell you that everything is going to be okay, but I'm not sure how to. All I can say is that I love you and we're going to get through this."

I wanted to say more, but I looked up and saw my father standing silently in my doorway. "Simon, my dad is here. Can we talk later?"

"Of course. I love you."

"I love you too."

I ended my call and invited my father in. He looked tired, so very tired. Who was I kidding? He looked more defeated than anything else. He sat beside me and let out a deep sigh.

"May I hug you?" he asked.

At first, I thought it was strange for him to ask, but then it wasn't. They acted this way in the hospital too, not knowing how I would react to being touched after being raped by Michael. I wasn't afraid then, and I'm not now.

I sat up on my knees and hugged my dad as hard as I could. He didn't know that I overheard his first argument over Uncle Jack, and he probably wasn't sure how much I heard of this one. I knew he was struggling and wanted to tell me. It was there, so close that I could feel it on him. Something that had been a weight on him.

I pulled away, looked directly into his eyes, and asked him point blank, "Is Uncle Jack, my father?"

He replied weakly, "Yes, he is."

"Feel better?"

"What? I'm not sure what you mean?"

"You just confirmed what I always suspected to be true."

"How did you know?"

When I went on to explain my reasons behind my suspicions, my father seemed very surprised by them. I looked more like Uncle Jack. Although they are brothers, I carried a stronger resemblance to Jack. For years, I believed that my mom may have had an affair, and I was the secret love child she played off as Mason's, instead of Jack's. Why break-up two marriages and hurt innocent people like my dad and Aunt Sara? Yes, it may have sounded a bit improbable, but he told me that I couldn't have been more wrong.

"Nicolette, if you are ready to hear the truth, then I want to be the one to tell you." I saw the pain behind my father's eyes and knew he was hurting. I was too and would sit and listen to whatever he had to say, no matter how hard it was to hear it.

"We wanted a baby, and although we tried for over a year to get pregnant, we were not able to conceive. Mom had a series of tests performed, and I did too. Her results were all normal, but mine proved to show that I was sterile and would not be able to father children. At the time, we believed our dream of becoming parents was simply over. We never entertained the idea of anything beyond your mom carrying a child of our own."

"How does Uncle Jack fit into all of this?"

"Jack offered to be our donor. You see, Aunt Sara had undergone a hysterectomy when she was in her early twenties due to a rare cancer that destroyed any chance of her and Jack having children of their own. When we made Jack aware of what was happening with us, he then approached Sara with the possibility of being a donor for us. Nicolette, when faced with losing the one person you love more than anything in the world, and you were powerless to help them, it changes you. I watched my brother suffer through a great deal of pain when Sara was sick, and then one day, she wasn't. Jack felt that he had been blessed with a miracle from God himself and never wanted to waste a minute of the gift he had been given."

"Why didn't they ever adopt?"

"I guess Sara didn't want to tempt fate. As happy as they were about being in remission, she also feared that her cancer could come back. If it had, and they did have a child, she didn't want to leave their son or daughter motherless. I believe they were just happy she was alive and they still had a life to look forward to together. After they traveled the world, another dream came true. They called it The Neighborhood Bar and Grille. And that's where he fits in."

"Daddy, I know there's more. What are you not telling me?"

"Nicolette, I have already told you more than I ever believed I would. Please, let's drop it."

"No, I don't think I can. What you don't know is that when I was in the hospital, I overheard you talking to mom about Uncle Jack, more like screaming at her. You were so angry. I had never heard you speak to her like that. You acted like you were afraid of him, or feared he may do something that would get him into trouble. Why is he so angry with you?"

"It's so complicated."

"It's not like I'm going anywhere. Daddy, you need to tell me all of it."

"Jack is my big brother. He was always there for me, and for your grandparents. My parents worked so hard to provide us with a good life, but it wasn't always enough no matter how much they tried. Jack worked odd jobs around the city and did some things that were questionable, to say the least, but that's his story to tell, not mine. My relationship with my brother is my own, as is yours with him. They are different, and I never wanted one to affect or come between the other. Do you understand?"

"Yes, daddy."

"Your uncle is a good man. He always tried to be a good son and brother to me. When I met your mother, I knew my heart would forever be connected with hers. We shared our mutual love for music and our work. Jack always supported our dreams, and there were many times I wished I could have been a better brother to him. When he agreed to help make our dream come true, it was the most generous and selfless act of kindness he has ever shown me. The only thing he ever asked in return was to be a part of your life. To live in your life and help us raise you. It's all he ever asked, and to this day, I will never be able to repay him for it."

After I wiped away my tears, I asked my father the very question he was having trouble answering. "Dad, what you've said explains a lot, but not why he is so angry with you now."

"Nicolette, I knew this day would come when I would have to tell you the truth, but not like this. He's left me with no choice, and I don't like it. Jack is very angry with me and your mother. When we made the decision to leave Chicago, something just broke in him. He masked his pain and hid his true feelings on how he felt about our move to California and what it meant for you. He begged me to leave you behind, but there was no way I would have ever agreed to that. He pushed and pushed, and then I pushed back. I reminded him who you belonged to, and it crushed him. I had only witnessed my brother cry once before, and that was when our mother died. He's angry because I took you away from him. I broke the promise that I made to him. And now he blames me for what happened to you. If I had allowed you to remain in Chicago with Jack and Sara, then this horrible act of violence you had to endure wouldn't have happened. As your father, it was my job to protect you. Nicolette, from the moment you were conceived, I promised my brother that I would always love and protect you. When you needed me the most, I didn't do that. Jack is right. I failed you, and that is one truth that I am going to have to live with for the rest of my life."

"No! he's wrong." I lunged forward into my father's arms and held him. He was crying. I was crying. "Don't you ever say those words to me again. What happened to me could have happened anywhere. I will not allow you to blame yourself. I have so much guilt inside of me, and I don't know what to do with it. I should have been honest with you. I should have told someone about Michael. This is on me, daddy, not you."

"No, Nicolette, don't say that. Listen to me. You didn't do anything wrong. This is on Michael, and him alone. I promise you that we are going to do everything in our power to see that justice is served."

He continued to hold me and do everything he could to comfort me, but I was at the lowest point of my life right now, and I didn't want to be held anymore. *My father blames himself, and I blame myself. He would have to search his soul for the absolution he needs to find his peace, as I would have to do the same. I knew I was loved. My family is amazing and there has never been a day that they didn't say it or show their love and devotion for me, but today it feels as if I am being suffocated by it.* I sat back and pulled my knees up to my chest.

"Daddy, you need to leave now."

The look on his face showed me that I had broken him even more, but I was exhausted. He placed a kiss on my head, and I jerked away. I didn't want to, but I was doing everything I could to hold it together. He told me that he loved me and then walked out of my room with his head down. I needed sleep. I didn't second guess my decision to take a valium that was prescribed to me. After all the revelations from tonight, all I wanted to do was quiet my mind.

I hit play on my iPod and drifted off to the songs that Simon had selected for me. The songs that made him think of me. The songs that were his words when he couldn't be with me to say them himself. I hugged my pillow, and when I closed my eyes, he was there smiling back at me. He was here with me in my dreams and kept the nightmares away, at least for tonight.

"I love you, Simon," I said, as I closed my eyes and dreamed of him.

Eighteen

Michael

Waking up to the reality that I just spent my first night in jail was surreal to me. I was lucky to have gotten any sleep at all with the combination of the smells and the sounds from inmates in neighboring cells.

This place is disgusting. I have to get out of here.

My head throbbed with a dull ache, as my stomach grumbled from hunger. I needed a hot shower and a decent meal. I was not going to spend one more night in this hell hole. I splashed some cold water on my face and saw the faint marks on my neck. Yeah, that was pleasant. Earlier, I was nearly choked to death by some guy who had to be connected to Nicolette. He kept saying over and over again how I hurt his girl, but he was wrong. I loved Nicolette, and I had to see her. I needed to know that she was okay.

A guard banged on the bars of my cell and told me to step back as he opened it. My lawyer arrived, and I was taken to a holding area to wait for my arraignment. John opened his briefcase and began to go over what would happen today. He asked me what my plea was as if he didn't know. I planned on pleading "Not Guilty," because it was the truth. He took his glasses off and held the bridge of his nose before addressing me.

"Michael, I was hoping you would consider a possible plea deal if it's offered."

"No. No deal."

"Be reasonable, Michael. The prosecutor's case is strong. They have compiled a long list of charges against you, and they have an equal amount of evidence collected to prove their rape case. Before we go before the judge, you need to understand what you are facing here."

I tuned him out as he droned on about my case. I kept telling myself that what happened with Nicolette was consensual. She got scared and freaked out, which led to a physical altercation, but not rape. I wouldn't believe it any other way. I loved her.

"Michael, are you listening to me? Your father has arrived. I will go meet him and bring him back here. Think about what I said, okay?"

"Yeah, whatever." I didn't have to think. I knew I was innocent.

Nicolette

"ood morning, how did you sleep?" my father asked as he sipped his coffee. I gave my body a much-needed stretch, sat up, and took the other cup he was holding. "I figured you might need it after last night."

Why is that? Because you told me that the uncle that I have loved all my life is really my bio dad? Yeah, I may need something stronger than coffee. No, I couldn't hurt him like that, so I said nothing.

"Nicolette, I'm going to be leaving in a few minutes for Michael's arraignment. The prosecutor phoned me early this morning, and it's happening within the hour."

"I know. Simon's father made some calls and knew the judge that would oversee the proceedings today."

"Do you want to talk about anything before I go?"

"No, I'm fine. I just want to be alone, if that's okay."

"No, but I'll respect your wishes. I love you. Mom and Uncle Jack are downstairs. If you're feeling up to it, maybe join them for breakfast, or I can have Gracie bring a tray up for you."

"Okay." A one-word answer was all that I could handle at the moment. He was trying, and I loved him for that, but I needed a second to breathe. I finished my coffee and I was about to call Simon when my phone rang. It wasn't his ringtone. Without looking at the number, I just answered it.

"Nicolette, are you there?" *OMG! It's Michael, but how is he able to call me, when he's in jail?* "You don't have to talk to me. I just wanted to tell you that I love you."

My heart was racing and my skin heated. Who the fuck does he think he is, calling me so casually as if all is well, and he didn't ruin my life? A life that was pretty close to perfect until he came into it.

When I finally found my voice, it wasn't pretty. "Love? You don't know shit about love, but hate, you do. That's one emotion you have mastered."

"No, Nicolette, you're wrong. I do love you."

"NO! Monsters don't love, and that's exactly what you are. You are a monster who preyed upon and savagely raped me. Love is the furthest thing from my mind when it comes to you. I hate you. Do you hear me, Michael St. Clair? I hate you. I hate you. I hate you."

As I screamed into the phone, my father, along with Uncle Jack and mom, rushed through my door. I was shaking uncontrollably by the time my father grabbed the phone from my hand.

"How dare you call my daughter!" he shouted, but the line went dead.

I fell to my knees and cried. Uncle Jack rushed over to my side and picked me up from the floor, carrying me back to my bed. My father looked lost as I allowed Uncle Jack to comfort me instead of him. Michael's phone call unraveled the safety net I found within my home.

"Uncle Jack, he found me. It was Michael calling me. I'm not safe here. I have to get out of this house. Please, Uncle Jack, don't let him hurt me again." He tightened his arms around me and then looked over his shoulder to my father. The look they had exchanged gave me a feeling of uneasiness, but I couldn't think about their issues now. Michael had called me, and all I wanted to do was to run and hide in a place that he could never find and hurt me again.

"Nicolette, we have you, and you are safe. I don't know how he managed to get his hands on a phone, but I promise that you will not be hearing from him again. I am going to call Prosecutor Jennings right now," my father said as he knelt down before me.

I was still with Uncle Jack, burying my tear stained face in his chest. I couldn't stop shaking. My father kissed my mom goodbye and then left to go down to the courthouse.

It took me a few minutes to catch my breath, and I thought Uncle Jack may have needed that as well. He wasn't saying anything, and when I finally moved off his lap, his face was hard and angry.

"I'm sorry for scaring you. His call just took me by surprise."

"Baby, you have nothing to be sorry for. I will never allow that bastard to hurt you again, do you hear me?"

"Yes, Uncle Jack." He looked at me with pained eyes? *Did he expect me to call him dad? I didn't know if I could ever do that.*

"Jack," mom tapped him on his shoulder. "Why don't we let Nicolette get dressed, and then we can all have something to eat, okay?"

"Are you okay? Do you need me to stay?" he asked me.

"I'm better now, thank you. I'll be down soon."

Once they left, I locked my door and then cried into my pillow. He called me. He actually called me and once again used words that he had no right to say to me. I felt dirty just thinking about it and took the hottest shower I could endure without burning my skin.

I walked into the kitchen, and all conversations and movement stopped. I took a seat at the counter and addressed the elephant in the room. "You can all stop staring at me. I'm not going to flip out. I just want to eat breakfast. Can we do that?"

Gracie handed me a plate full of pancakes, eggs, and bacon, along with a tall glass of juice. I was so hungry, I practically inhaled the food.

"Nicolette, we need to talk. Will you talk to me?" he asked. I dropped my fork to my plate, causing it to make a loud clattering sound. *I wasn't doing this right now, especially with these two double-teaming me.*

"Look, I'm not sure what you expect me to say, nor what you want from me, but as far as I'm concerned, nothing has changed.

I've already heard the story from daddy. I don't need to hear it again."

"Sweetheart, it's so much more than that, if you would please just give me a chance."

"Uncle Jack, the truth is, I have always suspected that you were my father. I thought you and mom had a secret affair, and she had pawned me off as my father's child instead of yours."

"Nicolette! How could you believe that?"

"I don't really know, it was just a feeling."

"Why didn't you ever say anything to us?"

"I didn't want to hurt our family, and I love daddy too much to ever destroy him with something that might have been true. No matter how I felt, I kept quiet and loved you both."

Uncle Jack was quiet and looked unsure of what to say next, but then mom asked me if I had any questions, and then I was done. "If it's all the same to you, I've had enough of family bonding time. You all need to just give me some time to process all of this. Have you forgotten what I've been through this past week? I was raped. I just found out that my uncle is really my bio dad, and just when I was beginning to feel safe, my rapist calls me this morning and once again professed his obsessive love for me. I think it's safe to say 'I have a lot to deal with right now' is an understatement, don't you agree?"

I tried fighting back my tears, but it was no use. I whispered, "Sorry" as I grabbed my keys and walked out the door. The expression on Uncle Jack's face was just too painful to look at. I regretted my words immediately, but it was out there now and I couldn't take them back. Mom called out to me, but I ignored her and sped off. I knew where I was headed and who I wanted to see.

Michael

I was led into the courtroom in handcuffs, in full sight of spectators watching and judging me. The press was not allowed in here, but I saw flashes of light from the photographers that were shoved away by the court officers. The door closed with a loud sounding thud.

I glanced over to see my lawyer in a heated exchange with who I believed was the prosecutor. I had only been allowed to visit with John and my father. Their conversation ended, and he took a seat at our table.

I asked, "You look upset, John. Are you sure you are the right man to handle my case?"

He gave me an incredulous look before answering me. "You know, I'm not so sure after that stunt you pulled this morning. Her father has reported the call you placed to his daughter, and now that man over there plans on burying you with it today. I'm not sure if I can say anything in your defense that will help your case. You did this to yourself."

I clenched my jaw and leaned in for no one else to hear what I would say, "You will get me released today on bond, do you hear me? Do your fucking job, and stop whining about it."

He muttered a curse under his breath and said nothing more. My eyes scanned the room and then were locked with Mason Vanelle's. If looks had the power to kill, then I would be dead right now.

The judge entered, and the room was called to attention. I stood quietly and listened to the charges against me. They included rape under the California Penal Code 261 in the first degree. It was combined with aggravated force and violence against the alleged victim. Other charges were stalking and various sexual misdemeanor counts.

I began to sweat as the prosecutor continued to list in great detail the crimes I had committed against Nicolette, although her name was never mentioned in today's hearing. He kept calling her my "victim," which made my stomach roll with revulsion. It was John's turn to refute the charges. After he concluded with his argument, the judge asked me to state my plea.

I responded, "Not Guilty," and the courtroom erupted into chaos after my lawyer requested bail on my behalf. I looked over to witness a strong reaction from Mason Vanelle. A clerk leaned in close to him and then he visibly calmed. The judge slammed his gavel down and quieted the entire room.

"I have never granted bail in a class one rape/sexual assault case before, and I will not begin today. Your request for bail is denied. You, Michael St. Clair, will return to custody in the L.A. County Jail to await trial." He looked away from me and then called the next case.

John said, "It's going to be okay, Michael. I'll work it out."

Before I could respond, I was being led away by two court officers, and then I saw her. Nicolette was standing against the back wall of the crowded courtroom. She stood in an enraged stance, as she stared at me with burning hate in her beautiful eyes.

Nicolette

I had already planned in my head how I would react if Michael had been granted bail, but thankfully, he wasn't. When he looked at me, I wanted him to see exactly how I felt about him and never be confused that I felt anything but pure hate for him after what he had done.

I drove not knowing where I would end up, and then acting on natural instinct, I parked my car in the lot that was used for the beach goers who owned cabanas at the club. I walked past the Paulson's, and my heart skipped a beat, remembering the last time I was here with Simon. I remembered how he held me when we danced to our song and then kissed me senselessly until I was out of breath. I wanted him so much that night, but he held back and assured me that our time was coming to us. *It's not anymore, is it?*

How could Simon ever want me again after what Michael did to me? I closed my eyes and tried to focus on Simon's beautiful face, but then it faded to black and all I saw was the frightening images of Michael and then my cries as he raped me.

"Why are you here? What are you doing?" I practically shouted to myself with no one in sight to hear me, just like that night. I'm sure my therapist would have a field day analyzing why I decided to return to the scene of the crime. I had nothing to gain by being here. All it represented now were memories of my assault and the extreme pain I was in.

I held out hope that the good memories I shared here with Simon and our friends would outweigh the bad. I fell in love here. Simon Paulson found a way into my heart while I broke his. Walking further down the beach, I saw that his boat was gone and the slip was empty. It was getting late, and the seagulls were feasting on the remnants of the day's bait.

The sounds of the ocean had always soothed me. I almost wished that Simon was out there surfing, and I was sitting here on the shore waving him in. Yeah, no. There were no happy memories here, just the ones that that reminded me of the life I once had, the same life that was taken from me. I prayed that I would survive this somehow and it wouldn't break and destroy who I used to be.

Nineteen

Simon

Looking at my phone every five seconds made my heart race. I couldn't concentrate, and school was the last place I wanted to be. I bailed on my track meet and knew I would have to deal with the wrath of my coach, but I didn't care. All I wanted was Nicolette, and she wasn't returning any of my calls or texts.

Sam practically dragged me down to the quad to join the rest of our friends for lunch, but I couldn't eat. I couldn't do anything but think of my girl. After the girls greeted and hugged me, Alexis said, "She hasn't called us, Simon."

"I know," I replied. "You have to give her time. When she's ready, she'll come back to us."

"What about you, Simon? How are you dealing with all of this?" asked Bailey. Her voice was layered with concern.

"I'm doing the best I can. I'm trying to hold it together for Nicolette and be anything she needs me to be to help her get through this. You just can't imagine what it did to me when I found her that night and saw what he had done to her."

"Oh, Simon, it must have been awful."

"Bailey, you don't know the half of it. She was beating the hell out of him while her body was naked, torn, and beaten from what that animal did to her. It was a horrific scene. Once I had her in my arms, her blood was all over me, then she just closed her eyes, and I freaked out. I thought she was dying in my arms. I was sickened by all of it and what she suffered through. God! Bailey, if I had just gotten there a few minutes earlier, I could have stopped him. I would have killed him dead. My beautiful girl was hurt, and I did nothing to help her."

Without thought, Bailey took me in her arms and hugged me with her arms practically cutting off my circulation. She was crying and pleaded with me to stop blaming myself for what happened to Nicolette.

"Simon, you can't go through this again," Jameson chimed in. "We all watched you suffer and blame yourself over Jennifer. This situation that's happening with Nicolette has the ability to rip your fucking heart out."

I turned away and then shouted, "It already has. Don't you all get it? What Michael did to Nicolette can never be undone. Don't worry about me. Focus on Nicolette, and how hurt she is. I'm so in love with her, and I am afraid that he has destroyed what we were trying to build with each other. Before this happened, every time I looked into her eyes or held her in my arms, I couldn't imagine my future without her in it. And now? I just don't know what is going to happen."

I finally surrendered to my pain and fell down to the ground, wanting the earth to swallow me up. The girls wrapped themselves around me as I tried to fight against their love and support, but that only made them hug me tighter. Once the guys joined in, I was practically tackled by all of them.

"Okay!" I shouted. "You can get off me now. If you break my back, you can tell the coach why I can't run anymore."

Bailey gave me another hug and looped her arm inside of mine as we took a seat under the tree. I only wanted Nicolette's arms around me, but she wasn't here, and our friends were. They asked me if she would return to school, and I honestly didn't know how to answer their questions. For all I knew, she could have been on a plane back to Chicago by now.

The last bell rang, and this fucked up day was over. I dropped my stuff off in my locker and carefully avoided the coach and my teammates. I would deal with them tomorrow, but for now, all I wanted to do was get on my Harley and ride.

Sam caught up to me as I was about to take off. He looked worried, but I assured him that I wasn't going to do anything stupid. He knew me best and realized that I needed to clear my head and riding my motorcycle was the best way to do that.

I stopped at the Juice Bar to grab a burger, and then lost my appetite when I saw our booth, and another couple occupying it. *Where are you, baby?* I thought, as I walked out from the restaurant and continued on my ride.

My heart stopped when I saw her car and where it was parked. Nicolette was here somewhere on this beach. I parked my bike and began looking for her. I checked the entire Beach Club and then down at the marina. I couldn't imagine why she would come here, but I had to check anyway. There was no sign of her, but her car was here, so I knew she couldn't have gone far. I jogged up and down the beach until I saw a flash of pink through the sand dunes.

I slowly made my way up the hill, and sure enough, it was my angel. She was curled up and sound asleep between the two dunes. If it wasn't for the bright colored hooded sweatshirt she was wearing, I might have missed her.

I blinked back my tears, as I tucked her hair behind her ear that had fallen over her cheek. She looked so beautiful. I prayed she was dreaming of good things. I didn't want to scare her, as I tried to remain quiet until she awakened on her own. The sun was setting and the temperature began to cool down.

I waited fifteen minutes, and then she slowly opened her eyes to see me beside her. She blinked a few times, with her long eyelashes feathering her cheeks. She looked around and realized it was only me that was here with her.

"How did you find me?" she asked.

"Don't you know? I will always find you because I love you. Your heart is forever connected with mine."

One tear fell down her beautiful rosy cheek and all I wanted to do was wipe it away, but I hesitated to touch her. I needed her permission, and she easily gave it to me with her beautiful eyes that answered my unspoken question. I ran my thumb across her face, as more tears fell.

"Baby, can I hold you?" I asked.

She hesitated at first and then let me do the very thing I wanted to do all day since I woke up. She nestled into her usual spot as I wrapped my arms around her. If I was certain of anything, I knew she belonged right here with me. I was never going to let her go again.

"Simon, we have to talk."

I responded to her question by pulling her closer to me. There would be no heavy conversations today, not if I could help it. All I wanted was to hold her, and I hoped that she wanted this just as much as I did. No, more like *needed* this intimacy between us. When she tried to move out of my arms, I naturally held on, but then she asked, and I let her go. I didn't want to scare her and tried with all my heart to be gentle, knowing how fragile she was. We both sat up and across from each other.

She had tears in her eyes when she whispered the words, I feared the most. "I can't see you anymore, Simon." The pain was written all over her face as she struggled with her words.

"No! Nicolette, I will never let you go."

Her face went ashen, and she pulled further away from me.

"What's wrong, baby? You're shaking," I said as I tried to move closer, but she pulled away again.

"I'm sorry. I don't know what's wrong with me. I have to go."

When she got up to leave, I practically sprang up on my feet. "Please, don't go. Stay and talk with me. I need to know what I did. What scared you back there?"

"I guess it was just the words you said."

"What? What did I say?"

I watched her deeply inhale while staring out at the breaking waves coming in along the shore. "You said you would never let me go. Simon, he said the same thing to me. He said it to me for months, but never more than the night I cried no."

Shattered...

"Nicolette, look at me."

I didn't want to push her, but I needed her eyes on me when I said the next words to her. She slowly turned around, and my heart nearly broke in half. She looked so sad.

I told her, "I'm not him. I love you, Nicolette, and I would never hurt you. I said those words because it's just simply how I feel. You can't just walk into my life, turn it upside-down, and then walk out without me trying to make you stay. I will fight for you. I love you too much to just walk away."

"Don't you see? I have no choice. I won't hurt you any more than I already have. I have brought you nothing but pain, and you are too good of a person to be with someone like me."

What the fuck? Hold it together. She loves you, and you love her. This is her pain doing all the talking here, not your girl.

"Nicolette, I love you. You are not going to break up with me because I won't let you. How could you ever believe that you have caused me pain? I came alive the day we met, and my heart has been yours ever since. Please look at me." My fingers were itching to touch her, but I stepped back and waited.

"I am looking at you."

"No, you're looking through me. Baby, you can trust me, I promise you. When you look into my eyes, I want you to see how much I love you. Here, give me your hand." She did with no hesitation and allowed me to place it on my heart. "You feel that? That's you, baby. My heart beats for you. I know you love me. There's no point in denying what we feel because I feel everything you feel. I know you believe this too."

"You don't have a choice. No matter what you say, I am not going to change my mind. I have to let you go in order to save us both."

"Have you heard a word I have said? Nicolette, you will only cause me pain if you walk away from me. Please, I am begging you to trust me and the feelings that I have for you."

"It won't work. I'm too damaged to be with you."

"No, you are not!" I finally shouted and reached for my girl. I was holding her as if she would disappear at any moment. "Baby, you have been through a traumatizing act of violence, and you need time to heal and recover. I can't imagine how you are feeling, and I can only speak for me, but I know that I love you. No matter what, my feelings for you have not and will never change."

"Okay," she said.

"Okay? What does that mean?"

"It means that I believe you. You just stood there and begged me to believe you, so this is me doing just that."

"You can, Nicolette. I promise you."

"I believe you, Simon. That's why I'm still here. I'm so screwed up right now and feel as if I have disappointed every single person in my life. The guilt has pulled me so far down into this black hole that I fear I may never be able to climb out of. It scares me, babe, and I'm afraid that one emotion is all that I will ever feel."

I said nothing more and just held her until the sun set over the Pacific. I left my bike down at the club and drove her home in her car. I was exhausted, but I didn't care. We needed this time to work out our feelings, and I was just relieved that she was still here with me, and we were together. I carried her into her home and upstairs to her room without waking her. She slept so soundly in my arms. I took her shoes off and placed her underneath the blanket. Before I left, I placed a kiss on her cheek, just breathing her in as if she was my lifeline.

"I love you, Nicolette. Please don't give up on us. Stay with me, and trust your heart in my hands."

She whispered, "Okay," and then fell back asleep.

I felt a thousand times better since our talk at the beach. Her family was relieved that it was me who found her and brought her home. They didn't know where she had gone after leaving early this morning. I didn't know that part, but I didn't need to. We were together now, and before I left, I made that fact very clear to her family. I wasn't going anywhere. We were part of each other's lives, and that wasn't ever going to change.

Nicolette

When I opened my eyes, Simon was gone, but his words were still with me. I loved him so much. I rolled over to look at my phone. It was just after three in the morning, and I was wide awake and hungry. I went down to the kitchen to get something to eat, and then I turned around to find my father sitting in the dark at the breakfast bar.

"Daddy! You scared me," I said as I clutched my chest.

"Yeah, I know what that feels like. Why did you walk out on your mother yesterday? Where were you?" his tone was cold.

"Don't you know? I know you saw me there at the courthouse."

"Why? You had no business being there. God! Of all the places you could have gone, you chose the courthouse? Answer me! Why did you go to Michael's arraignment?"

"What the hell do you want from me? I had every right to be there, and no one was going to stop me. That animal raped me, and he stood there and pled not guilty. He still believes that he did nothing wrong. You can't imagine how that felt to hear him say those words."

"You're wrong. I feel everything. When I saw you standing in the back of the courtroom, I thought I was going to have a heart attack. I was terrified that the media would figure out who you were. You took a huge chance being there. When I finally got home and was told that you weren't here, I was scared. You weren't even supposed to be driving, and you just took off without telling anyone."

"Well, I guess the worst already happened to me, so what's a car accident to add to the list?"

"This is not a joke. How could you put us through that?"

"Do you see me laughing? I can't believe you are turning this around on me. I didn't want to hurt mom or Uncle Jack, but I felt as if I was drowning from the mountain of shit that was piled on top of me. They kept pressuring me to talk about how I felt about my biological beginnings, and all I wanted was to eat my fucking breakfast in peace."

"I'm so sorry. I didn't know."

"Why would they tell you? When it's easier to blame me? When I woke up yesterday morning, I didn't know that I would end up down there at the courthouse, but I did. I wanted to look into his eyes and see if there was even a shred of remorse, but there wasn't. I wasn't ready to go home yet, so I drove. Simon found me at the beach, and I pushed him away. I hurt him. I told him that I wanted to break up with him, didn't want to be with him. I did everything I could to push him away, and then he pushed back and told me that he loved me. He loved me so much and begged me to stay and trust him."

I continued, "Daddy, I also trust you. I know you love me, and Uncle Jack does too, but you are my father. Do you hear me? *You* are my father. My feelings for you have not changed, will never change, just because my DNA did. Finding out about Uncle Jack doesn't have to change us. I love you, daddy, and I've been so lucky to have you as my father—my only father."

"Thank you. You don't know how much I needed to hear you say that." He held his arms out to me like he had done a thousand times before, and I allowed him to hold me.

"I think I do. I love you."

"I love you more, so much more."

I wasn't going to push him away like I tried with Simon. Daddy needed to believe that I didn't blame him. I loved him. I knew he needed this time with me. He was always there for me, and now the roles were reversed, and I had to be strong for him.

By the time I climbed the stairs back to my room, I was beyond exhausted. I collapsed on my bed and listened to Simon's newest special playlist he added to my iPod. I loved the title, "Nicolette's way through my heart." I smiled and let the beautiful melodies take me to another place that was reserved for only Simon.

Twenty

Nicolette

After I hit the alarm for the umpteenth time, I padded my way into the bathroom to shower and get ready for school. I had been home for weeks now, recovering from my attack, and when I thought of Simon and how much I missed our friends, I knew I was ready to face the world again.

After our talk on the beach, I concentrated on my therapy. I knew I couldn't hide in my room forever. Simon even convinced me to take a few rides with him. He didn't drive too fast, but it was just enough to make my heart race and give me the kick start I needed. I knew I may never be the person I was before my attack, but it was time to reclaim my life, whatever it may be.

"Where are you going?" asked mom. All eyes were on me as I walked into the kitchen.

"School," I replied, shrugging my shoulders.

"Honey, are you sure that's a good idea?"

"Daddy, it's time, and I'm ready."

"There's no rush. You can still work from home and stay on track."

"I know, but there's no need to do that. I'm all caught up with everything I missed, and I still have an A average. I wouldn't be going if I felt I couldn't handle it. Simon will be there and so will my friends. I'll be okay, trust me."

I kissed my parents' goodbye and glanced over to Uncle Jack. He looked so tired, and I knew he was missing my Aunt Sara. I asked him if he would walk me to my car, and just with one question, his eyes brightened. He's been here but kept a safe distance, never wanting to push me.

My therapy sessions were private, and I didn't share too much with my family. The semantics of my family had changed, but as I promised my father that we were okay, I did the same for Uncle Jack. He would always be my godfather and uncle. I told him that I would always view him in that way, no matter whose blood ran through my veins. He gave me one of his awesome hugs that I loved so much, and then I waved to him as I drove off.

On my way to school, I stopped at the Juice Bar. I lost over five pounds in the last month, and my body craved a foamy latte and chocolate muffin. I finished my breakfast and parked my car in its usual spot. As I made my way through the crowded parking lot, I heard my name called out by Bailey. She hit the pavement in a sprint and nearly knocked me over with her hug.

My first day back and one of my friends was already crying. It had been so long since I had seen the gang, but I was in no shape or the right state of mind for catching up. Simon was the exception, and I was happy they all gave me the time I needed. Her unspoken question was right there between us. I made it easy and just answered her.

"I'm okay and taking it one day at a time."

She smiled and nodded. After I was passed around for more hugs, I asked where Simon was.

Jameson was glassy-eyed until I gently shoved him. "If you don't stop crying, I will never shop with you again." They all laughed and continued to hug me. "Okay, where's Simon?"

"Oops! Sorry, I almost forgot. He's down at the track practicing. Coach has been riding his ass lately with the big meet this weekend."

"Okay, thanks. I love you all, but I need to go find my guy."

I had a few minutes before my first class. I didn't think it would be a big deal if I was late since no one knew I would be here anyway. I took a seat at the top of the bleachers and watched him clear the hurdles like no one's business. My boyfriend, the star of the track team. He looked amazing out there, as I quietly cheered him on from the stands. I didn't mind being his personal cheerleader. But the other fans hanging around him, well, they needed to go. It was time to make my presence known and show the blonde bimbos that he was very taken.

They failed at getting his attention anyway. I giggled as I reached the bottom. He saw me as he made his way around the final turn. His smile was gorgeous. He leaped over the fence and scooped me up into his arms and then over his shoulders. He continued to spin me around, he was so happy.

"Baby! What are you doing here?" he asked as he placed me down, but still in his arms.

"It's time to get my life back, and school was the best place to start."

Simon couldn't have been happier for me. He leaned in to kiss me but asked first if it was okay. My heart always said yes to him, as well as my eyes when he looked into them. Simon's kisses were always phenomenal, but now they were even more gentle and guarded. He didn't want to push me, and I was thankful for his patience and understanding.

"I wanted to watch your practice, not halt it altogether."

He laughed. "Don't worry about it, baby. I was done anyway. I am so happy to just be here with you."

"Me too, but I don't think your coach feels the same way. Don't turn around, but he looks pretty pissed."

"I don't want you to worry, especially on your first day back. Go to class, and I'll catch up with you at lunch. I love you."

"I love you too."

A few hours later, we were once again standing in the same place. Simon said to me, "I'm sorry about missing lunch. I really wanted to be there."

"It's okay. Sam told me that you were running laps. I guess the coach wasn't so understanding?"

"He eventually got there. He knew I was dealing with some stuff without asking me for details. It's none of his business, but it is when it affects the team. His bark is worse than his bite, and he wanted to make sure I understood my obligations. If that wasn't good enough for him, then I would be happy to step down as captain. Well, that didn't go over too well for the coach, especially with the make or break meet this weekend."

"I'm sorry it took an ultimatum for you and your coach to work it out."

"Forget him. We worked it out. Anyway, Sam was my ride today, and he seems to have disappeared. Do you mind driving me?"

"I would love to, but you drive." He caught the keys with one hand and then leaned in to kiss me. He looked so happy.

"I've missed the sound of your laugh, Nicolette. It's amazing."

"You're the one responsible for it. Let's go."

We walked hand-in-hand to my car, with Simon lifting my hand to his lips to kiss it. Simon took a detour, and we parked outside of the botanical gardens.

"Interested in the roses?" I asked.

"No, just backing up a wish that I made. I'll be right back."

I watched my boyfriend run over to the huge fountain and pull a coin from his pocket. The top was down on my car, so I could see him with no problem. He kissed the coin and then tossed it in the fountain. He was smiling when he got back to the car.

"You are adorable. May I ask what your wish was?"

"No, you may not. It's going to come true. I know it."

We stopped and picked up some dinner and then sat in my car while we ate. I caught him up on everything with my family. He laughed when I told him about my theory about the secret affair that I had suspected. Then the conversation shifted to a more serious one.

"Simon, I have to tell you something."

"Okay, what is it?"

"It's very important, and it's something that I have only discussed with my doctor, and now you. This is going to be difficult to say, but you need to know."

"Nicolette, you're scaring me."

"I'm sorry, I don't mean to, but I'm scared too. There is a strong possibility that I may be pregnant. Michael didn't use protection when he raped me."

His beautiful smile had vanished, and his face went ashen. I knew if I was going to lose him, then this revelation would do it. I prepared myself for the worst-case scenario, but that didn't happen. Simon pulled me close and wrapped his arms around me.

"No matter what, Nicolette, we will always work out whatever life throws our way. All you need to do is trust me and believe that I will always take care of you."

I believed him, and I felt safe. I trusted Simon and his feelings for me. He promised he would never break my heart, and without a doubt, I knew this to be true. He walked me to my front door with our hands once again linked with the other. Saying goodbye to Simon never got easier, especially after the wonderful hours I just spent with him. I choked back my tears and kissed him goodnight.

"I love you, Simon."

"I love you too, so much. Call me before you go to sleep. I want my voice to be the last one you hear before you close your eyes, okay?"

"That sounds perfect," I said.

When I walked through my front door, I wasn't sure if I was in the right house. It sure looked different since I left this morning. My home was transformed into a Christmas scene from Disneyland. I always wanted to visit but never had the chance to do so. And I may not have to since Disneyland had come to me, and it was in my living room. My eyes scanned the room and took in the beautiful lights and decorations. I even had a tree. I clapped my hands together like a little girl. This was amazing.

"Surprise!" my parents and Uncle Jack shouted out. My dad looked like he was going to combust, he was so happy. Before I could ask, mom told me that since we missed our first Christmas here in California, we would just make up for it today. They came up with the idea after I made the decision to return to school.

I wiped away my tears, all happy for a change. This was my family who tried to make me feel better. My heart was bursting with love for all of them.

One by one, they hugged me as I blinked back more tears. I thanked them for my surprise, as we sat in front of the fireplace while roasting s'mores. This night was perfect. All that was missing was my Aunt Sara. I didn't know how much I missed her until right at this moment with my family.

I couldn't have asked for a better day, and it was impossible to thank my family for all they did for me. Daddy promised me that when the day came when we could put Michael behind us, we would all go to the real Disneyland and celebrate our family. I smiled and remained optimistic that all would work out.

I got ready for bed and smiled as I waited to call Simon. I had a few minutes and decided to check my computer and send a few e-mails. I was horrified to see the breaking news alerts on my Google homepage, and then I saw my name. I clicked on link after link and found news about my attack all over the internet. I felt so sick reading my name in the headlines. I covered my mouth and ran to the bathroom just in time for my stomach to erupt. I never vomited so hard in my life. This sucked. Mom came in to check on me, and then I showed her my computer.

"Mom, how did this happen? It's all over the internet. I thought we had a gag order in place? My name has been released! Oh my God! Everyone is going to know what Michael did to me."

I started to hyperventilate and couldn't catch my breath. Not knowing what to do for me, mom shouted for my father. He had seen me have an anxiety attack before; this was my worst one yet. My chest felt heavy, and I began to shake. He wasted no time trying to calm me down and just took me to the hospital, calling out to Uncle Jack to follow. Dr. Jonas was on call tonight and paged per my parent's request. They wanted me to see someone I was comfortable with. This was the last place I thought I would end up, especially after the amazing day I had with Simon and my family.

I was taken in through triage immediately and examined by Dr. Jonas. I was placed on an IV drip and was given something to calm my nausea after I vomited several more times. My mom was freaking out while my father and Uncle Jack nervously paced the room.

"What the hell is going on with my daughter?" my mom shouted.

"Mrs. Vanelle, your daughter is suffering from post-traumatic stress disorder. I suspect seeing the news report may have been the trigger for her anxiety attack. I have never seen anyone handle a situation in the manner she has. Your daughter has been incredibly brave and strong throughout this ordeal. You said she returned to school today? That's a huge step in her recovery. To interact with her family and friends is very positive. It is my hope that her reaction to the news report doesn't set her back. I would like to keep her overnight for observation, and then she can go home in the morning."

"It's okay. Keep talking as if I'm not here," I mumbled under my breath.

"I'm sorry, Nicolette. I thought it was okay to speak freely in front of your family," Dr. Jonas said as she walked over to my bedside.

"It is, but can this wait? I'm not really up for a big debate right now."

"Of course, Nicolette. Get some rest, and I will check back soon."

"Dr. Jonas, may I speak to you alone, please?"

"Certainly. Please clear the room, everybody. I need to speak with my patient."

"Nicolette! What are you doing?" asked mom.

"It's okay. I just need a minute with my doctor."

Dr. Jonas said, "Okay, we are all alone here, although I don't think they are very happy with me at the moment."

"Yeah, join the club," I muttered.

"What is it, Nicolette? It's clear you have something on your mind."

"I do. I just don't know how to form the words."

"Take your time."

"Okay, I wanted to address the real issue."

"And? What might that be?"

"Can I be pregnant?"

"Yes, it's a possibility, but I will not know for sure until I run some tests. Do I have your consent?"

"Yes, but not to speak freely with my family. I want to be the one to know first. It's my right and my choice."

"I understand. I'll send in my nurse to draw some blood."

I knew my mom was going crazy out in the hall, but I just wasn't ready to share this with her yet, nor my father or Uncle Jack.

I knew they would look at me differently once we knew if I was pregnant or not, and I wasn't ready for that. And there was still...Simon! I missed my call with him! Where was my phone? I think I left it at home.

After the nurse took my blood, I was so tired and fell asleep for a while. When I woke up, Uncle Jack was there, holding my hand.

"Nickel, you're awake. How are you feeling?"

He looked tired and had been crying. "I'm okay, Uncle Jack. Please don't cry for me. I am so sick of everyone crying. It's too painful knowing that I'm the one responsible for all of your pain and stress."

"That's not true. You need to stop blaming yourself for this. For weeks now, that's all you have done. Don't you know that none of this is your fault? As for the crying? We cry because we love you so much. It's in the handbook, and it's too late to change the rules now."

I laughed at his joke and did feel better, but it was short-lived with Dr. Jonas walking in, followed by my parents. She had the test results in her hands, and judging by the grim look on her face, I knew what she would say. What I feared she would say. I was pregnant with Michael St. Clair's child. A child that was created from an act of violence. The brutality of it all made my heart and body numb. I had no tears. No reaction. I felt nothing, less than nothing. I gave permission for Dr. Jonas to share my results with my family, but not here in my room. I wanted to be alone. Mom argued to stay, but I sent them all away, even Uncle Jack.

I curled up into a ball and cried into my pillow. I prayed for absolution for my guilt and peace for my family. Having this baby would destroy them. I didn't miss the pain I saw behind Uncle Jack's eyes when he silently walked out from my room. They didn't say the words, but somehow, I felt that they already knew what Dr. Jonas would say. Mom had a copy of my chart with all the doctor's notes in it. I knew she read it from cover to cover and just remained quiet while hoping that what they feared would not come true. Yeah, me too.

Mason

"That sonofabitch! He has to die right now!"

"Will you keep your voice down. Our daughter is right through those doors," I said to my enraged brother.

"*Our* daughter? Is she *our* daughter now? That's generous of you, but it's too late. You and your damn judgments make me sick, but it's amazing how quickly you change your tune when it suits your purpose. The one Achilles heel that I possess, oh yes, even men like me have one, and you know exactly what it is. You're scared and will do and say just about anything to stop me."

"Yes, you're right. I will do everything in my power to not only protect Nicolette but my brother as well. You have to calm down. He's in jail where he belongs."

"You just don't get it. Open your eyes, Massimo! That animal raped our daughter, and now she's pregnant. We thought her life was forever changed with the rape, but now? She's pregnant with that pig's child. It makes me sick. What is going to happen to her now? She has to get rid of it and it has to be performed as soon as possible."

Nicolette

They didn't know I was there. How could they? I was good at hiding and going unseen, especially when it came to my family. No matter what they said, or how many surprises they had planned, what happened to me changed them, and it was clear to me after hearing what Uncle Jack had said. This was not the same man that I loved and viewed as my hero. He was angry, cold, and downright scary. I thought back to the first conversation I wasn't supposed to hear and just like this one, I was scared. I was beginning to understand my father's reaction when he found out how my mother went behind his back and called Uncle Jack. Did he really have the capability to go after and kill Michael? No, it couldn't be true. I wouldn't believe it.

I was so dizzy from all the vomiting I had done, and my head was beginning to pound again, but I needed to get the hell out of here, away from all of them. I called the nurse to come into my room. I ordered her to remove my IV, but she refused and paged Dr. Jonas. I didn't care what my chart said, I wanted out of here, and if she wasn't going to remove it then I would.

"Nicolette, you must calm down." Dr. Jonas said as she hurried into my room.

"No, I will not calm down. I am an adult, and you can't keep me here against my will." I tugged on the tube and cried out as blood shot out from my arm.

"Nicolette!" she shouted, and then with the assistance from her nurse and another, I was wrestled back down into my bed. My hands and legs were restrained, as they held my head in place to keep me still. Another IV was administered, as I watched Dr. Jonas inject something into the bag of fluids.

"You don't understand. I need to get out of here," I mumbled, as the sedation or whatever she injected me with began to work.

When I finally was able to open my eyes, I saw the most beautiful blue eyes staring back at me. Simon was wiping my forehead with a cool washcloth. My restraints were removed, and he was holding one of my hands in his. My world had returned right every time he looked at me. When the reality came crashing down around me, I jerked my hand back.

He calmed me and told me that he knew about the baby. He knew everything, thanks to mom filling him in. I felt ugly and ashamed and couldn't bear to look at him. He lifted my chin toward him, and when our eyes connected, all I saw was how much he loved me.

He said, "Hey, don't hide from me, baby. You know I can't take it when you refuse to talk to me. I'm not asking, I'm telling you to trust me, and please do not run. We will get through this, I promise." He held my two hands in a tight grip and would not take his eyes away from mine.

I asked, "Simon, how could you say such things to me? Especially after what happened here tonight. How? Why? Simon, after everything I have put you through. How do you still want me? I just don't understand."

Twenty-One

Simon

"Nicolette, I swear you are the most exasperating person that I have ever known. I just don't know how to get through to you. I am sick and tired of listening to you blame yourself. You are behaving as if you asked for this to happen to you. Why is that? You seem to believe that you are the responsible party for causing everyone's stress and pain. It must be exhausting to be that self-deprecating."

"That's not fair! How could you say that to me?"

"None of this is fair! Don't you see that? I am in love with you. I know you better than you think I do, and this is just another attempt to push me away in what you call saving me, but you are so wrong. I am not going anywhere. You need to catch up and get on the same page with me. I love you."

She chewed the hell out of her bottom lip, probably thinking of more ways to break-up with me. Damn! She was so beautiful. I didn't want to be angry with her, but she was so damn frustrating. She was sick and in the hospital, again, and trying to shut me out. I spent weeks now trying to convince her that I would never leave her, no matter what. Talking wasn't working on my stubborn girl. I had to do something to calm her down, but what could I do without shattering her even more?

"I'm sorry. I'm sorry," she kept saying over and over again.

I swear if I heard one more "sorry," I was going to punch a fucking wall. I couldn't take it anymore and slammed my mouth down to her perfect lips and kissed her madly until she was out of breath. I held her face and made her look at me. I needed to know that I didn't scare her, but I didn't know what else to do.

"Nicolette, eyes on me. Did I hurt you?"

My girl still wasn't talking, and it was beginning to scare me. She didn't look afraid, more like relieved? She finally responded by leaning into my touch and kissing me back. *Thank God! I could breathe again.*

"It's about time. Thank you, Simon."

I was confused. What was she thanking me for?

"What for?"

"Your kiss. It's what I've been waiting for," she confessed.

From our beginning, I have always been passionate in showing my girl exactly how I felt about her. She always responded to me and to my touch. I loved it, and so did she, but this time was different. I knew I couldn't get carried away with her, not after all she'd been through. The fire between us was strong and felt every time we touched each other. No matter what she was saying right now, I felt it was my turn to say sorry to her. Her eyes begged me to kiss her again, and holding back from her was not an easy thing to do.

"I know what you're doing, Nicolette, and normally your smile would take me down to my knees, but not today. You need to believe once and for all how much I do love you. My soul is connected with yours, now and forever. I'm telling you that I am not leaving you, not today, not tomorrow, not ever. Okay, now that we have cleared that up, you may kiss me. But control yourself, baby, we don't want to raise your blood pressure."

There was that smile again, and I knew she was back here with me. Her body calmed, and her cheeks reddened with a beautiful blush of pink.

"I love you. Thank you, Simon, for loving me too."

Her doctor came in a short time later and was happy to see my girl was in better spirits. She asked to speak to her in private for a few minutes, and I took the time to call my parents and grab a coffee. As I approached the waiting room, I walked in on a heated argument between her parents and her Uncle Jack.

"Don't let me interrupt you," I said, as Mr. Vanelle rose from his seat and walked over to me.

He put his hand on my shoulder and tried to lead me away from the room and the conversation they obviously didn't want me involved in. If that were true, then they should have picked a more secure place to talk. "Simon, this doesn't concern you. Please stay out of it."

"The hell it doesn't, Mr. Vanelle. With all due respect, your daughter is my entire world, and anything that involves her, involves me, sir."

"Simon, come and sit with me," said Christina, her mom. I took a seat next to hers and heard her out. "I speak for all of us when we say that we know how much you care about Nicolette. We also feel that you may be in over your head and have not considered all that has happened with Nicolette and how it will affect you and your future. I have spoken with your parents, and they have informed me of your full scholarship to attend Northwestern University. That's an amazing opportunity."

"I'm not taking it. I never planned on going, but my mom made me apply anyway. I'm going to school here in California, and I'm staying with Nicolette."

"Simon, all your decisions cannot revolve solely on Nicolette. That's not fair to you. You have worked incredibly hard in school. Do you even realize the gift you have been given? Not too many students are afforded the same opportunities you have. It's an incredible honor, and you should be very proud of yourself. Your mom told us that you may even be Valedictorian for this year's graduating class."

"Mrs. Vanelle, this is not your business, and with all due respect, I don't need you to be concerned about my future academics. I never agreed to Northwestern, and this was way before I ever met your daughter. It came down to the needs of my chosen field, and it was California University that won out in the end, and with my mother at the helm of the school, it's even better. I told my family, and I will tell you the same: I will decide what is best for my future. It's just not about me anymore. I have Nicolette to consider."

"Noted, you're right. What about the baby? Are you prepared to raise a child on your own? You are so young. How can you be so certain of anything at this point?"

"Mr. and Mrs. Vanelle, Jack, I'm done with the Q&A part of this conversation. I love Nicolette. She is my heart and soul. I knew from the first day on that beach when my eyes met hers, she was the one. I can't change what happened to her, nor can I erase the pain that Michael inflicted on her. I pray each and every day that she will continue to heal in mind and body. As long as we stay together, we will overcome anything. Whatever she decides to do about this child, I will stand by her. She has my unconditional support. You asked me how I can be so sure? It's an easy answer: Love. It's the love I have for your daughter, and it's the same love that will help me help her. It's that simple, and I have never been more certain of anything in my life. Yeah, you're all looking at me like I'm just some kid with his head in the clouds, but you're wrong."

"Yes, I'm only eighteen years old, but I have had my share of heartache and pain. I know what loss is, and I know what love is. I have found love with Nicolette, and I plan on including her in my future. I know how much you love her, but so do I, and you are going to have to come to terms with that. I am asking you to respect our relationship and give us your blessing. It will make things easier for Nicolette knowing she has her family's support. We're done here." I felt her presence before I could turn around. She was behind me with a shy smile on her face with eyes only on me.

"Are you ready to go?" I asked her. She simply nodded in response, and we left. Her family stood in silence and watched us walk away.

Nicolette said, "I love you, Simon. Thank you for standing up for me."

"Someone had to. I will always fight for you. Never doubt that." I lifted her hand up to my lips to kiss, and she visibly relaxed as I drove us far away from the hospital and the bad memories from the night before.

"Where are we going? I thought for a minute that you were taking us back to school."

"No chance of that happening. We are taking a vacation day."

"What about the coach? Won't he be mad at you for missing practice?"

"Nope, because I worked it all out and will meet up with the team tonight for a late practice. Don't worry about school, your parents, not a thing. Just concentrate on enjoying the day with me, and I'll take care of the rest."

I felt her hand tighten around mine as we got closer to the beach, but then she looked surprised to where we were. I drove off the main road down to a private beach entrance and drove a few miles more until we reached the tall gates. I punched in the code and drove us down the winding path that led to the beautiful beach house high on the hill. Her eyes lit up as she looked all around. There was not another house in sight for miles, and we were in our very own private bubble.

I helped her from my Jeep and took her hand as I led her up the small flight of stairs. Then we walked up to another twelve until we reached the top. We walked through a pair of French doors, which led to a huge living room. We were surrounded by floor-to-ceiling windows. The late morning sun shined through them while we heard the waves breaking along the shore in the background.

She sounded happy when she asked, "Where are we? Should we be here?" She was adorable and gave me that shy smile I adored.

I took her in my arms and simply answered, "A special place, and yes, this is exactly where we are supposed to be."

"I don't understand."

"Come, let's sit down, and I'll explain. Baby, this home belonged to my mother's sister, Aunt Grace. Next, to my mom, she was my second favorite person in the world. I loved her a lot and miss her every single day."

"What happened to her?"

"She died. She lived here until her passing two years ago. My aunt was an artist, and painting was her one true passion. She loved art and filled this home with works of art she always loved. As you know, we are from Colorado, but mom was a California native before meeting my dad. They met at college and married shortly after. Although she loved her new life with my dad in Boulder, it was always mom's hope to return to California. When my aunt was diagnosed with breast cancer, she knew where she had to be. My brothers were settled up at school, and we moved here. Mom only had a few months with her sister before she died. Aunt Grace was very wealthy and left her entire estate to her nephews. Trusts were set-up for my brothers, and I got this house."

"This is unbelievable. This home is huge, and the view is incredible. I don't know much about real estate, but I would guess you have agents begging you to sell. I can't even imagine what this property is worth."

"The last time my father ran the numbers, I believe it was just under four million, give or take."

"Holy shit!"

"Yeah, that's one way to describe it."

"Simon, why did you bring me here today?"

I waited for her to ask, and I couldn't wait to see the expression on her face when I told her my reason. "I wanted you to be open to the possibility of living here with me and sharing this home with me, as my wife."

"Holy shit!"

"Another surprised reaction. I'm hopeful," I said, but she looked nervous all of a sudden. "Nicolette, don't freak out. Just listen to me."

"Simon, we are moving way too fast here. I need to sit down."

"Just breathe, and let me explain. How much did you hear of my conversation with your family?"

"All of it."

"Okay, then you know about my scholarship, which I never intended on accepting. My parents are no different than yours. They have been planning my future for as long as I can remember, but my plan is very different from theirs. Dad wants me to go into law, and mom wants me to go into education. Neither career choice is what I want. I want to become a Marine Biologist. It has always been my passion, and the only one that truly understood that was my Aunt Grace."

I continued, "Aunt Grace was my biggest advocate when it came to me making my own decisions. My parents devised a plan for my brothers, and one for me. They complied, and I didn't. My entire perspective changed when I met you. You were the missing piece to a puzzle that I had been searching for. No matter what happens, we have to stay together. I don't want anyone else to share my life with. You are my puzzle piece and have been since the day we met. Say something, Nicolette. I need you to breathe, and tell me what you're feeling."

"I love you too, but I don't want to hurt you."

"Are we back there again? I thought we had settled all of that back at the hospital."

"We did, but you don't understand."

"Okay, then make me. I'm not going to know unless you talk to me."

"I love you, Simon, you know that I do, but I just can't be with you in the way you need me to be. Our families are right. I don't think you have considered what you would be sacrificing by being with me. Once you seriously think things through, you will figure out that I have too much baggage that will eventually weigh you down in the long run. Once you move on, you will meet someone who is worthy of your love and then forget about me."

"Nicolette, I know what you're doing, and for the last time it's not going to work." She wouldn't look at me and began walking toward the doors before I pulled her back to me. "No, I'm not letting you walk out the door this time. I made that mistake once, and I will never be so foolish again. I know who I am and what I want. It's you, Nicolette Elizabeth Vanelle, only you. I see the girl that I love, and all I want to do is share my life with her. None of this means a thing if you're not with me. This is just a house, but if you truly love and trust me, then we can make this a home...Nicolette? Answer me. Do you trust me?"

"Yes, Simon, I trust you."

We didn't need any more doubts holding us back. I had finally done what I wanted to do from the first moment she stepped into this home. I crushed my lips down to her sexy mouth and kissed her. I didn't stop there. I kissed her along her silky neck with heated want. I was undeniably in love with this girl, and when she returned my kiss, I knew there was no more doubt. I wanted to give her the world. She just needed to allow me to do so.

We kissed and kissed, as I repeatedly told her that I loved her. She was wrapped around me, and all I could do was dream about making love to her, but I would never pressure her into anything she wasn't ready for. She was still recovering, and her injuries were still visible. I never wanted her to be afraid of my touch, and she wasn't. She let out a contented sigh and placed her head on my chest as I ran my fingers through her long, thick hair.

"Are we okay now?" I playfully asked her.

"Yes, we are. Simon, we have so much to talk about. I feel as if I've been transported to a magical bubble here with you, but the reality is very different. I'm pregnant with Michael's baby, and I can't even begin to understand what to do about it."

"How do you feel about being pregnant?"

"I'm eighteen years old. I never wanted this for myself, and I never expected to be raped. This baby deserves so much more than what I could give him or her. If I keep this baby, he or she will forever be a reminder of Michael and what he did to me. How is that fair?"

"It's not fair, not at all. Children should always come from love. If you look at it from another way, maybe it will help you come to a decision. This baby was not conceived in a way it should have been. What Michael did was selfish and cruel. You are an incredible young woman, strong and full of life. He took something from you, and you need to reclaim it back. He may have taken your body that night, but he didn't take who you are. After everything he put you through, you still found the courage to fight back. Do you even realize where that strength came from? It's here in your heart and your spirit. This incredible miracle growing inside of you does not belong to Michael, it belongs to you. This baby will grow inside of you, feel your love, grow from your strength, and become an extraordinary person because of you. I promise you that whatever you choose, I will always be here by your side, and accept and support whatever you want to do."

My beautiful girl was crying, but smiling at the same time. I prayed that she heard the words I desperately wanted her to believe. I loved her with all that I was and would never leave her.

"You're exhausted. I know your head must be spinning right now, and that's okay. Let me take you upstairs and you can rest."

I carried her upstairs to the master bedroom and placed her down in the middle of the king-sized bed. I kissed her cheek and whispered, "Sleep, baby, I love you."

As soon as her head hit the pillow, I knew she was asleep. She was so tired, and I knew she needed some time to process all that we discussed. It was a pretty safe bet that she should be out for a while, so I took the opportunity to get some surfing in. I loved it and never felt freer than when I was riding a fifteen-foot wave into the shore. It was a high that I would never tire of.

I was only out there for about an hour. I showered outside on the deck and then threw on clean board shorts and a t-shirt. The weather was great for December, and I set up our lunch out on the deck. I heard her screaming by the time I reached the bedroom. She was having a nightmare.

"Baby, wake up," I quietly said. "Nicolette!" I called out to her, and she finally blinked her eyes open.

"Simon!" she called out.

"I'm here, baby. It's alright. It was just a dream." I scooped her up and into my lap. I loved how she naturally just fit with me.

"Simon, it was so real. I heard a baby crying. I kept trying to find it, but all I heard was the crying."

"It was just a dream. Come, let's eat lunch."

"You smell like the ocean. I like it."

"I love that you like it. I went surfing while you were sleeping. I love this beach, and this small part belongs to me. The ocean out there is a different story, but it wasn't too crowded today."

"I'm glad you did it. I don't want you to stop doing the things you love because of me."

"The best thing I love is you, and that is never going to stop. No worries, babe, okay?"

"Okay."

"Your mom called. They wanted to know where you were. I didn't tell them. All I said is that you were sleeping and you would call them when you woke up."

"I'm sure she loved that. She probably called your parents."

"Probably, but they don't know where I am. They are visiting my brothers up at school." I said, and then tossed another fry into my mouth.

"Thank you for bringing me here. It's been perfect."

"You're welcome. You don't have to decide anything right now. Just think about it, okay?"

"What about Michael? If he finds out that I'm pregnant, won't he want rights to the baby?" I tried not to show my disdain for him, especially to Nicolette. I moved my plate away and held her hands.

"He lost the right to anything the moment he decided to hurt you. Do not worry about him. I will never allow him to hurt you, or this baby. I meant what I said, I love you and want to share everything with you, and that includes this home. You will never have to worry about anything. I can take care of you, Nicolette, and this baby. This home is mine to do whatever I want. Aunt Grace made sure of that. We have plenty of time, okay?"

"Okay. I love you."

"I love you more. Don't forget that."

I finally felt as if I could breathe a sigh of relief. I managed to get through to her, and we spent the rest of the day relaxing and loving each other. I didn't care what anyone thought about us, or say how young we are. They didn't know who we were, and how we felt about each other, only we did. I promised my beautiful girl the world, and I vowed to spend the rest of my life making her happy. She deserved nothing less. We were one heart and one soul. It made me so happy to know that Nicolette believed it too.

Twenty-Two

Michael

There is nothing good about jail, but it allowed me one gift that I always seemed to take for granted—time. I had hours and hours of it. With my bail denied, I wasn't going anywhere anytime soon.

I stared up at the cracked ceiling, and all my thoughts were of Nicolette. *Why couldn't she have given me a chance? I'm not a bad guy, am I?* When I wasn't thinking of Nicolette, my mind shifted to another person in my life that I loved once—my mother, Lydia. *Why was my mother taken from me?* So many questions and I didn't have one single answer.

Did I actually do what I'm being accused of? I'm trapped behind these bars and suffocating in this tight space. It's easy to feel as if the walls are closing in around you because you have nowhere to go. What would my mother say if she could see me now? Would she turn her back on me? My father did, so why not Lydia? No, she was the only one that did love me, and then I lost her to fucking cancer that took her from me.

My father hadn't been back to visit with me since my arraignment. He was communicating through his lawyer. Yeah, I called that one. My father didn't do anything that didn't benefit him first or his fucking movie house. Did he think that I had forgotten about his new film debuting in a couple of months? The very same that her parents worked on, leading me right to Nicolette. All I wanted to do was love her.

With the adrenaline pulsing through my body, I punched the concrete wall, the very one that I felt trapped by. I looked down to my bloodied and broken hand as it finally registered what I had done. I wanted to shout at the top of my lungs, but I couldn't do that in here. It would look as if I was weak and then I would be marked. I couldn't show any emotion in here if I wanted to survive. I called out for the guard, and when my calls went unanswered, I ripped a t-shirt into pieces to wrap my hand. When the guard finally did show up, he didn't look all that concerned about me but called for a medic anyway.

After having my hand examined, I was told it was probably broken, and I needed to be taken to the hospital. My father and lawyer were contacted and met me at the hospital. I was surrounded by cops since my hand was too swollen to be handcuffed. I wondered which one of them was trigger happy if I made a move. I wasn't that stupid, so I concluded that all of them would have been pleased to shoot me if I gave them the chance to do so.

It was too swollen for a cast, and I would have to come back in a few days to have it set. They wrapped it and placed it in a sling for support.

After the doctor left the room, my father flipped out on me. *What else is new?* "What the hell were you thinking? Punching a brick wall? How could you be so reckless?"

What could I say to him? I could tell him that I was feeling sorry for myself and wished my dead mother was alive to hold me. My mother was an off-limits topic with my father, so I remained quiet and waited for him to stop yelling at me. He finished, and then I was taken back to jail. He slapped me on my back and told me to remain strong. *Yup! I'll do that, dad.*

I was back in my cell with a throbbing hand and all the time in the world to think. My father told me that his lawyers were working on getting the judge's ruling reversed on granting bail for me, and then they arranged for a team of psychiatrists to evaluate me. I didn't care what they had to do, as long as they got me out of here. If released, I would be restricted to house arrest and would have to wear an ankle monitoring device. I would agree to those terms without hesitation. I hated this place and just wanted to go home.

I was allowed one pain pill for my hand. After a while, I began to get tired and closed my eyes. I didn't dream about Nicolette; no, it was the other woman in my life that I loved. *"What's happened to my beautiful boy?"* I heard her voice, and it was so clear as if she was right next to me. *"Have you forgotten me? Who are you? And what have you done to my beautiful boy?"*

I begged her not to leave me again, but her image faded and she was gone. I woke up in a cold sweat. My breathing was ragged. My hand ached, but no more than my heart. How the hell did I get here?

Even with a nightmare, today was still perfect here with Si-mon. We talked for hours, and when we weren't talking, he was kissing and loving me. I loved him so much, and I wasn't going to doubt us ever again. I hated to leave the beach house, but Simon gave his word that he would not miss another prac-tice. My heart felt heavy, but he promised that he would call me as soon as he was finished.

I took a deep breath before I walked inside of my house. I knew they were all in there waiting for me, but I wasn't ready for yet an-other exhausting conversation on how fucked up my life had be-come. The first person that I saw was Aunt Sara. All the anxiety that I felt faded away the minute I ran into her arms.

"Aunt Sara, I am so happy to see you," I said as she hugged me back.

"I've missed you so much, and I am so sorry I wasn't here sooner."

"It's okay, you're here now."

She held my hand as we walked further into the living room, clearly interrupting yet another conversation about me. It's easy to guess since they weren't shy about how loud they were talking when I walked in.

"Honey, how are you feeling?" asked mom.

"I'm better, Simon took care of me today."

She smiled at my response and then looked over her shoulder to my father and Uncle Jack. It was obvious to everyone in the room that she wanted to say something to me, and five seconds later, she didn't hold back. "We have to discuss the baby." *Right on cue.*

My father sighed and folded his arms across his chest. "Nicolette, we have been discussing this all afternoon. We're worried about you, and we need to know how you feel about it. What do you want to do about this baby?"

I looked over to Aunt Sara, the only one in the room that seemed to care what I wanted. She told me that I didn't have to make any decisions right now, despite what my family wanted.

I wanted to simply say that I hadn't reached any decisions about the baby since I really didn't have any time to process the news. I told my parents that I wanted to go upstairs to lie down for a while and maybe after dinner we would talk, but that wasn't good enough for them, and that's when I lost it. I thought of Simon and how supportive he was to me, especially today at the beach house. I missed him already and wished he was here with me now.

"Nicolette, come back here and talk with us," my father said as he tried to approach me, but I put my hands up to him.

"No! I will not. What do you want from me? Do you think I can just magically wish what happened to me away?"

"Honey, calm down. We can work this out as a family."

"You are unbelievable! It's crazy how you all just sat here all day and discussed my life as if you were the ones in control of it. You don't have a clue to what I have suffered through and the daily hell that I am in. Every single day and night, I relive my rape. He did unimaginable things to me that night on that boat, and now I'm pregnant with his child. How the hell am I supposed to come to terms with this nightmare that I call my life? I just want to get through the next hour without any pressure from any one of you. You think you are helping me? Well, you're not. The only thing that you have managed to do is push me further away."

"Nicolette, that's not what we want. If you would just let us talk to you, I know we can help you."

"No, daddy, you can't. None of you can help me. I know you want to, but I refuse to be pressured and backed into a corner just to appease you. I tried that once, and look where it got me."

"What does that mean?" my father asked.

"Last year, I was living in Chicago, dreaming of going to college, and I looked forward to the next chapter in my life. Everything changed for me when you decided..." I pointed to my parents and then continued, "You decided to do what you felt was best for me."

"Honey..."

I interrupted my mother. "Quiet! It is my turn to speak, and I demand my voice to be heard. Mom, when you and daddy landed the amazing opportunity to work out here in California, I was happy for you, but then the new life you wanted forced me to leave the only one I ever knew. You didn't care how it affected me. You took my choice away, even after I begged you to allow me to stay and live with Uncle Jack and Aunt Sara. I have done everything you asked of me, and now it's your turn to do something for me. You need to back the hell off and give me some fucking space."

My mother glared at me and looked totally offended that I dared to raise my voice. "Nicolette, you will not use that language in my house, do you understand me?" she shouted.

"Or what? You'll punish me? Send me to my room without dessert?" I said as I glared back at her.

"Honey, I know you are upset, but we will not be disrespected. We love you and are only trying to help you," she said.

"Are you serious? You want to help me? If this is your version of helping me, then I don't want it. You are once again trying to control me and navigate my life the way you see fit. I have held my tongue for far too long now, and I will not be silenced. You keep asking me how I feel and what I plan to do. Here's your answer: I don't know. Just when I finally accepted my new life here in California, I never could have predicted what was going to happen to me with Michael."

I continued, "I have new friends who care about me, and then there's Simon, the boy who loves me. He's been my rock throughout this entire ordeal. I have tried to push him away, but he's here loving and supporting me. I don't think I would have made it this far without him. His love is saving me, mom, and it's everything I need to survive this. The last thing I want is to hurt any of you. You are my family, and I love you, but you need to give me some time. I need to heal and work this out on my own. I will not be pressured into making any decisions just because you want me to."

I started to cry and my father tried once again to comfort me. This time I let him.

"Oh, my baby, we never meant to upset you. You mean everything to us, and we just don't know how to help you. We have to know that you are okay." My father pleaded with me to understand they only had the best intentions when it came to me and how sorry they were for hurting me.

My father hugged me, and I closed my eyes and prayed that this conversation was now over. All I wanted was to go up to my room and wait for Simon.

"Nicolette, if you are calmer now, I would like to say something," mom interrupted my moment with my father.

I couldn't believe that after everything I had said, she still didn't get it. I stepped out of my father's embrace and turned to address my mother. "Mom, haven't you heard a word that I have said to you? How can you stand here and expect me to listen to any more of your thoughts and wants that pertain to my life? I am not ready to make any decisions, nor do I want to hear the word 'baby' again. Just leave me alone."

She pushed again. "Nicolette, whether you are ready or not, this baby is a reality, and we need to discuss it."

That was it. I was ready to explode. My head was spinning, and I felt nausea stirring all around in my stomach.

Aunt Sara handed me a glass of water. "Honey, please calm down. All this stress is not good for you." Bless her heart, my Aunt Sara, always the voice of reason.

"Thank you, Aunt Sara. I'm fine," I said and then turned back over to my mother.

"You wanted this conversation. Didn't you, mom? You just couldn't leave well enough alone. You pushed and pushed and backed me into a corner, a corner that I feel I have to claw my way out from. Let me be clear so we don't have any misunderstandings moving forward to how I feel. For the umpteenth time, this is not how I envisioned my life to be. Thank you very much for reminding me, yet again, on how my life has changed. Yes, I am pregnant. How did I get pregnant? Let me see," I said, as I tapped my chin with my finger. "I remember now, I was fucking raped! Just in case you didn't hear me, I'll say it again: **I. WAS. RAPED!** Is that clear enough for you? I was raped by the boy that you told me to be nice to. I'll never forget when you asked me to try to maintain a 'civil relationship' with him." I put my hands up in a mockingly way to gesture quotes. "You remember mom, don't you? We were all seated around the dinner table, and you said it would be good if I got along with Michael because it would make your working relationship with his father run that much smoother. Right, daddy? Yes, that same boy stalked me for months. He physically attacked me, not once, but twice. The same boy that I tried with my best efforts to let him down easy and tell him that I wasn't interested in him. No matter what I said, he wouldn't leave me alone."

I continued, "I tried, mom. I really did try. For the sake of your business, I followed your advice and tried everything in my power to do what you asked of me and be his friend. What you didn't know was that Michael never wanted to be my friend. He had this sick fantasy that he loved me and we were meant to be together. I told him that I was in love with Simon, which I believe only enraged him more. Every time I refused him, the challenge for him to get me had increased. I just never knew what he was capable of, and by the time I did? It was too late for me. That animal took what he wanted from me by force. Michael St. Clair raped me. I fought him with all the strength that I had, but he kept hurting me. He didn't care and certainly didn't show me any mercy as he continued to take what he wanted. Michael St. Clair has left a permanent mark on my soul with his child growing inside of me. You wanted to know how I feel about it? Now you do."

I fell to my knees and cried. I just revealed to my family intimate details that I tried to protect them from. They all walked closer to me, and I screamed at all of them not to touch me.

My heart was beating so fast, and it felt like it was going to burst right out of my chest. I ached all over. My beautiful day with Simon had now been reduced to a faded memory. They were all in tears, even my Uncle Jack. I hurt my family and caused them more pain. I didn't even recognize myself anymore.

I slowly rose from the floor on my shaky legs and began to walk away from them. Although I hated to be pressured, I also deeply regretted how I spoke to them, especially to my mom. She didn't deserve to be talked to in such a brutal manner, but the dam had been breached and I couldn't hold back my feelings any longer.

"My life changed forever the moment Michael St. Clair raped me. I know I will never be the same girl I once was. I don't know what you want from me, nor do I understand how you expect me to just carry on as if nothing has changed? If this is what you want me to do, then I can never give that to you."

I took a breath and continued, "I just found out that the man I have adored and loved my entire life is actually my biological father. I'm still processing and adjusting to that news while dealing with my rape. After I learned the truth, I didn't shut you out. I listened and understood all the reasons why you did what you did. I opened my arms to all of you because I love you so much."

I then turned to Uncle Jack, who was standing with Aunt Sara, who was crying beside him. "Uncle Jack, I love you. If it wasn't for you helping my parents, I wouldn't be here right now. You gave me life, and I am thankful for it. Having said that, you must understand that the life that I loved more than anything is just gone now. I have to figure out how I am going to rebuild it. This has been incredibly hard on me, and I'm trying to wrap my head around the fact that my family can just continue to make unrealistic demands of me. You all want to force me to fall in line and do what you want, totally disregarding what I want, which is…I don't know."

"I didn't ask to be raped. It's unimaginable, and I sure as hell didn't want to be pregnant at eighteen years old. As much as I want him to pay for what he has done to me, I also don't want to go through a trial and have to face him. You will never know how much I wish I could go back to that day where Simon and daddy actually reached me in time and stopped Michael from hurting me. I know that's not real, but the fact that I am pregnant is. I am the only one that is going to decide what happens next."

I looked over to my mother, who looked completely devastated. "I'm sorry that I hurt you, mom. I'm sorry that I hurt any of you, but it needs to be said. The days of planning my life and making decisions for me are over. I'm an adult now, and as much as I wanted to become one before, I never anticipated what I would be facing now. You all have a decision to make. You can support and love me, or you can let me go."

A couple of months ago, we were a happy family…but now? Everything has changed. After tonight, I don't know what we are.

Simon

My practice ran later than I wanted. But it felt really good to run and let off some steam. My team was so excited and ready for Saturday. This was what they had worked so hard for. My teammate Jimmy was hoping this win on Saturday would pave the way for his scholarship. College scouts would be in attendance, and I knew I would have to run my heart out for my team. This win would not be just for me, but for them.

After the team left for the night, I had a long talk with my coach, and we cleared the air between us. He told me that he was proud to call me captain. I promised him a championship win for the team and our school.

I quickly showered and got dressed. I saw that I had three missed calls from Nicolette. I dialed her number, and she picked up on the first ring. She explained to me all that happened since I dropped her home.

I clenched my fist to keep myself in check, or I would have hit something. I was angry that she had to go through all that stress and arguing with her family. She asked if I wouldn't mind picking her up and bringing her back to the beach house.

I knew she was upset, but it also made me happy knowing that she wanted to go back to the beach house. I promised her all the time in the world, but deep down inside, I wanted her there in that house with me. She had a bag packed and told me that she just wanted out.

I was at a loss for words and wasn't sure what to say. I urged her not to make any decisions based on hurt feelings. I also reminded her how much her family loved her, and they were hurting just as much as she was. I asked her to wait for me, and she promised she would.

We promised each other complete honesty, and no matter what our problems were, we would always find a way to work them out. I told her that we were stronger together than apart.

I rang the doorbell to Nicolette's home, and Gracie greeted me with a smile. She led me into the living room, where Nicolette's family was gathered. Her dad rose from his seat and walked over to me, shaking my hand. He thanked me for taking care of his daughter today. Uncle Jack followed and then introduced me to his wife, Sara.

"It's great to finally meet you. On my first date with Nicolette, you are all she talked about, and I hear you make a pretty awesome burger. I'll have to try it sometime."

"It's a pleasure to meet you as well, and just so you know, I have heard a lot of awesome things about you too."

"That's always good to hear."

The lighter conversation helped with what I knew was coming next. Her father looked grim like he just lost his best friend.

"Simon, I'm sure you know what happened here tonight after you brought Nicolette home."

I placed my hands on my hips and asked to speak freely. They all took a seat, while I remained standing. Her mom was quiet, but you couldn't miss her tear-stained cheeks.

"I just want to say that I know you all love Nicolette and want the very best for her, as do I. Having said that, you all need to just take a step back and give her some time. She needs to begin to heal and work through this. Now that she is pregnant, it will just add more stress to what she is already dealing with. I think that we can all agree that fighting with family is not going to make anything better, just the opposite. I love Nicolette. My future will include her, and if she decides that she wants this child, then he or she will be my son or daughter. She doesn't need a reminder on how the baby was conceived and the ugliness it came from. She is beautiful inside and out, and this baby will grow from within her. It will be just as beautiful, like its mother. How could it not?"

"Simon, you can't begin to understand the responsibility you are taking on," her mom said as she wiped her tears away with a tissue.

"Mrs. Vanelle, that's where you're wrong. I do understand exactly what I am signing up for. In fact, just this afternoon, I asked your daughter to marry me and share my beach house with me. She is my life, and I will not live my own without her in it. My feelings for Nicolette have grown stronger, and as long as we are together, she will be fine. I promise you."

Uncle Jack asked, "Simon, what if the child looks like him? How will you feel then? The baby will only serve as a reminder to Nicolette and to you. I just don't see how you will be able to raise this child as your own."

"Jack, do you think your brother felt that way when he raised Nicolette as his own? Knowing she was biologically yours?" His face fell, and I knew what I said may have shocked and hurt him, but it was the truth.

I continued, "We don't expect you to understand our choices, but we do ask you to respect them. Jack, Mason, you are honorable men, and family is everything to you, is it not?"

The two men looked at each other and then back to me and nodded in agreement.

"Well, it's the same for me. I'm going to take care of what's mine. Nicolette is mine, and I'm hers. We are together, and we will get through this. Again, I mean no disrespect, but I don't know how many more ways I can make this clear to all of you. When will you get it? What you did to her at the hospital, and then here at home, was just cruel. You ambushed her and completely bulldozed over her heart. Why do you think I took her away from here today? She needed rest and time to clear her head. I finally convinced her to wholeheartedly trust and believe in me to take care of her. I really hope that you have not destroyed what I have worked so hard for her to believe. We're done here. If you'll excuse me, I need to see my girl."

"She's upstairs in her room."

"Thank you, Mrs. Vanelle. I'll take it from here."

I took the stairs two at a time, with my heart racing. I slowly opened her door and called out for her. When she didn't answer, I turned on the brighter light and found her room empty. She wasn't in her bathroom. I ran outside to the balcony and saw that her car was gone.

"Damn it! Where are you, baby?" I cursed out loud.

I flew down the stairs and told her family that she was gone. Her mother gasped and hugged her husband.

"Oh, Mason, what have we done to our daughter?"

Nicolette

I know I promised Simon that I would wait for him, but I couldn't stand to be in my home after everything that happened tonight. I had planned on calling him once I was far enough away, but then I just kept on driving. He would be angry and disappointed, but I needed time to think. I didn't know where I was but then felt relieved when I saw signs for hotels and gas. I parked my car in the back of the motel and paid for a room for the night. I paid in cash so my parents couldn't track me through my credit cards.

They must have been out of their minds with worry by now, but it was better this way. I picked up take-out before arriving at the hotel, and once I was settled behind the locked door, I took a shower and finally had a moment of peace and quiet.

Before I left my house, I had called the one person that I knew would help me: Sam. He wanted me to wait for Simon, but when I said that I needed out of my house, he asked what he could do for me. My phone was turned off the entire time I was driving, and I didn't call Sam again until I was at the motel. He said he would call Simon, and then call me back on the room number. When Sam called back, he told me that Simon was still at my house at that time. Simon was beside himself with worry but disconnected the call and left to find me. My father demanded to know where I was, or he would call the police. Simon got angry and told my father that if he did that, then he would only push his daughter further away.

They had no choice but to let him go. A little more than an hour later, there was a knock on my door. I looked through the peephole and was relieved to see Simon on the other side. I slowly opened the door as he rushed through, scooping me up into his arms. He wrapped his arms around my body like a snake and didn't let go. He was crying. My love was crying.

"My God! Nicolette, you scared me."

He was still holding me in his arms when I tried to calm him. "I'm so sorry, Simon, but I couldn't stay in that house for one more minute. It was awful."

He placed me down and locked the door behind him. "So? Your only choice was to run? You gave me your word, and I trusted you to honor it. No more running, wasn't that our agreement? How can I trust you, Nicolette? When every single time we make a promise to each other, you go off and do something else."

My lip trembled as he continued to pace the room and yell at me.

"I know you feel betrayed and hurt by your family, but I was just with them, and they are not doing any better. Nicolette, what hurts me the most is that you went back on your promise and didn't trust me to help you. You decided to run. What scares me the most is the fact that you may have kept driving and decide not to call Sam again. I don't know what I would've done if that happened."

I didn't believe I could have felt worse about today, but the fear on Simon's face was gutting me to my core. He was the last person I wanted to hurt.

"Simon, please forgive me. I know I hurt you, but you must believe that I wasn't running from you. I do love and trust you with everything I have, and that's why I called Sam. I knew he would get my message to you, and then you would come to me. Simon, I wanted to wait for you, but after how my family kept pushing me to make a decision about the baby, I snapped. Do you think I wanted to fight with them? To hurt them? It was the last thing I wanted, and it hurt me so much to see how sad they were when I turned my back on them. Once I got into my room, I just started throwing things into my suitcase. It was a blur after that. Tell me you understand. I can't lose you, Simon, and not for this." I wrung my hands in my lap and waited for him to say something.

He did something better and pulled me up into his arms. "I forgive you, Nicolette. You never have to worry about losing me. I love you more than my own life." He continued to hold me and just allowed me to silently cry. I needed to let go of the stress of today and hold on to the better parts with Simon. He did this for me and without judgment.

He missed dinner, and I was thankful I ordered enough to share with him. We talked some more while we finished up with our late meal. He told me that he was staying with me tonight and not to argue with him. I smiled, and then looked over to the bed. This would be the first time I would share a bed with Simon, but I wasn't scared or panicked.

I prayed that tonight I would be spared from having any nightmares. We settled into bed with Simon holding me close to his body. I couldn't miss his erection pressed up against me, and when I looked at him, he smiled and didn't look a bit guilty for it. He just leaned in and kissed me, but not before telling me he loved me.

Tomorrow would be a new day, and he would drive us to school. It wasn't exactly where I wanted to be, but Simon told me that if I wanted to take my life back, then school was exactly where I needed to be. We talked about his upcoming track meet and how excited he was for Saturday. He made me promise that I would be there to cheer him on. I gave him my word and told him how I looked forward to meeting his brothers.

We skipped right over what happened with my family. We talked about the happier times we had to look forward to, which was us and our future. He felt that I cried enough of the sad tears tonight, and if I was going to cry anymore, then they would be only the good ones.

He held me all through the night, and when I opened my eyes, his legs were entwined through mine. His body felt heavy, and I was too warm. I managed to move without waking him, and I watched him sleep. I was itching to touch him, he looked so beautiful and at peace. I only leaned in to kiss his lips, which formed the perfect O. Simon had been so gentle with me for the past couple of months, and my heart was overflowing with love for him. He perked up his lips after my kiss and then opened his eyes and smiled at me.

"What are you up to, baby?" he asked and then gave his long-toned body a deep stretch.

"Good morning, I was just admiring the view."

"Oh yeah? Is it a good one?" he asked and then pulled me on top of him.

"It's the best."

He just stared up into my eyes as he held my face. *What was he looking for? And then I knew.*

"Simon, I love you."

He closed his eyes and let out a contented sigh. "I love you more. I came to life when I met you. Please stay with me, Nicolette."

He just about broke me with his words. I knew I had placed the doubt that I saw in his eyes because I did scare him last night by leaving. I wanted to stay right here in this bed with him, but he reminded me that we needed to get ready and go to school. Before he stepped into the shower, he asked me for my keys. I wondered why, and once again, I knew. I handed them over without hesitation, and he winked. The bathroom door was kept open. Every few seconds, he peered out from the curtain to make sure I was still there.

We drove in silence for a while, as I chewed the heck out of my thumbnail. I was worried about my family and how I just walked out on them. They must have been frantic. I had never done anything so reckless before. Simon assured me that when I returned home today, my family would be more understanding. I hoped he was right. When I didn't have any cuticle left, Simon finally reached for my hand and calmed me with just a simple kiss.

"Nicolette, stop with the worrying. Today is just another normal day. We will attend classes—and I mean all our classes—and then meet up for lunch with our friends. I'll go to track practice, and then I'll drive you home."

"You make it sound so simple."

He laughed and then kissed my hand again. "It is baby, I promise."

The gang was waiting for us at our usual spot on the quad. Sam asked me if I was okay, and I told him that I was and thanked him for the help last night. He just wanted me to be okay. They all did. We hung out for a few minutes, and the first bell alerted us that we needed to get going.

Simon walked up behind me and gave me a hug. "Time to go, babe. Say goodbye."

"Bye," I said and then took Simon's hand. "You know, Calculus could have waited another minute or two."

"I'll make it up to you."

"Promise?" I asked.

"Always."

After my morning classes, I checked in with the Guidance Department, per their request. My advisor, Stephanie Perkins, was going over my file when I knocked on her door.

"You wanted to see me?" I asked.

"Yes, I did. Have a seat. I haven't had an opportunity to speak with you since you returned to school. How are you doing?"

"As well as could be expected, but I'm here, so that's a step in the right direction."

"I agree with you, and I've been going over your file. You have completed all your missed work, and I am proud to say that you have maintained an A average in all of your classes. That's quite impressive, Nicolette."

"Thank you," I said quietly.

I walked the halls, and then I suddenly felt nervous, as if all eyes were on me. I knew that wasn't the case, but my eyes began to well up with tears. I ran inside to the nearest girl's bathroom. I locked the stall and leaned my head against the door, trying to catch my breath. My anxiety attacks increased since the rape, and the PTSD feels worse at times. I'm finding it harder to get through them. I'd have to remember to tell my therapist at my next appointment. She wanted to prescribe something for me, but I refused.

I was about to leave when I overheard some girls talking, and they were talking about me. I tried to be as quiet as I could, so they wouldn't know I was here. I looked through the space between the door and recognized the girls from the other day. It was the cheerleaders that were flirting with Simon.

"You heard, right? The party for this weekend has been canceled. I heard there will be no more anytime soon. I guess we have one person to thank for that."

"Brittany, what are you talking about?"

"Have you been under a rock? Michael St. Clair has been arrested, and he's in jail for allegedly raping some skank that should have been happy he paid any attention to her at all. Now our weekends are fucked because of her. Seriously, the charges are just absurd. He doesn't need to rape anyone because he can get any girl he wants."

"Jealous much?" her friend asked.

"Yeah, right. I was just venting. I can't believe this is happening to him."

"Brittany, have you considered that he may have done it? Don't be so quick to pass judgment on something you know nothing about."

"Kara, you are so naïve sometimes. Nicolette Vanelle is desperate and an attention seeking whore. How she landed a guy like Simon Paulson, is beyond me. She'll screw him over, just like she did with Michael. She should be the one rotting in jail, not him."

OMG! They know my name and believe that I'm lying about be-ing raped by Michael. I covered my mouth to silence my cries.

"You want to repeat that bitch?" shouted Alexis as she charged Brittany.

"What the hell is your problem?

"I'll tell you what my sister's problem is. You have a big mouth, and you don't know what the hell you are talking about," Bailey said, as she followed behind Alexis.

"You listen to me because I won't repeat myself. The girl you're trashing all around the school is our best friend. If we ever hear you say her name again, I will personally rip out every hair extension that is glued to your fucking head." Pushed to her breaking point, I saw Alexis shove the know-it-all cheerleader to the wall.

"Get your hands off me, Alexis or I will file assault charges against you."

"Do it bitch, and I promise you that you will never be able to cheer again," Bailey said, as she got in front of her sister.

"Yeah? And why is that, Bailey?"

"Forget about cheering, Brittany. You won't be able to speak af-ter I rip your disrespectful tongue from your mouth."

I felt so sick after hearing the exchange between my friends and the cheerleaders. How the hell am I going to be able to walk the halls of this school again? Kara stepped in front of Alexis and put her hands up to calm everyone down. She apologized for her friend's behavior, and then they got into a heated exchange. Kara finally found her voice and told Brittany to shut up because she was being cruel and pathetic. Brittany shot daggers at my friends and pushed out of the bathroom with Kara following her out.

I couldn't hold back the vomit that churned around in my stom-ach, I turned around and got violently sick. I was on my knees, as my stomach retched. I got on my feet, and I was a little dizzy. They didn't know I was in here, and when I walked out from the stall, Bai-ley and Alexis looked shocked and realized I heard every word that was said about me. I thanked them for defending me, and they promised that they wouldn't let anyone ever hurt me again. I wanted to believe that was true, but it was easier to believe the rumors than the actual truth.

So far, Michael was portrayed as the hero that had been wrongly accused, and I was the slut that was responsible for it. I never wanted to run so much in all my life, but I promised Simon that I would be strong.

I rinsed my mouth and splashed water on my face. Bailey texted Simon, and when I walked out from the bathroom, he was leaning against the lockers waiting for me. I just wanted to fall apart in his arms, but my strong boyfriend wouldn't let me do that. He pulled me in for a hug and didn't care who was watching.

"Let's get out of here," he suggested.

"You read my mind."

I didn't tell Simon that my stomach was bothering me. The vomiting was hard on my body, but then I felt a sharp pain that shot down my side. I hoped it would subside after I took something for it. We said goodbye to the girls, and I promised I would call them tonight. We drove to the Juice Bar and sat in our favorite booth. Simon leaned down to kiss me and said he would be right back. I gave our waitress our orders and then waited for Simon to return. I was looking at my phone and didn't notice that Seth was standing at our table.

"Hey, Nicolette, how are you doing?" he asked.

"Hi, I'm doing better."

"May I join you for a minute?" he was about to sit down, and I asked him not to.

"Seth, you can't stay. I don't have anything to say to you. I'm here with Simon, and I don't want a scene here. It's already been a bad day. Please don't make it worse for me."

"I'm sorry, Nicolette. I don't want to hurt you. I just wanted to say how sorry I am that Michael hurt you. I tried talking to him, I swear that I did, but he refused to listen to me. I'm sorry. I'm so sor-ry." He looked distraught after mentioning Michael's name.

Before I could say anything more to him, Simon was back and got right into Seth's face.

"Simon, Seth was just apologizing to me, that's it." I tried to calm him down, but he continued to glare at Seth.

"I don't want to hear it, nor do we need it. Stay the fuck away from my girlfriend, and that goes for your frat buddies and their bitchy girlfriends. Get the hell out of here, or I will physically re-move you."

Seth ran a hand through his hair and clutched the back of his neck. "I'm sorry. Nicolette, if you need me to testify in court, just let me know, and I'll be there."

I remained quiet while Seth turned to leave the restaurant. Si-mon was furious that he talked to me at all. I was trembling by the time he sat down beside me. When will this nightmare end?

"Nicolette," he said as he held my face. I couldn't hold back my tears and felt so ashamed. "Baby, look at me, please?" he said softly. "I need you to take some calming breaths for me, okay?" I shook my head and then after a few breaths, he pulled me closer as I breathed him in. "I love you, and I'm sorry for scaring you. It's going to be okay, I'll make sure of it."

Simon carried my suitcase inside and held my hand with the other. Uncle Jack was on the phone and gestured to us that he would be a minute. We went upstairs to my room, and I put my things away. I was exhausted from today and wished I could just fall asleep with Simon next to me. He knew what I was thinking and shot me a sexy wink.

A few minutes later, Uncle Jack was at my door. "Hey, sorry to interrupt. Can I have a few minutes alone with Nickel?"

"Sure, no problem. I'll be downstairs." Simon closed the door behind him, and then Uncle Jack immediately took me in his arms for a hug.

"You scared me. Please don't ever do that again. We are a family always and forever, and we are too strong not to work out our issues. My heart just about leaped out of my chest when Simon came running down the stairs. We knew we hurt you, but we never thought you would leave and not tell us."

"I'm sorry, Uncle Jack. I just didn't see any other way."

"We will always find a way, I promise you. I love you."

"I love you too."

By the time we got downstairs, mom and dad were home. When they saw me, they looked relieved that I was home too. Both hugged me with death grips around my body. More apologies were said, and then I finally called out, "Can we eat?"

Laughter followed and we walked into the dining room. Gracie had been cooking up a storm, and the smells coming from the kitchen was making Simon's mouth water. He was eating double his calorie intake to get ready for Saturday. He said he couldn't wait to eat more of Gracie's cooking.

I was about to sit down and take my place when I felt another twinge of pain on my side. I had to catch my breath. It didn't go unnoticed by Simon.

"What's wrong? Should I get your mom?"

"I'll go. You stay here and talk with my family."

"Nicolette, are you sure?"

"I'm fine. I'll be back in a few minutes."

He looked worried, but he let me go to talk to my mom. She was in the kitchen with Aunt Sara and Gracie when I stepped in to ask her to come up to my room.

"Are you sick?" she asked.

"I'm not sure. I've been feeling a weird pain come and go all day today, and then I did vomit a few times while I was at school."

She checked my temperature, and I had no fever. She explained that when you're pregnant, a woman's body goes through all kinds of changes. I wasn't bleeding, so she assured me that was a good sign.

"Nicolette, if the pain returns again, you must promise to tell me, okay?"

"I will, thank you, mom."

"I'll always be here for you. I'm just thankful you came home after we all behaved so badly. I know we were wrong and will have to work hard at regaining your trust. Please just allow us to do so, and lean on us for support. I promise I will not pressure you again."

"Thank you, mom. I love you too. I just want to put the last few days behind us, okay?"

"Okay, let's go eat."

"You go ahead, I'll be right down."

Once mom was gone, I let out the breath I was holding. The pain was back and this time a little stronger. I didn't want to scare anyone and going back to the hospital was the last thing I wanted to do.

I remembered what Dr. Jonas told me about risks of losing the pregnancy. I said a prayer and left it in God's hands. I changed into my yoga pants and a loose top and then walked back down for dinner.

Simon, always the concerned boyfriend, met me at the bottom of the stairs. "Are you okay?"

"Yup, all better. Let's go join the others."

We spent the next few hours talking, telling family stories, and just laughing and enjoying each other's company. I didn't know how much I missed all of this. It made me so happy to see how much fun Simon was having. He said his goodbyes to my family and walked me upstairs to my room.

"I want you to climb into this bed, snuggle under your covers, and get some real sleep." He kissed my nose and waited for my answer. I promised him no more running, and I would fall asleep to the playlist that he made just for me.

When he kissed me goodnight, it was so gentle, I almost didn't feel it. Taking him by surprise, I kissed him hard and sucked on his tongue. I knew this would drive him wild, but I didn't care. He once asked me to try it, but I was nervous and didn't do it. He tried to show me how, but then I never did it again until tonight. Simon's eyes lit up when he realized how I was kissing him.

Yes! He reacted the way I wanted him to. He had been incredibly supportive throughout this entire ordeal, and all I gave him back was stress and broken promises. I didn't want to see anymore doubt in his eyes, knowing that I was the one who put it there. From now on, I would show him how much I loved and wanted him, only Simon.

He let out a soft moan from his throat, telling me he knew. He waved his finger at me and said that I didn't play fair. I giggled, and we hugged each other until we heard a loud horn right outside my window.

"One sec. I'll be right back." He walked outside to my balcony and called down to Sam. "Hey, I'll be right there. Stop with the damn horn." I laughed. It felt great to laugh. "Nicolette, can you do me a favor tonight?"

"Anything, you only have to ask."

"Dream of me."

Dream of Simon? I've been doing that since he told me he loved me. I didn't think I would have any problem falling asleep tonight, not when all my dreams were of Simon Paulson, the man that I would marry someday. *Yeah, I guess I should tell him that my answer is yes.*

After I finished my homework, there was a knock on my bedroom door. "Come in," I called out. It was Uncle Jack with Aunt Sara. "Hey, going somewhere?" I asked.

"Yes, we are. May we come in for a few minutes to talk to you?" Uncle Jack looked so sad, tired, and withdrawn.

"Of course, come in."

Aunt Sara gave me a hug and then took a seat on the chair across from us, while Uncle Jack was beside me. He just sat there for a moment and looked at me with loving eyes. He then took my face in his strong hands and said, "I love you with all that I am. I will never regret helping my brother become your father, and I want you to know that you will always hold a special place in my heart. Forever, Nickel, always and forever. You are a part of me, just as I am part of you."

"I love you too, Uncle Jack. I'm so sorry for what I've put you through since you came out here. I'm ashamed of my behavior, and I hate that I lashed out on you and pushed you away when all you were trying to do was be there for me. Will you forgive me?"

"Baby, there's nothing to forgive. I've been out of my mind since your mother called and told me that you got hurt. I wanted to hurt that bastard for believing he could touch even one hair on your head. I would do anything for you, Nicolette."

His hands began to shake a little, and I saw that Aunt Sara had wiped away a few tears. "Jack, we don't want to miss our flight. This was supposed to be a happy goodbye."

"I'm sorry, honey, but how can it be when we are leaving our girl?" he tearfully said.

"Uncle Jack, please don't be sad. I need you so much, and Aunt Sara too."

"We won't be sad, honey, as long as we know you are okay. You will always have us in your life, and we will be here for you anytime you need us. I promise we will visit soon, and on happier terms. You are so strong. We love you."

"I love you, Aunt Sara."

My aunt gave me a few more minutes with Uncle Jack. I hated that he was leaving me, but I knew he had to return home to Chicago, as I needed to stay here in California.

"My girl, you'll be okay, right?"

"Yes, don't worry."

"Yeah, right. No matter where I am, I will always be looking out for you. If you ever decide to come back to us, your room is waiting for you."

One last hug, and then he left. I didn't know what the future held for me, and if I would ever return to Chicago, but one thing was for sure that I never had to question:

My home was with Simon, and wherever he was, is exactly where I would be.

Mason

"Are you ready to go?" I asked Jack as he placed his suitcases by the door.

"Yeah, our car will be here soon. We said goodbye to Nickel, and Sara is out back with Christina."

"Yeah, they never liked saying goodbye to each other. How did everything go upstairs? Is Nicolette okay?"

"Are any of us? There's a matter you and I need to discuss before I leave."

"Let's go into my office." I held my breath knowing what he would say. The last few days had been contentious at best, and with yesterday happening with Nicolette, my brother was hanging on by a thread. His decision to leave tonight surprised me, which led me to be concerned with what he would say or do next. He poured himself his favorite glass of bourbon and twirled the liquid around in his glass.

"Massimo, I need you to understand a few things before I leave your home."

"Will you please call me Mason. We have discussed this. I am not that person anymore."

"Yes, you are! People don't change, just circumstances. You've been reminding me of that fact your entire adult life. Massimo, you have forgotten many things about our past and our family. You sit here out in this godforsaken place, in your big home, and carved out a brand-new life for yourself, but it will never replace the old one you lived. All of this and your new and improved name will never replace who you truly are."

337

"Don't do this. Jack, we have been over this a thousand times already. Mama and papa changed our names to give us a chance at a new life. They didn't want the stigma of their past to cling to what they tried to build for us. We were their future. Their sons. They worked so hard when they arrived from Italy and settled us in that small brownstone. Mama loved it so much because it was ours. They worked so hard when they arrived here in America. Endless hours working and leaving us all alone, so they could give us a better life. You are my older brother, and you always took care of me, and our family. You gave me the most precious gift in the world, our Nicolette. I will always be grateful to you and never be able to repay you for that, but I need you to do something for me. Please, you need to allow us to continue to take care of our daughter and not interfere. If you need me to spill blood tonight and promise on it, I will. You have my promise, Jack. With every breath, I have in my body, I will not let her be hurt again. Never again."

I poured myself a drink and waited for him to respond. He was quiet, too quiet, and that was never a good thing when it came to my brother. I never knew what to expect from him.

"Massimo, when I first heard about Nicolette and how that animal raped her, I lost all logical thinking and snapped. I stepped outside of my body and returned to another place that I have spent years trying to forget. I wanted that fucker dead. I still do. All it would have taken would be one phone call, and then it would be over."

He poured another drink and continued, "As much as I was driven by my anger, I knew if I followed through with my intention, I would risk destroying another piece of my soul and hurt Sara. I was willing to take the risk for our daughter, just like papa risked everything by bringing us to America. It's what you do for the people you love most: you take the risk. Having said that, I won't lie to you and say that I have changed my mind about wanting him dead. That is a prayer I say nightly, but I will make you a promise, as you made one for me."

He said, "I will keep my word and not rain down the hell that Michael St. Clair deserves, for now. I will trust that he will be held accountable for his crimes against our daughter. If that happens, I will never go back on my word. Now, if the fucker walks, then all bets are off. I will not hesitate to make that one phone call to end this once and for all. You must understand. I will not be able to keep the promises I made to you here tonight. You need to agree with what I have just said to you. I need to hear the words, Massimo. Do you agree?"

"Yes. I agree with you, Jack."

We said our goodbyes, and then I watched as they left our home. I needed a moment to breathe and sent my wife up to bed while I took some time to remember every detail of my conversation with my brother.

I picked up a family photo of all of us together when we vacationed at Jack's cabin. Jack had his arm around Sara and Nicolette, and mine was around Christina. We were a family, strong and united. Although we talked, I'm still not sure how we were today, and that scared me. I know what he promised, and what I agreed to, but it was not enough. The doubt of the unknown still lingered deep inside of me. I'd seen the dark side of my brother, just as much as the love that was in this picture. He had the ability to flip the switch and become someone else. I prayed we would never see that side of him again. I knew that if that were to happen, then Michael St. Clair's days were numbered, and there's not a damn thing I could say or do to stop it.

Simon

Dreaming of my angel always made my heart race. I was having the same dream that blessed my nights for the past week now. It was our wedding day, and I had finally made her mine. Our commitment to each other was sealed forever. It was a beautiful dream, one I hoped to make a reality soon.

My voice was crystal clear as I recited my vows to her, and then I saw the tears in her eyes when we were pronounced husband and wife. My dream felt so real, and I never wanted to wake from it. But then the three giants that were my brothers had other ideas. They were huge beasts, so lifting my mattress to flip me didn't take much effort. They stopped bouncing the bed once I opened my eyes.

"Come on, track star, wake up!" my brother Andrew shouted. I tried to punch him away, but then Jacob and Cameron joined in on pulling me from my contented sleep to start my day. It was Saturday, the day of my track meet. I knew how important this day was, not only for me but for my coach and my teammates.

"Okay, I'm up. You three, get off my bed and get out of my room," I shouted, but they ignored me.

"Hey, baby bro, don't go crying to us now. We hope the Cali sunshine hasn't gone and whipped your ass into a little girl now," Andrew teased.

When all three of them decided to tackle me back down to the bed, I had enough of the brotherly bonding. "Get the fuck out of my room! How's that for not being whipped?" I shouted back at them.

Of course, my mom was always in listening range and came into my room to reprimand me. Shaking her head in disapproval, she said, "Simon, they're only fooling around. Must you speak to your brothers that way?" She then smiled up at Jacob, Andrew, and then Cameron. I swear she looked at them as if she was picturing glowing halos above their heads.

I was finally up on my feet, walked over to my mother, and kissed her on her cheek. "Yes, mom. That's exactly how I speak to your brawny spawns."

I ignored the laughter coming from my brothers and walked into my bathroom to get ready. Of course, they were still here when I finished my shower.

"When do we get to meet the love of your life?" asked Cameron.

"You will meet her today at the track meet. Nicolette will be there with her parents, so please be on your best behavior." That earned me a piece of toast thrown at my head from Andrew. "I mean it, guys. Don't embarrass me today."

I went back to getting ready and couldn't help but notice the air had shifted from a light-hearted morning to now a more serious one. Jacob, the leader of the trio, stood with his hands on his hips and asked to speak with me. I knew this was coming. My brothers had been worried about me since learning of Nicolette's attack, and because our father shared everything about my life with them, there was no way to avoid this conversation.

"Simon, can we talk?" Jacob walked up behind me and placed his hand on my shoulder.

"No, not today. If you three are going to talk down about my relationship with Nicolette, then forget it. I will not have this debate with you, not with my brothers who are supposed to have my back. Dad has already put me through it for months now, and I'm sick of it."

"Hey! Calm down and talk with us. We came all this way to see our kid brother, and we would never say anything negative about your girl. Can you please hear us out?" Andrew asked.

"Okay, I'll listen," I said to all three of them, and then Jacob took the lead.

"We always have your back, little brother, so let's get that straight right now. We love you, and we are only asking you to not shut us out, especially when we know you need us the most. We're sorry we didn't come sooner and haven't been here for you as much as we would have liked, but we are here now and want to help you any way we can," Jacob said and then gestured to Cameron.

"Simon, when you hurt, we hurt."

"Yeah, the four musketeers! One for all, and all for one. Right, Simon?" asked Andrew. "We don't need to get into anything heavy right now. All we want is to make sure you are okay with all of this. Are you?"

I threw my towel across the room and grabbed the back of my neck. This was the last thing I needed today.

I said, "Thanks for your support, but you don't have to worry about me. I am one hundred percent sure of my love for Nicolette, and I'm fully prepared for anything life throws our way."

"Like...a baby?" Cameron asked. I froze at the mention of Nicolette's baby. How did they know?

"How the hell did you three find out. I never told you, so that means mom or dad did."

"We overheard mom and dad talking about it. I think the bigger question is: why didn't you tell us? This is pretty big news, and it's a lot for you to be handling all on your own. Come on, Simon, get your head out of the clouds and join us here on earth. This is just crazy."

"I'm sorry you feel that way, Jacob, I guess you two agree with him? So much for the brotherly support. Yeah, she's pregnant, and she's not sure if she's keeping it or not."

"Simon, listen to me. Have you really considered how raising this kid as your own will ultimately affect your entire life? I mean, getting a girl knocked up under normal circumstances is a major life changer, but this is anything but normal. Your girl was raped, and now pregnant with her rapist's baby? Wake up! We know you, man, and you can't just stand here and tell us that you are okay with it."

"What the hell do you want from me, Jacob? Do you want me to just break-up with Nicolette? I will never do that. And before you make her sound as the girl trying to trap me, know this: she has done everything in her power to push me away, in the name of protecting me. Do you hear me? She's more concerned about my feelings than her own. She's my girl, my future. Do you think I prefer her to be pregnant? No, I don't. It's killing me, and the thought of Nicolette being tied to that animal in this way makes me sick. But I'll never tell her that. By choosing to love Nicolette, it means that I love all of her, and that includes her unborn child. As much as the knife continues to twist and rip at my heart every time I think of Michael, it's the love that we have that fights that anger I feel. And we both come out stronger for it."

I yelled back, "Satisfied? You wanted to know how I feel, and now you do. Get the hell out of my room and leave me alone. Fuck! I have the biggest race of my life today, and this was the last thing I needed. Leave me alone. Get out!" I shouted back, but they didn't even flinch.

These three were my brothers for life, and no matter what I said, they would never turn their backs on me. It just became too much standing in my room with them, and I finally began to slowly break. Andrew was the first to bear hug me, followed by Cameron, and Jacob. I had been holding in my feelings for so long now, trying to be strong for my girl, that I never knew this was exactly what I needed. They always had the ability to read me like a book and let me yell, hit, and scream it out until I finally began to calm.

My brothers laughed, and I couldn't help joining in after Jacob said a joke about not getting into a heavy conversation. Right! These guys didn't do anything halfway. They knew I needed them, and I finally allowed my guard down so they could help me.

Mom and dad were waiting for their brood of men to join them for breakfast. Dad raised his glass to me and wished me well today. I swallowed as much food as I could and then I had to get down to the field.

My phone had been blowing up all morning with messages from my team, including one very special greeting from my girl. She told me that she loved me and couldn't wait to watch me win the championship today.

"Come on, Paulson, get warmed up," Coach Johnson shouted. I told him that I was more than ready for my three events today and not to worry. I was hoping to get a few minutes with Nicolette, but Jimmy interrupted my plan.

"Dude! I am pumped for today. Did you see the stands? We have scouts, and one from Stanford."

"You will do great man. Good luck." I slapped him on his back and joined the rest of our team.

I looked around, and my eyes met hers watching me from the stands. My world was returned right again at the sight of my angel. She waved to me and then held up her signs, along with Bailey's. It

344

read: **TEAM SIMON**, while Alexis's read: **TEAM JIMMY**. Jimmy nudged me with his shoulder after reading the signs. My friend was in love, and I laughed out loud but was very happy for him. He finally managed to win the heart of Miss Ice Princess, and clearly, she was in love with him too.

Nicolette

His day was finally here. My excitement could be read all over my face, as the gun went off to begin the day's events. Simon was set to compete in the 100 and 400-meter dashes, and in the 4x400 meter relay race. That was his event to dominate in.

He was set to compete in the hurdles along with Jimmy, but he felt the tension in his Achilles tendon and didn't want to risk injury. He asked the coach if he could pick an alternate to take his place and prayed he made the right decision. He easily won the 100, and his team was on their way to winning the championship.

Simon knew he would not be running for his chosen college, but Jimmy would. Mr. Paulson only had football dreams in his eyes when it came to his three brothers, but Simon wanted something different, and now that future included me. He never wanted to disappoint his family, but he said he was his own man and had to follow the dreams that made him happy.

The loud snap of the gun startled me from my daydreaming, as the 400 dash began. Jimmy wore a determined expression on his face. He wanted to be noticed by the Stanford scout, but Simon was way ahead of him, as the cameras flashed on the track star, along with the attention of the scouts.

Alexis was holding her breath for Jimmy, but then I noticed how Simon slowed down, giving his friend an opportunity to pass him, resulting in Jimmy taking the win. Simon came in second, and the crowd erupted with applause for Jimmy after he had beaten the track star and team favorite.

Simon scanned the crowd, and then found me. He winked, and then caught his breath. I knew then what he had done for his friend, and I couldn't have loved him more than at that moment. His coach charged him and began yelling. Even over the loud crowd, he could still be heard.

"What the hell did you just do? Son, that was not our plan," he shouted at Simon, who was completely calm with his answer.

"Don't worry. I know what I'm doing."

"Yeah? I wish you would let me in on it. We are one race away from winning the title. Don't be reckless and take foolish chances again," he said and then stormed off.

Simon just stood there and allowed the coach to yell at him, but the coach didn't know everything. Simon was more than focused and ready to take the championship. He knew what this would mean for Jimmy and a few of his teammates who were hoping for track scholarships. He didn't need nor want any more validity for his accomplishments. He wanted this win for his team and was determined to get it.

While other events were taking place, Simon and his team had time before the final event. He walked over to the stands and was greeted by his parents, along with mine who were excited to watch Simon compete. I was nervous about meeting his brothers, but they were all very nice and all took turns giving me a bear hug. Simon had warned me earlier that they would do that and not be scared by the giants he called his brothers.

They were awesome, and I loved the signature Paulson greeting I had heard so much about. They were all over six feet in height and matched each other in weight. Andrew was the biggest out of the three and was close to 250 pounds. But you wouldn't know it by looking at them since they were all built and toned. They talked about Northwestern, and how much they hoped to be drafted into the NFL. This was their father's dream for his boys, and I somehow knew it would come true. These guys loved football, talking about football, and playing football. I was saved from more football conversation when Simon finally reached for me and gave me the greeting I've been waiting for all morning.

"Hey beautiful," he gave me a chaste kiss on my cheek, knowing all eyes were on us. I giggled under my breath. He was adorable. "Walk with me for a few minutes." He held my hand in his, and we made our way through the stands. He walked us away from the sounds from the crowd cheering him for the last race he would compete in.

Once we were alone, he asked me how I was feeling. I looked at him confused and wondered why he would ask me such a question.

"I'm fine, and having a fabulous time, might I add." I gave him my best smile, but my boyfriend sensed something off with me and asked again in a more serious tone.

"Nicolette, you look pale, and when I kissed you back there, I felt how warm your skin is. Now is not the time for jokes. Do you have a fever?"

How could I hide anything from him? Simon had a sixth sense when it came to me.

"Well?" he asked.

"A small one. Don't be mad. I haven't been feeling well for the past couple of days. I thought it was normal because I was pregnant."

"I'm not upset, but you should have told me that you were sick. I wouldn't have had you come here today had I known. Does your mother know you're running a fever?"

I wanted to come up with a lie, but he knew the answer just by looking at me. "No, I haven't said anything yet, and I don't want you to either. I'm fine, babe. Please don't worry about me." As I tried to convince him that I was telling the truth, I suddenly felt a sharp pain shoot down my side and below in my abdomen. I took a deep breath and fought through the wince, as the pain traveled through me.

He took one look at me and began to pull me back to my parents. I stopped and told him that I was fine. He didn't believe me, but I wasn't going to allow this to ruin his day.

"Nicolette, why are you being so stubborn about this? Fine, have it your way, but I'm not running anymore today."

"No! I won't let you do that. Simon, you have worked so hard for this day, and you are so close to winning the championship."

"Will you tell your mom?" he continued to push, and he refused to compete in the final race until I agreed.

"Yes, I will tell my mom. Happy?"

"No, not when I know my girl is sick. I love you. Don't be mad at me because I'm worried about you."

Bullseye! Right to my heart.

Now I felt bad because I knew I hurt his feelings. I gave him a kiss and assured him I was fine. Deep down, I knew what was happening and prayed for nature to take its course. I was cautioned by my doctor and read all the statistics about losing a pregnancy. I cupped Simon's face and kissed him again and again. I promised him that if I felt any worse, I would leave and go to the hospital. Using my best moves on him was the only way to calm him down. He couldn't resist when I gave in to passion and kissed him madly. He loved it, and with every kiss, he seemed to visibly relax...*well, not in every area of his body.*

He looked down to his shorts and winked at me. "Thanks, babe. You made sure all my assets were on full display for the cameras." I blushed and knew my guy was good to go. He gave me a hug and a moment to calm his body down before he walked me back to the stands. He was protective of me, and I didn't blame him for something that came so naturally for him.

Once I was seated, he shook his finger at me, making me keep my word to him. I smiled back and crossed my heart. He walked over to his brother, Andrew, and pulled him aside. They both looked over at me, and then I knew he was asking Andrew to keep an eye on me, never believing that I could take care of myself. I guess that was my fault for Simon doubting me. I wasn't always honest with him when he begged me to trust him. I saw Andrew nod his head and then bear hug his brother. Simon returned to the field and got ready for his final track event.

With the snap of the gun, they took off and ran the race of their life. Alexis was jumping up and down cheering for Jimmy, and I got up to join her and then felt dizzy. Andrew caught a glimpse of my almost stumble. He was by my side in seconds. He wrapped my arm around his neck and easily lifted me up from the bleachers. He was a bear of a man and began carrying me down. No one cared to notice since they were all too focused on the race.

"Andrew, I'm fine. You can let go of the death grip you have on me," I said, as he gently sat me down.

"Sorry, sis. I have my orders to take care of you."

I smiled, and then he gave me the Paulson wink, along with a cool bottle of water.

"Is it helping?" he asked.

"Yes, I'm much better. It was hot up in the stands, that's all. Thank you for taking care of me, but I am fine. Let's go back and watch your brother win the championship, okay?"

We cheered the guys on, as Jimmy handed off the baton to Simon. He was so focused on the finish line. It would be close, with two runners closing in on him. He sped up and crossed the line in victory. His coach and teammates rushed and lifted him up in the air, shouting their congratulations. They finally did it!

Our moms were crying, and our dads were high fiving each other. The brothers jumped down from the bleachers and ran toward Simon. I was close behind until my pain stopped me where I stood. This time it was severe, and I was bent over while trying to catch my breath. I called for Bailey, who came to my rescue.

"Bailey, you need to get me out of here, and I mean now!"

"Nicolette, you need to go to the hospital. I'm going to sit you down here and go get Simon."

"No! Bailey, you will not. He's the last person I want to see right now. He's earned his five minutes of happiness. Let him have it. Let me just sit and rest for a few minutes. This is Simon's day, and I will not spoil it for him. I've caused him enough stress."

"Nicolette, if you knew anything about your boyfriend, then you would know he would want to be here for you, especially when it's clear that you are sick and in pain. If something happens to you, how do you think he's going to react knowing I could have done something to help you? Please don't put this on me. He loves you something fierce, and I don't want to lie or piss him off."

"Bailey, I'm much better, see? I told you that the rest would help. It's hot out here today, and I didn't eat that much at breakfast."

"You are a bad liar, Nicolette. The minute you feel sick again, all bets are off, and I will tell Simon. Deal?"

"Deal. Now give me a hug before I start to cry. You're a great friend, Bailey. I love you."

"I love you, but not a big fan of your stubbornness. You drive me crazy. Go congratulate your hot man before a cheerleader steals him away from you."

I laughed. "No chance of that happening." I wasn't lying to Bailey. The rest helped, and I felt better. I was able to walk over to Simon's waiting arms with no pain at all.

"Hey, baby, give your man a kiss," he said as he reached for my mouth. I kissed him back with everything I had. He was completely adorable. He then lifted me up and squeezed me hard, causing me to wince with some pressure on my side. I inhaled a quiet gasp of breath and released it before he could see my face.

I said, "I am so proud of you. You were a rock star out there today. Look at Alexis. She's kissing the hell out of Jimmy."

"I'm happy for them, but I would rather be kissing and loving you more than anything in the world. I'm going to take a quick shower, and then I'll come find you."

"I'll be waiting for you."

"I'm counting on it. Love you," he shouted over his shoulders as he joined Jimmy, and followed the rest of his team back inside.

I let out a few deep breaths and walked over to the ladies' room. I gripped the sides of the sink and willed the pain to go away. I splashed cold water on my face and didn't miss my reflection in the mirror. My cheeks were flushed. I knew my fever was getting worse. I sat down and rested my forehead against a cool rag and hoped it would do the trick.

With how I have been feeling the last few days, I suspected my body was rejecting the pregnancy, and I was in the beginning stages of a miscarriage. The pain wasn't going away, as it intensified with each increased twinge to my side and abdomen. I had to believe and trust what my body was telling me. I just needed to get through the rest of the day without setting off any alarms to my family or Simon.

The girls were not convinced that I was better, but I told them to focus on the celebration that was taking place on the field and not to worry about me. He wasn't too hard to find standing next to his equally tall brothers, but Simon stood out from them. He was just as tall, but leaner with his muscular frame. He looked good enough to eat in his faded ripped jeans and a white t-shirt. His tanned body was kissable, and I couldn't help but swoon over him. He was easy on the eyes. It was no wonder why all the girls at the school fell all over him.

He must have felt my eyes burning holes through his back because he turned around and locked eyes with me. He gave me his best panty dropping smile and walked over to me. My boyfriend sure loved lifting me into his arms, and this time, he added a twirl. He was making me dizzy, as I begged him to stop or risk me throwing up on him. He slowly slid me down his body and made sure I felt every inch of his muscular frame.

He gazed into my eyes, studying every feature about me. It felt like he was trying to create a forever image. I was beginning to think he was right about our connection, just by the way he was looking and touching me now.

"Do I have something in my teeth?" I jokingly asked him.

"Yes, you do. It's big and green."

"Ha! I know you're teasing, but I love it. I love you."

"I love you so much that it can actually make me hurt when you're not with me. I know it's crazy. Just holding you in my arms is making my mind wander off to places it shouldn't."

I leaned into his chest and breathed him in. "Simon, I'm sorry."

Alarmed by my apology, he held my face in his strong hands and asked me why I was sorry. He looked worried.

"It's not anything you did. I'm just sorry because I can't be with you the way you want to be with me."

"Nicolette, you're not hurting me by not sleeping with me. Our time is coming, and I will wait forever for you. Please don't stress over sex. When it happens for us, it will mean so much more, I promise you. I don't want you to worry. And if you catch me staring at you, it's because I am so madly in love with you and say my thanks to God every single day that you're with me. You are responsible for all my smiles. I am going to make you so happy. You will never know anything else."

As he held me in his arms, I thought, *how could he be any more wonderful than he is right now? I am so in love with Simon Paulson, that I can't see straight.*

The celebrations continued as we said our goodbyes to our family and friends. Simon told me he had a surprise for me but wouldn't tell me what it was until we got there. He again blindfolded me and made me promise not to peek. When we finally arrived at our destination, he told me to keep my eyes covered until he removed the blindfold. He opened my door and carried me up two flights of stairs, and then I knew where he had taken me.

He placed me down and removed the cloth that was covering my eyes. When I opened them, I saw that we were at his beach house, and the deck was decorated in twinkling bright lights, with a table set for two. It was the most romantic gesture anyone had ever done for me. Simon wrapped his arms around me and asked if I liked it. I pulled his lips down to meet my own and told him how it was beautiful and amazing.

How could I not love my surprise and the man who arranged it for me? He walked me over to my seat and placed the linen napkin across my lap. We drank sparkling water from flutes. He looked so happy when he lifted the silver dome, and to my surprise, it was my Aunt Sara's Roof Top Buster Burger.

I asked Simon how he managed to arrange this surprise for me. He smiled and told me he worked it out with Uncle Jack before he flew home. It was prepared and shipped out right away. My mouth was watering just smelling the amazing burger in front of me. Simon already began eating his, while I was nervous about how my stomach would react. I managed to eat half, along with some of the steak fries. I was full and could eat no more, and then Simon cleaned his plate and finished off what I had on mine.

After dinner, Simon asked me if I would dance with him. It had been a while since we did this, and he looked so sincere when he held out his hand. He played our song, "Your Body is a Wonderland." Simon shared with me that on the day we met, he drove home, and this song played on the radio. He knew it was ours to have, and it had become his favorite to listen to every time he thought of me.

I had never felt more relaxed, and I was in no pain. All I felt was the gentle kisses he placed on my neck and shoulders.

We continued to dance through a few more songs, and then he asked me if I was ready for bed. I looked up at Simon, and he kissed my anxiety away.

"Relax, baby. I meant to sleep and nothing more."

"You mean sleep? As in, sleep here…at the beach house…with you?" I stuttered over my words, and it felt as if my tongue was beginning to swell. This wouldn't be the first time we shared a bed, but here in this house just meant so much more. The flowers, the candles, and the amazing meal we just shared was incredibly thoughtful of Simon to do for me. I just didn't want to disappoint him—not ever.

"Yes, we are both sleeping here tonight, and before you ask, your parents know we are here together. I love you, and so do they. Your parents trust us. No worrying tonight, okay?"

He led me upstairs to the master bedroom. I found a small bag filled with my pajamas, toiletries, and fresh clothes for tomorrow. Simon had thought of everything, and my heart was just bursting with love for him.

He ran a bath for me with my favorite lavender salts. While I was soaking in the tub, he got ready in the other bathroom. I wanted him to join me in the tub, but he laughed and said he didn't think that would be a great idea on account of how I worked him up on the field earlier today. He kissed me and left me on my own to relax. I felt amazing, so loved and cherished.

The bed had been turned down, and fresh flowers were on the nightstand. He was propped up on his elbows and invited me in to lay with him. Once I was there, he pulled me to his side and held me close to his body. I had never felt so safe.

Wrapped in his arms and legs entwined with mine, I couldn't have asked for a more intimate moment with the man I loved. Our breaths began to even out as we drifted off into sleep.

A few hours later, my skin felt like it was on fire. Simon must have shifted through the night, because he was sleeping on his side, hugging a pillow. My sleep tee and shorts were soaked in sweat, as I tried to move without waking Simon.

Once I reached the bathroom, I felt a pop and burst, as liquid ran down between my legs. Blood started to pour out of me, and then the pain hit me like a freight train. I let out a cry for help, and then I saw Simon burst through the door, shocked and scared at what he saw. I felt unsteady on my feet as my head began to spin. Simon caught me in his arms as I began to fall to the floor.

I was in and out of unconsciousness, and my eyes began to roll to the back of my head. Simon was screaming at me to stay with him as he dialed 911. The paramedics arrived, and I was placed onto a stretcher and lifted into an ambulance. I felt a sharp stick to my arm, and my face was covered with an oxygen mask. The sirens were loud, and I heard strangers read off what I thought was my vitals, and then I heard Simon. He was begging me not to die.

"Baby, please open your eyes and stay with me. Don't you leave me, Nicolette!" he continued to scream, as he begged me to stay with him.

I was so tired and could do nothing to keep my eyes from closing.

"I love you, Simon," I whispered as my eyes began to close, and I fell asleep to Simon's painful and panicked sobs.

Simon

I had never felt so helpless and scared as I watched Nicolette be taken away from me and put into an exam room. I had her blood all over me. My heart ached for my girl and what was happening to her. Dr. Jonas was the doctor on call tonight, and I was thankful for it. She knew us well, and I trusted her to take care of my girl.

With trembling hands, I pulled out my cell phone to call her parents. It was just after five a.m. when her father answered, half-asleep. I told him what happened and where we were. I heard her mother asking what was wrong in the background, as I assumed her father got out from their bed to get dressed. He said he would be with me soon, and then the call disconnected.

I paced the lonely waiting room and waited for someone to tell me something on my girl. Nicolette's parents came running down and stopped at the nurse's station, demanding information on their daughter. The nurse told them the same coded answer she gave me: "You will have to wait for the doctor."

When Mr. Vanelle turned around, I was silently standing behind him. His eyes took in the sight of me and how I looked. He covered his mouth and sobbed loudly, knowing whatever was happening with Nicolette was not good. He began to question what happened, and then I just fell apart. I couldn't hold back my emotions any longer.

"Simon, we're here now. It's going to be okay. Will you tell us what happened?" he questioned and was incredibly calm. I told him that we were asleep, and I was awakened by screams coming from the bathroom. Nicolette had been gripping the sink while standing in a pool of her own blood. She was in so much pain, I thought she was dying.

Her mother gasped and wiped away her tears. She said, "She's losing the baby."

I didn't know what to say. For the second time, I had Nicolette's blood all over me, and now she was going through a miscarriage. All I wanted was to be with my girl, but no one had come out yet.

We waited for more than four hours to hear news on Nicolette. I was beside myself with worry. When Dr. Jonas finally emerged from the O.R. doors, she told us that Nicolette had needed emergency surgery.

"How's our daughter?" her father questioned.

Dr. Jonas was removing her surgical cap as she walked us back into the waiting room. "Nicolette suffered a miscarriage, along with a uterine tear to her placenta. It caused a monstrous hemorrhage."

I would have fallen to my knees if I wasn't leaning against the wall for support.

"Mr. and Mrs. Vanelle, Nicolette has barely healed from the sexual assault she endured, which caused much damage to her uterine wall. As I explained to Nicolette, it was very rare to become pregnant after experiencing a trauma in the manner she did. This is her body's way of rejecting the pregnancy, resulting in miscarriage."

Her mother interrupted. "When did you have these conversations with our daughter? I knew nothing of these risks. Why didn't you tell us? We could have been better prepared, or even pushed harder for her to get an abortion."

"Mrs. Vanelle, your daughter is an adult, and I have to protect the rights of my patient."

I flipped out. Every word that was coming from her mouth was making my stomach heave. "That's such fucking bullshit!"

"Simon! Calm down, son."

"No! I will not come down. Mr. Vanelle, we should have known about her condition. If I had, I wouldn't have brought her all the way to the beach. What if we didn't get here in time? She could have bled out and died in my arms tonight." I let out a roar of pain mixed with screams and tears. All I wanted was my girl. I needed to see her and make sure she was truly still with me, but at the same time, I was so fucking angry.

Her mom rushed right over to me and comforted me as best as she could. "I'm so sorry, Simon, for you ever having to go through what you did tonight. I wish we could have helped her sooner. Had she been alone, she may not have made it. You saved her life tonight."

I couldn't speak, just sat there and listened to Dr. Jonas further explain Nicolette's condition to her parents. She told them that when she located the tear, a severe infection was evident, which would explain why Nicolette was running a fever. I never knew how bad it was; Nicolette hid it from me. Dr. Jonas went on to say that by the time she was inside her body, the infection was so severe, that she feared Nicolette may have gone into septic shock. Any longer, and she would have. Nicolette must have known what was happening to her, and she never said a fucking word to me.

I couldn't stand to be in their company for one more minute. I found the nearest bathroom and then proceeded to puke up my guts. I couldn't believe this was happening. *I'm here in this fucking hospi-*

tal, again, and I can't do anything to help her but wait. I needed air, but I wouldn't leave her, and I was still covered in her blood. I needed fresh clothes, so I called my mom.

My dad and brothers had gone hiking up in Big Bear, so when I reached my mom, she was just running early morning errands. Within less than an hour, mom arrived and found me outside the emergency room entrance. She took me in her arms, and I broke down and cried in defeat. This was atypical for me to do, as I always tried to control my emotions, but not today. I needed my mom to tell me that my girl was going to be okay, and we would get through this. I promised Nicolette.

"Simon, what happened?" I was sick that I had to say the words again, but I explained it all to my mom. She gave me words of encouragement that I needed to hear to be positive and strong. I knew she was right, but what could I do about my anger that I was feeling?

"Mom, she must have known something was wrong," I said, as my head throbbed with a headache. "After what Dr. Jonas said to her family, it all makes sense to me now. She wasn't feeling well at the track meet. I'm not blind. I saw the pain in her eyes when I held her, but she acted as if it wasn't anything to be worried about. Why did she do this? Fuck the track meet. My team would have won regardless if I'd been there or not. My girl needed me, and what does she do? She lied to me, again! How could she be so reckless with her health and not tell me?"

My heart began to race. I had to lean down and grab hold of my knees to catch my breath. Mom was over me and rubbed my back.

"Simon, take a deep breath. You are going to make yourself sick."

"No, I don't believe I could feel any worse. Mom, don't you get it? What if I didn't get her to the hospital in time? I could have lost her tonight, never knowing why she kept this from me. How many times have I asked—no, begged—her to trust me? She could have told me anything, and I would have understood. Why did she do this?" I was shouting uncontrollably to the point that I punched the wall with my fists.

"Simon, stop this right now. Come and sit with me. Punching walls are not going to help you, or Nicolette."

I hadn't done this in a long time, probably not since my aunt had died, but I needed comforting. I leaned my head onto my mother's lap and cried. She combed her fingers through my hair and whispered over and over again that she was here for me, my entire family would be. "Close your eyes, baby. It's going to be okay," she said, and then I did.

I didn't know how much time passed when I slowly sat up and began talking with my mom again. She handed me a bag of clothes and encouraged me to go clean up and change. I didn't feel like moving, but she told me to go and she would be here when I returned.

I lathered my hands with soap and watched the clear water turn red, as it ran down the drain. The sight of it made me almost ill again, but I tampered it down and cleaned my hands the best I could. I washed my face and then tore off my bloodied clothes, tossing them in the trash. Mom brought me jeans and another t-shirt. It was one of my favorites. How did she know to pick the one Nicolette loved for me to wear? Maybe it would make her smile when she saw it.

Mom told me that Nicolette's parents went down for coffee and brought one back for me. I wasn't in the mood for it, but I accepted it anyway.

"How are you feeling honey? Do you want to talk?"

"Mom, I really don't know how I'm feeling. I'm devastated for my girl and then angry with her all at the same time. How could she keep this from me? And how could I have been so oblivious not to see how sick she really was?"

"Simon, you don't know if Nicolette knew and understood how serious her condition was. She wasn't far into the pregnancy, and she's so young to comprehend all the new changes her body was going through."

"Mom, you make perfect sense, but you don't know her like I do. She's stubborn and so headstrong. She doesn't trust me, mom. If she did, then she would have never kept this from me. I tell her every single day how I feel about her, and I beg Nicolette to believe me. And now when she needs me the most, she still can't be honest and tell me what's wrong. It feels like the rape all over again. I was powerless then, as I am right now."

"Oh, Simon, I'm so sorry."

"Yeah, me too. Mom, when I'm around Nicolette, it's like all logical thinking goes out the window. I'm so blinded by my love for her, I see nothing else. Here we are, in this hospital again, and she's pushed me away and won't allow me to help her."

"Simon, anyone could see how you feel about Nicolette. I know it has taken me time to accept your relationship with her, and I'm sorry for that. She's a lovely girl, and I know she loves you too. I was just worried that you would be hurt again, but it's so obvious you two belong together. Please, son, take some time to calm down and give her a chance to explain. She loves you, and I know she trusts you. You have to be patient with her, and be very careful of her fragile heart. She's incredibly strong and inspiring. She has gone through so much in the last few months, and she's still standing. She's here and with you. What does that say about your relationship?"

"I don't know."

"Sure, you do, and you feel it right here in your heart. You love that girl with everything you have inside of you. Now go tell her that. She needs you, Simon, and you need her." All I could do was hug my mom and hoped that she knew how much I appreciated her being here for me. Just then my cell phone buzzed in my pocket.

I said to my mom, "She's awake and asking for me."

"You go, I'll stay behind with Mr. and Mrs. Vanelle. I love you, Simon."

"I love you. Thanks, mom."

I quietly entered Nicolette's room and pulled up a chair to sit beside her, carefully avoiding all the wires she was connected to. Nicolette had an IV in her arm with two bags of liquid going through it. She was hooked up to another monitoring machine with wires coming out from the top of her gown. I clenched my two fists to tamper down my anxiety seeing her like this. She looked so pale with a mist of sweat on her forehead. I felt the heat pump off her, as I leaned down to kiss her. I knew she was on a strong dose of antibiotics to fight the infection.

When I looked at my beautiful girl lying here so still, all I could do was fight back my tears for her. I was done with being strong. The sight of her last night, and now here in this condition, just weakened me. I placed my head down to her hands and prayed for her to come back to me.

The first words I heard were "I'm sorry," and then more tears fell between us.

"Why didn't you tell me, Nicolette?" I hated to ask, but I needed to know.

"In the beginning, I thought it was nothing and told my mom. After reading the baby book, we agreed that what I was feeling was normal and didn't give in to worrying about it. I experienced some sharp pains, but they always went away. I wasn't bleeding, so again, I didn't worry."

"Yes, but you were warned about the risks of carrying this pregnancy, right?"

"Yes, I was. I always knew there was a chance of rejection."

"And yet, you still didn't tell me."

"Yes."

God! I wanted to scream, but I held back not wanting to upset her. But I couldn't hold back on my questions, not when they were right there between us.

"I'll ask you again, Nicolette. Why didn't you come to me? Why didn't you tell me right away that you were sick and your symptoms were getting worse? God knows I gave you every opportunity to do so. The night we had dinner at your house, was that the first time you felt the pain?"

By the way, she looked at me, I already had my answer. I felt sick because that was days ago, and she had been suffering ever since.

"Simon, I'm sorry for not being honest with you. I should have told you the truth. You had the track meet to get ready for, and if you had known about me, then you wouldn't have been able to concentrate on winning the championship. You had so many people counting on you. I couldn't be the one to come between that."

Hearing her explanation to why she didn't tell me was like sticking a knife through my heart, and every time I heard her reasons, it twisted and gutted me more. She kept her pain hidden from me and knowing why she did it, just completely shattered me.

"Nicolette, I can't breathe without you. You are everything to me. Don't you know that by now? How can I make it any clearer to you? There is not anything, nor anyone in my life that is more important than you. I need you to believe that. You should have told me. Concealing your illness from me put your life at risk. You could have died, and I would have lost you forever. Where would that have left me? You need to always talk to me, and first and foremost, be honest."

When words failed me, I cupped her beautiful face and kissed her gently. I didn't know any other way to get through to her. So, I showed her.

Twenty-Six

Nicolette

After he kissed me, it felt as if he was literally holding on to me with everything he had. *He's afraid of losing me, and it's killing me to hurt him any more than I already have.* He's not saying much, he never does. Simon treated me so gently, and he was always saying the perfect words to make me happy. *But is he? How can he be? When I'm beautifully broken?*

"Simon, I was telling you the truth when I believed what I was feeling to be normal stages of pregnancy. Dr. Jonas, along with my therapist, explained the possible risk about being pregnant, after the injuries I sustained. My insides were still healing, and the possibility of a miscarriage was not ruled out. I was advised to take it day by day and try to live my life as normal as I could."

"Nicolette, this is exactly what I am talking about. Didn't you think your boyfriend had a right to know this information? Fuck! I had already accepted this baby as my own. I had a right to know, and

I'm so confused by your decision to keep me in the fucking dark. And what's worse is that I asked you repeatedly if something was wrong, and you lied to me every single time."

"I'm sorry, Simon."

"Baby, I don't want any more of your fucking apologies. I want your trust! Tell me what I can say or do for you to give me that?" He left my side and paced the room, leaning his head against the wall. If I wasn't trapped in this bed, I would have run to him, but he looked so lost, and it was completely my fault.

When he professed his unconditional love and his promise to help me raise this baby, I knew he meant it. He was generous and kind and always put me first. I loved him for that, and I did trust him. Maybe it was me, though, that I didn't trust. I'd been solely carrying the weight of my attack and all the stress Michael put me through even before that night on the boat. It's all been on me, and that was my choice. Then after learning, I was pregnant, it just became too hard to bear. Pressure mounted all around me, and there was Simon, the only one that gave me room to breathe and time to think. I didn't know if I could truly go through with having Michael's baby, no matter what Simon wanted me to believe.

He said that love was stronger than hate, and the baby would be part of me and that would be enough for me to go on, but I still doubted. This baby was created from an act of violence and madness. Its father was a monster that hurt me so deeply, and yet, I struggled to come to a decision on what to do about either terminating or keeping the baby. I tried to find the good, but I didn't feel I had any emotional attachment to it as new mothers would.

If this were Simon's baby, I would have been over the moon knowing I would always have a part of him, an unbreakable bond between us. It was a beautiful dream, and it was one of many I had before Michael destroyed everything I cared about. But I was still willing to take the chance of carrying his baby, and the shame that came along with it.

I knew Simon may never understand my reasons for protecting him, but I also had to protect myself. I knew the risks and accepted my fate. I had no control whether this baby would survive or not, and without voicing a decision, I just carried on and left it up to fate to decide.

He still hadn't returned to my bedside, and the way he looked was beginning to scare me. He remained quiet and detached. I finally decided to use his words against him, hoping I would be able to break down the walls that were between us.

"Simon, please don't hide from me. Will you talk to me?"

"I don't know what you want me to say here. For the first time, I'm at a loss for words, and I don't know how the hell I am feeling. I know I was scared to find you yet again standing in your own blood. I believed I would have lost you."

I told him that I was sorry over and over again until he finally shouted at me to stop. Was this his breaking point? Would he leave me and decide he's had enough?

I wanted to say more, but we were interrupted by our friends walking through the door. He must have called them while I was in surgery.

When I looked over again, Simon was gone, and my heart nearly stopped beating. I didn't know if this was the end for us, nor if I would ever see him again.

Simon

Walking away from her, especially now, was the hardest thing I could ever do. But I had to get out of there and breathe for a fucking second. The walls were closing in, and I felt trapped by the circumstances that put us in this state of loss and pain. All I wanted to do was love her, but there was someone in my way, and he needed to be gone.

I phoned my father and asked him to meet me at his law office. When he questioned why I told him that I needed a favor and it was to remain private and stay between us. I knew I was asking a lot since as a family, we shared our lives with each other, but there's always an exception to that understanding, and this was mine.

I waited outside in my Jeep until I saw his car pull up in front of the building. I stepped out to meet him, and he looked worried, but I shrugged it off and followed him inside.

"Okay, I'm here. What's this about Simon?"

"I need a favor, and you are the only one that can help me."

He sat down behind his desk and rubbed his chin, a tell that he does when he's in serious thought. "What do you need?"

"I need to see Michael St. Clair, and it has to be tonight."

"Why? What good will come to you seeing him?"

"Probably nothing, but I still need to. I can't tell you why. I don't know if I fully understand it myself, but I can't do one more thing until I see him."

"I don't know. What you are asking me to do is complicated, and maybe even unethical."

"I know, but you'll still do it because I'm your son. You said you would do anything for me, and now I'm asking. Please, Dad, I know you can make this happen."

"You're right, I can, but I'm not sure I want to. Look at what you've been through today. You're not thinking clearly, and that's dangerous. I can't risk you getting into trouble and risking your future."

"Dad, I don't know anything that, as of yesterday, I was sure of. All I have right now is this moment, and it's leading me to Michael. Are you going to help me or not?" I asked.

He said nothing in return but picked up his phone and made the call. An hour later, I was standing in a room with two double-sided windows that you could not see into, but knew you were being watched from the other side. I took a few deep breaths and tried not to second guess my decision to come here. I knew my leaving had hurt Nicolette, but I felt suffocated and needed to be away from her, not trusting what I would say or do next. It brought me back to our night at my cabana when I let her leave and I didn't follow. I was lost then and driven by my anger over Michael, and it's the same for me now. I only hoped when I returned to her, that she would forgive me.

He was led into the room in handcuffs, surprised to see me stepping out from the corner. The guard secured him to the metal loop that was on the table and forced him down into the chair. I took the seat across from him.

"What the hell are you doing here?" he demanded to know.

I looked over at him with cold eyes, and then I answered his question. "I have my ways, and that's all you need to know."

"What? You got daddy to pull some strings for you? I know he's a big-time lawyer," he mocked.

"That's irrelevant. I'm here for one reason only, and that is to look into your eyes. I need to see what a despicable human being you are. One that stalked my girlfriend for months. You couldn't accept her not wanting you, and you did the one thing only a coward would do. You brutally raped her and left her broken. You are an abomination who doesn't deserve to breathe the same fucking air as my girl. You robbed her of her innocence. Your ugliness has shattered her, and yet you still look as if you have no remorse for the life you took."

"I'm done here, Simon. Guard!" he called out, but no one came.

"No one is coming for you, Michael. We're here to discuss *my* Nicolette. Do you hear me, Michael? My girlfriend! She was always mine, and you fucking ripped her apart with your hate for me and the fact that she never wanted you. She will carry the scars of what you did to her for the rest of her life. I hope you are happy. You not only got your revenge on me, but you left a permanent mark on her. I'm here to tell you that she's all bled out; we both are. Nicolette has nothing left, only the shell of a person she used to be. If I could, I would break every bone in your body. I would do it slowly, so you would feel every iota of pain, and then I would inflict more on you so you could beg for mercy like my girl did. I would watch you bleed out, just how Nicolette did when you raped and beat her. One way or another, St. Clair, you will pay for what you did to her. As long as I draw breath, I will make sure you pay."

"Paulson, you were always the tough guy, right? As you can see, I'm still here, but not for long. I will get out eventually, and not you nor anyone else will stop me from getting to Nicolette again. You can huff and puff and try to blow my house down, but in the end, I always win. I proved it already, and it's just a matter of time before I do it again. Give her my love."

Something inside of me just snapped, and I became enraged listening to Michael and his delusions. My fist clenched, and then I punched him as hard as I could, knocking him backward off his chair and down to the floor. I hovered over him and hit him again and again until my knuckles were bloody and bruised.

"Don't you ever breathe her name again. You will get what you deserve, but it's not Nicolette! And your punishment will not come from me. I won't risk going to prison and leave the girl I love behind just to spite you. So, fuck you, St. Clair." I shoved him down and walked away. He was screaming for the guard for help, but no one came. As I reached for the door, he shouted one more thing to me.

"Go to hell, Paulson. You go to fucking hell!"

"I'm already there, thanks to you."

I didn't say anything more to him and walked out, closing the door behind me. The guard that helped me handed me the tapes from the conference room. "Tell your father that we're now even, and my debt has been paid." He then looked down at my hand. "Better get that looked at."

"What's going to happen now?" I asked.

"He tripped and fell, and that's all you need to know. Take care of that hand, and make sure you give your father my message." He didn't say anything more and turned toward the room I just came from.

My hand was messed up, but I didn't care. All I wanted was to get back to my girl. I headed back to the hospital, but not before calling my father. He was waiting by the phone, as I expected. After I gave him the guard's message, it was clear to me that our conversation was over.

I knew my father had made many contacts over the years, and this was why I was confident that I could go to him for help. He was a powerful lawyer, and tonight I used him to get what I wanted. I didn't know if he would talk to me about it later on, but it didn't matter. I was prepared to deal with the consequences, if any, after tonight. But he told me that I didn't have to worry about it. The mystery debt that was paid to my father tonight secured my entrance and exit from that building and my meeting with Michael.

I returned to the beach house to clean up. I needed to wash away the filth of that place and my visit with Michael. When I walked into the master bathroom, I had almost forgotten what happened in there.

The room had been cleaned, and the horrific scene had been erased. I found mom's note that she had it taken care of. Even our bed had been made. I stretched my body across our bed and inhaled Nicolette's beautiful scent. Our perfect night was a mere memory. I clutched her pillow and screamed out my pain until my throat felt raw.

I was crippled by my pain over Nicolette and my hatred for Michael. How would I help her? I knew I needed help so that I could be strong for her, but I didn't have the answers. I took a shower and cleaned my hand. It wasn't broken, just cut and bruised. I could take this pain easily, and it was not anything compared to what my girl already suffered.

When I got to the hospital, I picked up her favorite flowers and was just about to walk into her room, when Dr. Jonas stepped out. I didn't see her parents and assumed they went home for the night. I asked her how Nicolette was feeling, and her face had fallen a bit.

"It's been a rough few hours. She's suffering from a considerable amount of pain, but it's normal with the infection and the procedure we had to perform."

I felt totally sick after hearing that. I just abandoned her when I should have been here, but her doctor put me at ease. She placed her hand on my shoulder and told me that I was Nicolette's best medicine.

"She needs you more than you know." She smiled kindly at me and then walked away.

I took a few minutes to get myself in check before entering her room. Nicolette was sleeping. Her hair cascaded over her pillow, and her long lashes were fluttering between her breaths. Her cheeks looked rosy, and her lips were crimson and plump. She was beginning to look like herself again, and I was thankful the medicine was working on getting her well. She looked beautiful, she always does, and I never wanted to let her go.

I gently crawled in beside her, and I held her in my arms. I promised to love her forever, and I asked her to forgive me for leaving her. I didn't know if she could hear me, but there was a deep need inside of me to say the words.

I had fallen asleep holding her, and when I woke up, a pair of beautiful brown eyes were staring back at me. She leaned in, kissed me, and then asked about my hand. There was no point in hiding it.

"Are you okay? Does it hurt?" she inquired.

"Baby, don't worry about me, I'm fine. How are you?"

"I'm better, now that you're here. I was afraid I lost you when you left. Thank you for coming back to me."

"You never have to worry about me leaving you. I'm the one that should be sorry. It was selfish to walk out without talking to you first."

"It wasn't, and we were talking. It was just so painful for you to hear. Don't deny it, Simon. I know it hurt you to find me that way, and I know I scared you. You need to let me feel this along with you. I know you don't believe me when I said I was better, but that is something you will have to work out on your own. It's over now, and the baby is gone. I just need to know that you're still here with me, you will forgive me, and tell me that we will be okay."

I held her close to my body and kissed her for as long as my control allowed me to. "There is nothing to forgive. I love you forever, and we are going to be okay. These past few months, you have suffered and endured more pain than anyone should have to go through in one lifetime. You need to rest and get well so we can begin the rest of our lives."

She silently cried against me, and I tried to push away the nagging feeling that there was more to say. But I held her and prayed for a better tomorrow.

She never asked me where I went, nor the reason to my injured hand. She didn't need to, at least right now, and I wasn't going to volunteer it either. All that mattered was that we were here together, and that was the last promise I made to her before she fell asleep again.

Twenty-Seven

Nicolette

"Are you happy you're finally going home today, baby?" Simon asked as he buckled me into my seatbelt. Always the loving and protective boyfriend.

"I spoke to your parents before I picked you up. They want you to come right home instead of the usual detours we seem to make."

I laughed along with Simon because he was right. "We do tend to do that often, but I understand my family wanting me home."

Simon was telling me surf stories all from when he was younger, and how he spent the best summers of his life with Aunt Grace. He loved and missed her very much, but remained hopeful that I would share his home with him and we could begin our new life together. I still hadn't given him an answer, but I hoped he believed that my heart already said yes. I would get there eventually.

I spent days in the hospital and never wanted to go back there again. We walked into my home, and I was welcomed by Gracie, who took my things and led us into the living room. The happiness I felt was momentary when I saw who was waiting for me, along with my parents.

I felt Simon's grip tighten around my hand, as Prosecutor William Jennings asked to have a word with me. I took a minute to greet my parents, who both looked worried, probably knowing what he was going to say to me.

"Nicolette," he hung his head low, "there's no easy way to say this, but as of this morning, Michael St. Clair has been granted bail. He was released to the custody of his father. It took place in the middle of the night."

I guess they didn't know, judging by the reaction from my parents. My father cursed under his breath, and Simon's facial expression hardened while he continued to tighten his hold on my hand. I didn't pull away from him, knowing this was what he needed. All eyes were on me as I processed what I just heard. I was thankful for sitting down, but then I needed to get up and make sure I still had breath in my lungs after hearing about Michael. Simon didn't want to let me go, but I squeezed his hand, showing him, I wasn't running—*at least, not yet.*

I took a step closer to the bar and wanted a drink. I've seen my father and uncle do it on countless times, and I wondered what it would be like to feel the amber liquid burn my throat as I gulped it down. But I didn't. I just stared long and hard at the stocked bar and then turned back to Mr. Jennings.

"Will Michael be under house arrest with a monitoring device? Or is he truly free to go anywhere he pleases?" I questioned.

"Yes, he will be wearing an ankle monitor, but he will not be allowed to leave his father's estate. His movement will be closely monitored."

"Yeah, but that's not a foolproof solution, is it? Surely with the right adjustments, it can be tampered with to get around the system, and then he will be free to do as he pleases."

"Nicolette, I can promise you that will not happen."

"That's just it, Mr. Jennings, you can't promise me anything. He's free, right? I was told bail would never be granted, but yet, he's home and back in his Beverly Hills mansion. How is that justice?"

"We won't let him near you, Nicolette." My father walked over to hug me, but I refused him with a warning not to touch me. I was seething with anger and contempt for Michael. *When will this nightmare end?* I didn't hold back my voice and unleashed my wrath on the prosecutor whom I felt betrayed me.

"Mr. Jennings, you have no idea how you failed me today. How much money did Clayton St. Clair pay to get his son released?"

"Now, Nicolette, hold on for a moment."

"No, I will not. You're standing in my home, and you will listen to me." I took a sip of water and tried to calm my nerves. I did not want to have a full-on panic attack. "Not one person in this room truly knows and understands Michael St. Clair. But it has taken me months of going over every detail of every encounter I had with him to finally understand what makes him tick. He needs control, probably craves it. When I rejected him, he lost what he needed most. I tried to find the goodness in him, but it was not to be found. He raped me, and never cared about the lasting damage he inflicted on me. It's clear that he is not going to take any plea deals you offer to him. So, let me ask you: How the hell is Michael going to pay for what he has done to me?"

I then looked over to my father, and I thought I saw the answer in his eyes. I thought of Uncle Jack and remembered the threats that I was never supposed to hear. I didn't react, and I focused my attention back to Mr. Jennings.

"We go to court, and we fight him," he said.

I huffed. "Yeah, in a very public setting where everyone will know my identity, and I'll be attacked all over again."

"Nicolette, my office will do our very best to keep this trial contained and closed off to the media. We believe that it's Clayton St. Clair's intention to not have any negative publicity either."

I never wanted that scotch so much in my life. I shook my head and sarcastically replied. "No, he wouldn't want that. Not with Grammy season around the corner, and then the Oscars after that."

"I'm sorry, Nicolette. My hands are tied."

"Yeah? Mine were too, Mr. Jennings when he was raping me." I was never more disgusted. I turned to leave the room.

"Nicolette, please stay and talk with us." My mother called out.

"No, I can't be here anymore. This doesn't feel like home to me, and maybe it never was. Mr. Jennings, do I need to be directly involved in the preliminary hearings?"

"Well, no, not exactly," he stammered over his answer. I nodded in agreement, and then looked over to Simon, knowing what I would say next would devastate him.

"Okay, I guess that's that. I will be leaving town for a while, and it will be tonight. Any information can be directed to my parents, as I have already previously agreed per our last conversation."

It happened. The one thing I feared happened, and I knew I could no longer stay in this house. I had a backup plan in place and prayed I would never have to use it, but with Michael being free now, I knew what I had to do. I was still in pain and moved slowly up the stairs to my room. I didn't need much and reached for a smaller bag from my closet. My door swung open, and I turned around to see Simon, who looked so hurt and lost.

"Are you running again, Nicolette? You're going to just pack and leave and not discuss it with me first?"

I ignored his questions and kept packing my bag. He released a growl and tossed my bag across the room. I closed my eyes tightly, as I had known this would be exactly how he would react. Another secret that I kept from him.

When I refused to acknowledge him, he grabbed both of my arms and locked them behind my back. Tears were falling from his eyes, as his pain was slicing through my heart.

"Please, Nicolette, don't leave me. I love you, baby, and I know you love me. Fight for us, please," he pleaded, but I didn't dare look into his eyes, knowing he would break me down and I would stay.

"I'm sorry. I can't do this," I told him.

He released my arms and pulled away as if my touch had burnt his skin. He combed his fingers through his hair and pulled on the strands in vexation.

"Why? Tell me why? Is there anything I can say to you that I haven't already?"

"No, I'm sorry," I said.

"Yes, you keep saying that, but here you are, leaving me again. You know, Nicolette, I'm beginning to wonder if you ever loved me at all." His voice cracked with his words, furthering obliterating my heart into broken pieces.

"You know that's not true, Simon. How could you believe that I don't love you?"

"I believe it, Nicolette, because you won't stay with me. You promised no more running. You promised me that we would always find our way. I know we've been hit with another roadblock, but it's not anything we can't overcome. You can't just decide to up and leave me, and not expect me to fight for you, or us. I don't understand this. What about your family? Our friends? What about the life we have planned together?"

I said nothing and kept on packing.

"Where will you go?" he asked.

"I'm going back to Chicago to visit with my Uncle Jack, and from there, I'm flying to Switzerland."

"Did I hear you right? You're going on the other side of the world? When did this all happen? You can't just pick a place on the map and fucking fly there," he shouted, while I tried to remain strong and not allow him to break me down.

I knew if I gave in to Simon, I would be in his arms, begging him to forgive me for hurting him. As is, I would have to carry it with me and bear the consequences of my actions here tonight. My leaving could cost me Simon, but staying when Michael was free just was not an option for me now. I needed to heal, and I couldn't do that here.

I responded, "Yes, I can. Dr. Jonas has recommended a private clinic she knows of. It has everything I need."

He reached for me again and caged me in with his strong arms. I wasn't afraid. Simon would never hurt me. He was clinging on to me with every bit of strength he had.

"Dammit! Nicolette! I'm everything you need. Why don't you know that? Do your parents know?"

"They do. We talked about it after you left me in the hospital. I always knew it may come to this, and I wanted to be prepared. The idea of the clinic came later, after my miscarriage."

"I love you, and you're standing here about to leave as if I never meant anything to you. Your words have wounded me deeply, and I have to know if this is your way of punishing me? I might have left you for a few hours, but I never intended on leaving you forever, like you are doing to me now."

"I'm not punishing you, Simon. I would never do that to you. I just can't be here right now, and I am asking you to be okay with it."

"How can I be? Your leaving is tearing me apart! You don't have to travel to the other side of the world to feel safe. You have me, and I will never allow Michael, or anyone else, to ever hurt you again. If you don't want to live here, I will pack up your room right now and take you home to the beach house."

"Simon, I can't go back to the beach house. I'm not sure if I'll ever be ready. I need you to respect my wishes and just let me go. I need time to think and be on my own for a while. I'm so sorry, but this is how it needs to be."

"How long will you be gone for? Or am I not allowed to know that? And what about school? What are your plans?"

"It's already taken care of. I made arrangements with my counselor and Principal Davies, in the event that I don't return to school. I will finish the remainder of my classes online."

"You thought of everything, Nicolette, haven't you? You strategically planned out every last detail of your life and left me completely out of it."

He looked crushed. I hated to hurt him. I prayed that I never had to tell him any of this, but it was out there now, and there was nothing left to say.

He pulled me back and into his arms. I felt his tears wet my skin. His pain was breaking me. I loved him so much and never wanted to leave him.

"Please, baby, please, stay with me. I love you. I need you. I'll marry you tomorrow if I knew it would keep you here with me."

He cupped my face and slammed his mouth down to mine. He begged for entrance, and I easily opened up for him. I knew it was selfish for me to want this last piece of him, but I took it anyway. We quietly moaned together in our pleasure. I loved him so much and kissed him again before walking out of his arms. I prayed he would understand and forgive me one day. Although he continued to beg me to stay, I left him standing there, and I didn't look back at the man I had broken.

A car was waiting for me when I arrived downstairs. My parents knew what I was doing, and they promised they would never stand in my way again. I hugged Gracie and then said my goodbyes to my mom and dad.

"Take care of Simon. He's still up in my room."

"We will. You'll call us when you get to Jack's?" my mom asked.

"I'm not making any promises. I know you don't understand, and neither does Simon, but this is what I have to do to regain a part of me that Michael took. I love you."

I hugged them again. I hurried into the car, telling the driver to hurry and go before I changed my mind and ran back to the only man I loved and will always love.

Simon

S he left me. No matter what I said to her, I couldn't make her stay. She said nothing, not one fucking word to me. She just turned away and picked up the bag that I had thrown and finished packing. I wanted to just throw her over my shoulder and run away. I wanted to keep her safe and never allow her out of my sight, but I knew I couldn't be the one to make her stay. She would have to want that on her own.

When I watched her break from our kiss and walk out her door, I thought I was going to die. I never felt a pain like this and feared I may never recover from loving Nicolette Vanelle.

I didn't know how long I had been up there until her parents came and got me. They let me be on my own in her bedroom while I mourned her loss. Yes, that's exactly what it felt like. My heart turned cold the minute Nicolette decided to leave me. I clutched a framed photo of the two of us taken on the night of her birthday party. She looked so beautiful, and her ears sparkled with the diamond earrings I had given to her.

I wanted to go back to that perfect moment, instead of being stuck in this hell I was living with. She left, and with no promise of returning home to me. I couldn't move from off the floor. I was just numb. Finally, her mom kneeled down in front of me and pried the picture out of my hands.

"Simon, she loves you. She will come home to us. We need to trust and believe that when she's ready, she will come home. I know how you're feeling right now, but don't lose your faith. It is what I'm hanging onto until I can hold my daughter again."

She got up to her feet and extended her hand out for me to take. Once I was standing on my shaky legs, she pulled me into a hug. I cried on her shoulder and then Mr. Vanelle came in.

"Simon, I phoned your father. You should go home to your family. I'm so sorry, son."

"Yeah, that's what you keep saying, but it doesn't change the fact that she's gone. I know and understand that she needs to work through her pain, but she didn't have to do it alone." I said my good-byes and then left the Vanelle home, never knowing if I would ever be back again.

I made my way over to my Jeep and saw my three brothers waiting for me. They had extended their stay here in California after what happened with Nicolette and the baby. I was hurting, and they knew it. They made no move for me, just waited for me to react. When I finally broke, I charged them in a fast run, with Jacob grabbing on to me first. Andrew and Cameron followed his lead and held me in a cocoon of their love and support, while I fought through my pain.

When I finally got home, I saw my father. He had been waiting up for me ever since Mason called him. He knew I wasn't ready for "I told you so" and sent my brothers to help me, knowing I needed the distance.

I knew he wouldn't hurt me in that way, but it didn't stop me from thinking it. This was what they warned might happen. I would fall so deeply in love with Nicolette, and then she would break my heart. Yeah, that's exactly what happened, but it wasn't her fault.

I walked over to my father's liquor cabinet and pulled out his favorite bottle of 18-year-old Laphroaig Scotch. I knew it cost a fortune, but I didn't care. I always hated when people used alcohol as a way to solve their problems. At that moment, thoughts of Jennifer occupied my mind, but I pushed them away and took my first drink. I didn't believe I would ever come to terms with Nicolette leaving me.

This afternoon when I picked her up from the hospital, she was so happy, and now she was gone. I needed to dull the ache in my heart, and I poured and downed my second drink. It fucking burned like hot acid down my throat, but I wanted more. Anything was better than feeling this soul-sucking pain.

I felt his presence enter the room, as my back was toward him. I didn't want him to see me like this, not my father.

"Simon, drinking her away will not bring her back to you."

"You're right, dad. You're always right. This is probably not one of my finer moments, but at least I won't be able to feel anything."

After my fourth shot, I finally passed out. Jacob threw me over his shoulder and carried me up to my room, where he stayed with me, just in case I threw up.

I prayed that I would never wake from the blissful dreams I was having of Nicolette. The reality of tomorrow without her here with me was too great to ever be okay with.

PART THREE

Two months later...

Twenty-Eight

Nicolette

S aying goodbye to my life in California haunted my dreams. I missed my family and my new friends who became sisters and brothers I never had. The one person who never left my mind or heart was Simon.

The reality of knowing how much I hurt him, and the look on his beautiful face when I walked out the door, was never too far from my mind. I missed him every minute of every day to the point that I had become physically sick. My therapist advised me I was here to concentrate on my recovery and that it wasn't healthy to continue to blame myself. Anything else took a back-seat to that, but I disagreed. Simon Paulson was a part of me, just as much as I was a part of him, and I missed him.

He would have done anything for me if given the chance. I wasn't strong enough to stay with him, this was why I left. I was afraid and didn't trust my heart to lead me on the right path. I felt as if my pain was swallowing me up, and I fell into a deep despair. I was fooling myself into believing that I could handle all that happened to me with little help from others. Losing the baby was my breaking point, but I held on for Simon.

Justice was not on my side the day they released Michael, and that's when I knew I would run. Yes, a plan was in place, but it was one that I never wanted to follow through with. I tried to convince myself that it wouldn't be forever.

I kept minimum contact with the girls. My parents called me often, but half the time, I ignored their calls. As for Simon, I severed all communication with him. I needed to give him a clean break from me. I had hurt him too much, and I wanted him to forget all about me and move on with his life. Who was I kidding? That's not what I wanted, but it's what was best for him.

The last time I talked with Bailey, she tried bringing him up and told me how much he missed me. Simon changed since I left and only stayed close with Sam, while he detached himself from the rest of the world. Bailey was excited about the senior rankings, and how proud they were of Simon, who was named the Valedictorian for our graduating class. I was actually the second runner-up.

Throughout everything, I remained an A student. No one knew how I managed to accomplish that, including me. With school coming to an end, I had no idea what I wanted to do with the rest of my life. My friends had chosen their colleges and were excited for the next chapter in their lives. I imagined that Simon was ready to attend California University and without me.

One day, I accepted a long-distance call from Los Angeles. It was William Jennings, the district attorney informing me of my trial date. It had been set for July 13th, 2009. My presence was required, and I agreed to be there. Along with the trial that would begin soon, my parents filed a twenty-five-million-dollar civil lawsuit against the St. Clair family. No amount of money could ever replace what I had lost, but it gave them a small satisfaction to go after Clayton's wallet. I didn't care one way or another.

Physically, my body was now completely recovered from my injuries, including the surgery that followed my miscarriage. It was my heart that needed to be worked on. I never stopped loving Simon, not for a second. I considered calling to congratulate him, which was maybe not the best reason to talk with him, but I longed to hear his voice. My fingers trembled as I dialed his number.

I wasn't able to reach him and chose not to leave a voicemail. He never changed his cheery greeting. It made me smile, and miss him, even more, when I heard his voice.

"Hey, you've reached Simon. I'm probably surfing, or hanging with my girl. Yeah, I'm with my girl. You know what to do. Leave me a message after the beep."

My heart broke all over again after hearing his voice. I held my phone to my chest and cursed myself for leaving him.

Hours after I called him, I still hadn't left my room. My group therapist knocked on my door and found me crying over his photo. She held out her hand and looked at me with kind and understanding eyes.

"Come, Nicolette. We will talk it out in the group session."

Simon

"**H**ey! Thanks for getting me out there today." I high-fived Sam and then Jameson. "Those waves had to be over fifteen feet in height. I had forgotten how much of a thrill this was and how much I missed surfing with my best friends." I said, and then I realized the last time we did this—the day I met and fell in love with Nicolette.

I didn't want to ruin the day by bringing up Nicolette, so I rattled on about the waves and how I had missed surfing with my friends. When we made it to shore after the final run, I began to peel my wetsuit from my body and noticed my phone had a missed call.

I checked who it was from and literally fell to my knees. I had to fight for breath. Sam ran over to check on me and was just as shocked as I was. My heart had been shattered again, all because of one phone call. Nicolette called me, and I fucking missed it. I frantically checked my phone for a message, but she didn't leave one. I was so angry that I threw my phone against the rocks, causing it to smash into pieces.

"Simon, you need to calm down," Sam said.

"What's going on?" Jameson asked, as he walked over and picked up what was left of my phone.

"Nicolette happened!" I shouted. "She fucking called me after months of not hearing from her, and I missed it. Fuck!" I continued to shout and take out all my anger on my friends.

"Simon, call her back," Sam pleaded with me, but I shook my head.

"I can't do this anymore. If she wanted to talk to me, she would have left a message. Isn't it obvious, Sam? She regretted calling me and probably would have hung up if I had answered."

"You don't know that."

"It doesn't matter. She made her choice, and I have to make mine. This is not what I wanted, far from it. I want Nicolette more than anything, but I don't know how to get her back. I sure as hell couldn't make her stay."

"Simon, unless you call her back, you are never going to know why she called in the first place, and then how will that make you feel? That girl loves you, and you love her. Call her back."

"No, I can't do that. She asked me to let her go and to respect her wishes. I did that, Sam, and it's something I have been forced to live with since the minute she walked out on me. Fuck! I hate it, but it's how it has to be."

Nicolette

It took me two days to sleep off my jetlag, but waking up in Chicago was the best. I spent a few days with Uncle Jack and Aunt Sara. I had so much to catch them up on, and I knew I needed this time with them, just as much as they needed me here. I loved this home and the restaurant that was downstairs. It was my home away from home, but it was only my first stop.

I made my way downstairs from the loft bedroom and walked into the waiting arms of Uncle Jack. Aunt Sara was flipping pancakes and smiled back at me.

"Good morning, my beauty. You look well-rested and beautiful as ever." He kissed my forehead, and I hugged him in return.

"You are biased, you always were."

"I'm just telling the truth." He laughed and went back to reading his paper.

"You look amazing, Nicolette. The Swiss air really did wonders for you." Aunt Sara said, and then she served us the delicious breakfast she had prepared.

I agreed with my aunt. Being so far from the world I knew had helped me a great deal. I put myself through intensive therapy sessions. The therapist that Dr. Jonas recommended was amazing and always called me out on my shit. She was tough, and I never got away with anything. I needed that. The girls who were in my group were a diverse mix of women.

I explained to Uncle Jack how they all experienced a tragedy in their lives. All of them were determined to reclaim the lives that were taken from them. I learned so much. I leaned on them and allowed them to lean on me. He was happy that my therapy had such a strong impact on me.

After my last session, I made the decision to return home, but not before visiting my beloved hometown. After my visit with Uncle Jack, I would return home to Simon. Every time I thought of Simon, he equaled home in my heart, and I longed to be reunited with him. After the way I left, I had no way of knowing how he would react to seeing me again. I was praying that he would at least give me a chance to explain some things to him. I knew I had no right to ask, nor did I expect him to hear me out. It was my turn to put my heart out on the line for the man I loved. God knows, he did it enough for me.

I would be leaving first thing in the morning, so today was about Uncle Jack. We visited all our favorite places we loved, including the coffee house where I used to perform poetry in. I didn't get on stage this time, just enjoyed the eclectic mix of artists doing their thing. Over lunch, we talked about clearing the air between us, and all that happened when he was in California.

He knew I loved him, and knowing he was my biological father hadn't changed my feelings, only made me love him more. He was my hero, and there was not one day in my life that he wasn't there for me. I knew he was struggling with what happened to me, and he may never be able to move past it, but I loved him enough to reassure him that I was stronger and so much better from the last time he had seen me.

"Uncle Jack, these last days spent with you have been amazing. I certainly don't want to ruin the memory by bringing up the past, but I have to share something with you. It's something that has been on my mind for a long time now, and it needs to be said."

"Nickel, you know you can ask me anything, and I will always tell you the truth."

"What kind of truth, Uncle Jack? The one that you want me to believe in order to protect me? Or the other that protects you?"

"I'm not sure what you mean. Maybe you should explain it to me."

"After my attack, I overheard a conversation between my parents, and it was about you."

"Go on."

"My father was afraid of how you would react after learning about how I was raped. I never heard my father yell at my mother before, and never to the point of my mom crying with the same level of fear in her voice. I never questioned my father about it, and if it's uncomfortable for you to tell me, then consider the subject dropped."

He let out a deep breath and then reached for my hand. "Nicolette, when your mother phoned me about you, I stepped outside of myself and retreated to a very dark place that I swore I would never return to. Hearing the words, "Nicolette was raped" was carved out all throughout my soul, and I wanted to avenge you. I went to the hospital with all intentions on ending Michael's life and nearly did until my brother reminded me of what I would risk on losing if I did. I resent him for that, and maybe I still do. My past is my own, and it is one that I never wanted to touch you, nor my life with Sara. I stopped myself on that day, Nicolette, and your parents had every right to fear me."

"Why? Tell me, Uncle Jack. My father loves you. He admires and respects you, so does my mom."

"Yes, that may be true, but there's another side to me that they always shielded you from, and I'm not sure if I will ever be ready to share that part of myself with you. I love you, Nicolette, but I can't do that."

"I love you too and thank you for telling me. I promise you, Uncle Jack, that I am done with running away. I can't change the past, but I can promise you that I will fight for what I want and will no longer be afraid to be loved."

"When you first arrived here before leaving for Switzerland, all I wanted to do was hug you and make it all better for you, but I knew you were the only one that could do that. You were so brave, and I am incredibly proud of you."

"Thank you, Uncle Jack. It means so much for me to hear you say that. What happened to me did undoubtedly change me. Leaving everyone behind was the hardest decision I ever had to make. I knew in my heart that I couldn't return to the ones that I loved until I healed myself first. Uncle Jack, I am ready to reclaim what I lost, and that begins with Simon. I only hope that he will give me a chance to make it up to him."

"He loves you. I know that he does. You've both have gone through so much together, and hopefully, while you were away, he did some soul searching of his own. No matter what he's decided, I know for a fact that his heart will always lead him back to you."

"Let's hope you're right."

Twenty-Nine

Simon

Being with my friends made me happy. We had just finished lunch and were all seated around the tree, our favorite spot on the quad. It was hard not to think of Nicolette, especially in the company of the girls. They were rambling on about the amazing time they had at the prom and would not stop talking. Normally, I would have shut them up by now, but not today.

I loved Alexis and Bailey, and I was thankful for their friendships. They stood by me, even when I tried pushing them away. My friends deserved to be carefree seniors, and knowing we would be graduating soon was a happy milestone to celebrate. I was asked by dozens of girls to go to prom, but I always said no. The entire weekend was one party after another. I chose solitude and spent the weekend at my beach house. I surfed during the day, and I was lost in my memories at night, always dreaming of Nicolette.

There wasn't a day that had gone by that I didn't think of her. My feelings had not changed. I was deeply hurt and nearly destroyed myself after she left. I tried every day to understand her reasons for leaving, and I prayed daily in hopes that she was okay. Would we find our way back to each other? Only time would tell.

It seemed all our friends were doing well, especially Sam. On his trip to San Diego to tour his campus where he had been accepted, he met Brooke and fell hard for her. They spent the entire meet-and-greet together and have been attached at the hip ever since. I was happy for my best friend. He deserved to finally get the girl. Now, I just needed to get mine back.

Jimmy and Alexis were still going strong. He was awarded a scholarship to run track for Stanford. Alexis had been accepted at UCLA, and as for Bailey, she announced that she was on her way to Columbia University in New York City. She never believed she would get in, and after playing the dumb blonde part for far too long now, it was time to get serious. She was always smart but played the act to meet guys. She and Jameson went together to the prom, and they danced the night away after he had received word on being accepted into the Fashion Institute of New York. He was still buzzing about it, and he planned on sharing an apartment with Bailey.

Later that day, I was called in to speak with Principal Davies. He wanted to personally congratulate me on becoming this year's class Valedictorian. I thanked him for the acknowledgment and got up to leave when he stopped me.

"Simon, I know your years at our school have been plagued with unforeseen circumstances, and throughout it all, you have been an outstanding example to your fellow students."

Thanks for the recap, dude. Bringing up my most painful memories. Yeah, good times, I wanted to say, but I politely thanked him for his praise.

"Have you given any thought to what you will say at commencement?" he asked.

"To be truthful with you, I hadn't planned on giving a speech at all, but I know it is a time-honored tradition to do so. If I choose to, sir, then I would like to deliver one from my heart, and not the usual blah, blah, blah, that most people come to expect. I want to be different."

"Simon, you have earned your right to speak, and you have my blessing in choosing the words you are most passionate about."

"Thank you, I appreciate it."

Later that evening after a long discussion with my father, it was decided that I would speak from my heart since it was the only way I knew how. He gave me a strong squeeze on my shoulders and said how proud he was of the man I had become. I thanked him too, because if it wasn't for my father, then I wouldn't be half the person I was today. If it wasn't for the unconditional love and support my family had given me, then I honestly didn't believe I would have made it through these last few months. I owed them everything and wanted to deliver a speech that was deserving of everything they had given me. I was lucky to have had our friends, and even the Vanelles, keep in touch with me.

I must have written at least ten drafts until I got it right. I was still a little on edge for everything I wanted to say, but it was done. I checked my phone before going to bed. I had several voicemails from Bailey and Sam. I was too tired to listen to them now and figured I would catch up with them in the morning or at the ceremony.

"Thanks, mom, for my new jacket."

"My pleasure. It looks great on you. Just seeing you wear something other than board shorts makes me very happy."

"If I could, that's exactly what I would be wearing under this gown, but I wouldn't risk your beautiful smile. I love you, mom. You're the best."

"Okay, I love the compliments, but you're making me blush. Thank you for staying in your old room while your brothers are in town. I missed having my baby under our roof."

"I was happy to do that for you, mom, but you understand why I moved to the beach house, don't you?"

"I understand more than you know. I love you, son. Now let's get you graduated."

I wanted to say more to my mother but was interrupted by the three giants I call my brothers. They all barreled in and shouted together. "Let's go, baby brother! Time to make mommy cry with your speech."

That earned them all a slap to the back of their heads and an admonished glare from our mother. They all mumbled their apologies, and I just laughed out loud. I loved these guys so much. They told me they were proud of me today and still secretly hoped that I would change my mind about attending Northwestern. I knew exactly what I wanted to do in my life and with whom I wanted to share it. She was out there somewhere, and I intended to bring her back and reunite my heart with hers.

"Let's go, bro. We're going to be late."

"I'll be right there, Jacob. I just want to listen to my messages."

"Dude, we have no time. Let's go! The parents are getting antsy, and we're hungry."

I pocketed my phone and joined my brother. "You just ate less than a half hour ago, how could you still be hungry?"

"Um, Simon, have you seen me?"

"Yeah, okay, I take it back."

We were both laughing as we got into our waiting car.

Nicolette

"**W**ow, your guy is going to lose his mind when he sees you today. You look beautiful, honey." My father complimented me on my new dress, courtesy of mom and Zac Posen. It pays to know people, and he was our favorite designer.

"Thank you, daddy, but let's not get ahead of ourselves. I don't know if I even have a guy anymore to impress. We will see how things go after I speak with Simon."

"Well, we need to get you graduated first, Miss number 2 in her class. Nicolette, we have never been prouder of you. You just amaze us. We love you."

They double teamed me and hugged me until I couldn't breathe. I knew how happy they were now that I was home. I was only a mere few points shy behind Simon, but I didn't care, and neither did my parents. They considered it as first and repeatedly reminded me how awesome it was. I was proud of my boyfriend, and he certainly earned it. I had spoken to both Bailey and Sam this morning, but they weren't able to reach Simon.

Sam wanted me to call Simon before today's graduation, but I had a plan and hoped to high heaven that it would work. Sam was protecting his best friend, and he told me how much Simon suffered in my absence over the past few months. Everyone was worried for him, and just when he was finally coming up for air, I came home. He loved Simon as a brother, and I respected him for that. I promised Sam that if Simon did not want to speak with me, then I would walk away and never bother him again. He trusted that I was telling the truth, but I secretly prayed that it would not come down to that. I was madly and deeply in love with Simon. I never wanted anything so much in my life, and I prayed he wanted the same.

I texted Bailey to let her know I was here. We met at our spot on the quad. We hugged each other until all our tears were shed. I missed her so much. Alexis, Jimmy, Sam, and Jameson all joined in with the group hug. I was smothered in the middle, and I loved it.

"You look marvelous. No, darling, scratch that, you look hot."

"Thank you, Jameson. I love you too. Hey, before we go inside, I'd like to say something to all of you." They all gave me their attention, and I tried in earnest not to cry. "I just want to say how much I love each and every one of you. You are all so special to me, and today would not be happening without your love and support. I know I have been a terrible example of what a friend should be, and I'm hoping you give me a chance to make up for that. I should have been here with you this year, enjoying what should have been the best year of my life, attending Alexis's awesome beach parties, and dancing with Simon at our prom. I missed out on all of these experiences. I should have been sharing them with Simon and all of you. I am truly sorry. I am proud to call you my best friends, and I love you very much."

"Bring on the water works, and thank heaven for waterproof mascara," Bailey said and pulled me into another amazing group hug. I didn't want to let them go, but we needed to graduate, and I needed to reunite with my man.

"Sam, have you tried him again?" I asked.

"Yeah, he must have his phone off, and he's probably on stage by now."

"Okay, it will be fine."

I took my seat and scanned the crowd. I found my parents seated with the Paulson's and his brothers, along with Uncle Jack and Aunt Sara. My heart filled with joy seeing them all together as a united group. This was a good sign. Because my last name began with V, I was in the very last row. I wouldn't have been able to see the main stage if it wasn't for the big screens that hung on each side of the stage. Our school was huge, with a graduating class that totaled over 600 students.

As the cameras panned over the stage, I caught a glimpse of Simon. He looked so handsome in his cap and gown. His skin was a deep tan, no doubt sun-kissed from hours spent on the beach. His hair was highlighted with blonde streaks, again from the sun. I just wanted to charge the crowd and run straight into his arms.

Simon

I had to blink and focus on what I thought I saw. I was frozen to my spot and thought my eyes were playing tricks on me. I thought I had seen Nicolette, but how could that be? She was still in Switzerland, right? I was called to take my place, and I shook off the crazy thoughts that were running through my mind. I concentrated on what I needed to say. I took my seat and held the speech in my hand.

Principal Davies began addressing our faculty and graduating class. Awards and honors were handed out to many of my fellow classmates, including myself. I received honors for my athletic accomplishments. My proud family cheered every time my name was called.

My heart ached for Nicolette, as memories of her flooded my mind. I wanted her here with me today, not thousands of miles away on the other side of the world.

You could hear my brothers hollering from their seats, and I loved how our mom elbowed the triplets to be quiet. I couldn't help but laugh. They were who they were, three brawny guys from Colorado. When my moment finally arrived, Principal Davies stood to speak before introducing me. He spoke highly of me, and I was almost embarrassed by his praise.

"In a moment, I will introduce your Class of 2009 Valedictorian to you. I want to take a few minutes to tell you about this incredible and inspiring young man. Simon Paulson has been a student in our school and community for only two years. On his very first day, he made a lasting impression. He has been involved with many academic programs held here at our school. He has shown all of us his athletic abilities on the track, and for those of you who might have missed it, he, along with his teammates, brought home a victory for our Track and Field Team, breaking our ten-year losing streak!"

I wanted to find a rock and crawl under it. He was too much, but the crowd loved it. The sound of applause was deafening, and all I wanted for him was to stop talking.

"Without further ado, please rise and give your applause to Mr. Simon Paulson, the star of our school and your class leader in excellence."

I took a moment to breathe before standing up. I actually felt my face heating up, and I had never blushed before. Then I smiled knowing how untrue that was, as Nicolette's beautiful image was present again in my mind. I placed my hand over my heart and prayed I could get through this without breaking down. I stood at the podium and shook the hand of Principal Davies. I thanked him for his kind and gracious words.

I took a deep breath and began my speech, "When I learned that I had been chosen as your class Valedictorian, I was surprised, if you want to know the honest truth. I had believed that honor should have gone to someone more deserving of it, but nonetheless, I am honored to stand before you. I have never been one to want to stand out from anyone else. Like most kids, I just wanted to fit in. When you stand over six feet in height, it's hard to just blend in with your friends, but I managed. I was thankful that I was welcomed and accepted."

"Giving a speech at graduation is a rite of passage and a time-honored tradition. Up until yesterday, I wasn't sure if I wanted to say anything at all but was encouraged by Principal Davies to try anyway. I can't be the one who stands before you and tells you to follow your dreams. To make successes out of yourselves, and to make your parents proud. I can only speak for myself. I owed it to my parents to be here today, as well as my friends, who have been a constant presence in my life."

"I have broken my speech down into two parts. Hang in there, as I will try to make this quick and easy. The good part of my two years attending this amazing school was acceptance. I told you that I was thankful, but it's really hard to put into words on how I felt as the new kid and how I represented the total opposite of you. Principal Davies mentioned how on my first day I made a lasting impression. Well, he wasn't lying about that. Just ask Coach Johnson. He can back me up on this. I walked right into his office and asked for a tryout on his track team. He took one look at me and almost laughed himself off his chair. I remained firm in my plight and asked for a chance."

"He, along with the football coaches, all encouraged me to try out for the football team, which would have made my father and brothers very happy. Take a good look, because one day you're going to see them playing in the NFL. You heard it here first."

The crowd applauded and my brothers actually took a standing ovation, until my father shot one look and they sat back down. This gave me a moment to pause and take a breath before continuing.

"So, football was out. I wanted to run, and I knew I was fast. I guess some would say that I was a bit confident, but somehow, I knew I could deliver the wins and earn victories for our school. I just needed a chance to show the coach what I could do. He finally broke down and gave me my shot. I ran up against the fiercest competitor I know, Jimmy Taylor." I glanced down at my friend, who saluted me, while once again the crowd broke out into applause.

"With the sound of the whistle, I ran my heart out that day, leaping through hurdles and beating him by a few seconds. Judging by the look on his face, I knew I made the team. Coach Johnson, along with Jimmy Taylor and my fellow teammates, gave me a chance. From the deepest parts of my heart, I can't thank you enough for the opportunity to run for this school. You are my brothers, and I will always hold you in my heart. Thank you for accepting and allowing me the great honor to be your captain. A captain is one who leads his team, and I couldn't have done that without your support. Again, you have my deepest gratitude."

"Thank you also to my family. I couldn't have become the man you see standing before you without the love my parents have given me all my eighteen years here on this earth. They are amazing individuals who believe in education and have a deep love for sports and the skill set that develops in athletes. What you learn when you are part of a team will stay with you all throughout your life. It's what has been taught to me and my three brothers. Thank you, mom and dad, I love you. I'm sorry if I made you cry, but mom, this thank you was long overdue."

I saw my mom send me an air kiss, and I raised my hand to wave back. I had put them through so much this past year and shut them out when I shouldn't have. My family deserved this moment to celebrate together, and I was happy that I could do this for them.

I took another sip of my water and glanced over at Sam. He kept shaking his head and appeared nervous about something. I had no clue what it could be and continued with my speech.

Nicolette

I glanced down at my silenced phone and read a text message from Bailey.

Bailey: *You need to let Simon know that you're here. What he is about to say may hurt your feelings! Please go to him. Now!*

Whatever he would say, I probably deserved. I texted back my response.

Me: *Don't worry, friend. I'll know when to go to him.*

Simon

I shuffled my notes and began again. "I told you that I had written two parts to my speech. I believe that I covered the good part, and now I have a few things to say that are part of the bad. I guess I was considered popular around here, but like most kids, that doesn't make me exempt from bullying, nor does it save me from rumors. Here's the thing about rumors. Most times, you get it wrong."

"In my junior year, I dated a few of you lovely girls, until one became my first girlfriend here in California. Her name was Jennifer Williams. You all remember her, right? She was smart and very pretty. She loved her time here at this school, and I can recall when she shared her dreams with me about attending Harvard and how they would be lucky to have her on their campus."

"Sadly, Jennifer was killed in a car accident, taken from all who loved her, ending her dream of going to Harvard. Please join me in a moment of silence for our fallen friend."

The room had gone silent until I raised my head and began speaking again. "I only hope she is looking down at all of us here today, and wishing us well. Now, on to another person whom I would like all of you to remember here today, my girlfriend, Nicolette Vanelle. She was unable to be here with us today to accept her honors and awards. She should be standing on this stage with me as number two in our class, but she can't because she is on the other side of the world right now."

Nicolette

I knew I heard him right. He called me his girlfriend. He still loved and wanted me. I was so happy. As I sat in my seat, I felt many pairs of eyes staring at me. Our classmates were confused by what Simon was saying.

He didn't know that I was here and have returned home to him. I kept wiping away my tears. How could I have ever walked away from him? He was the most amazing person I knew. I needed to show my boyfriend how sorry I was for hurting him, and all I wanted to do was to love him for the rest of my life.

I knew our time was coming, but I just remained where I was and continued to listen to his speech. It was beautiful and heartfelt.

Simon

I took a deep breath and paced myself for what I was going to say next. My friends were staring at me, and I glanced over to my parents. For the first time, I noticed who they were sitting with. Nicolette's family was with them, *but how could they be? When Nicolette is not here?* I shook it off and continued. I swallowed hard and tried my best to keep it all together.

"Like myself, Nicolette was also a transplant and new to our school. She was born and raised in Chicago, her windy city that she loved so much. She feared nothing, and from day one walking onto our campus, she was confident and quickly made friends. I didn't meet her here, though. I was lucky enough to find her on my favorite beach. Remember, Sam, we were climbing over the wall to get a better look at the stunning beauty walking along the water's edge?" Sam smiled up at me. "I knew I was hooked from the first moment my eyes connected with Nicolette. She was like no one I had ever met, and she took my breath away. I never climbed down a wall so fast in my life. I knew I had to meet her."

"It was an instant connection, and I knew I wasn't alone in my feelings, as she felt the same for me. We talked for what seemed like hours, but that was because she was so easy to talk to. I may have even loved her then, but I was too afraid to tell her in fear I would scare her off."

"I mentioned the rumor mill early on in my speech, and sadly, my girl was not exempt from them. She found herself caught in a web of lies that were told by cruel individuals. It is my opinion that they never had a clue on what they were talking about. I will no longer be silent and will clear up the rumors once and for all. Ni-

412

colette Vanelle, the love of my life, is not here with us today because someone hurt her mind and body, and broke her spirit. Due to circumstances that were not her fault, she was forced to leave her family, her friends, her school, and me. I miss her every single day and have wished and prayed for her to come back to us."

I paused and took another breath. My heart was racing.

"When she left, she broke my heart. It felt as if it was shattered in millions of pieces. You can only feel that level of pain when you truly love someone. When I begged her to stay with me and trust me to take care of her, she left anyway. It wasn't her fault, and she was left with no other choice. I haven't spoken to her since the night she left, and with each passing day, missing her gets harder to bear. You know how they say, 'If you truly love someone, set them free? If they come back, they were meant to be yours.' You don't know how true I want to believe in that. After I leave this school for the very last time, I plan on getting on a plane and going to Switzerland to bring my girl home."

"I guess if you want some inspiration to leave with here today, then I suggest you go with this: Many of you will have lots of boyfriends and girlfriends. Don't worry about finding 'the one.' You will know when the right one enters your life and grabs hold of your heart. When that day comes, it will be magical, and I can promise you that. It was for me and Nicolette, and I'm hoping it will be that way again. I have so many things I want to say to Nicolette, and I'm just scared that I will mess it up and not find the right words to say to her." I looked up to my family, along with Nicolette's. All were in tears, smiling over at me.

"Principal Davies, thank you for allowing me to speak from my heart today." I was going to conclude my speech when I heard a familiar voice call out to me from the very far end of the room.

"What will be the first words you say to Nicolette when you see her?"

I took in a deep breath and slowly exhaled. I looked over to Sam, who wore a stupid grin on his face and nodded up at me. His expression said it all.

You're not crazy, Simon. You heard it right because we all heard it too. Your wish has come true. She's home and has come back for you.

Nicolette

If there was ever a perfect moment to speak up and let Simon know I'm here, this was it. After listening to his heartfelt words and his love for me, I found my courage and called out to him. I knew he heard me, as I watched him look out to the crowd.

I found my voice and repeated my question, "What will be the first words you say to Nicolette when you see her?"

His beautiful tanned face almost turned white when he heard my voice again. There was no doubt this time when I spoke again. He knew I was here. I slowly made my way through the long aisle, passing our friends and family. They were crying and cheered us on, as we were about to be reunited. It felt like a scene playing out from a movie, and everyone waited with bated breath to see what would happen next. This was real, though. It was our life, and I wanted it back.

I stopped before the stage, and my eyes locked on with Simon's. This was the first time we had seen each other since I left him months ago. His eyes were filled with tears, and he looked at me as if he didn't believe I was real and here with him. I smiled when I saw him blink a few times. He remained at the podium with his eyes solely on me.

"If I was given the chance to talk with Nicolette again, then the first thing I would tell her was that I loved her. I never stopped. Not one day has passed when we were apart that she didn't fill my thoughts or take over my dreams at night." Simon's tears began spilling down and wetting his cheeks. The room was so quiet, and no one made a sound.

I asked Simon, "Would you forgive her for leaving you?"

He replied, "There's nothing to forgive. I know now and understand why she did what she felt she needed to do."

"Are you willing to trust and believe when she says that she will never run again? Will you believe that she is completely and madly in love with you and would never leave you?"

Simon remained where he was and listened to every word I said. I walked closer to him.

I said, "I left because I was drowning in a sea of my own pain. I was riddled with guilt and couldn't trust my feelings for you. I needed to get well before I could allow myself to love you in the way you deserved. All you ever asked of me was to believe in our love and to trust you. You're right, Simon. I did run, but not from you. The truth is, I didn't trust me, and I doubted myself every single day. You professed your love for me over and over again, and it was that love that I carried with me. You never left my heart."

"Shame had taken over my soul, and I had no hope left. I never felt so lost. I knew in my heart that the only way I would ever be able to come home to you was to heal myself first. Once I did that, there would never be any question in my heart to where I belonged."

"You are home to me, and I love you. I am so sorry for hurting you, and I hope you will believe and understand that my leaving was never about you, or us. I worked every day to get better, and I have been fighting my way back to you ever since."

I had finally been able to breathe again, and I said everything I could to convince him that I meant every word. As he stood there with his tear-filled eyes, he never once broke contact with me.

Simon

I had never felt my heart beat so fast in all my life as I listened to my girl pour her heart out to me. Without caring who heard her, she stood in front of hundreds of people and spoke to me from her heart. I prayed on this every night since she left, and it wasn't just another dream. She was real and here with me.

All I could do was look into her beautiful eyes and feel her love run through me. I knew I had to move, but my legs felt like jelly. This was the magical spell I had been under since the day we met. One look into her eyes and I would submit to her without hesitation. I looked up to my family and to Nicolette's, and if I could have read lips, I knew my brothers were telling me to go for it.

Sam snapped his fingers at me and shouted, "Go get your girl, Simon, so we can get out of here already."

Our attentive audience broke out in laughter, followed by the roaring sounds of applause. I shook Principal Davies hand and ran straight for Nicolette. Even our astute principal was teary-eyed over our very public display of affection.

Nicolette stood there and anticipated my every move, and when I got closer, she knew what to do. I opened my arms, and she ran toward me. Once there, I folded her into me and breathed her in. I was so happy, I couldn't hold back the joy of holding my girl. I twirled her around, and never broke the firm grip that I had on her body.

I leaned in and whispered three words for only Nicolette to hear, "I love you."

She smiled, and then I crushed my mouth down to hers and kissed her as if I needed her breath to survive. We received a standing ovation for our very public reunion.

Principal Davies announced to our graduating class. "Our commencement ceremony has ended, and congratulations to all of you." As he said the words, the room erupted with our fellow graduates throwing their caps into the air, and the celebration began.

I was still holding onto Nicolette when I whisked her away and outside to be alone with her. I cupped her face as if I didn't believe she was really here with me. *My angel has come back to me, and I'm so in love with her.*

"Simon, say something. Are you okay? Will you tell me what you're thinking?" she said.

Thinking? If she only knew about the thousands of thoughts running through my mind at that moment. I still can't believe that this is happening. She's home. She really is here.

When my brain finally caught up to my heart, I simply kissed her gently on her lips and then answered her question. "Thank you, baby. For coming home to me." I looked lovingly at her and couldn't help but smile. I never stopped kissing my girl as I held her tightly in my arms.

"I love you so much. Please believe that I will never leave you again. I am so done with that part of our story. I just want to be with you."

"Forever, Nicolette?"

She replied with the one word she knew I needed to hear. She kissed me in earnest and whispered, "Forever."

We walked with my hand in hers and found our families, along with our friends, all waiting on us. My brothers each took a turn picking her up and tossing her back and forth to the other as if it was the most natural thing to do. I couldn't stop laughing.

I said, "Get used to it, Nicolette. It's a Paulson signature move."

It was wonderful to watch her smile and to hear her laugh again. My family would soon be her family too.

After we celebrated at the graduation luncheon, we all went our separate ways. Nicolette told me that she had planned ahead and told her parents that she wouldn't be returning home tonight, or through the weekend. If she worked it out with me, then they knew where she would be: our beach house. I watched as she said her goodbyes to her parents, along with Uncle Jack and Aunt Sara. They wished us well and couldn't have been happier for us.

"I'll be right back, baby. I'm going to say goodbye to my family. I love you."

"I love you. Go. I'll be here when you get back."

"Hey, Sam, do me a favor and wait with Nicolette until I get back."

"Sure, not a problem. I got your back," he said.

Nicolette

"I guess he's still a little skittish when it comes to me, isn't he?" I asked Sam.

"Nah, he's okay."

"Are you sure? I mean, he has you guarding me, when you should be with Brooke. I talked with her while you were with the guys. She seems wonderful."

"She is. I'm really lucky to have found her. You know we all are. He loves you on a level that he can't even explain, but we all see it, and that's why we understood his pain when you left. All we ever wanted was for you two to make it and be happy."

"Good to know my friend, because we're already there."

Simon

"We have some pretty amazing friends. I can't believe they all knew about your surprise, and I was the last to know," I said as I helped her up and into my Jeep.

"Yes, but it was a good surprise, right?"

"The best. I will never forget it." I brought her delicate hand to my lips and kissed her until I lost my breath. I couldn't wait to be alone with her and just love my girl.

A knock on my driver's window brought me back down from my high. It was my mom asking if I could take a minute to talk with her before we left. I groaned but then smiled. I would do anything for my mom and happily followed her over to the quad.

She opened her purse, pulled out a small velvet box, and placed it in my hand.

I asked, "Is this what I think it is?"

"Yes, it is. The love you have for Nicolette, and how she returns that love to you, was literally the most amazing sight these eyes have ever seen. As a mom, all I have ever wanted for my boys was for them to be happy and to follow their passions in life. Nicolette is yours, and you are hers. I love you so much. You are an amazing man and will be an amazing husband. It's time to pass on this beautiful ring that Aunt Grace wanted you to have. It's time to give it to the one you love. You have our blessing."

I clutched the ring box in my hand, and then pulled my mother in for a hug. "If I'm anything in this life, it's because of you," I whispered, kissing her on the cheek.

"Go be with your girl. I believe you have waited long enough," she said.

Once we left the school, Nicolette knew where we were going. The only place that I wanted to be with Nicolette was at our beach house, the beautiful home that Aunt Grace left for me. She knew I was the only one that could appreciate the house for its true beauty, and now it was mine to share with my future wife. *Yeah, I plan to make that happen very soon.*

When I parked the Jeep, I asked her to wait for me. I ran to her side and lifted her out and into my arms. She smelled like roses. I carried my girl all the way up the two flights of stairs and into our home. Her eyes roamed all around the room as if she was seeing it again for the first time. I gently placed her down and continued to be lost in her eyes.

She slapped my chest and said, "Stop it, already. Baby, I'm really here, and I am staying with you—forever." She reached for my hand and this time brought it up to her lovely, kissable mouth. She caressed my skin with the slightest touch of her lips, and then placed a kiss that had the ability to bring me down to my knees. She didn't let go of my hand, as I followed her up the stairs that led to our bedroom. She paused for only a moment, and then turned around and walked into my arms.

So lovingly she said, "Simon, I love you with all my heart and soul. I want nothing more than to be with you for the rest of my life. I want you to make love to me."

As much as I dreamed about this moment, I was scared of really wanting it, because I loved her so much. I held her in my arms, looked deeply into her eyes, and whispered my answer. When I said the words, her eyes filled with tears. She looked rejected, and I needed to explain my reasons before she misunderstood why I said no.

"Baby, you don't know how much I want to. I can't wait to make love to you and forever make you mine."

"Why say no then? I don't understand."

"I love and want you so much, and have since the minute we met. You are all that I want and will ever need. I'll cherish you until I take my last breath. But I just got you back, and I don't want to push you into anything you're not ready for."

"Simon, I am ready to be yours, and that means that I want to fully give myself over to you in every way possible. Making love with you would truly be my first time. It would wash away the scars that Michael left on me. Simon, show me what real love is. I have never needed you more than right here in our home. We are together now, and I will never leave you again. I'll say it as much as you need to hear it. Make love to me."

Piece by piece, she broke me down. I didn't know how I was still standing. My body immediately responded to hers. It was our undeniable connection that was always present when we were together. I ached and longed for Nicolette. It pained me to see her so desirable, and to have rejected her. I wanted her to be sure, though, so I had to ask again. I couldn't live with myself if I knew I hurt her. "Are you sure, baby?"

"More than anything in the world, I want this with you. It's our time, and I want you to make love to me and make me yours."

Her words, her eyes, and her body was my undoing. I was burning with desire for her. I wanted her so badly, but I knew I had to be gentle and not lose control with her.

She was right. This was our time, and it was on our side. She backed away from me, and then flashed her sexy smile. She slowly unzipped her dress, letting it fall down and around her feet. She gracefully stepped out and placed her hands on her hips. She wore silk stockings that were attached to a pink lace garter belt. Her bra and matching thong completed the look. She was sexy as fuck. I couldn't wait to taste every inch of her.

She lifted her leg onto the bed and ran her hands from the bottom of her ankles all the way up to the tops of her stockings. She was seducing me right before my eyes, and the sight of her made my heart nearly beat right out of my chest. I had never been so turned on before. She had never looked so beautiful. After the incredible floor show she just treated me to, she stalked over to me with hunger in her eyes. I licked my lips in anticipation on what she would do next.

I stood in front of her, and let her completely unman me. I could barely breathe, I wanted her so badly. She removed my jacket over my shoulders, and she placed it on the chair. Slowly and so sexy, she unbuttoned my shirt and removed it. I felt her soft fingers run down my chest, sending erotic shivers all throughout my body. She quickly removed my belt, freeing me from my pants and boxers. I removed my socks, and now I was on full display with a very hard erection for her to step back and admire. Her eyes began with mine, and she made her way down to the floor, taking moments of pause to bite and lick her bottom lip. As if I could read her mind, she was just as turned on as I was.

She was wearing too many clothes, and it was my turn to get her naked. I removed her bra, garter, and panties. She had a petite frame with skin so soft. Her breasts fit perfectly in my hand as if they were made for me. I lifted her up as she wrapped her arms around my neck. I placed her down on our huge king-sized bed, and I held my body over hers. She took my breath away as her gorgeous body was now under mine.

In this beautiful moment, a darker memory flashed through my mind. I would never tell her, but I was back to when I found her on the boat, and I remembered every spot on her body that was hurt. I knew I couldn't make love to her until I touched every part of her that he had hurt and marked. Today was our new beginning, and from this moment on, every time she looked at her body, I wanted her to know how much I loved and cherished it, and would never hurt her.

"Simon?" she began to question.

I told her that I needed this, to relax, and most of all…breathe. I kissed every inch I could cover, and then I kissed her there, down and in between her legs. She threw her head back and nearly screamed.

"Shhh, I know. I love you so much, Nicolette. You are the most beautiful woman that I have ever seen. I want to love you forever and worship you with my body."

She pulled me down to her and kissed me fervently. Our teeth collided, and she sucked on my tongue. I fucking loved when she did that to me. We have never been so intimate in this way before. I loved that she trusted me with her heart and body. I knew I had to be careful with her.

I kissed her left breast and took her pebbled nipple into my mouth. She let out a sexy moan as I cupped the other one. Her fingers pulled at my hair, as I continued to suck on her breasts. I pinched one in between my two fingers and took the other into my mouth. I feasted on her delectable body until she screamed out her pleasure. I didn't stop teasing her with my mouth. This was only the beginning. "Let go of your fears and just feel what I am giving to you."

She was breathing heavily and smiled back at me. She was absolutely adorable as she shyly looked into my eyes, and I answered her unspoken question.

"Yes, baby, that's exactly what that was, and I plan to give you many more."

She laughed, and I continued my exploration of her body. I kissed her flat stomach, and then onto her ribs, licking and biting all her erogenous zones. When I turned her over to her back, I noticed a tattoo. I was stunned to discover that my girl had marked her beautiful body. Her tattoo was a heart on the top of her hip, with an inscription written inside of it.

As I continued to stare at it, she asked me if I wanted to know what it meant, and I did. She explained that after she left me, not knowing if we would reunite, she wanted a permanent reminder of me that forever marked her body, replacing a mark that Michael had left. My eyes filled with tears as I pulled her closer to me. I didn't know how I felt about this. I wanted so desperately to know, but it always came back to Michael, and I hated that. Sensing my reaction to her tattoo, she kissed me.

"Simon, I'm sorry if I didn't explain it well. Let me try again. This tattoo represents you, and you alone. It was my way of keeping you close to me when we were apart."

I returned her kiss, and now more than ever, I needed to know what the words meant. She was fluent in several languages, and Italian was her favorite. When she recited the quote, I nearly came right there. It was beyond erotic listening to her words pass through her beautiful, plump lips that were slightly swollen from all of our kisses. *"Il mio cuore appartiene a te."* Whatever it was, it was beautiful.

She then said, "My heart belongs to you."

We entwined our bodies with one another. I loved Nicolette so much, and I wanted to show her, as she did for me with her tattoo. I leaned her down and kissed her tattoo, hovering over it with my mouth for a few minutes until she gasped and moaned. I kissed both sides of her ribs until I was at her opening and gently parted her legs, kissing her between her wet, slick folds. I was ravenous for her. I could feast on her for days, as she raked her fingers roughly through my hair, screaming my name. This was for her, and I wanted to please her, as I imagined her loving me with her mouth. I could wait. This was her time to be cherished, and I enjoyed every minute of pleasure I gave her.

"Eyes on me, baby." We never broke contact until she gave in to her orgasm and came again. Her skin was slicked with sweat, making me want to lick her sweet tasting skin. I reached for a condom and had her place it on me. She was nervous, as I felt her fingers tremble. I placed my hand over hers and helped her guide it down my length, never taking my eyes away from hers. She visibly relaxed as I continued to touch her. She let out a breath as I parted her legs slowly with mine. A few more breaths she released, and then I asked her again, "Is this what you want?"

"With all my heart."

Slowly entering, I carefully looked for any signs of discomfort on her face. She gripped onto my arms and took in all of me. Her eyes squeezed shut, and that one look pierced my heart. I began to pull out of her body, and she asked me not to stop. I pushed through her deeper this time until she got used to me. I kept up with this rhythm until she fully accepted me into her body, and I watched her visibly relax.

When I picked up the pace, our bodies molded with one another, and we matched breath for breath. I could feel worked up and close to my release, but I wanted her to come first, or both of us together. Our bodies moved in a synchronized dance until we both reached our moment and climaxed together. It was an unbelievable feeling that I had never experienced before. Thank you, God, for bringing her home to me. She was my girl. The love of my life, which made it a thousand times better.

Nicolette

I finally made love to the man I love. I was bone tired after our lovemaking and the very intense orgasms he had given me. Yes, my man did not disappoint. He was gentle, attentive, and put my needs above his own. As I drifted off into a blissful sleep, he called me his "angel" and then told me that he loved me, before I finally fell asleep.

My body was still entwined with Simon's as I slowly and gently untangled my body from his. It was no easy task since he was incredibly tall and strong like a bear. I didn't want to wake him, but nature was calling, so I made my way to the bathroom. The last time I was in here, it was a horrific scene with me losing my baby. I looked all around, and it was meticulously clean with not one thing out of place. I shoved those past memories away and focused on the now. I looked in the mirror, taking in all the love bites that Simon left on me. They were beautiful. He was amazing, and I have never felt more cherished and loved. I felt whole again. I wasn't afraid anymore when I looked in the mirror at my reflection.

The scared and guilt-ridden girl was gone and now was stronger. Her darkness had been replaced with light that shined all around her. I tiptoed out of the bathroom, not wanting to wake Simon. He looked so peaceful while he slept. I put on the shirt that he had worn earlier in the day and brought it up to my nose. It smelled delicious, just like him. I missed this while I was away. I didn't realize what comfort it brought me until I could smell his scent all over me.

I felt fantastic and only had some mild soreness. Simon couldn't have been gentler with me. Sex sure makes you hungry, and I was starving. Thank goodness, the fridge was stocked with fresh groceries. I found items to make a salad, and I saw that he had marinated chicken in a Tupperware container. After I placed the chicken in the broiler and prepared the salad, I looked up to see his ocean blue eyes staring back at me.

"Hello, baby. Sleep well?" I asked.

He walked around the kitchen island and lifted me up into his arms. "I woke up to a cold side of the bed. I didn't know if you had left, and then panic began to set in."

Hearing him tell me that made me take his face into my hands and kiss him madly. I needed to prove to him that I had meant every word I said before. "I am never going to leave you again. Haven't we had enough doubt between us? Please believe me. I love you, and making sweet love with you should have banished any doubt you may have felt. Simon, if you're scared, then be scared with me. I'm here, and I am not going anywhere. Am I truly forgiven for hurting you?"

"Don't ever ask me that question again. I love you, baby, and there is nothing to forgive." I was still in his arms as he shut the oven off. "The food can wait. I'm hungry for something else." I giggled, and he carried me back to our bedroom and made love to me again.

Today was about new beginnings. We were going to put the past behind us if only it was that simple. We still had to get through a trial with Michael and face our lives being aired out in the media with both sides fighting the other.

I wasn't looking forward to the day when I would come face to face with Michael. I wasn't afraid, though, not anymore. With Simon by my side, together we could handle anything. I finally believed what he had been telling me all along.

Simon

I lost count after the third time making love to Nicolette. It was an endless fight against my self-control when it came to loving my girl. How I survived these past months without her, I'd never know. The only thing that mattered now was that she was home for good.

Another first we experienced was showering together. We continued to explore each other and lathered one another with body wash. Running my hands down her perfect silhouette felt amazing. I couldn't stop touching her. Of course, she made me hard again and shocked the hell out of me when she grabbed hold of my throbbing dick. The head of my cock began to leak pre-come as she wrapped her hand around me and began to stroke. I didn't want to push her, but I wasn't going to lie and pretend that what she was doing didn't turn me the fuck on. I wanted her again, and then she pulled me down to her in a savage kiss. I lifted her up in my arms. I told her to wrap her legs around my waist as her body perfectly aligned with mine.

When I entered her this time, I pushed in deeper, as she cried out her pleasure. This was a different position, where it would be more intense for her, but she took all of me without complaint. I loved it when she ran her fingers through my hair. It was like a possession, and she was staking her claim.

"Open your eyes, baby. I want to see you as I make you come," I whispered.

Her eyes widened, as my dirty talk got dirtier with every hard thrust into her body. Her pleasure and comfort were my only priority, and I needed to have her eyes on me at all times. It would be the only way I knew that what we were doing was not too much for her. She read my mind so easily, as I could read hers. I pulled back to a more guarded pace, and then she showed me exactly what I was waiting for. Her body pummeled against mine, and oh my girl came and screamed out my name. I silenced her with my mouth as I came too.

After our shower, if that's what we are calling it, I carried her out to our bedroom, and I tenderly dried her body from head to toe, causing her to shiver. I promised to love her forever and continued to kiss every inch of her beautiful body.

She laid lazily against my body, as I twirled her long strands of hair in between my fingers. I couldn't help myself from smiling and fantasizing about the right moment to propose to her.

We already promised our commitment to one another, and making love has connected us. She mentioned staying with me forever, and she would never leave me again. She had to know that a proposal would be happening soon, right?

I just had to figure out when. *How do I surprise her?* When I heard her voice at graduation, no one was more surprised than I was. When her image came into focus and she was literally a few feet from me, I thought my heart may have stopped beating. I was that blown away by seeing her again.

Surprised? Yeah, you could say that. I didn't believe anything I could do would top hers, but I would try.

Nicolette

"**B**aby, your cheeks have to be hurting by now, since you haven't stopped smiling."

"You make me so happy. I can't believe I'm holding you in my arms right now. Even after all we shared since you came home, it still feels like a dream. The thought of you not coming back home nearly broke me. I never want to feel the way I did when I watched you walk away and left me just standing there. Alone."

Listening to my love express how hurt he was by my leaving pained my heart. He would never know how sorry I was for having done that to him. I shifted in his arms and leaned on my elbows. "Simon, were we ever really apart? I know we had many miles that separated us, but you always remained where it mattered most, and that's right here in my heart."

He held me tightly in his arms and kissed me breathlessly. I placed his hand over my heart so he could feel how it beat when he touched me. I said, "Baby, you are my heart. No one resides there but you. I meant what I said. I fought my demons, and my only focus was returning home to you. Can we truly move past our time apart, and start over?"

"Yes, we can. I promise you. Our new life began together the minute I heard your voice at graduation. You are my entire world, and I am never letting you go again."

"Good, because you have me for life."

"Can I ask you a question?"

"Anything, you know that."

"Will you tell me about Switzerland?"

"Yes, but not now, okay? Today is about starting over and loving each other. I just want to focus on us, not dwell on the past." He seemed to be satisfied with my answer and held me in his arms. I buried my face into his warm body and smiled. I was home.

We walked our beach and collected seashells along the way. The beach house was filled with unique shells and beach décor. Simon said every time his aunt traveled to islands around the world, she would always bring back something for her home. Her taste in art was amazing. The home was beautiful. I still couldn't believe that this was my life now, and I got to share it all with Simon.

After we enjoyed making s'mores in the huge fireplace that was on the far end of the deck, it was back to cuddling on the deck lounger. He was so relaxed and calm. When I woke this morning, I didn't know what the day would bring for us. Reuniting with the man I loved had been a long-awaited dream come true. We had survived throughout all of our pain and loss.

I couldn't stop looking at him. He was now sleeping peacefully. I didn't want to disturb him, but there was something I wanted to do. I looked through my suitcase and found what I was looking for. Only a few people knew that I had always loved to draw. I smiled, knowing it was another thing I had in common with his beloved aunt. Back in Switzerland, my love for art was renewed, and it was very therapeutic for me.

He didn't move since I left him. I began to sketch Simon's handsome features. When he shifted slightly, I held my breath to not make a sound, but then he settled back and I still had the image of him I wanted to capture. His jaw line was strong, and I concentrated on every detail of his face. Once that part was done, I worked on his body, taking in every toned muscle, especially his defined abdominal muscles. I had to clench my legs together when my eyes found his perfect V muscle at the bottom of his torso. His body was exquisite, and it was all mine.

He slept so soundly that I was able to complete several sketches of him before he opened his eyes and caught me. He leaned up on his elbows with his beautiful naked body on full display for me to admire. He raised his arms over his head, elongating his frame, and then gave me a sexy grin. "Sorry, I passed out on you. You wore me out, baby."

"It's okay, I was able to pass the time," I smirked.

"Yeah? What have you been up to?"

"That's for me to know, and you to find out." I giggled.

He took that as a challenge and leaped off the lounger. He lifted me up and placed me down on his lap and began to crazy tickle me until I couldn't breathe. "Okay, I'll tell you about Switzerland," I said in between breaths.

"While I was away, I began to use art in my therapy. I painted every single day, and it helped me a great deal. When I couldn't express in words how I was feeling, I painted it. Here are some of the sketches that I did."

I handed him the portfolio, and his eyes expressively widened with every sheet he looked at.

I explained, "In the beginning, I felt isolated from everyone else. I was alone most of the time."

He said, "I should have been there for you. I'm so sorry you had to go through that without me."

"It wasn't your fault, Simon. I made so many mistakes and completely shut you out of my life. I couldn't let you help me, and I alone chose this. I had to accept the responsibility of my leaving. Time passed, and slowly I began to feel comfortable and let the therapists help me. Lana, she was great. When I wanted to give up, she convinced me to stay with the program. I was the biggest pain in the ass, and she called me out on everything."

I continued, "I was there to recover first. I took yoga classes, long hikes in the mountains, anything I could to heal my spirit, and then onto my heart. I knew my way home was through you, Simon, but I needed to take care of me first. I know I've told you this already, but it's the truth. I was so broken after hearing about Michael, losing the baby, and all those horrible fights with my family. It was toxic. But then there was you, loving me throughout everything, and every time I believed I had taken a step toward healing, another obstacle would drag me back down. Do you understand what I'm trying to tell you?"

"More than you know. When you left, I shut down and tuned out the rest of the world. I didn't care, didn't want to hear it. I shut my family out and our friends. I was drowning just as much as you were, and I really didn't know how I could go on without you. Then one day, Sam came over and pulled my ass out of bed. We went surfing. I felt alive out there on the ocean, and it was thrilling to feel the board under my feet again. It hadn't been like that for a long time. When I got back to shore, I had seen that I missed your call, and my world shattered again. If I had answered your call, would you have talked to me?"

"I really don't know. It was a bad day to begin with, but then I found out from Bailey that you were chosen to be Valedictorian. I was so proud of you, and I wanted you to know that."

"You didn't leave a message."

"No, I didn't. I chickened out and hung up. My only comfort was listening to your voice on your outgoing message. You never changed the greeting on your phone, and it made me smile. It gave me hope."

"Baby, why? Why did you call everyone but me?"

"I wasn't ready, and I certainly was not strong enough. If I had heard your voice, then just the sound of it would have brought me home, and I may have ended up worse than before I left. I thought I was doing the best thing for you. If it were a clean break, then you could've moved on with your life and would've eventually forgotten about me. I knew I had caused you so much pain, but this would've been the last time. As much as it hurt me to let you go, I somehow convinced myself that I was setting you free."

He searched my eyes, and then took me in his arms. "How could you believe such a thing? After all the talks we had, you thought you were doing me a favor? Baby, it was quite the opposite. It felt almost like a part of me died, and every day that passed without you, I lost another piece of myself. Don't you know that you are my world…my every reason just to wake up in the morning…the missing piece to my puzzle? I couldn't breathe without you. I barely survived you walking out on me that night. It took me months to realize that you were the only thing in the world that could truly hurt me. It was because I loved you so much and willingly handed over my heart to you. You are the first girl that I have ever loved and will ever want to love for the rest of my life. Please, Nicolette. Don't ever leave me again, because, without your love, I will truly be lost."

We held onto each other and cried until we were empty. We needed this cathartic moment between us. Simon had held his feelings in for so long, and after everything we shared today, he still carried the weight on his shoulders. After we openly shared our pain, we vowed not to talk about this again and finally laid it to rest. Once we walked back upstairs to our bedroom, he held me throughout the night, never breaking our bond with one another.

Simon

If I was dreaming, then I didn't want to wake up. I slowly opened my eyes, and my beautiful sleeping angel was lying in my arms, sleeping so peacefully. It wasn't a dream. She was real and here with me.

We talked and shared so much of ourselves yesterday. Making love to her was amazing and exceeded my wildest dreams. I craved so much more of her and wanted to feel her naked and on top of me. I trailed my fingers up her naked back, as she stirred a little in our bed. She let out a breathy moan, and then opened her eyes and found mine staring back at her.

"Good morning, baby. How did you sleep?" I asked her, but not before kissing her inviting lips.

"Hmmm, I think you know." My girl was adorable. "I slept wonderfully, and so safe in your arms. Thank you for being my body pillow."

"I'll hold you for the rest of my life if you let me." I wasn't going to wait one more second to ask her. I leaped from our bed and told her not to move. She giggled again. I swear every time I heard that sweet sound, I wanted to make love to her again.

I grabbed the ring box from my jacket pocket and climbed back into bed with Nicolette. I sat up to face her, taking her hand in mine.

"Nicolette, you're a part of me, as I'm a part of you. We complete each other. I love you with every fiber of my being. You heard the story, right? I fell in love. From the moment, I saw you on the beach, the world I knew had shifted, and I was completely drawn into yours. You are beautiful inside and out. When you enter a room, I have to catch my breath and slow my heart rate down. You occupy my dreams at night, and you are the first thought that begins my day, each and every morning."

"When I accepted this home, I knew I could only live here if you shared it with me. I want to love you and take care of you for the rest of my days. I want children with you, to know that our love will create a son, a daughter, or you never know—both. Twins and triplets do run in my family. Just dreaming of that moment when you will tell me that you are pregnant with my child, brings me to my knees. I'm so happy. This is what you do to me. My future is with you, and the life we are going to make will be amazing together. Say yes to me, and give me the extreme honor of becoming your husband. Be my wife...be mine forever?"

I slowly opened the ring box that I was holding. Her eyes were glazed over, and she wasn't saying too much.

I said, "This ring belonged to Aunt Grace, another piece of her heart that she wanted me to have. One day while she was painting on the beach, she was wearing it, and I asked her about it. You know the painting in the upstairs entryway?"

"Yes, it's beautiful. A bouquet of roses."

"That's the one. It was also the one that she was painting right here on our beach. She never married, but that didn't stop her from wearing this beautiful diamond ring. It's a 3-carat diamond placed into…" I paused and then whispered, "…a rose-shaped setting. I told her that it matched the painting, and she smiled."

"It's beautiful, Simon. It reminds me of a blossoming flower. It matches my earrings."

"Yes, it does. Those came from me, but they were intended to match your ring. Nicolette, that day I spent with Aunt Grace, I will never forget. It was the day she told me that her cancer had come back and she only had a few months to live. Before I could even do it, she stopped me from crying, telling me that's not what she needed from me. I then asked her what she did want, and if I could, I would get it for her. She smiled again, and then told me about her wish for me to have this home and this beautiful blossoming diamond rose ring. I was sixteen years old, and I was being asked to make a promise to her, one she knew I would never break. She knew my older brothers were different from me. They had no emotional attachment to our life here in California. They were born and raised in Colorado, and someday, Jacob wants to own a ranch and build a house on it. As for Andrew and Cameron, they are too wild to ever settle down. Their love is football, and that's where they are headed. My life is here, with you, and on this beach, and living in this home. All I need now is your answer, and then I plan to make love to my fiancée for the rest of the day."

I sat back on my heels and waited for Nicolette, to say something. Her tears were falling, but I had a feeling they were happy tears. I wiped them away and more fell. She happily clapped her hands and then shook her head, but no words came out of her mouth. I finally kissed her to make sure she was still with me, and then she lunged forward, nearly knocking us both off the bed.

"Nicolette, baby? I need to hear the words. Will you marry me? Will you be mine? Because once you say yes, you are signing on for a lifetime of forever's."

She whispered in a breathy tone, "Yes, Simon. I will marry you."

Those six words were all it took to set my soul on fire. I rolled us over to the middle of the bed, removing the sheet. I caressed her naked body and loved her with mine, as we began to make love, sealing the commitment we had just promised to each other.

"You have made me so happy today, Nicolette. Always trust that I will love and protect you, every minute of every day for the rest of my life."

She knew how devoted I was to her, and with agreeing to marry me, she would never question my love for her ever again. The days of my girl doubting and blaming herself were over. I knew everything she felt was placed deep inside of her from Michael, and he would never have control over her again.

I was so in love with my beautiful girl and couldn't wait to marry her. We made love and were in sated bliss after our bodies were completely spent. She was sleepy but smiling at the same time. She placed her head on my chest, as I rubbed small circles on her naked back.

Surprising me, she asked, "Can we get married tomorrow?"

Awakening before Nicolette, I watched my beautiful fiancée sleep. Her chestnut brown hair cascaded over her pillow, and I loved how her long eye lashes sashayed like feathers on her big brown eyes. She accepted my marriage proposal and made me the happiest guy in the world. I knew we were young, and most people would think we were crazy to marry at our age. I didn't care, and neither did she. The truth was, most people hadn't gone through what we had. We fought through the darkest of times to come out on the other side and be together. That alone matured us way beyond our years.

I left her sleeping in our bed, and because she looked so peaceful, I didn't have the heart to wake her. We spent the entire night with our bodies entwined with each other and made passionate love until we literally passed out. I walked out onto the deck. The sun had risen a short time ago and left a bright glow over the ocean. I loved it out here. The waves looked awesome today. Maybe I would try to get my girl out on the water. Or at least watch me as I surfed. She never could resist me in my wet suit.

As I felt the sun on my face, a warm breeze swept on by. I smiled and believed it was my Aunt Grace. I looked up to the heavens and said a prayer in her name. "Your dream for me came true, Aunt Grace. I found the other half of my heart with Nicolette, and she's wearing your ring. She loves it, by the way. Thank you for believing in me, and helping me find my love. I promise to fill our home with children, and wherever you are in the universe, you will hear their laughter. I love you, and thank you for loving me."

I was so lost in my thoughts, and then I had the perfect idea to celebrate our engagement. My brothers were leaving tomorrow, and I wasn't sure when they would make it back out this way again. I phoned my house, and Jacob answered. He was grumpy that we hadn't spent that much time together, but I promised we would soon. I told him to be a team player and gather the troops for brunch today at the beach house. He said that he would, and then I called Nicolette's family next.

I spoke with her Uncle Jack, and he assured me that they would all be here for brunch. Before he ended the call, he thanked me for making his "Nickel" so happy. I could barely contain the joy I felt after I ended the call, but one more to go. I called the catering company to arrange for our last-minute brunch. I was lucky they could fit us in on such short notice, but since they catered many of my parents' parties, they were happy to help me out. I programmed their number on speed dial to use their services again, maybe even for our wedding reception.

I quietly entered our bedroom to find our bed empty, and my sleeping girl missing from it. I looked in the bathroom, and she wasn't in there. My heart began to race when I couldn't find her, and then I saw her through the French doors that led to another deck we have off our bedroom. She was sitting on one of the loungers with her knees pulled up to her chest. She looked deep in thought. I felt nervous all of the sudden and wondered why she didn't come to find me once she had awakened.

Thirty-Three

Nicolette

T he ocean breeze felt so refreshing on my face. All this time living out here in sunny California, and I'm still not tan. My porcelain skin refuses to darken, and I look a shade darker than ivory standing next to Simon.

The realization of my new life just hit me. *I'm engaged to Simon. How did I get here?* I'm going to be Mrs. Simon Paulson. When we first got together, I used to scribble what my name would look like using his last name, but who knew that dream would ever become a reality? If you were to ask me a week ago, if this was where I would be, I didn't think I could have honestly answered the question. I didn't know what to expect from Simon and how he would welcome me home when I returned to California.

Remembering the way, I had made my presence known to him at the graduation, I smiled and hugged my knees. I was relieved that he didn't pass out from the shock of seeing me. It was the total opposite of what could have happened. He declared his love for me in the most public way. Our graduation will go down in history with Simon's epic speech. We reunited in front of our graduating class, and hundreds of people cheered us on.

The words we said to each other were forever sealed within my heart. Our first time making love was beyond anything I could have imagined. Simon held me in his arms and promised me that making love to him was truly my first time. What Michael did to me did not change my virgin status. I didn't willingly give myself to him. He took it from me and against my will. Loving Simon and trusting him with my heart and body erased the ugliness that Michael had left on me.

I was madly in love with Simon, and he simply amazed me for the man that he was. We shared so much together. I would never forget how he took his time kissing and touching every spot on my body. He was so gentle with me, and I was never scared. I didn't know what I was doing and hoped that I wouldn't disappoint him. We learned together, and he never allowed me to doubt myself. Simon's love gave me confidence, and I didn't need to hide from him. He wanted me to never be shy about my body, nor ashamed of it.

I was not going to hide my feelings about it, but I loved when he enjoyed loving on my body. I was in awe of his. He was a work of art, my own personal Adonis. He had lean muscle throughout his tall physique, and his stomach was lined with layers of abdominal muscles, ending in a perfect and very kissable V. *Listen to me go on about lusting over him, I can't help it.* He was all I thought about when I was so far away. Simon belonged on the cover of a fitness magazine. This beautiful man was all mine, and I never stopped asking myself the same question over and over again: *"How did I get so lucky to have found him?"*

I felt his presence before I heard his voice. I turned around and smiled at my beautiful man behind me. My smile faded when he appeared to be worried about something. I immediately walked over to him, placing my arms around his waist.

"What's wrong, Simon? Are you okay?" I asked.

His expression was unreadable as he was very quiet. He held my face in his hands and searched my eyes as if he was looking for something. He allowed me to kiss him, but then without letting me go, he asked me the same question. "What's wrong, baby? Are you okay?"

I knew what this was, and I wasn't going down that road again. I quickly kissed him again to put him at ease. "Simon, I'm more than okay. I'm fantastic."

He said, "I was worried when I couldn't find you, and crazy thoughts ran wild through my head. I'm sorry."

"Stop, it's okay, and I understand. I love you. The minute you took me back, my world turned right again. I have never been so happy, and I am so in love with you. I will never leave you again, and I meant every word I said. I'll say these words to you every day like a prayer if that's what it will take for me to prove it to you."

His body instantly relaxed, as he pulled me into a death grip of a hug. Sometimes my man didn't know his own strength that I had to tickle his side to loosen his hold on me. When he finally pulled back, he gave me a proper good morning kiss that set me on fire and made me feel hot in all the right places. I shifted my legs, as my body so easily responded to his.

"Shower with me?" he asked in a low sexy voice.

"Absolutely," I whispered.

After our very hot shower, we sat on our deck and enjoyed the morning sun. Simon was stretched out on one of the loungers while only wearing his board shorts. *Damn, he should be illegal*, but I kept that naughty thought to myself. He told me about brunch and how excited our families were to be coming over to our house. *Our house? I can't believe this is real.*

"How do you think our parents will react to our news?" I asked.

"Happy! How can they be anything less? I don't want you to worry about anything. We have their blessing, and they support our relationship. It's just a matter of time before we make it official."

He blew me a kiss and went back to reading a surf magazine. I didn't want to spoil his mood, but there was another matter that I needed to discuss with him. I broached the subject very carefully. "Simon, before our company arrives, we need to talk about something important."

"No, not today. I'm happy and I don't want to talk about anything that is going to spoil our day. Please, babe, no heavy discussions today."

"I wasn't ready to talk about Switzerland, but we did it anyway."

He groaned and wasn't happy about it, but he gave me his full attention.

I said, "After I got home, all I wanted to do was get back to you, but before I did that, I needed to take care of something that couldn't wait."

"Which was?" he asked.

"While I was in Switzerland, I had spoken to William Jennings. You remember him, right? The prosecutor assigned to my case?"

"Yeah, what about him?"

"I had a meeting with him, along with my family."

"You're telling me this now?" he asked and then got up from his lounger and walked over to the deck railing.

No, not this time. You are not going to pull away from me just because you don't like something I say. I joined him and made him look at me. "Yes, I'm telling you now. As my fiancé, you have a right to know, and I always want to be honest with you."

"I'm sorry. I didn't mean to react the way I did and be harsh with my tone. You have to give me some room here. I just got you back, and I hate to admit this to you, but I'm still afraid this is all a dream. A dream that I'm going to wake from and find you gone. I can't go through that again. I won't survive it, babe. It will destroy me."

"Hold me, please," I said.

He did with no hesitation and carried me back over to the deck lounger. I curled my body around him and kissed his neck. I begged him to believe that my running days were over. He shifted my body and placed his head on my chest. I was holding him this time, and I promised to never let go. He slowly calmed, and his breathing became normal again. He was scared, and it took a lot for Simon to share that with me, but how could he be? After all that we have shared. I'm wearing his ring and have agreed to marry him. Isn't that enough? I put him through hell, I know that. I promised myself that I would try harder to be patient and understanding with his feelings. When he finally raised his eyes to look at me, he was back with me. My loving Simon.

"Will you tell me about your meeting?" he asked.

"Do you promise to hear me out?"

"Nicolette, you wouldn't be asking me to do that if what you had to say was good news. I'm sorry, but I am hanging on by a thread right now. I can't make any promises." He moved away from me and walked back over to the railing. I watched him for a few minutes as he watched the waves break onto the shore. I'd seen this side of him before, and I knew what he was doing. He wanted to protect me at all costs and didn't want me to be hurt, but that couldn't truly happen until we put Michael and our past behind us.

"Simon, will you look at me. I met with Mr. Jennings and requested a preliminary meeting with the judge, along with Michael's lawyer and my lawyer." I took a deep breath and ripped off the Band-Aid. "I also requested for Michael to be there."

Simon bit his lip, probably trying not to scare me with his reaction. He let out a breath and ran his fingers through his hair. "No, not happening. I will not allow you to do this. It will be a cold day in hell before I let you go anywhere near that piece of shit."

It was my turn to breathe. I twirled my engagement ring on my finger and looked for some kind of sign to help me find my way. I didn't want to lose my temper with him, but I never liked being told what to do. No matter how much I loved him, it was a trigger for me. I would never be able to give myself over to anyone if I lost my free will, not even for Simon. He was angry and withdrawn. I placed my hands around his waist and leaned into his naked back.

"Please, don't pull away from me. I need you." His body was hard as a rock and layered with tension. He wasn't letting it go so easy, but he did turn around to hold me. "We are less than two months away from going up against him in court. I am so scared to put myself out there and in such a public way. I will have to fight in front of a jury of strangers and convince them that he was guilty of what he's been accused of. He still believes what he did was not rape, but consensual and rough sex. I will not walk into that court-room and listen to his team of lawyers say that about me. It's wrong, and I'm trying to stop it."

"Yeah? And just how do you intend to stop him?"

"Do you remember the conversation I had with Jennings? The night I left for Chicago?"

"How could I forget? It was the night you left me."

"I know you are angry and frustrated, but please do not be this way. I need to tell you everything, and we can do without the sarcasm to your tone."

"I'm sorry, but what do you expect from me? We have been back together for only two days, the best of my life. Aren't we al-lowed to be happy for one fucking minute? And without making it about Michael?"

God! I hate this, and I hate him. I stood there and allowed Si-mon to scream out his frustrations. I needed to allow him to do this, or it would eat him up alive, and I needed him to know everything, especially the next part of my story.

I was trying to be strong and patient, but the tears broke through. I hugged him again and begged him not to be angry with me. "I can't bear this, please? Talk to me."

He said, "I'm not angry with you, and I never want you to be angry with me. Nicolette, I'm just trying to understand you and why you want to do this."

"If I had stayed when the first hearing took place, I could have been directly involved with all the proceedings involving my case, but I left. This is my chance to right that wrong. I need to speak with the judge and give my testimony in detail about what Michael did to me."

"I don't understand. That's what a trial is for."

"Yes, you're right. My testimony can be reserved for a trial, but a deal is on the table, and I can challenge it. I have a right to be there, and for my voice to be heard. Whether they listen to me, or not, I'm going to that court hearing."

"I can see there is no changing your mind. When is it?"

"Tomorrow morning at nine. I know this news is not what you expected or wanted to hear, but I need to do this. I'm ready to face him, and I am not afraid."

"Nicolette, what if I am? I can't make any promises that I won't leap over a table and beat him to a pulp. He deserves nothing from you. It's going to kill me to watch you in the same room with him."

"Here's the other part that you are not going to like," I said.

"I don't know how much more I can take."

"Let's hope that's not true. Because there is one more thing I need to tell you, and I know you are not going to like it."

"Nicolette," he said cautiously in his tone. "What will I not like?"

I released one deep breath and then said, "You will not have to watch anything because you will not be permitted inside with me. I will be with my lawyer and no one else. I'm doing this alone."

Thirty-Four

Simon

"**W**hy would you ever put yourself through that? Alone? I thought you were done living your life that way. You have me, and I can be there for you."

"I know that, beyond a shadow of a doubt, but this is something I have to overcome. It's on me."

"You don't know everything. You weren't the only one keeping a secret. I'm guilty of it too, and I just don't know how to tell you."

She knelt down in front of me and took my hands in hers. She loved me. I saw it in her eyes. She said, "Hey, don't hide from me. Isn't that what you're always asking me? Whatever you have to say, I will listen and understand, I promise. Was it someone else?"

"No! Never. How could you ask me that? You own me, body and soul. I'm bound to you for life."

"Okay, I'm sorry. It's just, I don't know, you look guilty of something. Talk to me, please."

I said, "The night you lost the baby, when I left the hospital for a while, I was out of my mind. I wasn't thinking clearly, sick with worry over you. I kept thinking how you were in the hospital again, and I was hating the person who was responsible for putting you there. All the pain and suffering you endured was all because of him. I believed you were dying in my arms, and I didn't know how I could go on without you."

"I'm here now, baby, and I'm not going anywhere."

"Yes, but I didn't know that back then. No matter how many conversations we have about it, I don't think I will ever be able to explain to you how I felt finding you in that condition. I had so much rage inside of me, and I knew I had to unleash it somehow. I drove around for a while and then I made up my mind to confront Michael." There it was, my truth. I finally told her. I watched her expression stay the same, and she gave me no reaction to what I just told her. What if she had known all along that was where I went?

"How did you manage to see him? I was told he was under strict restrictions, and only his father and lawyer had access to him."

"I went to my father and had him call in a favor with a contact he had at the jail. With his help, I was granted access to Michael."

"What did you do, Simon? Did you hurt him?" she asked. She looked lost at the moment but hung on to every word I was saying to her.

"I met him in a private conference room with the guard on the other side of the door. He was surprised to see me. I think I was the last person he expected to see. He was handcuffed to the table, and his other hand was inexplicably wrapped in a cast. He was defenseless against me."

"I asked you a question. What did you do?"

"Nicolette, it's nothing like you are imagining. The look on your face is gutting me."

"I'm sorry, but this is unexpected. I'm trying to work it out quickly, but it's hard. Go on, please."

"He didn't want me there, but I had plenty to say to him, and I wasn't going anywhere until I did. You have to understand. I wasn't in the right frame of mind when I went to the jail. I hated him and wanted to rip his throat out. I don't remember everything I said to him, but I punched him pretty hard. Then he fell backward with his good hand hanging from the table. I wished I would have broken that one too."

"I guess that clears up for me as to why your hand was bruised and swollen when you came back. I always wondered, but since you didn't tell me about it, I let it drop."

"Thank you for that. I never wanted you to know any of this. After I hit him, it was just a blur. He was screaming for help, and then the guard escorted me out of there. He wiped the video feed clean and handed me the hard copy. I went back to the beach house to clean up, and then I came back to you. That's all of it, I swear."

"Did Michael ever say anything to anyone about you?"

"My father never heard anything else about it. I'm assuming he kept his mouth shut. Who would believe him anyway? I destroyed the proof that placed me there. It would be his word against mine, and the guard would never say anything."

"Simon, did you tell Michael?"

"Tell him what?"

"About the baby?" My girl was crying, and it was breaking my heart for her to have to relive this again. I pulled her back onto my lap and held her close to me.

"No, I would never betray you like that. I'm sorry for leaving you that night, and my reason for it. I felt helpless and angry. I hated him so much. I just didn't know what to do."

"I'm sorry you ever had to go through that. It's over, Simon, and we are together now. We promised we would put this behind us, and after tomorrow, it will be. You're not the only one that wanted Michael dead. When I was with my Uncle Jack, he shared a secret with me, one he's been carrying around for a while now."

"Is it bad?"

"It could have been, but he stopped himself. He never confirmed it, but my uncle had many connections back in Chicago, and without actually saying the words, he may have been involved in the mafia when he was younger. It sure sounded that way, and he said that if he truly wanted Michael dead, he could have made it happen."

"Shit, that's crazy."

"I know, tell me about it. My father has never shared much about my grandparents, nor his childhood. When I would ask, I would just get bland answers and then the subject would change. When I got hurt, old feelings were resurrected for my uncle and my father. I didn't push my uncle to tell me anything else about it. It was clear that it made him uncomfortable, and we just went on to enjoy the rest of the day together. I'm glad you told me about going to see Michael. Let's not talk any more about it though. We have a great day to look forward to with our families, and a wedding to plan."

"God, I love you."

"I love you more."

I kissed my girl, and then she left to get ready for our company. She was so different from the girl that left me a few months ago. She came home with renewed strength and confidence. She'd proven that she could handle anything. I hoped that was still true for tomorrow.

Nicolette

O ur home looked great. The catering company arrived shortly after our talk and arranged a huge display of breakfast and lunch items all covered under large silver dome covers. We had a mimosa fountain surrounded by champagne glasses. Desserts and fresh fruit were on another table. Simon ordered roses and mixed flowers to line the railings. It was beautiful and perfect. I almost imagined that this setting would be perfect for our wedding. Our families were already here, but I didn't want to put any more ideas into Simon's head. Although the way he was looking at me, he probably was thinking the same thing.

Saved by the bell. Simon answered the door and welcomed in his family, but not before flashing me a sexy wink. *He knew, and I love him for it.*

He was greeted by his brothers, Jacob, Andrew, and Cameron. All four were high-fiving one another, as they made their way inside. They took one look at me and gave me that Paulson wink I love so much. Before I could blink, I was hauled over Jacob's shoulders. He twirled me around and then passed me to Andrew, who then tossed me like a football to Cameron. He caught me in his arms, and I laughed out loud. *Oh, my goodness! These guys are going to be my brothers. I can't wait. They are so much fun.*

"Put my girl down before I have to beat all of your asses," Simon jokingly threatened his brothers. At least, I think he was joking. I couldn't stop laughing.

Marina and Ted Paulson walked in next, just shaking their heads at their antics. I'm sure she was used to their horseplay, but I was a peanut compared to these giants. I was wearing my ring, and as soon as his mom saw it, I was pulled into a loving hug.

"Welcome to our family. We love you, Nicolette." I wiped away my tears and hugged her back. I truly had their blessing.

We all took a seat and waited for my family to arrive. Ted asked if he could make a toast to us, and we said it would be fine. We each took a glass and listened to the Paulson patriarch:

"Nicolette, I want to officially welcome you to our family. You have made our son a very happy man. We want you to know that as a Paulson, we will love you, protect you, fight for you, and most of all, cherish you. Congratulations to you both, and may you have a blessed life together."

"To the happy couple!" Simon's brothers shouted out, as we clinked our glasses together.

The doorbell rang again, and my family arrived. We welcomed them to our home. I hugged my daddy, and then more hugs to mom, Uncle Jack, and Aunt Sara. Everyone seemed so relaxed and happy.

"Can we eat already?" shouted Andrew.

"Yes, help yourself," I said, and the guys filled their plates.

I watched two families blend together as one. I was so happy. Nothing could have spoiled this day. Later on, I gave my mom and dad a tour of my new home here with Simon. They seemed happy but overwhelmed at the same time, especially when we got to our bedroom. The bed was made and the room was tidy, but it seemed as if I have been living here forever. My personal things were strewn around the room, and I think they knew I would not be coming home with them.

Before I came back to California, Simon had already moved out of his family's home to the beach house. He said by being here, he felt closer to me. I told mom that I already talked with Gracie about packing my things I would need right away, and then I would send for the rest.

"Wow, you really are so grown up. How the hell did that happen?" asked dad. We took a minute to catch our breath and walked on the beach.

"Daddy, I'm going to be okay."

"I know, it's just hard letting you go. You're so young and have gone through so much this last year, and now you are engaged to be married. I think I need some time to catch up."

"I'm not going anywhere, and we have all the time in the world. I told the same to Uncle Jack. We are fine. I love you, dad, and I hope someday you will be able to work out your differences with Uncle Jack. He loves you so much."

"You spoke with him about me?"

"Not in so many words, but the subject did come up briefly. He didn't say much, and I'm guessing you don't want to either. Just be brothers, and don't let what happened to me, or how I came into the world, affect your relationship. You two are too important to me, and I need you both in my life."

He pulled me into a big hug and kissed the top of my head. "You're so smart and wise beyond your years. How did I get so lucky to ever be your father?"

"That's an easy one. Fate stepped in and gave me you. You have been an amazing dad and role model for me. I love you so much."

"Let's go inside before the guys eat all the cake."

"Okay, dad, I'm right behind you."

Simon

"Can I have your attention please?" I couldn't hold back my smile as I asked everyone to grab a glass of champagne. My beautiful girl was beside me and never looked happier. "When I woke up this morning, I almost believed I was dreaming, because everything that happened in the past two days was just that—a dream. Not wanting to tempt fate, I presented my beautiful girl with this ring." I placed a kiss down to her hand. "I asked her to marry me, and I'm happy to say, she said yes. So, consider this a 'save the date' announcement. I plan on making Nicolette a Paulson very soon, and we will celebrate that union here at this home, and on this beach. We love you all." Our guests raised their glasses and each took a turn wishing us well.

We had a wonderful day celebrating our engagement, enjoying all the great conversations that flowed so easily between us. I held my girl in my arms, as we waved goodbye to our families. I already missed my brothers, but they promised to be back for our wedding. I loved this time of the day. The sun was just about to set for the evening over the beautiful horizon. Hues of orange and pinks cascaded out onto the water. If I were a photographer, this would be an amazing picture to capture. This would be amazing for Nicolette to paint for our home. *Our home.* I'll never tire of saying those two words.

"Can I ask you a question, Simon, and don't laugh at me."

"Baby, you can ask me anything, and I promise to never laugh at you. I will make sure to add that promise to our wedding vows." She kept her eyes trained out on the ocean, and then I finally had to turn her around to face me. "What is it?" I asked.

She inhaled a deep breath, and then her cheeks turned the darkest shade of red. With shyness to her tone that was barely above a whisper, she asked me to take her swimming. It didn't seem like an odd request, but then she looked embarrassed by the question and then it finally registered with me what she was exactly asking.

I said, "I never took you for the skinny-dipping kind of girl. Why all the dancing around it? You seem so nervous. Did you think I would say no?" I tried not to laugh, but my girl was adorable. She never answered my questions, just turned around in a huff, and tried to go back inside.

"Forget I mentioned it," she said over her shoulder.

"Hey!" I reached for her and pulled her back. "Walking away will never do. If I hurt your feelings, I'm sorry, but you have to stay and tell me that, not storm off."

"I'm sorry, I overreacted."

"Nicolette, I would love to take you for a sunset swim, and anything else you want to do."

That did it, and she blushed again. I knew what she was thinking. It made me so happy knowing how much she trusted now. I promised myself that I would never take her for granted and never forget how fragile her heart was.

Nicolette

fter I asked him to take me swimming—and I do mean the naughty kind—Simon was a man on a mission, and my shy blushing just made him want me more. He brought my hand to his lips and began kissing the back of my palm. I was thinking I should get a small tattoo on the inside of my wrist. I smiled at the thought of how Simon would react to seeing his name tattooed on my body. He was in love with the one on my side and kissed it every time we make love.

Our stretch of beach was private, and we had no neighbors on either side. Without even giving it thought, I let my inhibitions melt away and allowed Simon to lead me down by the water. Never taking his eyes off me, his eyes were practically glowing with an intense hunger. I never felt more wanted by Simon. He slowly removed my dress, and it felt just as slow sliding down my body and falling to the sand. I quivered with goose bumps that lined my skin as he continued to touch me. He gave me a wink, signaling it was my turn to undress him. I couldn't wait.

He lifted his arms over his head and helped me remove his shirt. Next, my hands found his waistband and with a forceful tug, I pulled him closer to me. Simon was in heaven, as I continued to touch and appreciate his body. Being bold was new for me, but I wanted to be everything for him. I pushed his shorts down, along with his briefs, and standing before me was a very naked Simon. I hungrily ran my tongue over my lips, as I continued to lust over my hot man. He knew what he looked like in clothes, and out of them, but it didn't faze him.

He only cared to make me happy and was a good sport about standing still for a moment so I could take in all of his beauty, but not before he removed my last two pieces of clothing. He loved to max out my pleasure, as he always did everything in a slow and precise art form. He unclasped my bra, and then he guided his fingers along the outline of my panties, sliding them down ever so gently. My head was spinning, and I was beginning to lose control of my senses.

We walked together to where the ocean met the water's edge. It was still a bit chilly, but it felt exhilarating all at the same time. Simon lifted me into his arms and carried me into the sea. He crushed his lips onto mine and made love to me while the ocean waves crashed around us. I had never felt freer in all my life, or more connected with another human being than Simon.

I completely submitted to the man I loved, and he did the same, as we solidified our commitment to the other. This intense feeling was incredible, with jolts of pleasure coursing through my body. I called out his name, as he silenced me with his kisses.

My body was spent after that round of lovemaking. He carried me all the way back to the house and didn't care about our discarded clothing. He said over and over again how much he loved me and could not wait until we could do that again. Another first that we would always have between us.

Once we were settled in our bed, we were entwined with each other all through the night. I knew Simon was worried about tomorrow, with me coming face to face with Michael, but I wasn't. My fear has been replaced with strength and courage. I promised myself that I would never allow Michael and what he did to intimidate or control me ever again. Facing him tomorrow in court would be a true test to that promise.

Simon tried not to show me how upset he truly was, but there would be no missing the way his muscles tensed up. I felt safe in his arms, and I prayed he felt the same way in mine. At times, his grip would tighten around me, but the more he held me, his tension lessened with each breath he let out. After a few minutes, he finally drifted into what I hoped would be a peaceful sleep.

I woke up before my scheduled alarm was to go off. Simon was still sound asleep, and I needed him to remain that way. Marina shared with me how little sleep he got after I left, and he ate even less. Her revelation pained me a great deal, but that's over now. He would never have to worry about me leaving him again. These moments with him were precious, and it was exciting to know that I could sneak in these stolen glances of him, and he would never know. He sometimes smiled in his sleep, and it made me wonder what he could be dreaming about.

I whispered, "I love you," and then I left him to sleep while I showered and got ready. I scanned my closet for something conservative to wear to court, but my choices were limited since all my things had not arrived yet. And then that's when I saw it. Bless my mom for knowing me better than I knew myself. I saw her carry a bag inside with her yesterday, but I quickly forgot about it once our party began. She must have slipped it into my closet when I wasn't looking: a navy blue fitted dress by our favorite designer, Zac Posen. I found matching ballerina flats to accompany my outfit. I kept the rest of my look simple. My hair was pulled back into a sleek knotted twist at the nape of my neck. I applied mascara and a touch of pale pink lip gloss.

Daydreaming of Simon took care of my rosy cheeks. I swear the more I thought of him, the more my cheeks blushed with crimson. I was ready, and I turned around to catch Simon staring at me.

"Good morning," he crooned. I said the same to him as he folded me into his warm embrace. "Are you okay this morning?" he questioned.

"More than okay, I'm ready."

Satisfied with my answer, he gave me a kiss and then went off to shower.

He was quiet when he joined me for breakfast. Not one word was said to me, as he drank his coffee in silence. He looked nervous and unsettled. What changed in the fifteen minutes he was gone?

I did my best to ignore the incessant tapping until he finally broke down the wall that was suddenly between us. He looked in pain, and my heart ached for him. I asked him to talk to me, and then he whispered the very name that had brought on this melancholy mood.

He said, "Michael." Of course, it was about him, and hopefully, after today, he would never be mentioned again.

"Baby, are you absolutely sure about today?" he asked, as I wrapped my arms around his neck and pressed my body to his. He needed to be reassured, and it was my pleasure to show him. I took his mouth in a passionate kiss and let him explore my mouth until I felt his erection. We didn't have time for anything else, that would come later then and for as many hours as he wanted. He pressed his forehead against mine, and then with my hundred percent certainty, I gave him my answer.

"Yes."

Thirty-Five

Michael

I finished dressing into my three-piece Prada suit that was select-ed by my father. Even with a broken hand, I cleaned up nicely. My lawyer encouraged me to write up a statement about the events that took place that night with Nicolette. If questioned by the judge, he wanted me to be prepared.

Today was for Nicolette. She missed all the pretrial hearings and requested to have a meeting with the judge overseeing her case. The original judge who was assigned to the case from day one suffered a heart attack and was replaced by a female judge, Erin Northwick, said to be ruthless and unforgiving, especially in sexual assault cas-es. I wasn't worried until my lawyer looked as if he was going to puke after learning of the change in judges. Judge Northwick took no pity on any offenders who appeared in her courtroom, especially men who hurt women, a fact that John had pointedly driven home to me.

It had been over seven months, the longest ones of my life since I laid eyes on Nicolette. She haunted my dreams each and every night, along with my mother. I couldn't seem to rid their images from my mind. I had been sitting here in this cell all these months battling the demons that plagued me each and every day. I had minimum contact with my father, and anything I needed to know was sent through his lawyer.

Any semblance of my old life was gone. My friends cut me off, especially Seth, who told me that I disgusted him. My freedom was short-lived after the Vanelles petitioned the court to have my house arrest revoked. Although my father had emphatically denied rumors of taking me out of the country, his promises fell on deaf ears. He was a wealthy man, had access to private planes, or other means of making me disappear. The judge was not willing to take that chance, and I returned to jail after a week of being home.

It didn't matter where I was, I was still a prisoner, and freedom for a guy like me was not to be found. I was hiding behind my father's wealth and his lawyers, but most of all, my guilt. It took me this long in isolation to finally come to terms with what I did to Nicolette. I calmed my nerves as best as I could, and then my father arrived shortly after.

"Michael, is your statement prepared?"

"Yes. I have written it in the way I was instructed to."

"Good, at least that's something. Michael, I want you to be fair warned that today may not end well for you. This man-hater of a judge could possibly take what Nicolette says and nail your balls to the wall. I have tried everything in my power to help you, but I have run out of options. The fact remains that you did what you are being accused of. You raped that poor girl, and every day you sit here and claim that you're innocent will be your downfall in the end. I should have made you accept the plea deal right away. Had I done that, maybe this could have been over by now."

I got up and turned away from my father. I hated to hear this again and again from him, but he was right. Today I would be judged for all that I had done.

Turning to face him, I said, "Father, that night with Nicolette, I detached myself from all logical thinking. At that moment, I hated you. You were rejecting and sending me away again, and I couldn't deal with being abandoned. What I needed was a father, and I hadn't had one since mother died and left us. I took all that anger and resentment out on Nicolette. I felt as if I had nothing to lose, so I hurt her instead."

I watched my father get up and walk toward me, slap me hard across my cheek, and then shove me against the wall. I wanted to hit him back, but I didn't. He then grabbed me by the lapels of my suit and pulled me into him. He was crying for the first time since I was fourteen years old. His arms tightened around my back, and as I tried to struggle away from him, his hold only grew stronger.

"I'm so sorry, son. I'm so sorry. Michael, every time I look at you, I see your mother. You have her eyes that were once so full of life. I know I have darkened them with my rejection for my own son. I'll never be able to apologize for making you believe that you were not loved by me. I could never hate you. I just couldn't feel anything after she died. You never left her side, and I felt robbed of the time you had with her. I was jealous and petty. I blamed a young boy for loving his mother. What kind of man does that to his own son?"

I watched my father cry into his hands and mourn the loss of his wife and son. Although I was still here with him, I hadn't been in other ways that should have mattered.

"Michael, I don't ever expect you to forgive me for the way I treated you, nor believe what I have said here to you today. If your mother could see me now, she would be ashamed and probably turn away from me forever."

"No, she wouldn't have. My mother was the kindest person I know. She loved us and believed there was good in every human being." With my final words to my father, I finally had broken through the cloudy image that was in my nightly dreams. If there was ever a time to feel my mother's presence, it was now in this room with my father.

He had finally broken down the walls that kept us apart after all of these years and took me in his arms. I needed to forgive him, and then I would ask the same of Nicolette.

John interrupted our moment and was with a court officer, who was here to take me down to face the judge. I entered the courtroom for Judge Northwick and didn't see any signs of Nicolette.

I took my seat and leaned in to question John. "Where is she? Could she have changed her mind?"

He raised his hand to me as he continued to read the papers that were handed to him when we first arrived. He then gestured over to me to look down at the paper.

"Why is she speaking privately to the judge?" I asked, but he offered no response in return. My father leaned in and gripped my shoulders.

"No matter what happens here today, I'm here, son. I am not going anywhere."

Normally, my old self would have told him to go to hell, but after our breakthrough, I wasn't going to shut him out, not when I needed him the most. Nicolette entered the courtroom and had taken a seat alongside her attorney, never once looking over to me. The court officer entered next, followed by Judge Northwick. He instructed us to all rise, as the judge took her seat.

"Good morning, ladies and gentlemen of the court. Let the record show that we are here to hear an official statement given by one Nicolette Elizabeth Vanelle. The testimony I am about to hear will serve in a future trial, the state of California versus Michael St. Clair for the charges of rape, and or sexual assault under California State Penal Code 243.4. I have had conversations with the defendant, Michael St. Clair, and was not introduced to the victim that is named in this case until this morning in my chambers."

I swear you could hear a pin drop in the room. I was beginning to sweat just being here in her presence, and then the judge looked over directly at me.

"Mr. St. Clair, I have read your account of what occurred on the night of December 12th, 2008. Today, I will hear from Ms. Vanelle and her personal account of the same night mentioned in your written statement. I also have in front of me documents pertaining to a revised plea agreement that has been presented to me by William Jennings, who represents the Los Angeles District Attorney's Office. Your lawyer has been given ample opportunity to peruse the document and discuss your decision to either accept or reject what has been offered by their office. It is my understanding that the previous deal was rejected when Judge Shire was overseeing your case. Having said that, Mr. St. Clair, I will listen to Ms. Vanelle's testimony before I sign off on any agreement that has been issued. I will make my final ruling after this morning's proceedings. Do I make myself clear on all matters that have been said here today? Or do I need to speak slower?"

"That won't be necessary your honor, we understand."

"That's wonderful, Mr. Scott, but I wasn't asking you. My question was for your client. Now, Mr. St. Clair, do you agree or disagree with what I have said here?"

I practically stuttered over my answer but managed to get out my words to her. "Yes, your honor. I do."

"Hallelujah!" she said and then directed her attention to Nicolette.

"Ms. Vanelle, when you're ready, please take your place over by the podium, and you may begin."

The moment of truth had finally arrived. She was now in the direct line of me, where I was forced to look right at her.

Nicolette

I took a few calming breaths before I made my way over to where I was to speak. I remembered the words of encouragement from Simon and my family, who were all waiting for me right outside these courtroom doors. I regretted my decision of not having them in here with me, and then I looked down to my beautiful engagement ring and felt Simon's love. This ring represented my commitment to only him and the life we planned to have. I needed to close this chapter of my story before I continued the next one with Simon.

I walked around from the table and looked over to Michael. His eyes were locked on with mine. Today was the first time since leaving the hospital that I had seen him. He looked nervous, and for good reason since my statement was the one that would decide his fate here today and for the rest of his life. I straightened my shoulders and began to read my statement.

"I would like to thank Judge Northwick and the officers of this court for allowing me the opportunity to speak here today. At the time of the original hearing, I was abroad recovering from injuries I had sustained from my attack, and then I required additional time to heal from an unexpected surgery I needed to have. Unbeknownst to me, I was very sick and nearly lost my life due to the very reason that has brought us all here today."

"I was raped, and this is my story…"

I looked over to Michael, who had visibly shifted in his seat. You could see his lawyer trying to still him. He knew what I was about to say was the total truth, and I was ready to tell it.

"I moved here from Chicago in May of 2008, along with my parents. At a summer party in July of that same year, I was introduced to the young man who sits here before you today, Michael St. Clair, the son of Clayton St. Clair, who was in a professional relationship with my parents. I never intended to have anything more than friendship with Michael, but for him, this was not the case. For months, he continued to harass me with an excessive amount of phone calls, text messages, and package deliveries to my home and later to my high school. I tried to be civil, but civility was not to be found with him. October 2008, I was physically assaulted in my home by the defendant, Michael St. Clair. I suffered a sprained wrist, but nothing could compare to what I felt in my heart."

"I didn't tell my parents until the next day. I was scared, and I didn't want what Michael was doing to me to come between their working relationship with his father. My parents confronted Clayton St. Clair and were given his word that his son would not bother me again. Unfortunately, Michael did not respect that promise and continued to stalk me."

"I truly believed I was doing the right thing by remaining quiet and not giving him the attention he craved. I figured he would stop and just give up. My last interaction with Michael St. Clair before he raped me was the night of my birthday party in November, a private party that he was not invited to, but was there allegedly with friends. He cornered me again and physically grabbed me and then forcibly kissed me. He promised he would be seeing me again, and he said I had to stop fighting what he believed we had between us. Again, I remained silent."

"The only thing that I am sorry for is this: I didn't trust my parents or my friends to help me. I remained quiet and was in constant fear of hurting my parents and jeopardizing all they had worked for. Time went on, and the holidays were near. I hadn't heard from him in weeks, and all communication had ceased. I breathed a sigh of relief that it was finally over, and I could go back to living my life, one that did not include Michael St. Clair."

"I was foolish in my thinking to believe that was true. My guard had been let down, and the next time I would face Michael would be the night he grabbed me and dragged my body along the cement walkway that led to the entrance of the marina, where his boat was housed. He held his hand over my mouth and prevented me from calling out for help. Once I was on board his boat and below in the cabin, I was thrown down to the floor. I had hit my head and hardly had time to regain my balance before he struck me again. This time it was the wall that my body had been thrown into, and I hit my head again. I was lying on the floor, and then Michael was there, holding me down."

"Through the pain, I tried to reason with Michael. Even with everything I had learned from taking self-defense classes, I was no match for him. He was angry, so very angry, and refused to hear me."

I took a minute to compose myself, drink some water, and then I looked over to Michael.

"What happened next was unimaginable. I was praying this was a nightmare that I would awaken from, but it was very real, and it was happening to me."

"You!" I pointed over to Michael. "You. Raped. Me." I could no longer hold back my tears, but I never took my eyes off him. He needed to see me.

"When your hand wasn't covering my mouth, I begged you to stop hurting me. I screamed over and over again the word 'No.' You took no mercy and inflicted an unmeasurable amount of pain on me. I was a virgin, and you took that away from me. A gift that belonged only to me, and it would be my choice to give that gift to a man that I loved, who was deserving of my heart. No, that man was not you. My heart never belonged to you. When you took my body in such a forceful manner, you literally tore my insides apart, and I needed surgery to repair the damage you left in your wake. My next surgery was the one that I mentioned earlier which I needed in order to save my life. It was to remove the remaining effects from the miscarriage that I had suffered. Yes, Michael, you impregnated me the night you raped me."

I placed my head down into my hands and then turned away for a moment. The judge asked me if I wanted to take a break, but I refused, just needing a minute to catch my breath.

"I nearly bled out from a tear in my placenta, and that caused a massive infection. I nearly died that night, all the while you claimed you were innocent. I said 'No.' I said that word to you for over five months and screamed it at the top of my lungs the night you raped me. You left a permanent mark on me that night, and still, I said 'No.'"

"The life I had known was changed forever. Your act of violence shattered all that was good inside of me. I suffered unimaginable pain, and then there was the guilt. I believed that I had done something wrong, but in actuality, you were the one that wronged me. I had to leave everything and everyone I loved and who loved me back. I was no longer the person I used to be. I ran far away to the other side of the world, and at the time, I never believed if I would return."

"I had to undergo intense therapy to heal myself physically and mentally. The moment I was finally strong enough to look in the mirror, the dark world that I had imprisoned myself in was shattered and broken through with light. I had a new sense of purpose to reclaim what you had taken from me. I returned to my family and my friends. I took back my life and promised myself to never give you any more control than I already had. As each day passes, I feel stronger, confident, and most of all loved. With each day, a little bit gets put back together, and it's one more piece that is mine again and not the one that you took."

"I thought I hated you. I gave it a great deal of thought while I was separated from my family. But to hate you would take too much of my energy and waste my strength, especially on someone like you. You had already taken up way too much space in my head, and I was done allowing you to do that."

"Before I conclude my statement, I would like to ask you a question. If you had the chance to go back and change what you did to me, would you? Because I would."

"I would have never allowed my fear of you to remain silent. If you ever want a real chance at redemption, you will admit what you did to me. You will stand like a man and accept responsibility for it. I no longer remain silent. I pray that you will find your redemption and do the right thing. Only you, Michael, can decide that."

As I released the breath that I was holding, I saw that Michael had tears streaming down his cheeks. For the very first time, he looked remorseful and sad. I returned my attention back to Judge Northwick.

"Thank you, your honor, for allowing me to speak here today."

Judge Northwick addressed our lawyers, as Michael's lawyer asked for a fifteen-minute recess. I didn't look back and hurried as fast as I could through the exit doors. They flew open with a force, as my eyes found Simon's worried ones. He began walking toward me, while I ran to him. Once I was there, he crushed his body against mine. I finally let go of all the emotion that I was holding back the entire time I was in there with Michael.

Michael

My body stilled as I listened to Nicolette give a detailed account of the night I hurt her. Yes, I did that, and the realization I would never be able to take that back pained me deeply to the point that I was sick to my stomach.

I sat there hanging on to every word she spoke, and so eloquently at that. She never faltered with her words, only taking a breath or two before continuing. She was incredibly strong and brave, and I was nothing more than a shameful coward. A coward who took what I wanted and didn't give a shit about how my actions hurt others, especially Nicolette. What kind of monster was I? She was pregnant with my child and lost it too.

The walls began to close in around me, and I began to sweat and feel dizzy. As I sat here this morning in silence, all the emotions I felt rushed through me, and I emptied all the contents that were in my stomach. I was on my knees in a $3000.00 suit, hugging a wastebasket that reeked from my vomit. After I had nothing left to expel, John handed me a handkerchief to wipe my mouth.

"If you are quite finished," John said, "a decision needs to be made right now, or the deal will be removed from the table and we move forward with a trial. Michael, this all could be over today, if that's what you want."

"John, how the hell am I supposed to know what I want? I thought I knew, and then one fateful mistake ruined not just one life, but two. You were right, and so was my father. I deserve to be punished for what I did to Nicolette. She wasn't lying. I did all those things to her, and so much more. If you want to know the truth, she was kind in her statement. I preyed upon a young girl and hurt her in ways that can never be undone. I have denied my crimes all these months because I am what she has probably always believed: I am selfish. I am arrogant. Her words made me realize what I never wanted to believe about myself."

I turned around to face my silent father. "I am so sorry for ever laying these two hands on you. I know I have hurt you deeply over the years, but to hurt you physically is something I never thought I was capable of."

"Michael, if you could forgive me for all the years I shut you out, then I could easily forgive you for a bump on the head. I am so sorry." My father hugged me and then held me by my shoulders. "I promise you that we will have time to right all the wrongs in our relationship, but that will have to wait until we figure out what path to take here today. You need to clear your head and listen to John. He needs to go over with what has been proposed."

"I understand. John?" I turned around to my lawyer. "What does it say?"

"It's a five-year mandatory sentence to the California State Prison, Los Angeles County. You would be required to pay a fine up to $10,000.00 or more depending on how the judge rules." *A small price to pay for what I did to Nicolette.* "Not right away, but you could go on to receive rehabilitation while incarcerated. You can finish your education, earn a degree."

"How low have I fallen? From Stanford to prison. Yes, that will look really good on a job application."

"Michael, it is what it is, and it will not get any better than this deal. As you continually remind me, your father pays me well to do my job. This is me advising you to take this deal, or you risk a bigger sentence if found guilty from a jury of your peers."

"John, I need to speak with Nicolette," I said.

"You can't be serious. Michael, that would be the last thing I would ever advise you to do."

"John, make it happen. Before I accept this deal, I need to talk with her. Please, I'm begging you."

He looked over to my father and then back to me, stunned at my request, but he told me he would see what he could do. He spoke with a court officer and then exited the courtroom, leaving me with my father.

I let out a deep breath and waited.

Nicolette

"**M**y brave girl, you did it," Simon said as he continued to hold me, not allowing anyone close to me. He wanted to make sure I was okay. He touched my face and wiped away my tears, and then his eyes roamed all over my body until his eyes met mine once more.

"God, I love you," he said and then crushed his mouth down to mine, as his tongue begged for entrance. When I opened up for him, he kissed me so beautifully and tenderly. My hands found his, and I slowly pulled away just enough for Simon to see me.

"Baby, I'm okay. I'm here, and with you. You're kissing me as if I'm going to disappear at any moment, but I can assure you that I won't."

"I'm sorry, Nicolette. I've just been out of my mind since you walked through those doors without me to protect you."

"I promise you that I'm okay. I could use some coffee. Would you mind?"

"Not at all. Let's go back to your family, and then I'll get it for you."

I hugged my family, and then we all took a seat on the benches that were adjacent to Judge Northwick's courtroom. Simon was back and handed me a cup. I took a few sips of the hot liquid and the chill that I felt while I was in there slowly dissipated, and I was warm again. We were talking in light conversation for the next fifteen minutes or so, and then a bailiff approached me.

"Ms. Vanelle, your presence is required in Judge Northwick's chambers. She would like to speak with you before she makes her ruling."

I turned back to Simon, who was apprehensive and tense again. I assured him, "I'll be back. Don't worry, okay?"

"Yeah, and maybe I won't breathe either." He smirked.

"I love you too," I said and then followed the court officer through the doors and back to the judge's chambers. My attorney, along with Mr. Jennings, joined me.

"Mr. Jennings, what's going on?" I questioned.

"Nicolette, a most unusual request has been made."

"What is it?"

"Mr. St. Clair would like to speak with you. We will be with you the entire time, and you can say no, and then we will continue on with the hearing."

"I'm okay, Mr. Jennings. We've come this far, and whatever he says will not derail me from seeing this through."

"Good. You are the bravest person I have ever known."

My hand was on the doorknob, and with one last exhaled breath, I made my way into her chambers. Judge Northwick rose and asked me to have a seat.

"Ms. Vanelle, you are a remarkable and incredibly brave, young woman. I have never met a more mature and poised individual with such grace, especially at your young age. You have been through hell, and yet you have the courage to speak here today, and you got through it from beginning to end. It's almost over, I promise. It is entirely up to you if you wish to speak with Mr. St. Clair. You can refuse his request. Let me be clear and upfront with you: he has agreed to the deal and will be sentenced today. Once you walk out of my courtroom, you will never have to worry about him again."

"Thank you, your honor. I will speak with him."

"Fair enough." She gestured over to her court officer, and he opened the door so Michael could enter.

I was well-protected between Mr. Jennings and my lawyer. Judge Northwick remained behind her desk, with Michael seated beside his lawyer, but in front of me. He swallowed hard and loosened his tie before speaking.

"Nicolette, I don't ever expect you to forgive me for the crimes I committed against you. I only hope you forgive yourself. You did nothing wrong, and I take sole responsibility for my actions. You were right. I did everything you said I did, and so much more. My delusions were greater than the reality, and I now see how wrong I was to ever believe that you would return my affections. I don't deserve the kindness you showed here today when I never did that for you. I am so very sorry for the pain I caused you, especially to your body. You don't owe me any explanations, and I don't have the right to ask anything of you, but knowing that will not keep me from asking my question."

"Go on, ask me."

"If our child had survived, would you have told me about him or her?"

"I honestly don't know. If you are wanting more, I don't have the answer for you."

"Thank you, it's more than I deserve."

"You're right, you don't deserve anything from me. Just sitting across from me is a gift, one that I willingly gave to you, unlike on the night you raped me. I survived you, Michael. I had to travel through the gates of hell and come out from the other side to survive. I had to fight my demons and regain who I was before ever laying eyes on you. I will not be the one that grants you absolution. You will have to find that all on your own, as I have to find mine. After this moment, I will never think of you again. Your honor, if there is nothing else, may I be excused?"

"You may. I'm going to call for a fifteen-minute recess, and then we will reconvene to conclude today's hearing."

I never turned back to look at Michael, and I left her chambers to find my family and Simon waiting for me right outside the doors. Simon hurried over to me and took me once again in his arms. I told him what happened, and I assured him that I was okay. I asked him to join me inside, along with my family. They didn't hesitate and followed me through the doors to the courtroom.

Simon held my hand on his lap and kept his eyes trained on the judge, not Michael. I knew he hated that I talked with him, but he kept his feelings to himself. We were so close to this being over.

The room was brought to order with Judge Northwick taking her seat. She looked over to where Michael was seated with his lawyer and his father behind them. I glanced over to Uncle Jack, who shot a dagger over to Michael with his eyes. I knew that my uncle had seen him, but never really knew what he said to him. I knew what he wanted to do but then held back for my sake. It was clear that Michael recognized him and was unnerved by his close presence.

"Michael St. Clair, you have agreed to the plea agreement that the District Attorney's office has presented to you. I have heard testimony from both sides, and I am prepared to hand down my ruling. I hereby remand you to the California State Prison, Los Angeles County. You will serve the full five years sentence without an option for parole. This time will not include time already served here in the county jail. You are required to pay restitution to your victim for the amount of $10,000.00 dollars. Forgive me, I was mistaken with my choice of words. The brave, young woman who stood before this court today, and spoke from her heart is no victim. She is a survivor."

She then looked over to me and said, "Ms. Vanelle, I wish you only the best. You are truly an inspiring young woman." Simon leaned in to kiss my cheek and wiped away more of my tears.

"Mr. St. Clair, you are one lucky man to be given this incredible opportunity to redeem yourself. I only hope you will take from what happened here today as no less than a gift from Ms. Vanelle and from me. If I ever see you in my courtroom again, I will not be so tolerant the next time we meet. This concludes today's hearing."

With the slamming of her gavel, I watched Michael be hand-cuffed and taken into custody to begin his sentence. He kept his head down and never looked back at me again.

I did it, the thought crossed my mind as I watched him leave the courtroom. I was calm, and any anxiety that I felt this morning was just gone. I felt as if I could breathe again, and it was an incredible feeling not to be afraid. He finally admitted what he had done to me. He faced his fears today, as I faced my own.

I fell right into my mom, dad, and Uncle Jack's arms, my heroes who never stopped fighting for me. We were all crying happy tears and had so much to look forward to. My father smiled over at me, and I knew what he was thinking: Disneyland!

The nightmare that changed my life was finally over. I'm sure that Simon would never forget what Michael had put us through and almost broke us in the process. I had to leave Simon to find myself and make me whole again. He stayed behind and lived through the memories each and every day. We made it, and we did it together.

Today was our new beginning, and I had a brand-new life that waited for me outside of this courtroom. It begins and ends with Simon Paulson.

PART FOUR

It's a beautiful life...

Nicolette

Three Happy Years Later…

As I sat in my office, I tried with great effort to calm my nerves. I couldn't believe that everything I dreamed and worked so hard for was finally here. Today, we opened the doors to the C.A.L.I. Women's Help Center.

After Michael was sentenced, his father asked if he could settle with our family privately. I never wanted any part of the lawsuit to begin with, but then after speaking to Simon and my family about it, I knew what I wanted to do with the money. I would help other women in need, and that's how C.A.L.I began.

He had given what my parents had asked for, but there was a catch to the settlement. Owing Clayton St. Clair was the last thing I wished to do, but all he wanted, in the end, was for me to sign a non-disclosure agreement. He didn't want any more publicity, nor did I for that matter. As soon as I agreed, our lawyers met, and the next day I received confirmation that twenty-five million dollars had been wired into a trust made out to me. The money would never replace what his son had done, but I knew I could use it for the greater good, and I couldn't wait to begin.

After the hearing, I said goodbye to my family, and for the next week, Simon locked us away at our beach home to plan our future. He had waited long enough, he said and handed me a notebook to begin making plans. He called it our "wish list" and began adding all of his ideas to the book. He didn't want to wait to get married, but I told him that although I didn't want a big wedding, I still needed time to plan. I was my parents' only daughter and wanted my mom to help me plan our special day.

After one too many conversations about picking a date, we agreed on February 13th, 2010. We married on our own private stretch of beach. We kept it small and only invited our close friends and family. Our wedding couldn't have been more perfect. Alexis and Bailey stood up for me as my bridesmaids. Simon chose both Sam and Jameson to stand beside him as his best men. We laughed when Jameson refused to be an usher. Sam conceded and shared the best man role with him.

Our friends were amazing people, and our wedding was perfect, being around so many people who loved us so much. Simon's real brothers, Jacob, Andrew, and Cameron, also stood up for Simon. I had Aunt Sara be my matron of honor.

We planned our wedding in reverse. College would begin in September, and we knew that once school began, we would be busy. So, it was Simon's idea to take a three-week vacation to Australia, a pre-honeymoon he liked to say. He always wanted to surf Australia's Gold Coast, and he did every day we were there. We snorkeled the spectacular waters with the color-bursting coral reefs. I was scared about the sharks since Great Whites were popular in those waters, but I was safe with Simon. When I wasn't in the water with him, I was playing photographer. He was fearless on a surf board. I must have taken thousands of shots, some of Simon doing tricks on the board, and others with him appearing as if he was surfing through a wave tunnel. Those waves reached over twenty feet in height, and I held my breath every time until he swam to shore. Our honeymoon before the wedding was magical every day we were there. I would never forget it for the rest of my life.

Simon promised me the wedding of my dreams, and it was. The stylist checked my hair and makeup one last time before my big reveal. I kept my breathing as calm as a bride-to-be could on her wedding day. The stylist slowly turned me around, and I couldn't believe how beautiful I looked. My long layers had been shaped into big bouncy curls that cascaded down my shoulders, a special request from Simon to keep my hair down. My makeup was not too heavy, but my eyes looked amazing with the smoky eye shadow that was applied.

I was about to become Mrs. Simon Paulson, and it took everything inside of me not to cry the happy tears I was feeling. He sent me flowers with a card that contained his beautiful words.

My beautiful Nicolette,

You are my angel, and today you will become my wife. I can't wait until I see you walking toward me. I will take your hands and entwine them with mine as we recite our vows to one another. I love you, baby. Always and forever.

—Simon

"Nicolette, it's time," said Uncle Jack, as he entered my dressing room. "Nickel, you have never looked more beautiful."

"Thank you, Uncle Jack. I feel beautiful."

"Well, your father is waiting for you. Let's get you married."

I hooked my arm inside of Uncle Jack's, and we made our way to where my father was waiting for us. To honor both men who had raised me to be the woman I am today, it was only fitting to have them both walk me down the aisle to my future husband.

"Am I really looking at my daughter, who is about to become a married woman?" my dad said as he placed a kiss on my hand.

"That would be me, and you both look very handsome."

"We do, don't we?" I smiled at my uncle's comment, and then it was time.

I had chosen an ankle length form-fitting dress with an open back. Daddy nearly had a stroke when he first saw me in it, but mom talked him down. All the men were wearing white slacks with white linen shirts and blue ties that matched the ocean. My straps were sequined in ocean blue to complement Simon. My gift from my besties was a pair of Louboutin jeweled encrusted sandals.

We opted not to go with the standard wedding march and chose a song that seemed meant for us. "On This Day" by David Pomeranz. The lyrics were beautiful, describing two lovers on their wedding day. My two dads walked me gracefully to Simon, as he reached for my hand, but not before wiping away one of his tears.

"Nicolette, I love you. You are stunning," he whispered and then placed a kiss along my neck before coming to attention in front of the minister.

We recited our written promises to one another, then rings were exchanged, and we were bound together by the very words we said to each other.

Simon could hardly hold back once we were pronounced husband and wife. He leaned into me and cupped my face as he delivered the kiss that put all kisses to shame. He lifted me up into his arms and kissed me again and again.

"We're married. I love you, Nicolette Elizabeth Paulson."

We made our way down the flower-lined path and were greeted by our family and friends in endless hugs, until Jameson shouted, "Let's get this party started!" and we all laughed and did exactly that. We were toasted with rounds of champagne, speeches from our parents and friends, and as the night came to a close, Simon had one last surprise for me. I was bouncing in my chair, I was so excited.

"On behalf of my lovely bride and myself, we thank you for sharing our wedding day with us. You are all so special, and we love you very much. Our lives are blessed because we get to share our life with you. Now, you all got a chance to dance with my girl, and I was a pretty good sport about it, but there is nothing more special than the official dance to our song. I never had to think about what I would choose for Nicolette, because this song has been with us from our beginning, and now I'm going to dance to it and hold my beautiful wife. Please welcome our friend, John Mayer."

Our guests clapped their hands, and a roaring sound of applause welcomed John. He took his place on stage, but not before stopping to give me his congratulations and, of course, a jab that only I could appreciate.

"Hey, Nickel, still want to go back to Chicago? Or has California grown on you?"

"I think it's safe to say that I am an official Cali girl. Thank you for my surprise."

"You're welcome, but all thanks go to your husband. He was quite persistent with my manager." He winked and then began to string his guitar and sing, "Your Body is a Wonderland," our beautiful song.

Every little girl dreamed of her perfect wedding day. My dream came true today when I married Simon. Simon's love brought me back to life at a time when I believed the light would never break through my darkest days. Simon Paulson was my missing puzzle piece, and now that we were married, I was complete. My days were blessed just loving him and our life together. To love him was easy.

I would always remember the boy who climbed down the wall to say hello. When we met on the beach that day, I had no idea that he would become the keeper of my heart.

A knock on my office door brought me back from my wonderful daydreaming.

"Hey, what are you thinking about, sitting in here all by yourself?" Simon asked as he leaned down to kiss me.

"Hello, husband," I said as I kissed him back. "I was just remembering our beach wedding and how beautiful it was."

"Every day with you is beautiful, and I'm not sure if I will ever be able to put into words just how much I love you. You are my life, and I thank God every day that I get to share my life with you."

How does he do it? He makes me feel so cherished. "Simon, can I ask you a question?"

He smiled at me and always answered with the same response. "Anything."

"How did we get here?"

He simply replied, "Together. And I would never want anything more than this moment with you. If you're ready, it's time to open the doors, but before we do, I just want to say how incredibly proud I am of you. Nicolette, this is your defining moment. I always believed you were larger than life, and now all your hard work is going to help so many others that need it. Are you ready?"

"Yes, I'm ready."

He took my hand, and we made our way out to the excited crowd. In attendance were both our families, along with our friends who had made the trip for our grand opening. After I was introduced, I made my way up to the podium and received a standing ovation. Simon was right by my side, and sensing my nerves, he leaned in to place a kiss on the special spot on my neck, and I instantly calmed.

He winked at me and then said, "You can do this. I love you."

"Thank you all for coming out here today to join me and the amazing staff standing behind me to officially open C.A.L.I., a center for women. This has been an indescribable journey that I have been on, and I still pinch myself just to make sure that it is all real. Over the years, I have traveled around the country and shared my story, and now I will share it with you. The life I had known at the age of eighteen had changed forever. I was raped. I never believed I would ever get back who I was before my attack. I had to travel very far to find myself again, and with the help of Dr. Inga Jonas, I found my way."

"She had been my doctor from the very first moment I was admitted to her hospital. She never left my side and gave me the help that I needed to move forward from what happened to me. I wasn't kidding when I said I had to go far away, so far that I ended up at a private clinic in Switzerland. All I wanted to do was run and hide. I felt ashamed and guilt ridden. I was suffering so deep on the inside that I didn't want to hurt the ones who loved me on the outside."

I looked over to Simon, who blew me a kiss. My husband saved me in more ways than I could ever express into words. I mouthed to him, "I love you."

"While I was away, I met incredible women along my journey. They shared their stories with me so openly, and willingly gave me their trust. I felt connected to them in a sort of way. We shared a common bond, and with a renewed purpose to heal and move forward with our lives, friendships were made for life."

I looked out into the crowd and saw Ariel. She was standing beside her husband and her young daughter who looked just like her. Ariel, like me, was raped but survived her attack, only to be threatened again, which resulted in killing her rapist. I smiled at her and was so honored that she made the long trip to be here today.

"Every day that I was there, I wanted to give up, but the courageous women in my group, along with my therapist, threatened to kick my ass every time I refused to talk it out. They convinced me that I no longer had to be afraid and showed me how to take back what he took from me. I'm just not talking about being raped, it goes so much deeper than that. The day I walked away from my family, friends, and the love of my life was my rock bottom. I completely detached myself from them and left with not one ounce of remorse to how they were feeling, even after they begged me to stay. I wasn't strong enough, and I didn't feel safe."

"When I didn't believe I could fall any deeper down into my despair, my therapist dragged me to the group session, and I met Ariel."

I looked over to my friend, and she held her little girl's hand up to wave back at me.

"I listened to her painful story, and that session changed my life. It was as if I received the awakening I was praying for. The next day I made the decision to return to my family. What Ariel and those women did for me will be a debt that I can never repay. I was one of the lucky ones to have received so much support and love throughout my entire ordeal. To simply say 'Thank you' will never be enough. I have been asked many times what C.A.L.I. stands for. Today, I can share it with you. It actually means two things."

"The word 'CALI' comes from California, which was where I met and fell in love with my husband, Simon Paulson. We've built a life here, and it's a good one that has been tested over and over again, and with each challenge that we have faced, we're still here. In love and together. I survived what happened to me, and I truly believe in my heart that this center will assist so many that are in need of the same help I needed four years ago. So, C.A.L.I. means this: Courage, Acceptance, Love, and Inspiration. These four points got me through the most difficult times in my life, and it has become my daily mantra. As we open our doors today, I hope it will give anyone in need of help the strength to move forward and carry on with their life. We are in this together, and I look forward to continuing my journey with all of you. With God's blessing, thank you."

Before I could wipe away one fallen tear, Simon was there to lift me in his arms. "I am so proud of you. Baby, I love you."

"I love you more. Let's cut that ribbon." With a roaring sound of applause from my family and all our invited guests, I took my golden scissors and cut the ribbon to officially open the center that I would make my life's work to give back.

They say everything happens for a reason, and I may never understand why Michael hurt me the way he did. All I know is that I survived, and I survived him. I would walk out of here today with another chapter to my story that will be complete.

As this momentous day came to a close, I remembered my earlier question to Simon. His answer was always the same. He made me believe that if I trusted and believed in our love, we could conquer anything. He never broke his commitment to me, even when we were apart, and he didn't know if I would come home. Simon was my lifeline, and I was strong because of the love he had for me.

"Ready to go home?" he asked as he pulled me in for a hug.

"Yes, let's go home," I said and kissed him earnestly with all that I had.

With our hands linked together, we made our way home to our beach paradise. It had been an amazing journey falling in love with Simon Paulson, the boy from the beach. He was right. We got here together like we did with everything in our life.

I woke up every day and got to share it all with my forever love. I couldn't wait to see what would come next...

The End

Did you love Simon & Nicolette?
Are you curious to know what happens next?
Read on for a chapter excerpt from *An Unfinished Life*.
In that book, you will learn more about Uncle Jack
and reunite with Simon & Nicolette…after their happily ever after.

Jack

The man behind the mask...

If you had the power to turn back the clock, would you? Hit the rewind button on your life and just start over? A man can dream, can't he? Yeah, I would definitely do it if I could. I would pick certain parts...the harder ones I wished I could erase from my mind and never think of again.

As I descended the stairs to the main bar area on the first floor, I saw most of Chicago watching our Bears destroy the Cardinals and sending them back to Arizona in tears. You could feel the energy in the bar as the game went on to a winning victory.

I loved this bar. I loved that Sara, my wife, the love of my life, convinced me to open it and give back to the neighborhood that always had my back. This was why our bar was called The Neighborhood Bar and Grille. It was a place to have a laugh with a friend, to blow off steam after a hard day's work, and it was a place that kept me honest, whereas, in my younger days, I wasn't always. I hated to admit that I did some things that I wasn't proud of, things that no matter how hard I tried to forget, would always be present in my memory.

"Jack, you need to do me a favor, and I don't mean picking up a few packages for me. This is something of a different nature and one that requires a different approach. Do you think you can help me out here?"

Johnny leaned back in his chair and blew out puffs of smoke from his Cuban cigar. I didn't hesitate at all with the request. Johnny paid me well, and I was in his debt. I agreed immediately without knowing what he wanted me to do.

He continued, "That's what I wanted to hear, my friend. You are exactly what I need for this job. Go see Carmine. He will give you the details, and once the job is done, you come back here. Understand?"

He took another deep inhale on his cigar, and he waited for my answer.

"Yes, sir. I won't let you down."

"That's good, Jack. I was hoping you would say that. I'm counting on the right message being sent so our other associates understand what it means to fall in line and never fuck with my business. You make sure they know that crossing Johnny Carlucci is a grave error in judgment, one they will regret."

After Carmine gave me my instructions, I left to find Mikey. He was holed up in some shitty motel on the east side. As Carmine kicked down the door, Mikey made a run for it. He didn't know I would be waiting for him on the fire escape. He was trapped with nowhere to run. I shoved him back through the window as Carmine pulled him up from his shoulders. He was scared, just a kid who didn't know any better, but he should have, working for Johnny Carlucci.

Carmine punched him in the gut, making him fall down to his knees. He was crying and begging for his life. I wasn't there to end his life, just to send a message. Johnny told me to make it hurt, a pain he soon would not forget. Carmine taped his mouth, and with my height and weight compared to his small skinny frame, I must have looked like a giant to him. He tried to struggle and fight me back, but I was too strong to be knocked down.

I picked him up with all my strength and smashed his back against my raised up knee. He shrieked in pain, and I dropped him to the floor. I instantly knew what the force of my attack had accomplished. I felt sick. I needed to get out of there.

Carmine pulled the tape from his mouth and whispered into his ear, "You get to live, Mikey. If you're stupid enough to cross the line again, I'll come for you and finish what my boy Jackie started."

His voice was cold, scary as fuck, and downright vicious. We just left him there crying in this rat-infested motel room. We made it outside, and I bent over and vomited all over the sidewalk. Carmine wasn't fazed by this at all. He hit me on my back and assured me that I would get used to this real quick.

"It's the life, Jackie."

I returned that night to Johnny's office, and he was pleased with me. He handed me an envelope and took me in his arms like a father. I felt sick and disloyal to my own father.

"You did good, Jack. Really good."

I didn't say anything in return and walked out of his office feeling sicker than I ever had before.

Once upon a time, I didn't think I had a choice, so I took a different road and made my peace with it. I convinced myself that my actions were justified for the betterment of my family. If mama and papa were taken care of, then that meant they didn't have to work the usual fourteen hour-plus work days that sadly was their life. The only day they didn't work was Sunday. They spent half of it in church, and then mama would spend the rest of the day cooking over a hot stove so we could have one dinner together that week. We would bow our heads while holding hands and reciting the Lord's Prayer.

This was important to my parents, so although I was the one at our table committing sin after sin, I silently prayed that I would be forgiven for them. Again, if what I did benefitted my family, then I could live with that.

I'll never forget when the truck pulled up in front of the brownstone we lived in, and out came a second-hand piano. Papa nearly knocked my head in for that one. He didn't believe the story I told him that it was tossed on the side of the road and free to anyone who wanted it. I just happened to know some guys that could get it to me. This was one lie that I didn't feel bad about telling. My kid brother, Massimo, was a musical prodigy and needed this piano to show the world his gift. The look on his face was priceless, one I would never forget.

Although they didn't like it, my parents allowed my brother to keep the piano. Of course, the first song he played was "Ava Maria." My parents wouldn't say it, but they loved hearing music resonating through our small home. It made them smile, convincing me once again that what I did was justified.

My parents tried with all of their heart and soul to live the American dream. They worked from the sun up to the sun down and never complained about it. I was the one that had a problem with it and did what I had to do to make things better.

This was how I lived every day of my life. I worked the streets—some say I owned them—but whatever. I did what I had to do to survive and make things better for my family, no matter how much my soul suffered for it. If someone needed my help, I would give everything I could and hope it was enough. I would still fight the good fight and give you the shirt off my back, but I'd like to think that I'm a better man today, someone, that papa could be proud of.

No one's life was perfect—hell I knew that better than any-one—but the life I was now living came pretty close to perfection. It was clean with no ugliness in it. I was blessed with two gifts: one being my beautiful Sara, my miracle, and the other was my girl, Ni-colette.

Nicolette was my entire world, my sole reason for waking up every day. She made me smile, and Sara made me want to be a better man who was deserving of her love. With all the sins of my past, I probably didn't deserve either one of them, but I have blessed anyway with their goodness and love.

The dream of becoming a father ended on the day my wife was diagnosed with cancer. I nearly lost her and begged God I would try to be a better man if he would spare her life. Sara beat her cancer and thankfully was still in remission and doing well. From then on, I would not live by past sins that used to define me. I would simply move forward with Sara and live happily and thankful for what I'd been given…another chance to make it right.

I maintained to keep that promise, and when my only brother was struggling, I found a way to give back. Our family meant everything to me. All he and I had was each other after our parents passed away almost back to back. I gave him and his wife…a life. They were childless and were not able to conceive on their own. It was probably the only unselfish act I ever did in my life. I never claimed her as my own, because she was never meant to be mine. It was an act so pure and beautiful, knowing I was part of a living miracle that blessed our family, erasing the ugly parts that I longed to forget.

I never felt I was deserving of anything good, but Sara proved me wrong by just loving me unconditionally. When Nicolette was born she would forever be my niece. You would have to be blind not to notice the strong physical resemblance we shared. But again, I shared the same likeness with my brother, so no one ever questioned it. I nicknamed her Nickel because the day she came into the world, I said she was shiny and new like a brand new coin. It always stuck, and she loved the term of endearment, as our beautiful girl grew into her own.

Nicolette and I were very close, almost inseparable at times. There wasn't a single moment or milestone in her life that we didn't share. My brother never reneged on our agreement. I would always play a role in her life as long as we understood our roles. Biologically, I was her father, but only one man would claim her as his, and that was my brother, Massimo.

Our given names were Vanelli, but our parents changed it to Vanelle. They thought it would be easier on us if we lost the vowel sound at the end and this way we sounded more American. I resented them for that, and for the first time in my life, I was disappointed in my own parents. They took that choice away from me, but even though I promised to accept our new name, I always used Vanelli. Another lie they didn't need to know about.

After they died, my brother changed his name to Mason. You couldn't get more preppy than that, but he was building a life for himself, and it was separate from the life we knew. I never liked it and most of the time called him the name our parents had given him. He would get angry with me and accuse me of being stubborn and unwilling to change my ways. Oh, if he only knew how much I changed to be the man he knew me to be today.

I was at peace with the decision we made about Nicolette's parentage. I also knew that if Nicolette ever questioned it, then we would all explain how she became our entire world. So, you can imagine how I felt on the day my brother announced a relocation from our home in Chicago to California, taking our girl with him. I, of course, fought him on every talking point he made. I already felt disconnected from them, and they hadn't even left. Mason explained that they were given an opportunity of a lifetime, one he and his wife could not refuse. I knew deep down how talented they both were, and I was proud of his accomplishments, but that didn't give me peace at night knowing our life as a family was about to change.

No matter what assurance Mason had promised me, my heart was breaking with the thought of not seeing Nicolette daily and listening for hours to all the great things that she was experiencing as a teenager.

I waged a war against my brother and his wife. I said no. I wouldn't allow them to take her away from me. Then, in what was probably the most vicious argument I had ever had with him, my brother painfully reminded me who she belonged to. Nicolette was their daughter, and I was just Uncle Jack. She was theirs, this was what we agreed, but tell that to my heart that always believed she was mine. My gift from God. My miracle. My redemption.

Mason and Christina promised me that I would always have her in my life. I tried to believe his words, but I was still angry deep inside. I promised Sara that I would not react and take it out on my brother.

Once his family was secure in the car, he patted my back and tried to once again reassure me while trying to mask his doubts on what I already believed to be true. Our lives would change, but Mason being Mason, he said, "The only thing that will change is our address, and everything else will be the same."

I watched her tears fall as Nicolette waved goodbye from the backseat of their car as they headed to the airport to begin their new life, a life I was so sure I wouldn't be a part of. I knew this was madness on my part, but it was my heart that was hurting and I needed my brain to catch up.

My brother was wrong. The picturesque life I was living with Sara, owning my bar, and being a staple in Nicolette's life changed the day she left. Then it was shattered and forever changed with one phone call...and three words:

NICOLETTE WAS RAPED.

It was as if time had just stopped. I was back there again, pulled deeply into a dark and ugly world, a world that was ruthless, cold, and unforgiving. I was all those things once upon a time, and for a little while, I actually believed that I wasn't anymore. One phone call destroyed that belief.

I wanted vengeance against the animal that hurt my girl. I couldn't believe I was back there again. Did I really ever leave? My blood had run cold. I felt no warmth on my skin. I saw red...blood red and I thirsted to destroy the monster who hurt her. I had to be the one to do it. She was my daughter! Fuck! It was my job to protect her, and I had failed her.

God, forgive me for what I wanted to do. I'd hurt and killed that bastard in my mind so many times. How was he still breathing? He shouldn't be, and if I had my way back then, his corpse would be a pile of dust by now.

The day after the Bears versus Cardinals game, I had errands to run outside. Winters in Chicago were brutal. The temps never reached above thirty-two degrees. I should know, I'd lived here all of my life. I loved walking through Little Italy on a Sunday morning. You could smell the fresh baked bread and pastries for several blocks. I always picked up my papers, cannoli were my weakness, and then I would have an espresso with Gino and the rest of the guys from the barbershop before I made my way home to Sara.

I didn't deserve my beautiful wife, but she loved me anyway despite what I'd put her through these last years. A dark period in our lives that I wish I could forget, but still a very present memory that I think of every single day.

My heart still felt the heavy burden of the promises I made to my brother, my wife, and my Nickel. Massimo knew better than anyone that once I found out what happened to her, I would want to seek vengeance, act before thinking, and not feel a bit of guilt when it was over. I knew I could live with my choices, but Massimo threw all my past sins in my face that day in the hospital, and my hand was forced by the love I felt for my family.

I'd never forgotten that day…

"How could you let this happen to my girl? How could you?" I screamed. My voice was menacing, while still clutching my brother's throat.

"Jack, get your hands off of him!" my brother's wife screamed at me.

Security officers rushed toward us. I didn't care and kept my hands on his throat. Christina kept repeating the "misunderstanding" to the security guards, and we were allowed to remain in the hospital. My brother fell to the floor gasping for air, as I tightened my fists. Standing back on his feet and supported by his wife, Mason continued to let out some calming breaths. Trying to keep her voice down from the now curious onlookers that were in the hall, Christina tried to reason with me, but I didn't want to hear her excuses.

"Jack, I didn't call and tell you about Nicolette just so you could fly out here to beat the hell out of your brother. What the hell is wrong with you?" Christina asked and then slapped my chest.

"How did you expect me to be, Christina? You all avoid my calls for days, and then when you finally do call me, I'm told that my beautiful girl has been raped by some animal. How the hell did you think I was going to react? You should know me better than that."

"I didn't think you would act this way, Jack," Christina answered.

"If you thought I was going to be anything else, then you don't know me at all, woman. I love that girl more than my own life!"

After our hallway brawl, all three of us left the hospital to speak in private. We had already put on a large enough show, and we didn't want to call any more attention to ourselves.

"Mason, I need to see Nicolette. She needs to know that I'm here."

"Jack, after the way you just behaved up in there, you are in no shape to see her. You need to calm down, and let us take care of our daughter."

"No, Mason, that's where you're wrong, Nickel is as much my daughter as she is yours. I have played it your way all these years, and today we are going to do it my way. You failed her, but I will not. I should never have agreed to let you take her here to this place! She would have been fine had she stayed with me and Sara. You in-

sisted that she would be okay out here and that you would always protect her."

"Jack, she has been protected from the minute I held her in my arms. What happened to Nicolette was beyond my control. I had only now just found out what was going on the night she was raped."

"That is bullshit, Mason! Where the hell were you? How could you be so oblivious to what was going on in Nicolette's life? Beyond your control...my ass! You're her father, for God sakes, and yet you did nothing! Why, Mason? Explain it to me! Why didn't you protect our girl? Was it because you were too busy with your career!?! I should take her back to Chicago, with her real family!" I taunted him with a vileness in my tone.

"Please, Jack, stop this," Christina was pleading with me. "Blaming Mason will not change what happened to Nicolette. Please don't reveal the truth to her. She has been put through hell. I don't know if she has the strength to take another shock to her system. Jack, I am begging for you to wait and give us time to explain it to her."

I ran my hands through my hair and sighed.

"Christina, you have had nothing but time—eighteen years to be exact—and I will not wait any longer. I will seek justice for Nicolette, my way."

"No, Jack. Please don't go after Michael. How will that help her if you're in jail?"

"Don't worry about me, Christina. I will do whatever it takes to right this wrong for my daughter. You sure as hell can count on that."

"That's your answer for everything, right Jack? Hit first, think later. The police are taking care of Michael, so you need to stay out of it," Mason screamed at me and pounded his fists on the wall beside my head.

That took balls, but I would not be deterred to why I was really there. I then leaned into Mason and quietly spoke to him so his wife *could not hear what I was about to say. There was nothing more important than family, and it painfully hurt me to remind my brother of that fact.*

"Remember who you are, brother. Papa may have changed our names, but that doesn't change who we are and where we come from. You, Massimo Anthony Vanelli, remember who you are. Stop hiding! Stop running! Remember who you are!"

Stepping back from me with a calm expression on his chiseled features, he turned to Christina. She was trembling in his arms.

"Honey, will you please give me a moment alone with my brother?"

"Are you sure that is a good idea?" she questioned.

"I'm sure. Please go sit with our daughter, and I'll be along soon."

"Come with me, please?" she pleaded, pulling at his arm to make him follow.

She was afraid, and I couldn't blame her for fearing me. I knew how I sounded, and I could only imagine how I looked to her.

"Christina, go to Nicolette, now! You were the one that called him here, and now I have to deal with this."

I watched my brother change before me. I knew he already regretted his harsh tone with his wife. He watched her turn away from him with tears in her eyes. Once she was out of sight, he turned back to me.

"Jack..."

"I don't want to hear it, Mason. There is nothing you can say to me right now that will change my mind. That fucker has to die!"

"Jack, I get that your first instinct is to want justice for Nicolette by causing harm to her rapist, but you are not thinking clearly right now. Remember who you are, Jack. The man that is standing before me right now is not Johnny's guy anymore. This hit-first-and-ask-later approach may have been your way in the past, but you let that

go a long time ago. Don't let this bring you back to the world that you never belonged in."

I hit the wall and then turned to slide down it. I looked up at my brother.

"What do you know about my old life? You were just a kid who followed me around like a lost puppy."

"I know enough, Jack, and I know you got caught up in a life that you didn't want, but you lived it until you had a chance to break free from it."

"I couldn't stand how hard mama and papa worked. They always kept saying that they worked this way for us and we will understand one day. I never did, and then Johnny asked me to do him a favor. All I had to do was make some deliveries for him when he asked me to. I would get paid, and paid well, he said. How could I refuse the money? He said, 'No one would get hurt. Just make the deliveries and report back to me.' I did it with no questions asked, and Johnny always kept his word."

"It wasn't just deliveries, Jack, was it? They always wanted more from you, and you had no choice but to do what they asked of you."

"Mason, you make it sound like I was a hired gun. I think your imagination is running wild."

"You can play it off as much as you want, Jack, but I know you were their muscle when they needed someone to be taught a lesson. Don't lie to me, Jack...I saw you."

"What the hell are you talking about?"

"You know exactly what I'm talking about. It was the night that I had my concert at school. Mama was sick, and papa was working late. You promised them that you would take me and be there while I performed my solo piece, but you never showed up, because Johnny had yet another 'errand' for you to run. When you finally got home, I saw your bloodied knuckles, and as much as you tried to hide it from mama and papa...they knew, Jack. I knew, Jack! I hated you at

that moment because I know what you did to Mikey Marino. That poor kid never walked again, because you did Johnny a favor."

"I'm so sorry, Mason. I didn't know any better back then. I never meant to have you disappointed in me, but I was just trying to make a better life for our family. I knew I was in over my head after that, and I went to Johnny and asked to be let go. He laughed at first and said no, but then I stood there with no fear and asked again. He said…no man ever asked him this and lived to tell about it, but I was different and he always knew this day would come. He did let me go but always promised to have my back, and if I ever needed anything, I could come to him or any one of the guys in the crew."

"Jack, you are a better man now, and maybe I didn't always see it growing up, but I do now. You are my brother, and I love you. Please don't let what happened to Nicolette bring you back to those dark days. Think of Sara, who loves you, and think of how she makes you better every day."

"That's a low blow, Mason, even for you."

"Jack, I'm not trying to hurt you, but you need to see that as much as you're angry about what happened to her, you can't let this insanity become your life again. I want to rip that boy apart with my bare hands, but it won't change anything and will cause more hurt for Nicolette. We need to be here for her now and not let this separate us. Please, Jack…I'm begging you. Let the police handle this, and stay out of it. Can you do that? If not for me, then for Nicolette and Sara?"

Walking away from my brother that day was the hardest thing I ever did in my life. He broke me down piece by piece and wasn't even sorry for it. I knew he would say just about anything to protect his family and keep me from hurting them even more, but I didn't start this…that animal did. And I couldn't harness the overwhelming feeling that I needed to finish it.

"Hey, you're back," I heard her call out from behind the bar.

My angel. My moral compass. That's what she was. Goodness radiated off of her, and anyone who met her could see what I have known all of my time loving her: Sara was light. I didn't deserve her, this I knew, but she was here with me and never once left my side.

I was the one always leaving her. I ran from our life when I heard about Nicolette. I shut her out and didn't allow her to console me, but I lost that battle and she came to me anyway. She wouldn't allow me to fall and lose myself to the pain that I was feeling. She knew who she married but also trusted that I would never hurt her. Her faith in me was astounding. I tried every day to live up to my vows and be an honorable man who was worthy of her.

I placed the bags down onto the bar and removed my hat, coat, and gloves. Sara practically leaped into my arms and kissed my cold cheeks. "Wow! How long were you out there? Jack, you left hours ago. You must be frozen down to your bones."

God! I loved this woman. I kissed her passionately and held her close to me.

"How about we go upstairs, and you warm me up?" I asked her with a hope that she would agree.

"I was thinking more along the lines of a brandy. Don't tempt me, Jack! There's a big game on today, and you know this place is going to be packed to the seams with customers. We have to prep and get ready to open."

"Let the staff take care of the prep today. I need you, Sara. Please let me make love to you."

I know how desperate I sounded, but I needed my wife to bring me back to the light. For days now, my mind had been retreating to a place I didn't want to be, but no matter what I did, the nightmare was always there.

She never took her eyes off of mine. What was she looking for? I hoped when she looked at me, she saw the love I had for her.

"Okay, take me upstairs."

Sara led me from the main bar area to our private apartment upstairs. Our restaurant was two floors, but we had added a third floor to get away to. We practically lived here. Sara was our head chef, and my presence was always required out in the open. I had a great staff that took care of everything when we couldn't be here, but it was to the point that we liked to be here. We were surrounded by our friends and customers who had been coming here since we opened. This was home. The only thing that was missing was Nicolette.

I was lost in my thoughts. Sara knew it but did everything to please me. She held my face in her small, delicate hands and said she would help me forget, if only for a little while. There were moments when I almost didn't trust myself with Sara, afraid I may hurt her. She never denied me her touch. We made love for hours, and then we showered and went back to our bed, where I held her.

"Talk to me, Jack, please. What can I do to help you?"

I didn't answer her. I just tightened my hold on her and breathed her in. Just having her here with me was all I needed and forever wanted.

"We have to get up," she said.

"Five more minutes."

"Jack, I need to get back to my kitchen. Do you really trust the guys to make Sara's famous Roof Top Burger?"

She buried her face in my chest and giggled.

"I love you, Sara. Please don't you ever forget it."

"I won't, Jack, not ever."

Her words put my restless mind at ease. We dressed and made our way down to our restaurant. Sure enough, it was a full house. Both sides were filled, and the pool area was lined with college kids knocking back beers and having a great time. I kissed Sara, and she made her way into the kitchen. Then I heard someone call out for me.

It was my longtime friend, Max, the one person who knew all my sins and then some. He stood up as I got closer and asked if we could speak privately. I checked in with Tommy, who was behind the bar and managing the crowd.

Everything seemed to be under control, and I led Max to my office. You couldn't get more private than what I had built downstairs in the basement. It wasn't convenient, but when I needed space, this was where I retreated to.

"You look good, my friend," he said before lighting up a cigar.

I declined one and instead poured myself a drink.

"I have news for you, Jack, and it isn't good."

An Unfinished Life is now available!

Acknowledgments

W riting my first book, *A Changed Life*, has changed my life in so many ways, I still find it hard to express into words. I'm incredibly blessed to have the life I have and to be able to do what I love and feel so passionate about.

I always wanted to pursue writing as a profession, but as you know, life sometimes leads you down a different road and dreams change. I'll never regret my choices because they have led me here and are my greatest accomplishments in this life.

First and foremost, I need to thank my husband, Henry. I remember telling him at the time that I was happy just reading other authors' books. Thank you, Henry, for encouraging me to write my own. I don't know if it was fear holding me back, but here I am finally publishing my first book! Thank you for making sure I didn't starve while I was writing for hours in the basement. Thank you for being an amazing father to our boys and picking up the slack around the house when, again, I was writing. Your support means everything to me, and I couldn't have this today without you. I love you with all of my heart.

For Zachary, Christopher, and Cameron, I wish many things for you and your future. I want you to believe that dreams do come true. Always follow your heart, and when you face difficult obstacles, don't give up. Keep moving forward to achieve your goals. It took mom a very long time to get here. Everything happens for a reason, and for me, this is how it was supposed to be.

It's been an amazing journey chasing my dreams. I have met so many amazing people along the way. I have been grateful for their friendships, guidance, and the occasional shoulder to cry on. You have all been a part of my dream, and I love each and every one of you: Joe, Julie, Mindy, Kathleen, Wendy, Alice, Karen, Trudie, Nancy T., Nancy M., Flo, Donna, Angela, and my angels in heaven.

Xoxo,
Mary

MARY A. WASOWSKI is a best-selling author who writes adult contemporary romance. Best known for her *Forever* Series, Mary loves creating sexy Alpha book boyfriends for you to swoon over. When she is not writing her happily ever after love stories, she is an avid reader of all romance titles on her Kindle.

A romantic at heart, she shares her zest for life with her husband, Henry, and their three sons. Proud to be an Indie Author, she lives in North Carolina and works as a full-time writer.

Stay in Touch!
I would love to hear from you.
Please stay connected wherever you are.

EMAIL:
AuthorMaryAWasowski@gmail.com

FACEBOOK:
https://www.facebook.com/Author-Mary-A-Wasowski-332971356804341

TWITTER:
https://twitter.com/wasow6

INSTAGRAM:
https://instagram.com/authormaryawasowski/

GOOGLE +:
https://plus.google.com/+MaryWasowski

Other Books by
Mary A. Wasowski

Forever Series:
Forever: Book One
Second Chance at Forever: Book Two
Our Forever Promise: Book Three
Happily Forever After: Book Four
Forever More: Book Five

Standalone novels:
All Roads Lead Home
An Unfinished Life
Return to Kildare
Revive
You Belong to Me

www.ingramcontent.com/pod-product-compliance
Lightning Source LLC
Chambersburg PA
CBHW051055030726
47504CB00006B/1642

* 9 7 8 0 9 8 9 6 2 3 8 0 3 *